CROSSING THE DATELINE

CROSSING THE
DATELINE

Carrie Hannah

ISBN: 1548428957
ISBN 13: 9781548428952

Library of Congress Control Number: 2017910284
CreateSpace Independent Publishing Platform
North Charleston, South Carolina

This book is dedicated to
My parents, Hank and Evelyn, who made my childhood
such an adventure ....
And to my husband, Charles, for continuing that adventure with me

Cover graphics by Hilla Hartenstein
Editing by Charles Hannah
Author's photograph by Norman Seeff

*B*y 1:00 AM Justine returned to her apartment and is startled by the stationary figure standing near the arched windows. A scream rises in her throat until she remembers it's only a mannequin dressed in an elaborate late 19th century costume.

"Hey, Mama," Justine intones to the mannequin. "It's only me. Arriving late. And alone. Again..."

The heat is unbearable so she switches on the fan, unleashes her bushy hair from its large clasp, and strips off her clothes, pulling on pyjama shorts and a tank top. She makes her way to the alcove that is her kitchen and while studying the contents of her refrigerator, becomes aware of a terrible odour emanating from the garbage, which she's forgotten to remove and which has fermented in the heat.

"God, girl, take out the trash!" she commands herself. And tired as she is and late as it is, the stink is enough to motivate her.

Glancing out the window overlooking Hicks Street, the elaborate white stone building directly across the street, catches her eye. It sits unceremoniously squeezed between the dark, brooding brownstone on one side and *the unsightly flat brick building on the other. The street is deserted at this late hour.*

The brownstone where she resides is unusual in that a narrow alleyway runs along the north side, through to the next street. Justine scans the alley out of her high, arched windows. Confirming it's empty she grabs the offending garbage and heads outside.

The summer humidity hangs weighty like a blanket, masking normal city sounds. A lone taxi passes, heading south. Its headlights momentarily pierce the darkness, blinding her.

In the dark alleyway, large garbage bins sit hulking like a herd of bison. As she hefts the cover open, heaving her trash inside, she hears a voice behind her:

"Need some help, mama? I could help you good."

Her head whips around. Two large boys approach in the shadows. She doesn't need to see them to know they're trouble. How much trouble, she isn't sure.

"I like them shorty shorts," one of the boys says, sniggering.

They pause about five feet from her, tall and menacing, blocking her way back to the street. Time stops, waiting for what will happen next.

Justine briefly considers her cursory self-defence training, but when one of the boys takes another step closer, she lets the heavy garbage lid slam and shoots further down the alley heading towards Willow Street, the boys feet pounding after her.

She never makes it to the next block. Instead, she is assaulted by sounds unlike anything she's ever heard before – low hums and high pitched howls – sounds that pierce not only her ears but through her clothes and into her skin. At the same time an unseen energy field propels her forward, faster than she was running and further down the alley.

Then her whole body smashes into a kind of invisible membrane; viscous, hard and porous all the same time. All sound ceases, as if she'd been sucked into a limitless emptiness bounded by blackness - all the while feeling as if she's still running forward, hurtling ahead.

And then suddenly, unbelievably, she's propelled out of the horror filled tunnel and is running in her flip-flops on fresh snow and ice. A weak winter sun reflects off the cold whiteness causing her to squint against the glare and the bitter chill of a winter morning bites into her exposed flesh.

One

Sweat dripped from a tendril of Justine's hair, running down her chest and into the crevice between her ample breasts. Her unruly, thick hair, which she had forced into a twist, had come loose in the heat. She had the urge to wipe away the sweat but her hands were occupied with delicately slicing a vanilla bean, the flavor she'd chosen for her herbal cough suppressant. The rich aroma filled her nostrils. At the same time she was intensely aware of Dr. Dan, her herbal remedies teacher, standing next to her, smelling as he always did of cinnamon.

New York City was heaving under a dense summer humidity coupled with record high heat and the *School of Naturopathy and Herbal Medicine's* ancient air conditioner had decided this was a good day to die. The windows were wide open but the air was thick and still.

"Hot," she heard him say and could almost feel his breath on her neck.

The temperature on top of the heady scents of vanilla and cinnamon, plus Dr. Dan's masculine proximity left Justine feeling light headed. She looked up but he was walking towards the front of the room, addressing the whole class:

"It really is too hot to concentrate," he said. "And the herbs will be compromised. So we'll end early today."

Wiping the sweat from his forehead, he ran his fingers through his dark hair. He'd said 'hot' in reference to the temperature, not her. Justine felt ridiculous; a familiar feeling resulting from misreading other people's signals.

It wasn't that she desired Dr. Dan. He was great looking and bursting with health and fitness - but he's happily married. That's a line Justine doesn't cross. Someday she hopes to be number one to someone, like Dr Dan is to his wife.

"Read the chapter on Tisanes, Tinctures and Teas," Dr Dan suggests. "And I'll see you next week when I hope either the temperature has dropped or the A/C has been repaired!"

As Justine descends the stairs to the street, some of the other members of her class pour from the building moving around her as if she were the boulder in the river.

"See ya, Josephine," One of them says, in an offhand way.

"It's Justine," Justine replies. But quietly, to herself.

She watches them head toward the East Village, assuming they're going for coffee. She suspects she could join them, she just doesn't know how.

Instead she walks to New York University and the office of Aubrey Linklater, Professor of U.S. History for whom she's been doing research. *It's an income*, she tells herself, when she gets depressed about where her life is heading. And Justine's good at research.

Later, waiting for the A train at Washington Square, Justine paced the platform. She'd been doing this a lot lately. Pacing. At 28 she felt she should have a better sense of what she was doing and where she was going. She liked her course in natural medicine but wasn't convinced she'd be able to translate it into some kind of real job. *Career*, was not in her vocabulary as it related to herself. Other people had careers. Justine would settle for a job she might be able to make a living at. Her lack of enthusiasm caused her to give up on things easily, underscoring her uncertainty and self-loathing.

Since graduating from NYU with a degree in history, she'd tried a variety of things telling herself she needed to look forward, not back. She was restless and if she allowed herself to admit it, lonely. It wasn't the kind of loneliness common to young woman her age. It was probably the most familiar feeling in Justine's lexicon of emotions. It began the day her mother left her at the age of 6 in a small hotel room in New Orleans.

The A train roared into the station bringing with it a rush of air even hotter than in the subway terminal.

Getting out at High Street Station, Brooklyn Heights, Justine crossed Cadman Plaza. Having spent most of her life in and around this neighborhood, Justine knows it intimately. She self-consciously ignores the men hanging out in the Park who follow her shapely frame with interest, and disregards the comments of adolescent boys gathered in groups, trying to look tough.

Deftly crossing between buses, bicycles and angry motorists she makes her way along Middagh Street. At street level, tucked into a three-story brick building is a charming old wooden store front with carved posts supporting 3 sided display windows; *Heights Antiques*.

"Hey, Ducky," she shouts, carefully shutting the delicate doors firmly behind her and relishing the wash of cool air inside.

"Lower your voice, love," comes back the expected, clipped British response. Albert Ducksworth 'Ducky' Fitzroy is Justine's much beloved *step-in-father* (as they like to call him). It was he who rescued her from the hotel in New Orleans when she was 6 and then became her family.

He pokes his greying head out from behind an intricately carved chaise lounge,

"Come here, Parcel and tell me what you think," he entreats.

Parcel is what he's been calling Justine since the day she was born.

"You were wrapped like a parcel and delivered into my arms," he told her. "I never thought in my entire life I would receive such a precious gift."

Justine hunkers down happily beside him to study the sofa more closely.

"Definitely 18ᵗʰ Century," she mutters. "But something's off about it…"

Ducky nods. His profile, like his last name, suggests royalty – with a high forehead and long, slender nose.

"That's what I thought – but it's a bloody good job – I can't find the fakery."

She stands casting her eyes over the lovely piece.

"It's from Pankhurst, isn't it?"

Ducky purses his lips, as if he hasn't heard her.

"I thought you were done buying from him," Justine admonishes. "I seem to remember you calling him a crook, amongst other things."

"*Miscreant*," Ducky corrects her as he leans in to inspect a sofa leg.

"Whatever – you said he couldn't be trusted and this sofa just goes to prove it!"

His shoulders sag and she is instantly sorry for her reproval.

"My dear, Simon Pankhurst and I have what one would call a healthy rivalry," Ducky defends himself. "It causes each of us to strive to do better."

Ducky's breadth of knowledge about antique furniture far outstrips Pankhurst's. But Ducky lacks Pankhurst's ruthlessness. His gift is in the lasting relationships he forms with his clients and their willingness to trust his impeccable taste. One of life's gross unfairnesses, as Justine sees it, is that Ducky's business is suffering while Simon Pankhurst thrives on the Upper Eastside.

"Never mind," Justine insists. "One day, you're going to show him. I just know it!" She hugs him close.

"Thank you for your vote of confidence," Ducky says, kissing Justine's forehead. "I've made tea, would you like some?"

Justine mouthed these supportive statements but underneath, she was growing impatient with Ducky and annoyed by his lack of backbone. She was annoyed mostly because she recognized the same lack of self-esteem in herself.

"I'm doing Paul's show tonight," she said. "So I'd better get going,"

"Take a *Lyft* home, won't you!"

They both know this is beyond their stretched financial means at the moment, but he likes to say these loving things and she likes to hear them. But it also makes her irrationally angry - at him, at their circumstances, mostly at herself.

The first six years of Justine's childhood were spent living above Heights Antiques – Ducky's small, two-bedroom apartment with windows overlooking the street. She and her mother shared a bedroom. The memories from that time were fading as Justine grew older; tea parties at the round antique table in the utilitarian kitchen, her mother's long dark hair smelling of lavender and falling over her face as she laughed at something Ducky said.

When she was 19, the landlord gave the apartment to his son and Ducky decided it was time for Justine to live on her own. What this meant was relocating to a subdivided brownstone on Hicks Street in which Ducky took the top floor attic apartment and Justine moved into a second floor unit.

Justine lets herself into the building on Hicks, aware of the oppressive silence but grateful for the relative cool offered by the solid stone walls. They'd lived here for almost 7 years when a developer sent notification that he intended to buy the building and proceeded to purchase leases from most of the other tenants. The building was now virtually empty but for Justine, Ducky and Margaret, the one-time street lady who'd moved into the wreck of a basement apartment and was currently squatting there. They'd steadfastly refused to move but had stopped talking about what would happen when they could no longer afford the rental increases. That time was fast approaching.

Two

Justine showered and changed but was dripping in sweat by the time she arrived at the theatre. As usual, Paul was in a *tizz*. A *tizz* is what Ducky called it. Paul Bellamy and Ducky had been together as a devoted couple long before it was even something most people could conceive of. They were like chalk and cheese - another of Ducky's sayings. Whereas Ducky was calm and always considered, Paul, by his own admission, was a drama-queen.

Tonight was no exception. Justine found him backstage *tsk-tsking* about the actresses' costume; one of his frothy, lacy creations that kept catching on the set and needing to be repaired. His beleaguered assistant stood steadfastly by, awaiting the next set of hysterical instructions. In spite of all this Paul blew Justine a sincere and grateful kiss.

Paul was a sought after costume designer and much in demand. This show however, was an off-off Broadway passion piece of Paul's and Justine had agreed to lend a hand with the numerous costume changes. She made her way in the semi-dark to the tight space just off stage, which was designated as a costume change area. The show was already underway. She listened to the now familiar lines delivered by the actors as the anticipation arose unwelcome inside her.

The good-looking young actor she assisted would soon squeeze into the small space, pressing his six-foot frame against hers, his breathing coming fast from his on stage exertions. Just as she picked up the tunic for his quick change, he appeared - the sweet scent of his sweat like burnt marshmallows. He was already unbuttoning his trousers, which fall easily to the floor, as she ripped open the Velcro on his shirt, exposing a well-developed, smooth chest.

In the dark, Justine has the impulse to run her hands over his skin like a blind woman exploring it's meaning. He's 18 and relishing the effect he has on her. Her breath comes in short bursts as her heartbeat quickens. His eyes watch her, lips grinning, as she pulls the tunic over his head. It's hot in this small space and their bodies are both on fire.

His change of trousers is on the floor where's she's arranged them so he can easily step into the leg openings. But because of his size, there's only room for Justine to bend down and pull up his pants. Which she does. Tonight as she stands, she stares back into his eyes, holding the waistband in each hand, defying him to do something. She feels his breath on her face and a searing, hot sensation whiplashes from her groin to her head. His hands wrap around hers, pulling his trousers together so that both of them can feel what's inside. His eyes glitter in the darkness, his lips curl into a knowing smile. Then he zips up the zipper, grabs his hat and races back on stage.

The vacuum he leaves in his wake is palpable. Not just the empty space but also the aching and longing coursing through her veins. *He's too young*, she reprimands herself - only half listening. At the beginning of the run, she was surprised and titillated by this backstage rendezvous. But a powerful urgency is now playing havoc with her sense of balance and her sense of reason. A similar dance will be enacted once more before the play is over, intensifying her restlessness.

Three

By 1:00am Justine returns to her apartment. She is startled, not for the first time, by the stationary figure standing near the arched windows. She is about to scream when she remembers it's a mannequin dressed in an elaborate late 19th century costume. Paul expertly repaired the outfit and he and Ducky presented it to her for her 28th birthday. Ducky's explanation of where it came from was emotionally unsettling but she was glad to have it.

"Hey, Mama," Justine intones to the mannequin. "It's only me. Arriving late. And alone. Again…"

She switches on the fan, unleashes her bushy hair from its large clasp, and strips off her clothes, pulling on short pyjama shorts and a tank top. She makes her way to the alcove that contains her kitchen. While studying the contents of her refrigerator, Justine becomes aware of a terrible odour emanating from the garbage, which she's forgotten to take out and which has fermented in the heat.

"God, girl, take out the trash!" she commands herself. And tired as she is and late as it is, the stink is enough to motivate her.

She glances out the window overlooking Hicks Street. As always, the elaborate white stone building directly across the street, catches her eye.

Built in the Beaux-Arts style it possesses a real turret and intricately carved balustrade leading up to a massive engraved double front door with heavily decorative cartouches and medallions clustered above the windows. It seems unceremoniously squeezed between the dark, brooding brownstone on one side and the unsightly flat brick building on the other.

The brownstone where she and Ducky reside is unusual in that running along the north side is a narrow alleyway through to the next street. Justine scans the alley out of her high, arched windows. Confirming it's empty, she grabs the offending garbage and heads outside.

The humidity hangs weighty like a blanket, masking normal city sounds. A lone taxi passes, heading south. Its headlights momentarily pierce the darkness, blinding her.

In the alleyway, large garbage bins sit hulking like a herd of bison. As she hefts the cover open, heaving her trash inside, she hears a voice behind her:

"Need some help, mama? I could help you good."

Her head whips around. Two large boys approach, the street lamp casting them in shadow. She doesn't need to see them to know they're trouble. How much trouble, she isn't sure.

"I like them shorty shorts," One of the boys says, sniggering.

They pause about five feet from her, tall and menacing, blocking her way back to the street. Time stops, waiting for what will happen next.

Justine briefly considers her cursory self-defence training, but when one of the boys takes another step closer, she lets the heavy garbage lid slam and shoots down the alley heading towards Willow Street, the boys feet pounding after her.

But she never makes it to the next block. Instead, she is assaulted by sounds unlike anything she's ever heard before – low hums and high pitched howls – sounds that pierce not only her ears but through her clothes and into her skin. At the same time an unseen energy field propels her forward, faster than she was running and further down the alley.

Then her whole body smashes into a kind of invisible membrane, viscous, hard and porous all the same time. All sound ceases, as if she'd been sucked into a limitless emptiness bounded by blackness - all the while feeling as if she's still running forward, hurtling ahead.

And then suddenly, unbelievably, she's propelled out of the horror filled tunnel and is running in her flip-flops on fresh snow and ice. A weak winter sun reflects off the cold whiteness, causing her to squint against the glare.

And at the same time she notices four extraordinary things:

- The elaborate, white Beaux-Arts across the street, is standing solitary with no other buildings on either side.
- A dappled horse waits at the curb tethered to a large, black hansom cab on top of which sits a man holding the reins, wearing a top hat and uniform.
- About to enter the cab is a rather short, middle-aged woman in a late 19th century dress more elaborate than the one on the

mannequin in Justine's apartment, complete with a bonnet fringed in fur.
- A man in a bowler hat, high, stiff collar, waisted, dark green, wool jacket and red cravat seems to be pursuing or pleading with the woman.

Justine tries to halt her forward motion when a series of events next transpires:

- The woman turns to the man, shouting vehemently, "Scoundrel. You're all the same!" and with great fury scoops up and hurls the contents of her small purse in his general direction.
- The man ducks to avoid being hit by the flying objects.
- Justine instinctively reaches up to block the objects hurtling towards her head.
- The man swivels around and sees her.

His glance travels up the long length of her unclothed calves and thighs, taking in the exposure of braless breasts and cold, pointy nipples. His shock at her near nakedness is evident. When his golden green eyes arrive at her face they lock onto her dark almond ones. Justine is literally frozen to the spot; held by the electricity and hunger in his look. She feels more exposed than mere nakedness and compelled to remain there by her own strong desire in response to his look. His eyes consume her.

The driver starts the horse and the carriage moves forward, pulling Justine's attention just long enough for her mind to try and process the inexplicable things that have just happened and for her body to register the severe cold.

The hazel-eyed man takes a step in her direction reaching out a gloved hand and Justine spins instinctively away, glancing furtively at the brownstone on her left. Shocked, she recognizes her building, with the uniquely arched second story windows. But it's also different in a way her mind can't process. In one of those windows, in what would be Justine's own apartment, a woman is looking out from behind lace curtains, wearing a high-necked, white blouse with wide blouson sleeves, her dark, red hair piled high on her head. Their eyes meet.

Justine can't begin to comprehend any of these utterly bewildering events. She can, however, feel the cold. It's bone chilling. So when the man cries out, "Please. Please don't go!" she instinctively runs back in the direction she came unable to stop herself even when she discovers she's running directly into what looks like a stable for horses.

And then she's propelled forward into absolute, complete and utter silence. Silence so thick it's blinding together with the acutely painful sensation of being pulled in all directions in a colorless darkness full of light.

Four

Justine can't remember falling asleep and is completely disoriented when she awakens, emerging from a distant dream of a man's desirous face filled with bottle green eyes. And then she is startled by a small, shiny object lying on her pillow. Leaping out of bed, she steps on something pointy and sharp. Hopping away from the painful object, she feels something fall out of her hair, run down her chest and land with a tinkle of metal on the hardwood floor. Justine screams at this final unexpected surprise, backing up to the wall, awaiting the next assault.

She is now fully awake, heart pounding in her chest. The sun glares through the window, onto the object on Justine's pillow, glittering and refracting a rainbow of light onto the sheets. Realizing it isn't a large cockroach but an inanimate object, she moves cautiously towards the bed, noticing at the same time the small object that fell from her hair. It too is glinting in the sunlight. She bends to look more closely, discovering it is a ring; an ornate cluster of rubies and emeralds with a large sparkling diamond at its center. Mystified, Justine notices the sharp object she stepped on lying nearby. It too is a piece of elaborate jewellery. As she picks it up, she seems to remember holding an object, perhaps this object, in her hand ....

And then she is bombarded with confusing, surreal memories and the room begins to spin. Managing to sit down on the bed, head between her knees, she has a faint recollection of running and strange sounds and then suddenly – snow - and being disoriented in a scene that is at once completely impossible and absolutely real: a woman throwing things at a man whose eyes devour her. Dripping with sweat and gulping air, she barely avoids passing out.

A dream, Justine's mind insists.

But her mind bombards her with images of a woman in a fur-trimmed bonnet throwing things.

Clutching the very real object in her hand, she reasons, "*These things … this jewellery … weren't here before.* Furrowing her brow she rationalizes unreasonably, "*I must have caught this.*"

A shudder creeps down her spine as she opens her hand, revealing the most beautiful brooch she's ever seen; a delicate hummingbird in flight, pavé set with cushion shaped pink diamonds, rubies and old, brilliant cut diamonds. The tiny bird's beak and feet are yellow gold and its eye is made from a cabochon emerald, pure and deep, deep green. Antique jewellery is not her area of expertise, but it's clear the brooch is old – and probably very valuable.

Holding this extraordinary piece is miraculous enough, but the ring is another thing entirely. She picks it up and can't believe it's not costume as the square cut diamond is larger and clearer than anything she's ever seen before and the emeralds on either side are dark and rich and absolutely, perfectly matched.

Hesitantly, her eyes travel to the pillow on which is lying a miniature, gem-encrusted egg. This was the projectile she caught in her hand… and which… travelled back with her.

"*Back...*" she whispers aloud, letting the word hang in the heat and rising humidity.

Then, not being able to complete the thought, she focuses again on the brooch.

"*It must have caught on my clothing or something,*" she concludes, nodding in agreement with herself. "*Yes, that makes sense. And the ring caught in my hair,*" she explains, inserting her fingers into her thick, bushy mop. "*And fell out again this morning.*"

The possibility of how these objects, glittering in gemstones and gold, might have been transported did not provide much comfort because the mystery of their existence was utterly beyond her ability to comprehend.

She reaches for the tiny bauble lying on her pillow, knowing what an egg shaped piece of jewellery might mean. Cradling it gingerly in her hand, she is awed by its exquisite craftsmanship. The shell is made from pink enamel melded with gold covered in a delicate open-work design of woven strands in white, yellow and pink gold spun around and around the egg. At the center is a large rose diamond surrounded with delicate, brilliant cut diamond. The hasp of this exquisite pendant forms a heart crafted out of tiny diamonds and pearls.

Justine remains seated on her bed for most of the morning, mesmerized by these jewels, unable to process how they could have come into her possession. She gets up to stand at the arched windows, surveying the alley. From her vantage point on the second floor she can see the bare dirt and weeds that make up the garden strip along the side of her building and the wall that separates it from the alley. And she can see at least ¾ of the way down the alley to the next street. There is absolutely nothing unusual or different to be seen. Just an empty, dusty alleyway with two large garbage bins pushed up against the wall.

She is startled out of her reverie by a knock on the door, followed by a gruff woman's voice,

"You there, sweetie-pie? It's me, Margaret, from downstairs…"

Justine shakes her head, smiling. Who else would it be with that ex-cigarette smoker's rasp calling her *sweetie-pie*? She hastily stashes the jewels into her nightstand and opens the door. Margaret stands in the hallway, all 4 foot 9 inches of her, fanning herself with the Daily News.

"J – M – J!! Bullshit artists telling *me* there's no global warming!" Margaret announces.

JMJ was short for 'Jesus, Mary and Joseph', which Margaret was often in the habit of uttering but which was anagrammed due to the heat. She has opened the front door to the building and is moving outside, assuming that Justine will follow. Which she obediently does.

"They came sniffing round again this morning," Margaret gruffs, seating her ample bottom on the top step.

Justine can guess who '*they*' are: the developers, intent on evicting them all from their homes. She plops down next to Margaret.

This was exactly where Justine was sitting, over a year ago, when she'd noticed Margaret trying to drag a mattress, twice her size, into the basement apartment.

By definition Margaret is homeless but refers to her homelessness as a *'life-style choice'*.

"Walls just confine me," Margaret insists, underscoring her bigger-than-life personality.

The truth is, she's devoted herself to helping those on the street by becoming one of them. But now, at the age of 65, she needs a bit more protection - walls and a roof have become a necessity. And, unlike Justine and Ducky, Margaret has no legal basis for staying in the building. Having devoted her life to others, Margaret has no safety net. So, when Justine helped her carry the mattress inside, she'd taken possession of the abandoned basement apartment and was squatting there. When the developers throw her out, she'll be forced to return to the streets for good.

"They're hunting way outside their hood," Margaret continues, eyeballing Justine. "Makes 'em desperate and dangerous."

"What?" Justine has lost the thread of the conversation.

Margaret clearly wasn't talking about the developers anymore.

"You might take one of 'em. But not two," she warns.

Then it comes back to Justine like a nightmare remembered; two tall, hooded figures, the garbage lid slamming shut. And running. Running into ... winter. Had Margaret seen something?

"Hallo, lovelies," a familiar voice chirrups as Ducky approaches bearing three cups of coffee from Vittorio's.

Ducky has been taught by Paul to relish good coffee almost as much as he cherishes a well-brewed cup of tea. According to Paul, only Italians know how to make a proper latte. The Vittorio's Café, owned by Benito Bianchi was over on Montague Street but, according to Paul, well worth the walk.

As Ducky passes out the recyclable cups, Justine notices his slender hands, marked now with liver spots and a dusting of grey hair. She thinks, not for the first time, what a pain in the ass she's been over the years. At 14 she'd blamed him for not being the mother she needed as she navigated the treacherous teens. Never popular and not striving to be top of her class, school had been painful for Justine and the loneliness of after school even more so. And yet, while her fellow classmates' parents were divorcing and tearing them apart in custody battles, Ducky and Paul had been a loving constant in her life.

More recently she'd felt the need to push Ducky away as she tried unsuccessfully to find herself. She accused him of hovering and being over-protective. Even the hurt in his eyes hadn't stoped her from dumping onto him all the dissatisfaction of her life.

Ducky's passion for the past and antiques, had given her a skill at research and a love of history. But short of joining him in his business, her BA didn't translate into any kind of viable future that she felt her own passion about. She knew she was being selfish and self-involved, but she was angry and resentful about so many things.

She would like to apologize to Ducky but Margaret is asking what their plans are if they can't stay in the building. She's concerned about them, even though she herself might end up in the street. There isn't a break in the conversation and Justine feels too hot and sticky to make one.

She prays whatever Margaret may have seen she won't say anything to Ducky. Justine doesn't know how or what she will tell Ducky, as she can't comprehend what happened. What ever is said, it had to be done tactfully and that was not a word in Margaret's vocabulary.

Five

Two days later, Justine ventures half way down the alley and, once past the garbage bins, thinks she hears or feels the strange sounds again, but when the sensation of being sucked into some kind of vortex begins, she runs back inside so fast she isn't sure she'd heard anything at all.

"I got the box at a junk sale a while ago," Justine explains to Ducky, sitting in his attic apartment a week later, sweating from more than the heat. She presses a hidden lever inside one of the drawers, adding, "I only just discovered it had a false bottom."

She'd never lied to Ducky in her whole life and while this was more a lie of omission, it made her very uncomfortable to be doing it. In spite of their recent difficulties, Justine trusted Ducky more than anyone in her life. After a week of staring out her window and fingering the jewels, she'd decided this alteration of the truth was her best option. The undeniable reality of the pink hummingbird was incontrovertible so Justine bought the antique box and placed the jewel inside the secret drawer.

"It's valuable, isn't it?" she asked. "Old and valuable."

In fact, in the intervening week, she'd done some research herself. The kind of research Ducky had trained her to do. She knew how and where to look. And what she'd found surprised her even more.

Sun poured in from the slanted windows in Ducky's attic apartment, highlighting dancing dust motes and glinting off the many faceted diamonds. With one hand he picked up the brooch and with the other he pushed his spectacles up onto his balding scalp. It was an action Justine had seem him do over and over throughout her life. Ducky had perfect vision up close but had always worn glasses to see distances.

The same could probably not be said about how he'd conducted his life but at the moment, his eyes narrowed as he studied the back of the brooch and then they widened in wonder. He glanced up, seeming to see her and be looking beyond her at the same time. Justine couldn't look into his eyes, which had loved her and protected her for as long as she could remember.

After a long, scary afternoon waiting alone in that New Orleans hotel room, it was Ducky's familiar voice at the door and his tall, lanky embrace that had reassured 6-year-old Justine she was going to be okay. From that moment on he was the only family she'd known. And he had filled that need as good as, if not better, than a real father.

Looking at her now, Ducky's eyes seemed both surprised and alarmed. Not the reaction Justine had expected, making her even more uncomfortable.

"Junk sale means, it's mine. Right?" she asked, standing up, moving away, keeping the conversation on the future, and avoiding more questions about how she'd come by this extraordinary jewel.

"Yes. It's definitely yours," Ducky replied, staring off.

"Then I can sell it. Can't I?"

"You want to sell this?" he asked, incredulous.

"Yes!" she answered, sitting down again.

What had finally convinced her to reveal the brooch to Ducky was their dire financial circumstances. Even though she was now in her twenties, Ducky continued to try and protect her, just as he'd always done. This meant keeping things from her; like the precarious state of his antiques business.

The economic downturn negatively impacted luxury businesses, but the betrayal by his former partner, Simon Pankhurst, had almost put Ducky out of business. Much to Paul's chagrin, Ducky had gone into business with Pankhurst and taught him everything he knew. Pankhurst had systematically stolen one client after another right from under Ducky's trusting nose, and then broken their partnership by employing an expensive lawyer and moving to Manhattan.

Among the many things Justine daily berated herself for, not being able to rescue Ducky was top of her list. Justine was no longer a child and she knew exactly how bad things were.

"There's one more thing," Justine added, handing him the photo-copy she'd taken off the Internet.

It was a photograph of Princess Marie of Edinburgh, the granddaugh-ter of the last Tsar of Russia on her mother's side and Queen Victoria on her father's. Born in 1875 the photograph was of a young Marie wearing what appeared to be a hummingbird brooch. There were two additional photos of Marie when she became Queen Marie of Romania wearing the same brooch.

Ducky gazed at the pictures and then at the jewelled bird, cradling it as if its preciousness were more than it's monetary value. He studied Justine for a long moment as if seeing her in a new light. Then he closed his eyes, ruminating. When he opened them again, it was with a distinct twinkle.

"Pankhurst knows jewels better than anyone," he said, suppressing a grin.

Six

Simon Pankhurst carefully removed the magnifying loupe from his eye placing it deliberately back in its velvet case. Ducky was a naturally elegant man, tall and stylishly dressed. Simon, by contrast, was a short, portly person, ill suited to his bespoke three piece Savile Row suit. With pudgy fingers, he meticulously folded the hummingbird brooch back into the silk fabric and gingerly slipped it back into the antique brocade pouch Ducky had transported it in.

Years had passed since these two men had sat in the same room together. Tonight, Ducky waited, seemingly impassive, sipping the aged port Simon had offered them, patiently anticipating his moment of triumph.

For greatest disruption, Ducky had timed their arrival at Pankhurst's exclusive Eastside shop just before closing. A fastidious, inflexible man, Pankhurst disliked any interruption of his routine.

"Sorry to bother," Ducky exclaimed, upon entering the store. Making his way to the back of the shop, he flourished the brocade pouch, temptingly. "Something I think you'd like to see..."

Ducky paused long enough to allow Pankhurst's natural avariciousness to overcome his irritation. He escorted Justine and Ducky into his back office where they now sat. Over stuffed with expensive antiques reflecting his success rather than his taste, there was clearly no economic downturn on the Upper Eastside of Manhattan.

Pankhurst switched off the Tiffany desk lamp, lifted his glass of port and sat back in his chair. Aware of the sub-text going on between these erstwhile partners, Justine was ready to throttle Simon Pankhurst and his painstaking precision. The silence was deafening and her patience at an end.

"So…?" she asked.

"How did you come by this piece?" Simon spoke to the room in general.

"It was an inheritance," Ducky replied quickly and definitively.

Justine's head shot around. She and Pankhurst eyed Ducky.

"There's no provenance, but no illegality," Ducky asserted with finality. "I've included that photocopy as guidance for your evaluation. You know I can be trusted." He looked directly at Pankhurst, daring him to disagree.

Pankhurst glanced away, downing the rest of his port. He took a deep breath.

"What can I say? It's … it's nearly priceless," he confirmed.

Everyone stared at the brocade pouch sitting passively on the desk containing the priceless hummingbird. The antique enamel Chinese clock elegantly tinged the hour. Ducky stood abruptly scooping up the pouch in his hand, peering down his nose at Simon Pankhurst.

"I will let you know if we require your services in the sale of this item," he announced. "We thank you for your time. "

Ducky was halfway out the door by the time Justine was able to gather herself and follow.

And he didn't stop there. Pausing long enough to ascertain her wishes, Ducky moved with greater speed than Justine had witnessed in a very long time. He organized for Paul to contact an influential theatre owner friend, who put them in touch with New York's best real estate lawyers who met with Pankhurst's snooty business law firm, who oversaw the private and very hush-hush sale of the brooch to an anonymous buyer and co-ordinated for a portion of the transaction proceeds to go directly into the account of the building developers who, after years of struggling to clear the brownstone, were more than happy to meet with the attorneys and negotiate a considerable cash settlement. In the end, on a very hot Friday in June, the brownstone they were about to be thrown out of became the property of Albert Ducksworth 'Ducky" Fitzroy and Justine Bonnie Fitzroy.

Seven

While all of this was underway, Margaret had gone to visit her friend, Joe, who was living in a terrible state run home for the elderly. Justine, without revealing too much, had assured Margaret that it was safe for her to go – that the developers would not swoop down and lay claim to the basement apartment.

Once the acquisition of the building was complete, Justine and Ducky decided to inspect their purchase. Making their way down the broken concrete stairs that ran beside the stoop and along the cracked concrete path to the basement door, Justine whispered,

"I feel like we're invading Margaret's privacy."

Ducky was now in possession of keys to everything but the key to the basement door was useless as vandals had broken it long ago. Justine stood in the open doorway, which along with one dirty window was the only source of light.

"This is worse than I thought," she spoke into the gloom.

"It's shocking even for a squatter to be living in!" Ducky agreed, surveying the space.

Paint peeled from walls alarmingly mottled with mould. This might be the cause of Margaret's recent bout with upper respiratory complaints. The faucet dripped into a sink stained and pitted and the carpet smelled of cat piss. There was a chill in the space, even in the deadly heat of this June day. In places there were suggestions of Margaret's attempt to clean and repair but no amount of effort made even by one stubborn old woman, could impact the neglect, deterioration and disrepair.

"Well, then, we begin here," Ducky, announced.

Relieved by Ducky's acceptance of her story about the hummingbird brooch, Justine next produced the diamond ring, alluding to the fact that it was also discovered in the same secret compartment in the same box purchased at a flea market. Ducky's hand shook when he accepted it from her but, in the current flurry of events, he didn't seem to require any further explanation.

The ring was also sold through Pankhurst and they were able to pay off Ducky's debts on his store and buy new stock. Both were delighted with how quickly things could be arranged when one had cash to spend. Designs were drawn up, contactors hired and the renovation and transformation of a once grand lady, their building on Hicks Street, began.

"Yes. Stay another week," Justine insisted, sitting on the stoop, iPhone pressed to her ear and a coffee in the other hand. "Margaret, I promise you everything is absolutely, positively fine here," she persisted in response to Margaret's infallible sense of something amiss. "And Ducky agrees," Justine assured her. "Yes. Absolutely get Joe out of that place. Take your time. We'll see you both soon!"

Justine hadn't slept properly in days. But not because of the insomnia that occasionally plagued her. Or the bad dreams. She was on fire with excitement. A sense of purpose and focus suffused her in a way she'd never felt before. She didn't have time to put on make-up or fuss with her hair, determined to be the first into the basement before the workers arrived. She felt resolute and alive. And, she admitted to herself, it helped that Brad, the head contractor, was drop dead gorgeous, toned and tanned and worked only in a pair of shorts due to the heat.

Once the mould had been professionally removed and old pipes replaced and electrical wiring made safe, Brad and his team ripped up the old, rotten floorboards, laid blonde bamboo flooring throughout, then replastered and repainted the walls. Upstairs, they were opening up the back of the brownstone into the garden and building a large terrace. This resulted in enough living space underneath to expand the basement into a two-bedroom apartment with two ensuite bathrooms.

New windows were cut into this extension, allowing more natural light into the space and Justine chose a new door with a frosted glass insert to replace the rotting old one. A decorative wrought iron gate allowed the front door to be safely left open in the summer months.

Justine stood in the new empty space smelling the clean, fresh scents and smiling with a deep sense of satisfaction.

"You should smile more," Brad commented.

"Not a lot to smile about," she snapped at him.

She hated being told what to do, especially by good-looking men around whom she felt uncomfortable and inadequate. Inevitably she complied, doing as they suggested, then hating herself for it. Now she just felt stupid for having said such a stupid thing.

In fact, there was a lot to smile about. Brad and his team had done a really good job. She came back later with iced coffees from Vittorio's as a peace offering.

Margaret and Joe arrived in the cab Ducky insisted they take. Joe was a Veteran, who'd never readjusted to life and ended up living on the street. Margaret had known Joe a very long time. He was a tall man, but carried his height cautiously as if not wanting to disturb others.

"You two are up to something," Margaret announced, eyeing Ducky and Justine as she got out of the taxi.

Ducky kept a neutral face but Justine couldn't help beaming from ear to ear.

"So I assume me 'n Joe still have somewhere to sleep tonight?"

Justine nodded, picking up their meagre baggage and leading the way to the basement apartment.

"C'mon Joe," Margaret encouraged her silent companion, guiding him by the arm. "Watch yer step going down …. Hey, someone fixed these …" she remarked, eyeing the erstwhile broken stairs.

Justine was practically bursting with excitement, waiting for Margaret and Joe to make their way to the entrance to the basement apartment.

"What's with the new door?" Margaret asked.

"Nothing gets by you, Maggie, 'ol lass," Ducky commented, opening the door and welcoming her inside.

Margaret entered warily, taking in the astounding transformation, making a complete circle to observe everything before she faced Ducky and Justine shaking her head in wonder.

"I think we've rendered her speechless," Ducky commented, chuckling.

"Fer the first time in my life," Margaret agreed. "What's going on here?"

"I, um, I came into some money," Justine explained "and Ducky and I – well, we bought the building."

Margaret's eyes widened, registering this information.

"The whole building?

"The whole building. And this is your new home for as long as you want to live here."

Again Margaret cast her eyes over the sparkling new kitchen and cosy sitting area with fireplace and comfy chairs. She glanced towards the front bedroom, whose door was ajar.

"It's two bedrooms now and two bathrooms," Justine explained.

Margaret noticed the door at the back and then remembered Joe who'd remained outside, waiting patiently.

"Joe?" Margaret said, moving to the doorway. "Did you hear that Joe? There's a room here just for you!"

Ever so gently, she guided him inside, steering him towards the back room. Opening the door, she gasped.

"Look at the size of that bed Joe. It's a big bed all for you!"

Joe moved gingerly towards the bed, then hesitated.

"You can sit on it. It's yours now," Margaret encouraged.

Joe looked back at Ducky and Justine for permission.

"It's your bedroom, Joe," Justine confirmed. "I hope you like it."

Joe sat on the bed, caressing the bedspread with his hand. Then he smiled, the biggest, sweetest smile Justine had ever seen.

Eight

The clock clicked over, it's red digital numbers flipping from 11:59 to 12:00. Midnight. Why it seemed important to wait until midnight, Justine didn't know; something to do with dressing up and Cinderella and the likely possibility that this was, in fact, just an aberrant fairy tale.

She stood up feeling the corset's whalebone stays, suck away from her damp skin and reposition themselves. The long, woollen skirt with another heavy underskirt, hung weighted to the floor. She wasn't used to wearing so much clothing, especially in summer, but the layers felt strangely protective.

Added to that was the fact that her mother had worn these very garments. On her 28th birthday, Ducky had decided it was time to present them to Justine along with the story of their provenance. All he said was that she was wearing this dress when he'd found her. He knew nothing more.

She opened the front door to her apartment. As part of the renovation, walls and a partial ceiling had been removed. During the day, the once dark, enclosed foyer was filled with light. She and Ducky were creating what would become an open plan living area with soaring ceilings. Painter's scaffolding cast looming shadows in the unfamiliar space. She hesitated. *What about Ducky?* She didn't even know what the question meant as she truly didn't know what she was doing or where she was headed.

The bizarre events, which resulted in the acquisition and subsequent sale of the hummingbird brooch and diamond ring, still seemed utterly impossible and unreal. But being unable to deny the reality of those 'trinkets', as Paul insisted on calling them, had finally forced Justine to take action. She peered into the wide-open space. Ducky was still living in his attic apartment but the building was theirs now. Ducky had a roof over his head and money in the bank. Ducky was safe.

She tiptoed to the front door, skirts rustling against her legs. Outside the night air was heavy with humidity and scented with saltwater. She made her way quickly down the front steps. The street was empty and the stillness was almost more than she could bear. Her heart beat in protest against the foreign pressure of the corset. She gulped thick air, trying to fill her lungs but prevented by the restricting stays.

Panic was rising in her belly in undulant waves of nausea so she broke into a run – racing around the corner of her brownstone and into the narrow alley alongside. It was a deeper darkness here but she didn't have time to think about hidden dangers because the high-pitched clamour had begun, growing stronger and louder and piercing not only her ears but through the layers of her clothing, slicing like razors into her skin. And even if she'd wanted to escape, the invisible force field dragged her forward, faster than she was running and further down the alley.

Then her whole body smashed into the membranous wall, viscous, hard and porous all the same time. Sound was sucked away as if into a limitless emptiness. All the while Justine felt as if she were still running forward, hurtling ahead. And then just as abruptly, she broke through onto a blindingly white, snow covered street.

She was still running forward, gripped with a terror so complete the scream was choked in her throat when a sharp wind blew painful icy flakes into her face, causing her to stop. Wiping her eyes brought her back into her body and an awareness of her surroundings. She found herself in the exact same spot as the last time, filled with the utterly disorienting sensation that she had made a U-turn and end up precisely *where* she'd started. But not *when*.

She noted the familiar white turreted building across the street, incongruously free standing. A shuttered stable blocked the alleyway she'd just run down and beside her she recognized her own brownstone.

It was daytime but the sky was dark and low and the blizzard blocked out what sun there might have been. She was alone. *Who would be out in such weather?* Justine thought, shivering and trying to steady herself.

The driving snow was beginning to melt against her warm body. The wet would soon seep through the layers of clothing. She had not planned what she would do if she'd successfully returned here. Her rational mind hadn't allowed her to believe it was possible. But here she was, figuratively frozen to the spot and growing colder by the minute.

Surprisingly, Justine didn't panic. Instead, she headed up the familiar steps of her building, noting that they were not worn in the familiar places. The front door was different too, a heavy dark hardwood with two small cut glass windows at eye level.

She knocked. A face appeared briefly in the glass and then, almost immediately, the door was pulled open and a red-haired young woman, poked out her head, her round, blue eyes wide with in astonishment.

"It's herself!" she stated, breathlessly.

Flinging the door wide open, she revealed herself to be a buxom young woman, in her mid-twenties dressed in a high necked, white and dark green striped blouse with mutton chop sleeves. Her full-length white apron was tied around a surprisingly small waist and worn over a long, dark green skirt. Except for the red hair, she was very pretty but not remarkable. Until she smiled. Which she did now, causing the freckles across her small nose to wrinkle into matching dimples in her round, rosy cheeks.

Reaching for Justine's arm she at once pulled and assisted her inside, saying as she did with a distinct Irish lilt, "I knew you would come. I just knew it."

Justine allowed herself to be guided into the dark but not entirely unfamiliar entry. A thick, golden Persian runner covered the honey oaken floors leading to the stairway, which wound grandly upwards with familiar, beautifully carved newels and polished oak banister.

"You must be chilled to yer very bones, miss," the woman was saying. "Come into the parlour, there's a nice fire going."

She'd opened the door to what was Justine's apartment and as in a dream, Justine entered. A lovely fire was indeed burning in the hearth. But this was not Justine's room. The floor was covered with red, 19th century Persian rugs and the room was filled with red velvet, over-stuffed seating and delicately carved wooden tables. If she thought about it, Justine could probably identify each piece of what, to her, was antique furniture – its manufacturer and its era. But she wasn't thinking now because she'd stoped dead in the middle of the room, staring at the oil painting hanging above the fireplace.

"That's how I knew it was you." the woman confided to Justine, nodding towards the portrait. "And just so's you know, I don't let just anyone into the … into *your* house," she added, confidentially. "I've been looking at your lovely face for a very long time. Hoping. Praying you'd come home. And now you have!"

Justine tore her eyes away from the painting and stared at the young woman, who was smiling again, causing the dimples to reappear. Her face drew you in with its translucent skin, steady, clear eyes, and engaging smile all surrounded by a halo of red and gold. Her look was so sweet and full of such genuine relief, that Justine felt herself relaxing slightly.

"My name's Margaret, miss, but I'd be pleased if you'd call me Maggie."

Maggie waited but Justine was having trouble keeping up with the conversation. So Maggie continued:

"I expect you'd like something nice and hot to drink to get the blood moving - you being out in the storm with no cloak or nothing."

Justine looked down and was momentarily shocked to see herself wearing what she still considered a costume, which didn't include a cloak.

"Hot cocoa …?" Maggie suggested.

"Yes," Justine managed to reply. "Hot choc – cocoa, would be nice."

"Or perhaps you'd prefer something a wee bit stronger?" Maggie offered, moving to a polished wooden drinks tray tucked into a corner with an array of crystal decanters sparkling in the colors of whisky and brandy.

A strong shot sounded like just what the doctor ordered, but Justine felt the need to keep her wits about her.

"Cocoa, I think. Thank you … Maggie," Justine replied, attempting a smile of her own.

When Maggie left, executing a small, bob-like curtsy and shutting the door quietly behind her, Justine turned once again to the fireplace and the painting hanging prominently above it. She had seen photographs, precious photographs, which she'd lingered over and dreamt about. It was a lovely face - heart shaped - a gentle widows peak, dipping into a broad forehead with two, perfectly arched eyebrows framing almond colored and almond shaped eyes. She remembered those eyes, filled with love and so much sadness. A long, noble nose set off the wide, sensual mouth. The artist had done justice to this beautiful, exotic woman. His use of oils and brush strokes suggested an appreciation, even a love, for his subject. The portrait's eyes twinkled with intelligence and a hidden secret that played delicately around the corners of her mouth. In memory the dark hair was thick, long and lustrous, worn wild and free. In the painting, it was piled high on her head with wisps of curls, lightly framing her face and exposing the full, voluptuousness of her décolleté. To Justine it was a beloved face. The most beloved face in the world. It was the face of her mother.

Nine

Before her mother left her in that hotel room in New Orleans, they'd sat together in the armchair, little Justine on her mother's lap. Her mother gave her a 24-carat heart shaped golden locket with a small diamond in the center. It had a secret clasp, which opened the heart revealing two tiny pictures of Justine on one side and her mother on the other. She remembered spending the last hours of daylight practicing over and over how to open the clasp. She never took the locket off and unconsciously reached for it now.

In the painting, around her mother's neck, hung that very same locket. The artist had managed to depict the way the diamond caught the light.

"I didn't know if you'd had your tea so I brought some ham and biscuits as well," Maggie was saying as she laid a table near the fire complete with porcelain cups and saucers, linen napkins, real silver and, from the smell of them, freshly baked biscuits.

Justine watched this whole undertaking as if in a dream. She didn't think she could eat but it was important to keep Maggie talking – so she sat down.

"Who's house is this?" she asked, reaching for the steaming cup of cocoa.

"Yours, miss," Maggie answered, looking confused. "I mean, hers ..." she explained, nodding to the painting.

The cocoa was so utterly rich and delicious, *'real tasting'* is how Justine would later describe it, that she suddenly felt ravenously hungry.

"And you think I'm her?" she asked, reaching for the knife.

"Aren't you?" Maggie's eyes widened, staring at the blade in Justine's hand.

Justine quickly stuck the knife into the thick slab of butter and purposefully slathered it onto a hot biscuit, her mouth watering as the butter melted.

"I think - I'm her daughter," she mumbled around a mouth full of the most delectable biscuit she'd ever eaten.

Maggie's eyes darted from painting to Justine and back again.

Justine was having difficulty concentrating. To say this was the most unbelievable, strangest situation she'd ever been in was an understatement. Added to that was the impact on her taste buds from the mixture of 100% real butter, rich cocoa and mouth-watering, hot biscuit.

"This is possibly the best meal I've ever eaten in my whole life," she spluttered, grinning and chomping on more biscuit.

The genuineness of her tone caught Maggie off guard and she blushed with pleasure from what could be seen of her neck all the way up to her freckled cheeks. She quickly reached for the flowered porcelain pot, pouring Justine more cocoa.

"Don't you want some?" Justine asked.

"Oh, no ..." Maggie replied, with surprise. Then added, "Thank you, miss ... I've had my tea."

"Okay. But will you sit down. Please?"

Maggie's eyes shot around in confused panic once again.

"I'm just as confused as you. Maybe more," Justine confessed, as calmly as she could. "I think we need to talk, and it would be easier if both of us are seated. Don't you think?"

Maggie eyes landed on Justine as if seeing her for the first time. Her gaze was direct, without the subservient artificiality. She nodded consent, sitting in the opposite chair and crossing her small hands in her lap.

With some reluctance, Justine pushed away the food and drink. With as much self-possession as she could muster, she managed to get Maggie to explain that as far as Maggie knew this house and everything in it was purchased by a man for the woman in the painting. For years, Maggie explained, young women just like herself were hired to look after the house while waiting for its owner to return and take possession. Maggie didn't know how long this had been going on but the lawyer who'd employed her was an older man who didn't seem terribly confident that the woman in the painting would ever return.

"Who's the man who originally bought the house?" Justine asked

"I don't know, miss."

"Please don't call me miss," Justine insisted.

"I'm sorry, miss, but I work for you – now that you've returned and …"

"I'm haven't returned. I'm not the woman in the painting."

"But you look just like her," Maggie insisted.

"I'm flattered you think so – but it's virtually impossible, trust me."

Maggie had removed the white handkerchief she kept in her apron pocket and was wringing it between her fingers.

"Think about it," Justine said leaning forward, gently placing her hands on Maggie's wrist. "That woman in the painting is about as old as I am now. You said this house has been waiting for her for years.…"

Maggie stopped wringing her hankie and again looked Justine directly in the eyes.

"Yes. I see. You're right, of course."

While the truth was dawning on poor Maggie, Justine was no closer to feeling herself on solid ground. It was getting hot near the fire so she stood and went to the window. Long, red velvet drapes hung dramatically to the floor. She knew they covered a casement window with a window seat. She'd sat it in many times before. She drew the curtains aside, thinking to herself, *Many times before? Before now? Or should I say, since now? Or would it be more correct to say, after now? Or…*

"What's today's date?" she asked out loud, trying to sound as casual as possible.

"December 26, of course." Maggie responded.

Justine held her breath, not moving. The silence went on just long enough that Maggie felt compelled to fill it.

"1905." she added.

Then Justine saw him through the snow fall, across the street, just inside the obscured light cast by the gas street lamp, making visible the unmistakable green of his jacket, which she knew was reflected in the pools of green that were his eyes. She stepped back from the window with an intake of breath.

Maggie was quickly at her side, with a comforting strong arm to support her.

"It's your man again, no?"

"What? Why do you call him that?" Justine demanded.

"I - I saw. You," Maggie began. "I saw you. And him. It was the day that angry woman arrived - wanting to destroy the place."

"What? What woman?"

"The wife. I finally got her to leave then suddenly Himself's there demanding money and she's screaming at him … and then … then you was there … and…" Maggie stopped speaking, waiting for Justine to start breathing again. "I saw you. I saw your face as you – ran off and – and …"

"Disappeared?" Justine proffered.

Maggie nodded, unable to offer a better explanation.

"Why's he out there?"

"He came back the next day wanting money. For the painting. I told him to bugger off. He could see I didn't have any money so he left. But he comes and waits."

"He'll freeze to death."

"Then he's a fool. And that's what happens to fools."

Ten

She hadn't intended to spend the night. Now that it was morning and she found herself in an upstairs bedroom in a four poster bed under a toasty down comforter and lace lined sheets, she didn't know what she'd intended. The sheer impact of so much unexpected information directly related to her, coupled with the impossible reality that she had somehow managed to travel back in time, had left her so exhausted that when Maggie suggested they call it a night, Justine had simply agreed.

She'd slept well. Too well in fact - as the light streaming in from the window suggested it was rather late in the morning. She sat up only to feel the sharp cold creep inside the frilly nightgown Maggie had given her to wear. She desperately needed to pee and was considering what to do when there was a discreet knock at the door and Maggie entered with a tray, filling the room with the scent of bacon and coffee.

"Good morning to ya," Maggie chirped, settling the tray near the bed. "Here's your breakfast and I'll just remove the ...." She reached under the bed. "Oh, you didn't need this?" she asked, brandishing a white porcelain bowl with a lid. "Meself, I just can't make it through the night without getting up at least once."

Justine watched as Maggie pushed the bowl back under the bed.

"Is that a – a …?"

Maggie waited, uncertain why Justine was having trouble identifying the object.

"Piss pot?" she offered. "Sorry, miss – or, um, dearie – or um, not sure what I should be calling you. But, yes, it's yer chamber pot."

Justine's eyes widened in horror.

Maggie glanced around the room, "Did you find something else to use, then?"

"No, I … didn't … but I sure could now! Is there a – a room? A toilet room?"

"Well, there's the outhouse in the garden but it's as cold as buggery …."

Justine stared at Maggie uncertain what to do. The frost on the windows was testament to the outside temperature.

"I grew up with lots of brothers and sisters and it don't bother me, but if you're wanting privacy I can come back to make the fire."

The pressure on her bladder finally decided for her. "I was an only child, so …" Justine explained. "And, please just call me Justine."

Maggie nodded and left Justine alone to make use of the pot.

When she returned it was with a large bowl of hot water. Justine was literally licking her lips after finishing off the entire plate of bacon, eggs, toast and pot of coffee. The taste was even better than the smells and erased any past noble intentions of becoming a vegetarian.

"You are the BEST cook in the world!" Justine enthused.

"Being the eldest, when me mum died, it was up to me to cook and clean. But it's nice to be appreciated," Maggie added, blushing. "I brought some water fer washin' and then I'll help you ta dress. You shouldn't arrive too late as he takes a rather long lunch."

"Who, does?"

"Mr. Brewster. The lawyer."

"Oh. And why am I going to see him?"

"So you can present yourself and claim - well - this…" Maggie explained, spreading her arms to indicate the house around them.

"But …" Justine protested.

"Of course you'll have to prove you're her daughter. But just look at you. Anyone with half a brain can see the likeness."

While she was speaking, Maggie had gone into and returned from an adjacent enclosure, which proved to be a closet, bringing with her a long, rich auburn colored skirt, matching tailored jacket, white, mutton sleeved blouse with full lace jabot and all the various necessary underclothing.

"This is a good color for you," Maggie continued, holding the jacket up to Justine's face. "Just like your mum in the painting."

Justine had gotten out of bed at the suggestion of washing herself, but was now rendered speechless.

"Oh, I'm so sorry, miss – I mean, Justine," Maggie, stuttered. "If you're wanting privacy to wash, you can go into the next room. The floor's tiled so's you can splash around a bit. "

"No, it's ..." Justine began. "Well, going to this lawyer. I'm not sure I'm going to be around much longer ..."

Maggie's hand flew to her mouth in shock. "Are you not well?" she asked.

"What? No. I'm fine. It's just ... I'm not ..." She was unable to finish the sentence. What could she say? How could she explain?

Maggie had reached into her apron pocket and was twisting her handkerchief, clearly in distress.

"What is it, Maggie? What's wrong?"

"Well, Miss Justine, to be honest. I need this job. I came to this country on me own – but me family back in Ireland - they depend on me sending what I can. I've been that worried if you, or your mother, or someone didn't show up soon – Mr. Brewster would let me go and find another girl to look after the place."

"Oh. I see," Justine replied.

This was becoming more and more complicated by the moment, but the look of sheer panic on Maggie's otherwise sweet face was enough to compel Justine into action.

"Well, then," she said. "I guess we should pay Mr. Brewster a visit."

Maggie immediately stopped fretting the handkerchief.

"On one condition." Justine added. "You must come with me."

Lacing and tying on unfamiliar clothes with the help of a skilled dresser was much easier than trying to do it on your own. As Maggie arranged Justine's thick hair up onto her head and attached the matching hat, Justine had to admit, the outfit was stunning. In fact all the clothing in the closet fitted that description. All of it, according to Maggie, provided by the same man who'd built the house.

Admiring herself in the ornate, full-length mirror, Justine, like her mother, had the perfect hourglass figure to fit this fashion in all the right places. It was wonderful to feel clothing fitting and flattering you, something Justine had rarely experienced.

Eleven

As they made their way out the front door, Justine was relieved to find the street empty - no man with sea green eyes frozen beneath the lamp. The blizzard had passed, leaving behind a street covered in a thick blanket of snow and an eerie silence to accompany it.

"There's a nice carriage in the shed, but no horse to draw it," Maggie explained, "So I had the neighbor boy find us a cab."

Justine glanced expectantly up and down the street. The sky was grey and the air, though fresh, was freezing. It was going to snow again or worse.

"We could walk to Cadmon Plaza." Justine suggested.

Walking to and from New York in her Nikes was something she did often. These leather boots, though a good fit, wouldn't provide the same comfort or protection. But if they stood here much longer, they'd freeze.

"Where's Cadmon?" Maggie asked.

But as Justine was about to answer, a Hansom cab pulled around the corner. It came silently, the horse lifting its feet in and out of the drifts of snow. Cold gusts of vapour escaped from the driver's mouth, perched as he was with little or no protection.

He stopped the cab as close as he could to the steps. "Wait for me, ladies," he called out with a distinct Russian accent. "*Ostorozhno*. I'll help."

They waited as he climbed gingerly down from the cab. One of his legs was stiff or worse and Justine found herself wincing in pain as she watched him. He was tall and stood erect as he gallantly offered his hand, assisting each of them down the icy stairs and safely into the relative warmth of the carriage.

The novelty of the carriage ride wore off quickly as the horse drew them onto the Brooklyn Bridge. The wind whistled fiercely and Justine grew more and more concerned for the well being of both the horse and the driver.

Luckily Mr. Brewster's offices were near to the Bridge on the Manhattan side and they were soon pulling to a stop. While there was more activity here with people coming and going, bundled into coats and scarves, the roads were dangerous and there wasn't much traffic.

When the driver opened the door offering his hand to help her down, Justine spoke to him: "We will need a ride back. Can you wait for us?"

He nodded. "Of course."

"I don't know how long we will be," she continued, "but I'd feel better if you got yourself and your horse inside somewhere and got yourself something hot to eat." Justine put the coins Maggie had loaned her into the man's hand.

The driver glanced at the coins and then up at her, speechless. To Justine he looked to be perhaps 40 with dark hair greying at the temples, a surprisingly aristocratic, clean-shaven face, high cheekbones and intelligent blue eyes.

He bowed his head for a moment and whispered, "*Spasibo*. Thank you. I will be here."

Once inside the brick, four story building, Maggie commented, "I wouldn't be surprised if he scarpers with the money, but that was a very kind thing to do."

As they travelled up in the gilded, caged elevator Justine noticed the brass plaque: *Built by Otis. 1895.* The disorienting reality of where she was, but more importantly, when, made her feel suddenly light-headed.

As if she could read minds, Maggie's strong arm was suddenly around her, and in a soft, sympathetic voice she said, "Are you alright, Miss Justine?" The elevator came to a halt. "We don't have to do this, if you're not up to it," Maggie added, soothingly.

"No, no. I'm fine, Maggie. Thank you. I want to do this. For you." And she meant it. Without knowing when or why, this red-haired young woman had become very important to Justine. She stepped from the elevator, focused and determined.

Twelve

"We would have telephoned," Justine explained to the stout secretary, trying to keep the irritation out of her voice, "But we don't possess one!"

Nonetheless, the woman seemed genuinely offended by her tone, hunkering into her bulldog neck, she pursed her lips and repeated, "Mr. Brewster always takes his lunch at this hour."

Justine was about to retort when Maggie cautioned her with a light touch on the arm. But Justine's nerves were already on edge and, raising her voice, she said:

"You might *ask* Mr Brewster if he would like to see us because we are *not* crossing that bridge in this horrific weather without seeing him!"

"Is there a problem Miss Singleton?" a deep male voice inquired.

Justine and Maggie turned to see a well-dressed, elderly man with a well-trimmed beard and round, metal spectacles, standing in the office doorway. When he saw Justine, his eyes widened and his hand went to his heart.

"Oh my," he said. "I truly never thought … It is you, is it not?"

"Well, sort of …" Justine replied. His polite manner and kind, brown eyes dissipated her previous irritation, leaving her feeling somewhat guilty and exposed.

"It's her daughter, sir," Maggie explained. "As you can see."

They were ushered into Mr. Brewster's office. Windows divided by six small panes overlooked a wintry garden courtyard and a friendly fire crackled in the hearth. Cups of tea were provided by a silent but perturbed Miss Singleton.

Justine was having trouble recovering her focus. *Ducky would absolutely adore all this Eastlake furniture,* she was thinking to herself, sipping the fragrant tea and glancing around the elegant but comfortably furnished office. Each piece was in excellent condition. 'Circa 1890 or 95,' she could hear Ducky say. *But of course it's in good condition,* she admonished herself, *it's only 10 or 15 years old!* That thought brought her abruptly back to the present moment.

She looked up to see Mr. Brewster staring at her, shaking his head.

"It really is quite unbelievable," he was saying.

"Yes. It is. Isn't it," Justine agreed, until she realized they were speaking of two very different matters of unbelievability. She took a deep breath, which was hampered by her unfamiliar undergarments, and tried to concentrate. "What I mean is," she continued, "The situation is most unexpected." She was aware of how her choice of words was changing, becoming more considered and proper, as if someone else were speaking. "Maggie informs me that the house on Hicks Street, belongs to my ... my mother."

Mr. Brewster produced a leather file but seemed hesitant to open it.

"This is rather awkward," he began, interlacing his fingers over the file. "I was not aware there was a daughter."

As she often did when nervous, Justine was fingering the locket she always wore around her neck. Without thinking, she removed it, opened it and offered it to Mr Brewster.

"Perhaps this will help," she said.

The lawyer studied the contents of the locket and nodding in satisfaction, continued speaking, referring to the open file:

"Mr. McGowan built the Hicks Street property for his – for your mother."

"Mr. McGowan? May I ask who he is?"

"Well, he ... and your mother ... that is ..." Mr. Brewster looked down, discomfited.

When she was old enough, long after her mother's disappearance, Ducky had revealed to Justine how he'd found her mother in New Orleans, alone and pregnant. Justine had dreamt of one day discovering the identity of her father. But until this moment, had never really believed it might happen.

"They were lovers?" she blurted out.

The silence that followed was deafening, but Justine heard a small window of possibility cracking open - she might not only discover who her father was, but actually meet him. So she blundered on:

"I would very much like to see him. I would like to meet Mr. McGowan. Can you arrange it?"

"He died, I'm afraid. In the winter of 1900," Mr Brewster said sadly, watching her face turn from excited anticipation to crushing disappointment. He took his own deep breath as if making a difficult decision. Rising from his chair, he turned away to stand at the window. "Mr. Henry Warren McGowan was a long time client and friend," he explained, his voice full of regret and longing. "Like all of us he was human and had his faults. He had a family, you see, a wife and two children. But he loved her - your mother - very much. Too much."

Justine was clinging to the thickly cushioned arms of her chair, the painful, unexpected words pouring over her like hot syrup; sweet and stinging.

"When she disappeared," Mr Brewster continued, "He built the house, believing it would draw her back. He set up an account for her as well, which I was instructed to invest and I have continued to serve him even in his absence." It seemed important that he impress this upon Justine.

"Thank you," was all she could think of to say.

"Your mother is currently worth quite a substantial amount." He paused. Took another breath. Then continued. "When she didn't return …" He removed his wire rimmed glasses and Justine could see the pain etched in his soft, brown eyes. "I believe it literally broke his heart."

Maggie reached into her pocket producing the ubiquitous clean handkerchief. Handing it to Justine, she bustled out with the teapot murmuring:

"Another cuppa's what's needed. With plenty of sugar."

Thirteen

The Winter solstice, the longest night of the year, had just passed. Daylight was brief and the nights were still quite long. It was dark by the time the Hansom cab turned into Hicks street and stopped in front of the brownstone.

Though not old, the driver once again clambered awkwardly down from his perch his left leg stiff but not from the cold. His clothing hung on his long frame as if they belonged to someone else and he carried no extra fat to protect him from the elements. He had a distinctly patrician manner about him – as if his current circumstances were unfamiliar and therefore problematic. He assisted Justine and Maggie up the stairs and safely inside.

The blizzard had passed but the temperature had dropped and the driver stood shivering on the doorstep as Justine paid him.

"Thank you for waiting for us today?" she said, placing coins in his half gloved hand.

"*Ka-nyesh-na,*" he said. "Of course. This is only correct."

He nodded and was turning to go when she said, "Tomorrow I need some help. Can you come tomorrow?

"You need cab?"

"Well. No. To be honest, I need some help with - plumbing …"

"Ah. I can recommend good workers for you," he said.

"I – I'm new at this," Justine explained. "And I trust you. Can you come with these workers?"

He glanced away, furrowing his brow, struggling with how to answer. He did not look up, but said finally:

"I am driver. Horse and cab and me – we belong to the boss." Then he looked at her and she could read the discomfort in his face. "Do you understand?" But there was something else – something like dread in his eyes as well.

"What's your name?" she asked.

"Alexander Alexandrovich."

"My name is Justine. What would it cost, Alexander Alexandrov- ich, to pay for your services, for the whole day tomorrow – as a driver?"

That night Maggie gave a guided tour of the house Justine now owned – in this century and the next. After much soul searching, Mr Brewster had finally decided this was the right thing to do. Once again, as in her own time, Justine went from having nothing but the clothes she stood up in to owning this brownstone and a great deal of cash in the bank.

Justine insisted on getting comfortable so both women now wore heavy woollen dressing gowns and fur lined slippers. Minus the basement apartment, which Maggie insisted was too cold to inspect, and including the attic, which Justine thought of as Ducky's, the building was 4 storeys high. Built in 1881, the same year work began on the Brooklyn Bridge; it was a demur Queen Anne style brownstone. The first floor parlour looked out proudly onto Hicks Street through two grand bay windows. At the rear was a formal, wood panelled dining room and the kitchen, overlooking an enclosed garden, which was too dark to inspect.

To Justine, the kitchen was a marvel of heavy iron appliances, exposed piping, deep ceramic sinks, marble covered counter spaces, hanging brass pots and pans and a variety of contraptions who's purpose she was not sure of.

"It's perfect," she exclaimed. "It smells as good as your cooking!"

In spite of all the dark wood on work surfaces, cupboards and floor, the room sparkled and Maggie virtually sparkled too when Justine expressed her pleasure at the sight and scent of it.

Tucked behind the kitchen was the room where Maggie slept. While it was rather large in size, it was clearly not built for this purpose.

"There's no windows," Justine said, aghast.

"No," Maggie agreed, "but the oven's against the wall so's there's always heat."

"That must be awful in the summer," Justine argued. When Maggie didn't reply, she added, "You are not sleeping in this room. Not in my house!"

The staircase had always been Justine's favorite part of the building - its heart - and inspecting it now confirmed that the original survived intact for over 100 years. From the front door entry it wound upwards towards the second floor like the long train of a women's dress, graceful and seductive. Off the second floor landing was the room in which Justine had spent the night. As this brownstone was the last in the row, it uniquely possessed arched side windows overlooking the alley. It was from these windows, Maggie explained, that she had witnessed Justine's first arrival.

Across the hall were two more large rooms. The one at the front was designed as a kind of study/library and the one at the back another bedroom. They were decorated in a less overtly feminie style.

"My father's rooms, don't you think?" Justine suggested.

"They're surely a man's," Maggie agreed.

The word, 'father' felt strange to Justine, but held within it all the buried hopes and dreams of a small girl whose only family was an older gay man, who loved her with all his heart.

Mr Brewster said that Mr McGowan never lived here. No one, in fact, had ever inhabited these rooms, but Justine felt drawn into the library with its dark panelled walls, filled with books and curios.

Maggie murmured about a getting a 'nice cuppa' and discreetly disappeared. Justine was sitting in one of the tufted brown leather Chippendale chairs facing the cast iron grate, when something caught her eye.

Above the heavily carved wooden mantel was an ornate framed mirror. On one side of the mantel sat a bronze Ormolu clock correctly indicating that it was 4:44 in the afternoon. On the other side and beautifully reflected in the mirror was an exquisite porcelain Meissen statue, only about 3 inches tall. Justine tiptoed to the fireplace. The figure was a fine 18th century gentleman in a long purple jacket with gold buttons over a delicately painted flowered vest with lace sleeves. But it was the outstretched left hand, alabaster white like his face, that made her eyes widen and her heart beat faster. The figure's eyes gazed in the direction of his left hand, as if reaching for something, or someone, who wasn't there.

The clatter of Maggie and her tea tray startled Justine and without thinking, she grabbed the small figure and stuffed it deep into the pocket of her robe.

"Why don't we go back to the kitchen," Justine called out. "It's warmer there. We can continue the tour tomorrow!"

Fourteen

Justine had so much to think about she didn't want to think. So after tea and dinner, she suggested a drink in the parlour.

"I couldn't," Maggie balked. "It wouldn't be proper!"

"Is the impropriety drinking or drinking with your employer?"

"Well, certainly not the drinking," Maggie agreed, with a sly smile. "I'm Irish and was born with the whisky in me blood and according to me father the drink heals all what ails ya. He took his own advice very much to heart, I might add."

"And it might be considered rude to turn down my offer ..." Justine added, with a sly smile of her own. She was liking this Maggie O'Reagan more and more.

Later, when Maggie got up to draw the parlour curtains, Justine went to the second set of windows to do the same. She stood for a moment, scanning the street. The lamps were lit and the street was empty. *Tomorrow night*, she assured herself, drawing the heavy curtains and returning to her seat by the fire.

Maggie was stoking the logs, weaving a bit, tipsy from the whisky but stirred by the story she was in the middle of telling:

"He was just a wee thing," Maggie was saying. "With tiny little hands and feet but not the strength to survive without his mam. It was me mother's 7th child. She'd been unwell since the 5th was born; me sister Dawn."

Maggie sat down, sipping from her glass, remembering.

"She was beautiful, me mother," she sighed. "I got the copper top from her - but not much else," she confessed, pushing a stray strand of that copper top behind her ear. "She came from a good family. They lost everything in the famine, but she'd been raised well and wasn't ever suited to the life of a farmers wife."

Maggie sighed again, thinking about her mother and staring into her glass of whisky.

Justine glanced at the painting above the fireplace but quickly returned her attention to Maggie. It was easier to listen to a true story, however sad, than to contemplate one that was utterly inconceivable.

"Me father loved me mother more than life itself," Maggie continued. "And then the baby died. A son. So he goes off – disappears - for nearly 6 months. God knows where. Into a bottle. Then he returns one day, just like that, announcing he's arranged this job for me – in America."

Justine reached over and touched Maggie's arm, "I'm very glad you're here," she whispered.

Maggie grabbed Justine's hand, her voice taking on an edge, "He wouldn't stay away from her in spite of what the doctor said and then, well, there was the Catholic Church …." Maggie looked at Justine, confusion and anger distorting her sweet face.

Justine nodded. "The Catholic Church has a lot to answer for in my opinion."

Maggie's hand came up to her mouth and there were tears in her eyes. "I've been so angry for so long – angry at him and at the Priest - and so afraid to say anything - because it's a sin."

"I don't think it is," Justine said. "I think it's just common sense."

Once alone in her room, Justine stared at the ceiling, unable to sleep. She'd helped a resistant Maggie to bed in one of the rooms on the third floor. Very simply furnished with a bed and dresser, it was located at the back of the house, adjacent to a large, unfurnished room. *He'd run out of steam,* Justine supposed, closing the door on the empty space, *…when she didn't return.*

It was such a sad story. She thought about them now, these two people who were her parents but who she didn't really know.

"The Catholic Church," she said out loud in disgust. Evidently her mother had found herself unmarried and pregnant and fled in shame to New Orleans where she somehow came across a 'bridge' like the one at the end of Justine's alley. And this ability to 'travel' across such a bridge was something she'd passed on to her child. *Common sense,* Justine snorted.

She turned over, gazing out the window. She'd left the curtains open in spite of the cold. There were not so many lights in the city in 1905 and the sky was a brilliant black and full of stars.

"He loved her, very much. Too much," Mr Brewster had said. Yes. This house and the overwhelming hope he'd placed in it was testament to that.

When the lawyer revealed her father was dead, she'd asked to meet his family – her half sister and brother. Mr Brewster flatly refused. He was a kind man and very sympathetic to her request, but it seemed their mother had only died recently and - well - Justine's existence was clearly unexpected and rather awkward.

There's more than one way to cook an egg, she told herself, using Ducky's quaint and reassuring expression. Then she let herself think of Ducky. She closed her eyes, whispering into the darkness the prayer they said together every night of her childhood:

> "*Where ever I am, God is.*
> *I am One with Divine Love.*
> *Wherever I am, God is.*
> *I Belong. I am Loved.*
> *Wherever I am, God is.*
> *Today and everyday, I know who I am.*
> *I am a child of God.*"

She wasn't so certain about knowing who she was, but it had the desired affect. Sleep took her in its embrace.

Fifteen

She'd overslept again and woke abruptly to sounds emanating from below, accompanied by the scent of coffee. Throwing on her robe, Justine padded downstairs. She was just finished twisting her hair in a knot on top of her head when she entered the kitchen.

Five men dressed like workers, including Alexander and a boy of about 14 were squashed around the table all completely absorbed in eating the porridge in front of them. Alexander scraped back his chair, standing almost at attention to greet her.

"Good morning, Alexander Alexandrovich," she greeted him heartily, extending her hand for him to shake.

The other men stopped eating to watch; their rough faces alight with interest. Alexander hesitated a moment, then took her hand and, covering it with his other one, shook with firm satisfaction. He seemed to stand even taller afterwards, stepping back to introduce the boy,

"May I present, my son, Sasha Marco …"

The boy arose, unfolding his long limbs awkwardly like a new born calf. Though tall for his age, the baby fat still clung to what would become angular features like his father's. But where Alexander was blond, going grey, the boy was olive skinned with shiny black hair.

"Sasha Marco. What a poetic name," Justine declared, extending her hand.

Sasha stared at her outstretched arm as if it might bite him. When his father gave him a small nudge, he managed a quick grab of Justine's hand and a slight bow from the waist. The other men applauded, laughing and adding their approval in raucous Italian. The boy blushed then began coughing deep in his lungs.

Justine was about to express concern, when Maggie entered from the pantry with a basket of fresh apples and screamed. Slamming the basket on the table, where they spilled and rolled, she grabbed Justine by the arm and forcibly dragged her from the room.

"What's wrong, Maggie?" Justine spluttered over a chorus of laughter that followed them out of the kitchen.

When they were far enough down the corridor and out of earshot, Maggie stopped. She was in such distress she couldn't speak. Letting go of Justine's arm she pursed her lips, extracting her hankie for support:

"I don't know who raised you, poor orphan child that you were, and it is really not my place to presume – but …"

"Oh dear. What have I done? Whatever it is, Maggie, you can tell me. I probably need to know."

"As I say, I don't know anything about – well, about anything, really. But Miss Justine it is highly improper, even scandalous, for a lady to appear in bedroom attire in front of men. Especially strange, foreign men!!"

Justine's hand covered her mouth and her eyes opened wide. But it was not with the requisite shame or mortification. Rather it was a supreme effort not to burst out laughing. But the genuinely horrified look on Maggie's face was testament to the level of Justine's error, and she managed to swallow her mirth.

"I'm sorry, Maggie. I – um – I wasn't thinking. I think it'll be fine. They are, as you said, only strange men." She waited a moment before grinning.

Shaking her head, in utter bafflement, Maggie said, "You do and say some of the strangest things, Miss Justine."

"Yes. I suppose I do. I really don't know anything about anything either. And I am so grateful to you for your guidance." And she meant it.

The prospect of fresh air and a walk gave Justine the patience necessary for Maggie to clothe and coif her appropriately. With the excess of undergarments to both protect the wearer from the cold and to protect the clothing from the wearer Justine had no idea how anyone managed to dress on their own. Even a brief shopping expedition, it seemed, required the correct attire. Today Maggie selected a dark blue outfit with wide black velvet lapels on the ¾ length jacket and matching black velvet trim at the hem of the skirt.

"I don't know what you're used to wearing, but this is suitable to your station," Maggie declared, admiring her handiwork in the mirror.

"What's my station?" Justine teased, "As the daughter of ..."

"*Tsch*!" Maggie interrupted, and by the fierce look in her eye, Justine understood it wasn't a joke for someone like Maggie.

An overly large hat complete with ostrich feather and bows completed the outfit. This required a bit of balancing to get used to. Justine found that walking like a 'noblewoman', with neck and head held high and erect, made things easier. *Okay*, she said to herself, *noblewoman, it is*!

A weak sun tried to peak through the overcast grey skies as Justine and Maggie made their way cautiously around the corner of Hicks and Orange Street. The side streets had not been cleared and the snow had turned to ice in many places. Maggie took Justine's arm in a friendly and helpful way, guiding her around the slick spots.

As they approached what was called Columbia Street, Justine stopped in her tracks. A magnificent 10-storey building dominated the landscape, spanning the entire block from Orange to Cranberry and Columbia to Willow. It was balconied and recessed and the deep brown red of its brick harmonized beautifully with its ironwork all topped by large, rectangular towers. Although Justine had begun to accept that everything was different, she'd been depending on what was the same to ground her.

"That isn't there," Justine said adamantly.

Maggie glanced at her with concern.

"It's the Hotel Margaret," she explained. "Me namesake," she added, hoping to humor Justine.

But Justine was looking up and down the street trying to orient her self. This very large building was definitely not a feature of Columbia Heights, in her time.

"Why would they take down something so large and so beautiful?" Justine murmured, shaking her head, gazing up at Brooklyn's only 'skyscraper'.

"Well, it most *certainly* is there," Maggie, insisted. "We could go inside if you like."

Maggie's tone was so insistent and unlike anything Justine had heard her utter before, that it brought her back to the moment. Maggie was watching Justine with open distress and bewilderment.

"I'm sorry," Justine said, shaking her head and linking her arm through Maggie's, "I'd rather do the shopping."

Maggie led them down to the water, where the stench of seafood and the sharp aroma of salt water mixed with the shouts of fish wives in heavily accented English and a cacophony of other tongues. Black and white photographs of *times-gone-by*, were nothing like the real thing. This was alive and at times very disturbing as poverty mingled with sickness and despair. Maggie knew her way around, leaving Justine to gawp and ingest. It was an assault on all six senses.

Next they made their way to the fruit and vegetable market; a street of heavy wooden horse drawn wagons filled with winter produce. Here too, Maggie had established friendly relations with the farmers based on garnering the best deals for the best price.

Sixteen

As they walked back up Hicks from Joralemon Street, they passed a small alley where Justine noticed a shop with a sign that read 中医. She recognized the Chinese characters.

"Let's go in," Justine suggested.

"I'm not going into that heathen shop," Maggie insisted. "Jesus, Mary and Joseph only know's what's for sale in there. And that's that."

"Buddhism is an older religion than Catholicism, Maggie dear. Making the owners of this shop anything but heathen. And the shop will be filled with herbs and concoctions for healing."

Maggie crossed her arms implacably over her chest, but Justine sensed she was thinking about what Justine had said. Maggie had a good heart. People feared things that were alien to them.

"Okay. I'll be quick," Justine said, pulling open the rickety door.

She was drawn into the utterly familiar and totally exotic interior. She'd spent time in Chang's Chinese medicine shop, on assignment for her herbal remedy classes. While she thoroughly abhorred some of the practices used to obtain the medicines and had always been a bit dubious about the efficacy for Westerners of remedies designed by Chinese for Chinese, she respected this ancient form of healing. And more often than not, they sold herbs that were used in Western medicine, as well as the expected range of weird and indescribable things in jars and baskets.

This shop was no different. It was quite small and the familiar musty, even mouldy aroma was the first thing she noted. Followed by the floor to ceiling shelves with small wooden drawers the contents of which were described in engraved Chinese characters highlighted in red paint.

A young Chinese man made his way down a very steep and very narrow spiral staircase. Wearing a traditional long silk gown and pyjama style trousers his slippered feet made almost no sound. If he was surprised to see her - a rather well dressed, white woman - his handsome, raw-boned face showed no indication.

"Good afternoon," he said in heavily accented English. "You are welcome in the shop of Zhang Zhu."

"Thank you. I am Justine. Are you Zhang Zhu?"

"I am son, number one."

"Then may I call you Zhang Ming?"

This time a faint glimmer of surprise turned his lips up in a grin, which he quickly quelled by licking them with his tongue. Justine and Zhang Ming were standing quite close in the small space and the unexpected intimacy of that brief exposure of his tongue, sent a quiver into her groin. He was probably Justine's age, maybe older, and unlike some of the men she'd passed on the street, he smelled clean with a hint of sandalwood.

She smiled at him, "There are a few things I wish to buy."

She heard herself speaking in that odd formal way again, but it seemed to flow naturally so she continued. Zhang Ming listened attentively to her requests, his dark head bent in thought, his hands crossed inside the wide sleeves of his gown. When she finished, he nodded, dragging a ladder that was attached to the ceiling by a railing along the wall of drawers. The floor space was tiny but the walls were quite high and this library style device was very cleverly employed.

Ming climbed up four rungs to reach the drawer he required. This gave Justine a direct view of his backside and broad shoulders, which she didn't tear her eyes from until he landed softly on the shop floor. At which point she realized that the clothing she was wearing was extremely unsuitable to sexual thoughts or arousal as she was having great difficulty breathing.

Zhang Ming took her elbow solicitously, guiding her gently to the only source of heat in the room, a brazier next to a small table with a bench against the wall. She sat while he proffered something like smelling salts for her to inhale. He withdrew while she pulled herself together. She'd made smelling salts in one of her classes but this was ammonia plus something else - peppermint, perhaps? It was very pleasant and made her feel momentarily giddy. When he returned, she blurted out:

"To be honest, I'd prefer wearing what you're wearing. Much more comfortable."

He moved suddenly to the opposite wall, as if to search through the drawers, but really to try and pull himself together. Letting him know she was attracted was the wrong thing to say and she instantly regretted it. She'd forgotten where she was – and when.

At the same moment an old Chinese man seemed to materialize out of nowhere. Moving from the shadows cast by the stairs, he tred even more silently than Ming and was suddenly standing in front of Justine, studying her closely.

His unexpected appearance startled her but his scrutiny unsettled her even more. He dressed similarly to Ming except for an intricately embroidered padded vest worn over his gown and a round cap on his head. Like Ming, his hair was pulled back into a long ponytail at the back, but the old man's hair was grey as was the long beard growing sparsely from his chin. But it was his eyes that flustered Justine. They seemed to see her and see through her.

"Hello," she managed to say. "How do you do?"

The old man said something in Chinese then sat at the small table, never taking his eyes off Justine.

"This is my grandfather, Zhang Zhi," Ming translated, from across the room. "He offers to read your fortune."

Justine glanced from the old man to Ming and back again.

"This is a great honor," Ming cautioned her. "My grandfather does not read for everyone."

She was about to thank him politely, saying that she didn't believe in such things – when it occurred to her that six months ago she didn't believe in time travel either. And yet here she was. Eyeing the old man, she was beginning to appreciate that beliefs were just that, whatever you believed. And that reality was simply a reflection of those beliefs.

Thinking about where she was, caused her to suddenly remember Maggie. And in that same instant, the shop door opened and Maggie strode defiantly inside. Obviously believing that the heathen had taken possession of her charge, Maggie's face was as red as her hair and her strong body tensed for a fight.

Maggie's bright blue eyes shot around the small shop, taking in Ming standing near the door just as surprised to see her as she was to observe him - and then the old man who continued to watch Justine as if nothing had changed and finally landing with great relief on Justine, herself.

"Oh, Miss Justine, there you are…" Maggie huffed in cautious relief.

Justine was unable to stand as that would require pushing the table away and the old man wasn't moving anywhere. So she spoke to Maggie comfortingly from where she sat,

"I'm so sorry, Maggie, my friend. It seems Mr. Zhang wants to read my fortune."

Maggie's mouth opened and then closed. The old man muttered something and Ming moved swiftly from the room.

"You look frozen to the bone," Justine observed. "Why don't you sit here with me? There's a small brazier." She smiled encouragingly, moving to make room on the bench. "It'll be fun!"

The old man was muttering to himself now, removing joss sticks from inside his gown and lighting a few on the hot coals. Maggie moved gingerly around him, inserting herself next to Justine on the bench. She gave Justine's knee a small squeeze as if to say, 'I'm here to protect you.' Justine's heart bounced as it often did when love was expressed towards her. She grabbed Maggie's hand to protect her in return.

Smoke rose from the incense, scented with cinnamon and sandalwood. Maggie coughed, rummaging in her sleeve for her handkerchief, which she pressed to her nose and mouth. Ming returned with a delicate Chinese teapot, pouring the hot brew carefully into small cups.

Maggie watched perplexed as Justine sipped from her cup.

"*Xie. Xie,*" she said formally, thanking Ming and the old man. She had drunk this delicious black tea many times with Chang in his shop, which, when she thought about it, was located very near to here, in Montague Street – but over 100 years from now.

'Try it," she suggested to Maggie. "It's not that different from what you drink at home."

Maggie stared dubiously at the small cup. "I prefer me tea with milk," she protested.

"It's considered rude not to drink," Justine whispered.

"Just like in Irish home," Ming added.

Maggie looked up at him, mortified, but he was smiling warmly at her.

"You're right," she relented, "It would be rude."

She picked up the small cup, hesitated, then took a sip. Justine and Ming waited. The old man closed his eyes and retreated into an absolute stillness.

Maggie nodded and took another sip.

"It's not bad," she said. "Could do with a splash of milk. But not bad at all!" She took another sip. "*She. She,*" she mumbled in a poor imitation of the Chinese *thanks* she'd just heard Justine utter.

Ming bowed, smiling and was about to reply when the old man's eyes popped open and he began to speak. He was looking directly at Justine, but this time he really did seem to be *seeing* her or seeing into her. Justine grabbed Maggie's hand and Maggie squeezed back. Justine didn't understand anything the old man was saying but she had the sensation that he knew, everything. She felt at once alarmed and relieved.

"He says you living double life," Ming translated. "You from here and not from here. You know the future and you know the past."

Justine leaned against the wall. That about summed up the truth. But what did Zhang Zhi make of what he was 'seeing', or Ming, or

Maggie? Justine didn't dare look at anyone. The old man was still watching her with his penetrating eyes, when he spoke again:

"He says you will find yourself," Ming translated. "And your lover and your enemy and then you will find them again. They are you and yours. Now and in the future."

Justine had no idea what this meant but the mention of an enemy sent chills up her spine. She clung to the warmth of Maggie's hand.

"*Yīnguǒ bàoyìng*," the old man said.

"I don't know how to explain this," Ming said, eyebrows furrowing. "It means… it means … following, as effect from cause. Do you understand?"

"Karma?" Justine suggested.

Chang used this word all the time, in English and Chinese. She felt the weight of it in her mouth and in the room and from the old man who silently vanished as mysteriously as he had arrived.

Seventeen

It was late when they returned, the street lamps were already lit and the temperature had dropped considerably. But seeing the small tiled room next to her bedroom fitted with a new white porcelain toilet and sink made Justine smile. Maggie eyed it suspiciously.

"I promise you, Maggie, dear once you try it, you won't look back!" Justine assured her.

The room behind the kitchen, which had once been Maggie's bedroom, was now tiled across the entire floor and halfway up the walls. A large claw foot tub sat regally in one corner and a freestanding cast iron stove had been installed against the opposite wall. A toilet bowl was waiting to be walled in to create a water closet with a brand new sink nearby. The only thing remaining to do was connect the plumbing. Justine eyed the tub longingly not having had a real wash in real hot water for over two days.

"I can't believe you accomplished so much in such a short space of time," Justine praised Alexander.

"Yes. They are good boys. They work hard," Alexander beamed, and then translated for the benefit of the 'boys'.

The men continued to work, sweeping up debris and cleaning off surfaces, but they voiced their thanks in voluble Italian.

Admiring the work, Justine secretly wished she could bring this team of craftsmen forward to work on this house in her own time. Thinking of her own time, brought up thoughts of Ducky, which made her heart turn over and Karma, which made her stomach queasy. She was glad to be distracted when Sasha began to cough.

"I bought some tea for that cough," she explained to Sasha. "I think it will help."

Back in the kitchen, the mixture of thyme and crushed garlic was steeping in a pot of boiled water as Justine added the Chinese herbal powder she'd purchased from Zhang Ming.

"That should make it taste better," she said, adding some honey and smiling at Sasha as she handed him the steaming mug.

Sasha cautiously took the cup, looking to this father for guidance.

"You are doctor?" Alexander asked. His tone was more surprised than suspicious.

"No. I'm not a doctor," she replied, chuckling.

Alexander pursed his lips, dubiously.

"It's just simple herbs," Justine assured him. When he didn't seem convinced, she added, "I studied the making of herbal medicines. In school."

She'd studied but never seriously believed she'd do anything with what she'd learned. Natural healing was another in a series of attempts to 'find herself'. But the sound of Sasha's probable bronchitis and his father's apparent inability to afford a doctor plus coming across Zhang's shop and she'd been inspired to do something.

"Your son has a very congested chest. These herbs will help. I promise!"

Alexander considered for a moment, then nodded his head. Sasha took a sip of the mixture, liked what he tasted and drank some more. When he finished, he gave Justine a great big smile, licking his lips. Alexander laughed, hugging the boy, then nudged him towards Justine.

"Thank you, Miss Justine," Sasha said, sincerely. "I liked it very much!"

"You're very welcome. Please take this with you," She said, handing him a small package. "Have your mother make it."

Sasha took the package, executed a brief bow but glanced with concern at his father. Justine noticed the look but Maggie was placing a large pot on the table so they joined the other men as the kitchen filled with the tempting aroma of fish stew.

Eighteen

It was close to midnight and Maggie and Justine were sitting again in the parlour in front of a crackling fire, under the painting of Justine's mother. The men had left with Alexander promising to return in the morning.

Justine glanced out the windows. It was too dark to see anything but she couldn't stop looking.

"Shall I pull the curtains?" Maggie asked.

"NO!" Justine responded, a little too emphatically. "I - I like watching the snow fall."

"Back in Ireland," Maggie said, "Me Dad would take us kiddies out the first night of the snow. We'd wrap up as warm as we could and head up the hill behind the barn. He'd tell us stories."

"What kind of stories?"

"You know about the faeries and the angels and how the snow flakes were them in disguise."

"Sounds nice," Justine sighed.

"That's the Da I like to remember."

"One Christmas, when I was about 10," Justine reminisced. "Ducky and I walked across the Brooklyn Bridge."

"I thought you lived in New Orleans," Maggie said.

"I did. Do. Well ... I live here, don't I?"

"Yes. Thanks be! And who's Ducky, then?"

"I – um – oh, Ducky was the man who raised me."

"*Ní maith liom do thrioblóid*," Maggie exclaimed in Gaelic making a sign of the cross. "When did he pass?"

"What? He didn't. Hasn't... He's still alive!"

"*O mo Dhiadh*, my God. I'm that sorry. You said, 'he *was*' and I assumed ..."

Maggie was mortified and got up to stoke the fire. *Ducky was, still was*, Justine assured herself. *Just not now. Or just not yet.* They watched the old log split where it had burned through and the crackling and snapping filled the silence.

Then Maggie asked, "Why did you come?"

"What? Where?"

"To New York?"

Justine got up from her chair.

"I – um, I don't remember ..."

She'd never been a good liar and she didn't like doing so with people she cared about. She went to the window, hoping Maggie wouldn't ask anything further.

Looking out, she noticed people moving in the white building across the street. The fire in their room cast a warm glow and she could make out a slender woman in a dark dress moving to and fro and a man entering from another room. He planted a kiss on the woman's forehead and she stopped to speak with him. It was a lovely, intimate moment that made Justine feel warm and a bit voyeuristic.

In the time she came from, high-density living was the order of the day and you learned to avoid making contact with your neighbor. She'd never given the white building or its inhabitants a second thought.

"Who lives across the street?" she asked.

"I don't know them but I've seen the sign on the door. *'Doctor Feingold'*."

"What kind of doctor is he?

"You do say the strangest things," Maggie declared.

"Yes. I suppose I do," Justine replied, apologetically.

Coming to stand beside her, Maggie shrugged.

"He's just a doctor."

Justine moved closer to the window. It was dark out but the light from inside highlighted the falling snow.

"Faeries and angels," she whispered.

"Yes," Maggie agreed.

They stood together watching the white flakes float past, piling up in drifts along the street.

It took some time but Justine became aware that the street was no longer empty. She squinted into the dark, sensing a presence. Then, just as she was telling herself it was her imagination, a figure stepped through the streetlight, heading across the street.

"*Mother-of-God!* It's himself again!" Maggie confirmed.

But Justine was already heading to the front door, wrenching it open as an icy blast of wind and snow hit her face. She stepped out just as the man arrived at the foot of the stairs.

"Who are you? What do you want?" she demanded.

"I want what's mine!" he shouted into the wind, grabbing the stone banister to drag himself up the steps.

Maggie was standing in the doorway, the feeble light from the foyer spilling onto the landing. As he got nearer, the man's green eyes became visible to Justine and at that same moment he recognized her.

"It's YOU," he said, with amazement. "It *is* you," he repeated almost with relief.

His eyes fixed on her and she was unable to move, unable to speak or stop him from climbing all the way to the landing, where he came to stand in front of her. In spite of the cold there was heat coming off him and an electricity sparked between them. He stared at her with intense, fevered eyes and she felt those eyes devouring her.

Wrenching herself away and stepping back into the doorway, Justine said, "You'd better come in."

He stumbled inside, moving past a very wary Maggie, into the parlour. Justine followed, trying to pull herself together. She'd been anticipating, even hoping for his return, but now that he was here she was uncertain how to proceed.

Seeing Maggie's horrified face she consoled, "We couldn't leave him out there to freeze!"

Maggie shrugged doubtfully, following Justine into the room.

The man was standing defiantly in front of the fire, steam rising off his wet clothing, which were dripping onto the carpet. His eyes were wild and bloodshot and his hand wavered as he pointed at the painting of Justine's mother.

"I want what's mine," he declared.

Then he began to shake uncontrollably from head to toe and would have toppled over had Maggie not caught him under the arms, helping him into a chair.

"He's sick and feverish," she said. "I'd best get him something hot to drink."

"No," Justine stopped her, "Whisky, I think."

Maggie nodded going to the drinks tray to pour a healthy shot. Justine took the glass from her and, kneeling down in front of the chair, handed it to him. He drank it down in one gulp and it seemed to calm him momentarily.

"How are you feeling?" Justine asked.

He began to shiver again and his eyes rolled up into his head.

"I think he needs a doctor," Justine decided, heading to the door.

"Where are you going?" Maggie asked.

"To get Doctor Feingold."

"NO!"

"Yes!"

"No. You can't! He's not …."

"What, Maggie? He's not, what?"

Maggie opened her mouth, but couldn't find the words. The man in the chair moaned, loudly. Both women stared at him and then at each other.

"I'm going," Justine said, turning again to the door.

"NO. Why don't you understand? It isn't proper," Maggie pleaded.

"This man could die, Maggie!"

Glancing back at the sick man in the chair, Maggie's brow furrowed in panicked confusion.

"I'll go," she decided and pushing past Justine, grabbed her coat and was out the door.

Justine stood at the window, watching Maggie make her way across the street in the storm and up the steps of the white building. Justine shook her head, dismayed. The dictates of propriety seemed to outweigh everything, including a man's life. Justine didn't mind rules. She liked things to be safe and organized. To a point.

Turning back to the sick man, she began removing his wet scarf and hat. Even in his wild state, even debilitated with illness, she felt a compelling attraction to him. At her touch, his eyes opened, focusing on her. His pupils were so dilated, the green was almost black.

"My name is Justine," she told him, trying to keep him from passing out again. "What's yours?"

"James Gray," he answered with difficulty.

He continued to shiver with cold but all the force had gone out of him.

"The doctor's coming, James," she assured him.

She could feel his breath on her neck as she knelt over to remove his arms from his jacket sleeves.

"I need to know about the painting," she whispered desperately into his ear. "I need to know about the woman in the painting."

His head lolled back so she grabbed his shoulders.

"Please. Don't pass out again. Stay with me."

At that moment the front door opened and Maggie entered followed by a slight man with wire rim glasses perched on the end of his arched nose, thinning black hair with a yarmulke stuck to the pointed dome of his head. He nodded, politely, almost hesitantly to Justine. She rose to welcome him, extending her hand.

"Dr. Feingold. Thank you for coming."

He looked at her hand, perplexed and then shook it.

"I am so sorry to bother you on such a terrible night," Justine went on, "but...." she indicated the man in the chair.

"I am happy to help," he said sincerely. "Just surprised." He had a soft, educated voice with the hint of a German accent.

"His name is James. James Gray," Justine explained.

Dr. Feingold did as much of an examination as possible. He was gentle and respectful, murmuring for the benefit of those present what he was doing and why. Not unexpectedly he suggested James be put into a warm bed and allowed to sleep.

Maggie sighed, disapprovingly but said, "The Master's bedroom." And helped the doctor support James to the stairs.

"Can you give him something?" Justine asked, plaintively, standing in the foyer. "Antibiotics? A shot?"

She heard her requests echo in the stairwell, between the grunts from Maggie and the groans from James as they struggled upstairs. Then she remembered where she was and when. Not invented yet. James could die.

She followed them hurriedly up the stairs as Maggie was gently closing the door to prevent Justine from entering.

"We need to undress him, Miss Justine," she cautioned.

"It's okay, Maggie. I've seen a man naked before."

Maggie's eyes widened in shock but Justine had already moved into the room to help Dr. Feingold. To voice her further disapproval, Maggie noisily got a fire roaring in the hearth. Justine opened and removed James' shirt. In spite of the illness he smelled masculine and clean as if he'd washed recently and she couldn't help but appreciate his strong build, only slightly wasted from diet or sickness or both.

As soon as she and the Doctor tucked him under the covers, James fell asleep.

"Elderberry is a good idea," Dr. Feingold said, responding to her suggestion. "Make sure he drinks some every couple of hours."

"Will he be alright?" Justine wanted to know.

They were standing in the foyer as Dr. Feingold was pulling on his coat. He studied her over his spectacles, pausing before he spoke. His eyes were clear and kind but a chill went up her spine. Finally he said,

"*B'yadai El-o-him*. It is with God."

She knew her need for James to live was selfish. He had information she desperately wanted. But it was compassionate as well. She didn't want him to die.

"He is young and strong," Dr Feingold added. "If he survives the night ..." his hands opened out in a shrug. "I will stop by tomorrow. If you would like."

He turned to go.

"May I ask you something?" she said.

"Of course." He turned toward her, patiently.

"Why were your surprised that we asked for your help?"

He shrugged, patting the yarmulke on his head.

"Because I am a Jew," he explained. "Most Gentiles would - well, they wouldn't choose to come to me."

There was something so resigned and absolute about the way he expressed this terrible truth that Justine couldn't help but reach out and squeeze his arm.

"I'm sincerely thankful you came," she said. "And I'd be most grateful if you'd stop by tomorrow."

She stood in the dark entry after he'd left, feeling the weight of the house around her and the time in which it stood.

Nineteen

The windowpanes rattled as the ferocious storm gusted through Brooklyn. Maggie had built a fire that would last the night, casting moving shadows on the walls and light on the sleeping man. Justine convinced Maggie to go on to bed, insisting she wanted to stay with their 'patient'. Sitting in the cushioned leather chair Justine watched James Gray with rapt attention.

Aside from his interest in the painting, it was clear he'd been waiting for her. Maggie said he'd been standing in the street on and off since their first encounter. *So,* she reasoned, *in a way, his illness is partially my fault. Well. Less than partially,* she consoled herself, considering he'd chosen to stand in the snow. *To some extent? Somewhat to blame? Not completely?* She considered, drifting.

Suddenly he cried out and woke her with a start. He was sitting up in bed, his naked chest heaving with fright, his eyes casting about the room, trying to comprehend where he was.

"It's okay," Justine said soothingly. "You're in my house."

His green eyes landed on her and the confusion softened to relief. He fell back against the pillows and she pulled the blankets over his shivering body.

"Cold," he whispered. "So cold."

"Drink some tea," she suggested, pouring a cup of steaming elderberry.

Sitting beside him on the bed, Justine cradled his head in her arm, supporting him. His full lips trembled as he sipped the hot beverage. He was weakened now by comparison to the half-raving man he seemed earlier and his body rested gratefully against her breasts. His head of rich brown hair fell in thick waves to his shoulders, curling over his forehead, spreading across the pillow as he lay down again.

"Thank you," he whispered, shuddering.

It was warm in the room, almost hot and there were no more blankets to cover him with. Justine stood over the bed watching his whole body tremble, not knowing what to do, feeling utterly helpless and very afraid.

Suddenly she couldn't stand it any longer and began tearing the clothes off her body. Discarding vests and skirts, untying shoes and stockings, ripping at petticoats and stays, until she stood naked by the bed.

Quickly she crawled in beside him, drawing the covers over both of them and spooning her warm body up against his. She wrapped her arms around his shivering length and held him close.

His body was muscular beneath the uncontrollable shaking, his skin smooth and his scent was of soap and sweat. Justine snuggled her face into his abundant hair, whispering:

"It's okay, James. It's going to be okay."

Slowly, as her warmth seeped into him, he began to calm. She held him while his exhausted body relaxed and he finally fell into a deep sleep. Relieved, the tension began to melt out of her. She felt protecting and protected, wrapped in the warmth of a fire, blankets and a slumbering man and soon she drifted off to sleep as well.

Sometime later he turned over and brushed her face with his fingers. His touch drew her up from sleep and she looked at him. The fiery passion in his golden green eyes was alight again and melted her down to her core. They reached for each other as if each had been holding their breath and were only able to breath again, together. His mouth covered hers, pressing hard against her lips, his hands reaching for her hips and full breasts. Her fingers reached back, diving into the rich folds of his hair and relishing the sinew of muscle and skin down his back and arms.

They didn't speak. There was no need. Their hands and eyes and bodies communed in a language of sensuality and a dance of pleasure and pleasuring.

Their ferocity rose to a crescendo but they weren't sated yet and the dance began again. This time with gentleness, touching and caressing until neither could wait another second, she pulled him once again on to her and into her, both of them riding that fine line between violence and joy.

Twenty

"Always remember that Mama loves you. More than anything."

Little Justine nodded, eyes wide, sensing, as small children do, that something was wrong. Something was very, very wrong.

"Can you say it again for me?" Justine's mother asked. Her voice was always deep and throaty but now it was struggling to hold back tears.

They were sitting together in the single overstuffed, flower-upholstered chair, Justine on her mother's lap. The only other furniture was a small double bed with a frilly, flowery polyester spread, a nightstand and battered dresser. The décor was meant to evoke an *olde* style charm but succeeded only in looking cheap and tired.

"Mama loves me. Forever and always." Justine repeated, obediently. She clung to her mother's neck with a bottomless pit of fear inside her belly.

"That's a good girl. You are my beautiful, precious girl." Her mother said, almond eyes filling with tears. "Forever and always."

They sat holding each other for a while longer. Justine could smell the shampoo her mother used even though her hair was tied on top of her head in a strange way she'd never worn it before. In fact everything about the way her mother was dressed was different - the long wide skirt, the tight bodice, short, tie boots - only adding to Justine's sense of dread.

"You remember what I told you to do?" her mother whispered in her ear.

"Yes, Mama. Call Ducky."

"Good Girl."

"And wait here until he comes."

"That's my brave baby."

She kissed little Justine and hugged her one last time. Then she was gone. Justine watched the hotel room door closing behind her mother and even at 6 knew she would never see her again. The bottom of the pit opened and little Justine fell in.

Justine sat up in bed, the black maw of that gaping pit trying to suck her down. She'd been to that precipice many times in her dreams, reliving that scene in the dreary hotel room over and over. It never got easier or less frightening or painful.

For a moment she didn't know where she was. The room was dark and cold and only faintly familiar. Then she noticed the man slumbering beside her and it all came back. All of it. Where she was. When. And what had happened last night.

Instinctively she crawled out of bed. Silently collecting her clothing, she tiptoed out of the room and across the hall to her room. It was disconcerting to think of it as 'her room', much as she couldn't think of this house as *hers* though she recalled saying it to James last night.

Then last night washed over her in waves of confusion and desire. Tossing her clothing in a pile on the silk brocade fainting couch, she threw on a nightie and ducked under her bedcovers.

Moments later, there was a discreet knock on her door and Maggie entered with a steaming bowl of water to wash with.

"Last time you'll be needing this," Maggie chirped.

Justine was intensely relieved she was back in her own bed. She knew that in the short time she'd been here she'd said and done things outside of Maggie's ken. But Maggie was a true individual, probably unlike most women of her time and had rallied. Rather than judging, Maggie tried to adjust. But Justine knew what had happened last night with James was not something Maggie would be able to accept. And Justine dearly wanted Maggie's acceptance.

"The patient's sleeping soundly," Maggie announced, as she sorted through Justine's discarded clothing. "That's a good sign. And those foreign workmen are here."

"Already?" Justine said, leaping out of bed. "What time is it?"

"Half-eight, Miss Justine. I'm feeding them porridge while's we wait for Mr. Alexander."

"Half-eight means, 7:30am. Right?" Justine was in the tiled room that now contained her brand new toilet, which didn't work yet. She was doing her best to wash, rubbing lye soap into the cloth and using it to scrub parts of herself. This brought unbidden sensations of James and the touch of his hands and lips.

Her private reverie was interrupted by Maggie, shouting from the bedroom, "Someone's at the front door, making a racket like a cockerel."

Moments later Maggie returned.

"Something's happened, Miss Justine," Maggie told her. "It's Mr Alexander wanting to speak to you. I had to practically bribe him to have some porridge so's you can dress first."

Twenty-One

"This is outrageous!" Justine declared.

Now properly dressed, she was standing in the hallway outside the kitchen with Alexander, whose face she couldn't discern as his head was bowed.

"How can he fire you?" she exploded.

"Today is my last day," was all he replied.

But I paid you for the entire day! And I assume you paid him?"

"But, of course," Alexander replied, raising his head to stare down his long nose at her, deeply offended.

"Of course," Justine countered, not wishing to further disgrace this dignified, honest man. "Then why?"

Alexander's awkward silence expressed volumes. From the way the workers deferred to and respected him as their natural leader, to the way he had escorted Maggie and herself that first day – Justine suspected this was an intelligent, possibly educated man, who found himself in the untenable circumstance of needing to do menial work to support his family.

"I am going with you," she declared. "To speak to this person, your boss."

Alexander looked down at her aghast and was about to protest when Maggie peeked her head out of the kitchen.

"And I won't take no for an answer," Justine insisted to both of them. "It's my fault, after all."

They didn't have a chance to argue because there was another knock on the door, which Maggie hastened to answer. Dr Feingold stood framed in the doorway wearing the same dark woollen coat as the night before.

"Good morning, Doctor," Maggie said, formally.

"Miss O'Reagan," Dr Feingold replied, with equal formality.

If he'd been wearing a hat he would probably have doffed it, Justine thought and assumed one didn't use a yarmulke in this manner. Not trusting herself to be in the same room with James, Justine hailed the doctor:

"Good morning, Doctor. Thank you for coming back. I've not had my breakfast yet and I'm about to go out. Do you mind ….?"

"Not at all, my dear," he said, following Maggie upstairs to check on his patient.

After wolfing down some porridge, Justine quickly inspected the work underway in the downstairs bathroom. She listened as Alexander gave instructions to the Italian crew, trusting that they would do as he said. She met Maggie and the Doctor once again in the front foyer.

"Mr Gray is exhausted, but much improved," the Doctor reported. "He needs to rest and from the way he consumed Miss O'Reagan's porridge, I'd say he hasn't eaten properly in some time."

"Everybody eats Mag – Miss O'Reagan's food like that," Justine said feeling responsible in part for James' exhaustion. "It's so delicious!"

Maggie snorted but was pleased by all the flattery.

"I must be off," the Doctor smiled. "I do double duty in my small community as the Rabbi."

Maggie helped him with his coat, waited until he'd made it to the street before turning to Justine and declaring; "He's like the priest, then, isn't he? Oh my," she added much impressed, waving to him politely before turning to collect her own coat.

"Where're you going?" Justine wanted to know.

"With you, of course!" Maggie replied, defiantly. "You will not wander the streets of this God-forsaken town, nights before the New Year, all on your own."

Maggie reopened the front door and they descended into Alexander's waiting cab. The sun was out, shining on a city blanketed in snow.

Unlike the first carriage ride, Justine was able to enjoy the passing sights and not be too concerned about Alexander freezing to death as he expertly guided the horse across the bridge.

The streets were much busier than the first time she'd been to Manhattan. Cars, though not in great abundance, vied with horse drawn carriages for throughway on the streets. Melting snow and pedestrians added to the confusion. Although jaywalking was a time-honored practice in the New York she came from, there was a semblance of order to motorized modern day traffic. Now, men in bowlers with canes and a few women in long skirts with cinched waists and large, decorative hats stepped out anywhere they pleased into traffic moving in both directions and on whatever side of the street provided an opening. As far as Justine could tell it was absolute chaos. But the very fact of it, of her being here in it, was exciting, daunting and still unbelievable.

When Alexander turned off The Bowery into Pell Street a crowd had gathered outside the stables into which he directed the carriage. Mostly young boys, they peeked curiously into the cab as it passed but quickly returned to their original fascination. On the street lay the carcass of a dead horse.

Alexander had warned her that this was not a place for women and Justine steeled herself for what else they might encounter. And she didn't have long to wait. The cab company was housed in a long, narrow mews with stables on one side and unhitched hansom cabs parked on the other. The entrance was through a stone archway and Alexanders' arrival made it difficult for another horse and carriage to depart. The driver waited patiently for Alexander to manoeuvre around him in the grey, sludgy snow.

Another man appeared, sporting a thick moustache, thinning hair sticking out from a worn derby hat and with a stout mid-section protruding from his frame. He began barking a tirade of abuse at the driver and whipping the horse.

Without thinking, Justine jumped from the cab, shouting at the man, "What the hell do you think you're doing?

She realized later that a well-dressed woman hollering in bad language had stopped him in his tracks and he swung around to face her. His skin was badly pocked and even from afar his body odour was enough to keep her at a distance.

"And just who the hell might you be?" he shouted back.

By now all her senses were assaulted with the sight of near starving horses shackled in their pen or attached to carriages, coupled with the stench of unwashed animals and unclean stalls. Her blood was boiling.

"Are you the owner of this godforsaken, shit-hole?" she demanded.

"I am. Declan Puttuck's me name. And what's it to you?" he challenged her, eyes narrowing. Slapping the whip against his thigh he swaggered menacingly towards her.

Alexander and Maggie moved in on either side of Justine. Puttuck squinted at Alexander but before his slow mental facility could put two and two together, Justine launched a verbal attack.

"I am employed by the law firm of Harold R. Brewster," she informed him, withdrawing from her small beaded purse, the gold embossed business card Mr Brewster had given her. She waved it in front of Puttuck's confused face, before stashing it back in the bag. Noticing Maggie's shocked look, Justine headed to the horses stalls followed closely by Puttuck.

"I am here to investigate improper and illegal labor practices, cruel and unhygienic conditions for both animals and employees as well as bullying, exploitation and the use of violence."

She turned abruptly to face the owner accusingly, breathing from the mouth to avoid his stench. She was 99% certain that none of her claims were either relevant or illegal in 1905 but when Puttuck opened his mouth to speak, slapping the whip against his thigh, Justine cautioned him sternly:

"Do not interrupt me Mr Puttuck. Violence might make people fear you but it will never get you their respect."

The only reason she'd said such a thing was because she was completely terrified of him. And it was only the familiar look of underlying stupidity she'd seen in the eyes of other bullies that gave her the courage to continue with this insane and dangerous charade.

"This establishment is in a shocking state," she informed him. "These animals are suffering and your employees are being abused. This will not be tolerated."

"Yeah? And what're ye gunna do about it?" he asked, threateningly, stepping closer to stare at her, then hawking, spitting and just missing her shoe.

Now Alexander stepped in. He was taller by a head than Puttuck but Justine had no intention of allowing this to escalate.

"May I remind you that there is a dead horse in the street?" Justine said accusingly.

"Yeah. And?" Puttuck spat back.

His utter indifference to this heartbreaking fact alerted her that she was on the wrong track.

"Alright, Mr Puttuck, I'm going to be very frank with you. While you're practices are beneath contempt, I assume you're a reasonable man and I'm going to make you a one time offer."

What movie script was that line from, she wondered, knees shaking beneath her skirts. Puttuck was glancing from Alexander to Justine and back again, slapping his thigh with the whip, trying to decide what to do but looking like he was choosing which of them to eat first.

"Not only do I work for a powerful and prestigious law firm that is preparing to sue you," Justine continued, "I am also the daughter of Henry Warren McGowan. My father's relationships in high places could ruin you with or without a law suit."

Clearly this statement had meaning for Puttuck because he stopped slapping the whip, peering at her and pursing his thick lips with concern.

"In order for me to stop the law suit and speak to my father – in order for none of this to happen - here's what I need you to do."

She paused long enough to ascertain that he was listening and therefore interested.

" #1," she began "Clean up this filthy place. Wash your horses and start feeding them properly. #2. Learn how to handle horses in a way that respects them. I promise you, when you treat any living being with kindness, you get more out of them. #3. Pay your employees a decent wage and improve their working conditions. If you were to provide warm uniforms in the winter, I guarantee you'd increase their ability to work."

Puttuck took a step back as if he was about to protest so Justine raised her voice and continued on:

"I hope you're listening to me, Mr Puttuck. I don't want to come back here ever again. And if I do, you'll be very sorry you didn't heed my words the first time."

Puttuck grunted. His mind didn't work fast enough to keep up with her so she pushed her advantage.

"Number 4," she continued, "Mr Alexandrovich is not being fired. He did nothing wrong and there was no basis for severing his employment. However, Mr Alexandrovich no longer wishes to work for you as he is now employed as my chauffeur. Therefore he is leaving your employ of his own volition."

She was certain Puttuck didn't fully comprehend everything she'd just said but glancing sheepishly at Alexander, she knew *he* did. He stared at her for a moment, then nodded his head once in consent. It was important to Justine that this was Alexander's decision and she was relieved that he'd agreed. Turning back to the befuddled Puttuck she knew she didn't have much time before his confusion escalated into anger.

"To that end I am going need a horse," she explained.

Out of the corner of her eye she saw Maggie surreptitiously raise two fingers.

"Two horses," she corrected herself. "The one we have and Alexander is going to select another. You are going to sell these horses to me for a reasonable price."

Horse trading was something Puttuck understood and he watched carefully as Alexander headed to a nearby stall, leading out a tall horse that had been so badly treated its hide was covered in whip marks and it's ribs poked through its flesh. Justine had to keep herself from crying out at its condition and surprise that this was the horse Alexander chose.

"$200 for the two," Puttuck spat out.

"$50!" Maggie countered, authoritatively. "That one's nearly dead and the other one might as well be!"

Maggie's small frame puffed up to her full height as she eyeballed Puttuck, daring him to disagree. Bargaining was something Maggie understood.

"$150," he spat.

"$60," she snorted. "And you're lucky to get it!"

"$100," he demanded, slapping his thigh with the whip.

"Are ye deaf, man?" Maggie inquired. "Have ye not understood that yer getting away with murder, here? Take the $70 we're offering and thank yer lucky stars that's all it cost ye."

Alexander was tethering the pitiful horse to the back of the hansom cab when another driver pulled in, hopped down and spoke urgently to him. Alexander looked towards Justine with panic in his eyes.

"What's wrong, Alexander?" she asked, moving quickly to his side.

"It's my baby daughter," he said. "I must go."

Justine withdrew eight $10 bills from her purse and handed them to Maggie. Maggie turned to Puttuck, grabbed his hand and stuffed the money into it saying:

"It's more than they're worth and way more than you deserve."

"Where do you think you're going with my cab?" Puttuck demanded, as Justine and Maggie climbed inside and Alexander mounted the driver's seat.

"It'll be returned," Justine assured him. "And if not, come and speak to my father about it!"

Alexander expertly turned the horse and cab around and with the newly purchased horse tethered behind, headed back toward The Bowery.

Twenty-Two

Alexander navigated the horse and cab north along the danger-ously slushy street with anxiety filled speed. Pedestrians and other vehicles made it necessary to stop and start and Justine and Maggie were tossed to and fro inside the cab.

This was a sleazier section of the Bowery, with squat two and three story grimy buildings housing a variety of workers pubs, transient hotels with rooms for 15cents a night and storefronts offering questionable forms of entertainment.

Holding tightly to the velvet strap as the cab swayed and bolted, Justine saw evocative signs like:

GRAND CAKE WALK   **SEE INTO THE FUTURE**

MINSTREL   &   **BELLA CORSO**

BURLESQUE   **FORTUNE TELLER**

That last one piqued her interest but Alexander suddenly steered sharply to the left forcing her concentration back into the cab and the urgent mission they were on.

It was as if the sunlight had dimmed as they pulled into a battered cobble-stoned street crowded with broken down wooden wagons selling small things poor people might afford. One lopsided metal van boosted a handwritten sign in very bad English offering *'neibors laundry 1ct 100 ct'*.

They drove past a warehouse and small factory spitting dark, bilious smoke and stopped in front of a row of five storey brick buildings dotted with the occasional tiny wrought iron balcony on which forlorn laundry was hung to dry in the wet winter air.

The few people in the street huddled in threadbare coats, staring out of sunken eyes carrying on the business of living under the pitiless burden of poverty.

Justine watched Alexander leap from the cab and dash up the front stairs, disappearing into the building.

"I think we should go with him," she said.

"No, Miss Justine. You do not want to go into that building," Maggie assured her, crossing her arms defiantly across her ample chest.

Justine waited impatiently studying the garbage disposed of in boxes in front of the building. She could see the rotting carcass of an animal, potato peelings and mud. Even in the cold, she could smell rotten oysters and rancid butter.

A young boy appeared on the street dressed in shorts and long, repeatedly repaired stockings stuffed into worn shoes much too big for his feet. He studied the cab and it's passengers with an appraising eye. Justine got out to speak with him:

"Can you be trusted to watch the horses and cab?" she asked.

He waited passively, looking at her with hooded eyes.

"There's a penny in it for you," Maggie said from inside the cab, "and a penny if it's all still here when we get back."

His boyish face came to life and his small, grubby fingers reached out for proof of payment. Sighing, Maggie got out of the cab, giving Justine a world weary shake of her head, and placed the promised coin into the boy's hand.

They opened the front door to the building, revealing an unlit, wooden staircase climbing up into deeper darkness. No sound came from the two apartments at the front and back so, grabbing Maggie's hand, Justine led the way up the stairs in the increasing gloom. The faint sound of a baby crying was all they had to guide them.

The boards on the second floor landing creaked in a manner suggesting rot and the airless dark intensified the claustrophobic effect. Squinting into the shadows, they could make out a strange set of internal casement windows and further down a black passageway, what might have been an open door. The baby's wail was coming from there.

Pushing open the door revealed a small, crowded room 12 feet by 12 feet with two grimy windows looking onto an airshaft and the brick wall of the next tenement. The gloomy room was crammed with a small cast iron stove, a tiny table with two rickety chairs, a makeshift crib plus a single bed on which sat a lean, dark haired woman holding the fretting baby.

Beyond was another room, more the size of a closet, which had the same internal windows through which negligible air and light might travel. Standing in the doorway was Sasha and a thin, young girl holding a rag doll.

While it was as clean as possible, the peeling walls and everything about the cramped apartment was worn and patched and gave off a heavy, exhausted air as if the room was as fed up as its inhabitants.

Kneeling beside the woman with the baby was Alexander. The tableau was so heartbreaking, Justine cried out causing Alexander to glance up. His sharp look suggested she'd done the wrong thing by intruding.

"Please forgive me, Alexander Alexandrovich," she said with as much respect as she could muster. "I only wanted to help."

He didn't speak but took the baby from his wife's arms, holding it protectively. It stopped crying.

"Is this your daughter?" Justine asked, stepping closer to look.

The child's nose was red and running and her dark curls surrounded a little face flushed with fever. Her rosebud mouth was compressed in concentration and then she coughed, deep in her throat and much too loudly for such a small being. The woman, Alexander's wife, stood up, and Justine was surprised to hear her speaking in Italian to the child, trying desperately to calm her.

"She needs a doctor," Justine said. "Is there a hospital nearby?"

Alexander's wife inhaled sharply.

"No, 'ospitale!" she said, shaking her head adamantly.

"But your baby needs a doctor!"

"It's not the doctor, she's afraid of," Maggie explained. "It's the hospital. It could kill you!"

Then Justine remembered reading somewhere about mortality rates in turn of the century hospitals. She also seemed to recall disturbing black and white photos to accompany the article.

"Ok, then what about Dr. Feingold?" she asked Alexander.

He closed his eyes, shaking his head. His face was etched with such pain, Justine thought he might drop the baby. Maggie reached for the bundle, suggesting causally to Alexander's wife:

"As Mr Alexander works for Miss Justine now, he can of course afford the best doctor for his child. Isn't that right little one?" she added, to the baby.

Alexander's wife looked at him questioningly. His eyes opened but he stood motionless, staring at the floor.

"We'd better hurry," Maggie said gently to the baby. "You need to see that doctor right away, don't you?"

Everyone looked to Alexander who finally nodded consent.

"You know," Justine said, thinking out loud. "It's a long way to Brooklyn and I'm wondering …. as you're going to need to be nearby, Alexander …. to chauffeur and things …"

Out of the corner of her eye, Justine could see Maggie subtly shaking her head, trying to stop her from whatever harebrained scheme she was cooking up now. Justine was vaguely aware that her grounding was slipping everyday she remained in this time and that the events of even the past 24 hours were too crazy to even try to comprehend.

But she threw up her hands defensively to Maggie, "They can't stay here!" she insisted, indicating the two other children and the miserable environment. "It doesn't make sense, anyway … to stay here, I mean. Does it?" she asked Alexander, reasonably.

"But where…?" Maggie started to ask.

"There's room," Justine interrupted. "There's plenty of room. There's an apartment - or at least there's space - below the main house. Right?" she conferred with Maggie.

"How do you know that?" Maggie asked, surprised.

"Well. That settles it then. If Maggie doesn't mind helping to pack up your family then you and me and your wife can be on our way to the doctor now…" Justine said, moving encouragingly toward the door.

Everyone once again looked to Alexander whose strong, proud eyes had filled with tears. The baby coughed again and that decided it. He helped his wife into her coat, giving instructions to Sasha in Russian, then, taking the baby back from Maggie, followed Justine with his wife out the door.

Down in the street, the urchin was nowhere to be seen and Justine was surprised that he'd not waited for the balance of his payment. But when she opened the door to the hansom cab, there he was fast asleep tucked into the blankets. He woke with a start and the wild look on his youthful face of an animal ready to attack.

"It's alright," Justine assured him. "I have another job for you. Do you think you can handle it?" she asked, placing the promised payment into his hand.

Eyeing the coin for authenticity, the boy jumped out of the cab, awaiting instructions.

"Can you find a horse and wagon and some men to help load up the stove and things from the second floor apartment?"

"My father has a wagon," he assured her.

"Good boy. My friend, Miss O'Reagan, is up there with this man's family. If anything is broken or stolen, you'll have to answer to him," Justine cautioned, pointing to Alexander.

The urchin eyed Alexander's full six feet and nodded his head in understanding. Justine placed another coin in his hand. She wished she could take him too and give him a bath and an education. She glanced up and down the littered, broken street overwhelmed with the suffering and need in just this small corner of the city. 'You can't save everyone,' Maggie had cautioned.

She helped tuck Alexander's wife and baby into the blankets as he turned the carriage around, finally heading for home.

"What's the baby's name?" Justine asked.

"Liliya. And my name is Rosa."

"It's very nice to meet you Rosa," Justine said. "And you Liliya," she murmured to the baby. "It's going to be ok," she comforted Rosa. "I promise."

How could she promise such a thing? The life of a small child was precarious enough in the time she came from. Now, in 1905, infant mortality was off the charts. Justine sat back rather than fighting the swaying of the carriage and stared unseeing at the passing city.

What am I doing? She asked herself. She would have returned to her time and her life if it weren't for the knowledge of a family that existed now, in this time and to which, in spite of everything, she belonged. The emotional pull of that connection was stronger than anything she'd ever felt before. It colored every encounter she'd had over the past few extraordinary days.

She was also experiencing a dislocation that comes when one is transported out of one's familiar life and surroundings. It was as if she was suddenly free to reinvent herself, moment to moment, out of deeply buried longings but at a barely conscious level. From the way she spoke to the way she acted, a transformation was underway.

When the lawyer told her of the existence of a half brother and sister, her heart had cracked open in a manner she'd never allowed to happen before. The desire to belong was so alluring she'd been trying to connect with everyone she met. Justine glanced at the mother and child across from her. She was changing; and was changing everything around her.

Twenty-Three

Waiting for someone to answer the door, Justine noticed the small, silver *mezuzah* placed on the right side of the doorframe. There were enough Jews in New York in her time that she'd seen many of these religious icons before. But noting it on the Feingold's door, made her wonder how large or small their community was and if they felt isolated or unwelcome living here.

The slender woman Justine had seen the night before answered the door. The delicate features of her face were accentuated by the way her hair was pulled back from her face and tied in a simple, large bun at the nape of her neck. She had intelligent, dark blue eyes, the precise color of the soberly elegant dress she wore. These somewhat haughty eyes regarded Justine for a moment before they glinted in recognition.

"You must be our new neighbor," the woman said, with a similarly educated tone as her husband's, with just a hint of her German upbringing.

"I'm Justine and I'm once again very sorry to bother you and the Doctor but we have a very, very sick baby," Justine babbled.

Mrs. Feingold was the sort of effortlessly pulled together women that always made Justine uncomfortable.

"*Oy va'avoy*," Mrs Feingold gasped upon noticing the emaciated Rosa, standing in the street holding her child. "Please come inside at once," she instructed, disappearing into the house.

Rosa hesitated staring up at the large, impressive white house but Alexander placed his hand on her back with encouragement. His face was set and Justine was unable to determine what he might be feeling. She led the way inside where she saw Mrs Feingold summoning them into a room off the foyer.

Sparsely furnished, it was clearly Dr Feingold's office. Located opposite the larger front room, it had the same high windows looking onto the street, which even on this winter's afternoon, allowed light to pour in. There was a large, neat roll top desk against one wall with floor to ceiling bookshelves and chairs along the opposite wall for patients to wait in. The lack of a rug gave the room a clean, open feel and the abundance of wood and cheery fireplace added a touch of safety and comfort - much like the doctor, himself.

A tasteful wooden Japanese screen stood towards the back of the room. Mrs Feingold waited for Rosa to approach with the baby.

"It's alright, my dear," she said, encouragingly, "The doctor is coming now."

Behind the screen was a wooden examination table complete with deep drawers and a padded, brown leather covering for the patient to lie on. Mrs Feingold was collapsing the metal stirrups used for female examinations so that Rosa could place little Liliya on the table.

As soon as she did the baby began coughing again, a sound that rattled in her tiny chest and distressed every adult in the room. Except for Dr Feingold who entered calmly from a rear door.

"Good evening, Miss Justine," he said softly.

"Yes, it's me again," Justine, said somewhat sheepishly. "This is Mr Alexander Alexandrovich, his wife Rosa and their daughter Liliya."

But the doctor had already turned his attention to the child. His murmured explanation of what he was doing accompanied his gentle but thorough examination. Mrs Feingold had donned a long, white apron and stood by his side efficiently assisting and anticipating his every need and occasionally offering a comment or suggestion. Clearly she knew much about medicine and he respected her knowledge.

Justine observed this elegant couple noting that they were a team; a loving, competent, intelligent team. It made her heart ache with longing and admiration. This was what she wanted in her life.

Dr Feingold stepped from behind the screen, motioning for Alexander and Justine to join him at his desk. His wife was subtly distracting Rosa as they washed and diapered baby Liliya.

"Your daughter is very sick, Mr Alexandrovich," Dr Feingold said. "Probably *keuchhusten* – pertussis, in English. Belladonna is often used to calm the spasm but my wife and I believe the proper remedy is drosera, a *homöopathisch*. If you agree we can administer immediately."

"Oh, my God – Belladonna!!?" Justine cried out. "Homeopathy is much, much safer for your baby, Alexander," she declared with conviction.

"I am glad you confer," Dr Feingold murmured, sardonically, turning away to write something down and so as to cover his grin.

Hunching his broad shoulders, Alexander pleaded, softly. "I am not doctor. Please save my Liliya."

Dr Feingold touched the big man's arm, comfortingly. "I am going to do everything I can. She will need to stay here tonight so we can monitor her."

"We will be right across the street." Justine confirmed. "Mr Alexandrovich and his family are moving into my building."

The doctor paused for a moment to digest this unusual piece of information, and then continued in the same reassuring voice:

"We will need to do a suctioning of the lungs. I do not think you or the mother should witness this. While it is generally not dangerous, it can be rather distressing to watch."

Alexander nodded and went to speak with his wife. A short argument ensued in both Russian and Italian. Rosa clearly did not want to leave her child. Trying not to eavesdrop, Justine glanced out the window and noticed a motorized wagon draw up across the street, followed by a horse drawn carriage out of which Maggie stepped.

"Alexander, Rosa, look, your son and daughter have arrived!" Justine announced.

Alexander guided his wife to the door.

"Thank you," he said, humbly to everyone in the room.

There was a great deal of moving and organizing ahead of them so Justine took her leave of the Feingold's and met Maggie in the street. The first thing she did was apologize:

"When this has all settled down, I have some things I want to share with you that might help to explain why I've been acting the way I have. But in the meantime, I'm sorry. I'm sorry and I cannot tell you how grateful I am to you, Maggie, my friend."

Maggie blushed from the neck of her high white collar to the roots of her auburn red hair.

"As I said the night you arrived – I am just so happy you're here."

"Good. Let's get this organized."

"Those workmen are still here. They've finished the bathroom."

"Would you send them out here to help and then please make sure Rosa and Sasha and their other daughter bathe and respectfully get every bit of their previous residence off of them. I bought some powder from Zhang that you can add to the bath water and wash through their hair. Take good care of Rosa, she's terrified."

"They'll need clothes …"

"Do whatever's necessary."

127

"You'll be needing this," she said, picking through the collection of barrel keys attached to a metal loop she always had with her. She handed Justine a ring with a couple of intricately designed brass keys attached.

Understanding each other perfectly, they moved as one towards Alexander and Rosa who were standing in the street with Sasha and their daughter, looking shell-shocked.

Twenty-Four

"I'd like to show you something Alexander and perhaps Rosa and the children can go with Maggie?"

Justine headed for the door to the basement apartment followed by Alexander. She had no idea what to expect and had a preternatural flash of déjà vu as she opened the door with the big brass key. 100 plus years from now she would open this same door to witness how her friend Margaret had been living, squatting inside these same walls – seeking protection and sanctuary in much the same way Alexander and his family now were.

Brownstones of this era had living quarters with entrances below the external stairs and windows at street level. These windows shed sufficient late afternoon light to make visible the central main room off of which were three doors and an exit to the back garden where Justine and not yet ventured. She whispered a prayer of thanks to the extraordinary Maggie O'Reagan. The interior was in good condition, cosy and spotlessly clean.

A deep stone kitchen sink and counter stood against the same wall as in Margaret's apartment with shelves and cupboards above and around it. A rectangular wooden table and 6 chairs were placed near the right wall and a sofa and armchairs surrounded the ample fireplace. No one had ever lived here so the simple furniture appeared new.

"Do you think this would be alright for you family?" Justine asked, crossing the room and opening a door to inspect the small front bedroom that actually contained a bed.

Although the ceilings were tall for a basement apartment, Alexander's height filled the space. He stood in the middle of the room unable to speak or to move.

Justine headed to the second door, opening onto another room also with a bed.

"Oh, look. Another bedroom! With windows looking into the garden," she exclaimed.

The emotional energy welling up inside Alexander threatened to overwhelm both of them. The best Justine could do was keep moving to the next door, which opened onto another room, small, but containing yet another bed. Her mother's lover, her father, intended a full staff of servants to wait on and serve her. Justine was almost as overcome as Alexander.

She waited for him to respond. Moving Margaret and Joe into this place had been more than the right thing to do. It had completed the space. It was as if emptiness had supported the building and then life replaced it.

As she watched Alexander, for a brief revelatory moment, she suddenly saw Ducky; the noble nose and bright, blue eyes that seemed to see more than they saw. It was so real and her connection to Ducky so deep that she spoke his name:

"Please, Duc …." she blurted out.

Alexander glanced at her and the 'vision' faded. She shook her head and was once again looking at Alexander Alexandrovich - a strong capable man reduced by unknown circumstances.

"I don't know how to say this," she mumbled, covering the confusing moment. "No one is living here. It's a space begging for life and a family to inhabit it."

Alexander's large, rough hand went to his heart, expressing the gratitude he couldn't speak. Then he nodded and went to oversee the installation of the cast iron stove and the rest of his families' few belongings.

For Justine the impression of Ducky lingered in the room.

Twenty-Five

The light had all but faded as she made her way upstairs. It always seemed coldest to Justine just as the sun disappeared over the horizon. She shivered. *Another day out of time*, she mused, not quite knowing what she meant.

An unfamiliar weariness slowed her steps and rather than heading for the kitchen she detoured into the parlour hoping for a moment alone. But what confronted her shocked her out of her exhaustion. The painting of her mother was gone!

Then she remembered James and the creeping sensation of dislocation flushed through her like vertigo. How could she have forgotten James? She raced upstairs fearing the worst, knowing somehow that the worst had already happened.

Throwing open the door to her 'father's' room, James was gone. The bed was unmade and the closet was ransacked.

"No! No! No!" Justine cried in absolute frustration.

James was the key. The reason she was still here: the hope of finding her family. And whatever his connection to the painting of her mother, it had been the bait to lure him to reveal what he knew.

"How could you do this? You snake. You fucking bastard!"

"*Trócaire*, Miss Justine, I don't know where you learned to swear like that ..." Maggie said entering but was stopped mid-sentence by the mess in the room and the absence of her patient. "Where's ...?"

"Gone! And so's the painting!"

"The ...? He stole the painting?"

"We shouldn't have left him here alone."

"He wasn't alone. The house was filled with workmen."

"I know and I thought he was too sick to move."

Maggie's eyes widened. "You don't think one of the workmen ....?"

"No. Why would they?"

"You can't tell about foreigners," Maggie confirmed.

"Maggie, dearest, you are a foreigner. I am a foreigner. Everyone who lives in this country comes from somewhere else – except the Native Americans."

"Yes. Well. I never thought about it that way..."

"Anyway, what would they do with a painting like that? Whereas we know it had some kind of importance for James – for Mr Grey."

Justine sat on the bed letting her head fall into her hands. "Oh damn, damn, damn…" she sighed.

In this bed she and James had …. But she didn't want to think about that. It just intensified the sense of betrayal. Men had left her before, after having sex. Men had said they would call and didn't. This felt different somehow. Not only had he gotten under her skin, he'd stolen something of rare personal value.

"The family's in the basement – gone to bed, I imagine, God bless them." Maggie said soothingly. "And I've run a hot bath for you. Then some supper and a nice hot cocoa and then …. and then we'll figure out what to do."

Justine sighed, gazing up at this warm, capable young women whom she'd only just met but who seemed to understand her almost as well as Ducky. Maggie was trustworthiness itself. She nodded, following Maggie downstairs.

The brand new bathroom floor sparkled with ceramic black and white tiling. White tiles ran up the walls around the tub and sink. The heavy iron stove gave off ample heat and Justine allowed herself to sink gratefully into the deep claw-foot tub, promising herself a bathroom just like this when she got home.

Not bathing everyday was extremely unpleasant and necessitated added implements to be worn under arms and elsewhere to protect clothing from body odour and stains.

"New rule of the household," she announced drowsily to Maggie. "Regular bathing and cleanliness!"

"I'm not sure how your new tenants are going to take to that idea."

I have tenants, Justine told herself, sinking deeper into the water and blowing bubbles like she had as a child.

"I had quite a task getting the daughter into the tub," Maggie continued. "She's a strange one to be sure. Doesn't speak. What's her name now …. Ann – lika? No. That's not right. There's another sound in there. I'm sure of it. Ann –silka?

Justine sat up ready at last to get out of the tub.

"Why do foreigners have such troublesome names?" Maggie wondered, collecting the towel from where it'd been warming near the stove.

Justine stood up reaching for the towel and Maggie quickly averted her eyes.

"Oh, my Miss Justine. Have you no shame?" Maggie cried, holding out the towel but refusing to look at her directly.

"We're all girls here," Justine said, chuckling, taking the towel and covering her nakedness. "But if my nudity offends you, I'll meet you in the parlour once I'm decent."

Twenty-Six

In spite of the empty space above the fireplace, Justine was bathed, fed and with a stiff whisky in her hand, felt much, much better. She'd convinced Maggie to have a bath and they were now curled in their separate chairs, in bedclothes and robes. With a fire crackling in the fireplace and the velvet curtains drawn against the winter chill, Justine had a strange sense of calm. She took a sip letting the alcohol burn slowly down her throat.

"Maggie," she began, "There's something I need to tell you that I'm quite certain you won't believe. You may even suspect that I'm insane or worse. And I wouldn't blame you. I find it totally incredible myself. But what I'm about to tell you is absolutely, 100% true."

Maggie turned not only her eyes but her whole compact body to focus on Justine.

"Because you're so observant and sensitive to others, you've noticed that many of the things I do and say are – well, strange – and often inappropriate. Right?"

"I'm just a girl from Kilkenny, miss. What do I know about what's what?"

"Nonetheless, if you were honest with yourself and with me, right now in this moment, you'd have to admit that while you might like me, you find me – odd."

"I don't know that's it's appropriate for me to have an opinion about you miss. And may I add - you're scaring me."

"I'm sorry. What I'm about to tell you is very disturbing and completely wondrous and impossible and occurring all at the same time."

Justine stood up. This was not going to be easy. She turned her back to the fire, looking at Maggie and taking a deep breath.

"Do you remember when you first saw me? Out there on the street? "

Maggie nodded.

"Do you remember that you saw me and then I sort of – disappeared?

Maggie looked down, remembering but unwilling to confirm it. She shifted uncomfortably in her seat, pulling her handkerchief from her pocket.

"Well, that's what you saw. Because the truth is - I crossed the date line. I crossed into another time and then I crossed back. I don't know how and I don't know why. I come from the future, Maggie. I was born almost 100 years from now."

Maggie glanced up at Justine with sunflower blue, saucer-like eyes, trying to perceive deception. Finding none she continued to stare as if her brain were attempting to catch up with what her eyes were seeing and her ears were hearing.

"It seems my mother may have been able to do the same," Justine went on, her hand referring to the portrait that was no longer there.

"Dear Mother of God," Maggie breathed out slowly, making the sign of the cross for protection. "It's not possible."

"I know. That's what I would've said a week ago. But the fact is, here I am!"

Maggie took a gulp of her whisky, then began wringing her handkerchief. Justine continued because she didn't know what else to do.

"I don't think anyone could ever have said anything more ridiculous or outrageous than what I've just said and I completely understand your distress and disbelief."

She sat down again, reaching out her hand:

"Considering what little you know of me, Maggie, do you think I'm a liar or a con artist or untrustworthy?"

"I don't know what that second thing is," Maggie replied, "but no, I consider you an honest, respectable lady, down deep."

"Thank you. That means a lot to me."

Justine stared into the fire and Maggie worried her handkerchief.

"When I came back the second time I didn't know what to expect," Justine explained. "I certainly didn't think I'd be living here in this house, with you and..." her hand made a big circle including everything that had happened and all the people involved. "I live in this same house over 100 years from now."

Maggie gasped. Justine nodded in agreement with how extraordinary it was.

"Until Mr Brewster told me about my brother and sister, I had no plan. But now, oh Maggie, I really want to meet them. My mother left when I was six. I never knew why. I was raised by the most wonderful man in the world. I call him Ducky. He's not my real father – more like my best friend. I never had a real family."

"Families are good. Families are also not so good," Maggie advised. She'd been sipping nervously at her drink and her words were faintly slurred.

"And then James – Mr Grey – and the portrait …. He was the key, you see, to finding my sister and brother," Justine went on. "But now that things have become a bit complicated … It just didn't seem fair anymore not to tell you. And to be honest, I've come to rely on your wise advice to navigate this time when things are – well – very different for me."

Justine looked at Maggie to determine if she'd said enough or should continue. Maggie shifted in her seat again and stared at her empty glass.

"I don't know what to say, Miss Justine. I – I don't know what to think."

"I'm sorry. I get it," Justine replied. She was the slightest bit disappointed that Maggie wasn't able to rise to the occasion and just suspend disbelief, but she also completely understood. "Ducky always says, 'why don't you sleep on it' – so why don't we go to bed and talk about it in the morning?"

Justine said goodnight to Maggie on the second floor landing and watched while she ascended to the next floor, swaying ever so slightly.

Twenty-Seven

Justine was surprised that she'd actually fallen asleep when she was awoken some hours later. By what, she couldn't say. The house was silent around her, the darkness interrupted only by a faint light, which at first she imagined was spill from the street lamps. She sat up feeling the chill – but there was something else. Something didn't feel right.

Padding around in the dark for her robe and slippers she glanced out the window, suddenly aware that the light wasn't coming from the street at all. It was coming from the floor above.

Tiptoeing, she made her way as silently as she could up the stairs. She didn't know why she felt the need for stealth but she winced every time a floorboard creaked. The third floor was pitch black; no light appeared from under any of the doors, including the room Maggie now slept in.

Justine wasn't familiar with this part of the house, now or in her own time and the darkness reminded her of the horribly claustrophobic landing in the tenement where Alexander had been living with his family.

There was another floor above. She knew that. It was the attic, which was large enough to have housed Ducky for many years. But Ducky had a proper set of stairs, obviously built sometime after the original construction. Justine remembered from Maggie's tour that there was only a narrow spiral staircase at the end of the landing leading to a trap door.

Loathe to go up there in the dark, Justine felt her way across the landing and stood listening for any sound indicating there was something up there; something or someone she needed to investigate.

The wind had picked up as it often did, heralding the dawn, brushing its frigid fingers against the casement windows. Justine shivered as much with the cold as with the unremitting sense that something was not right. Holding her breath, she reached for the stair rail, placing her right foot on the first step. Blindly her left foot found the next stair and then the next. She only knew when to stop when her head hit the ceiling. Fumbling around overhead, she finally located a metal loop. Slipping three fingers through it, she pulled, softly at first and then much harder. But it wouldn't give.

Justine had never liked the dark. She'd waited alone in the New Orleans hotel room at the age of six for Ducky's arrival. When night descended she'd been too scared to move or turn on the lights. Tonight her fear was intensified by the feeling of floating high above solid ground, with only a narrow iron step beneath her feet. Panic caused her to pull angrily again and again at the metal ring and then push it in frustration – which resulted in the trap door springing open.

Justine winced as the hinges creaked, screaming like alley cats in the silence. Terrified, she poked her head into the attic, locating the source of the light and also discovering Maggie, collapsed on a wooden box head resting against the incline of the roof. She was dressed in a long white apron with her hair tied up in a white scarf and white woollen gloves on both hands. Her lantern gave off a powerful glow, casting shadows up the slanted walls and out through the long dormer windows. Justine knew those windows; Ducky had made them into French doors with a small balcony onto the roof.

A bucket and broom were propped nearby and a feather duster had fallen from Maggie's hand. Her face was as white as her clothing and her eyes opened only partially when Justine pulled herself all the way into the space.

"Maggie?" Justine whispered, approaching gently not sure what was wrong and not wanting to startle her.

Maggie's lips were blue but moving so Justine knelt down, leaning closer, trying to hear what she was trying to say.

"As – ma," Maggie murmured. "Can't breathe."

"On, my God. Maggie. You're having an asthma attack!!?"

Panic shot through Justine like white heat, pumping endorphins to every cell in her body. This was followed by an explosion in her head of every nightmare, bad horror movie and childhood terror she'd every experienced about death and dying. For precious seconds Justine froze, unable to think or to act. Then just as suddenly, her body centered itself and her head cleared into sharp focus.

She took in the entire room at a glance, locating a small brazier. Using the fire from Maggie's lantern, Justine managed to get the coals burning. It would have to do while she was gone.

"I'm going to the kitchen to get you a steam pot. It will help clear your lungs. I won't be long," she added, squeezing Maggie's hand.

Getting down the spiral stairs wasn't easy but once back on the third floor landing, Justine raced to the kitchen. Grabbing the kettle she heated some water, while rummaging frantically through the herbs stored in a small cupboard next to the stove. In her rush to find something that would work she spilled other things onto the floor. Then she remembered the small vial of eucalyptus oil Zhang had included with her purchases. It was too precious and too unusual for her to offer to Sasha, but it was exactly what Maggie needed right now. She found it in the cupboard with the spices, hidden behind the vanilla. She couldn't wait for the water to boil so she poured warm water into a pot and secured a lid on top.

Racing back up to the second floor, she stopped to collect blankets and towels, hauling everything back up the frustrating and precarious attic stairs. Maggie was just where she'd left her, eyes closed, struggling with the effort to breathe as her body tried to shut down her airways.

Justine placed the pot on the brazier. The attic was used for storage but as no one had ever lived here it was relatively empty. However, she was able to locate a small arm chair stashed in the far corner, which she dragged closer to Maggie.

"Maggie, sweetheart, can you shift to this chair? You'll be more comfortable." Justine suggested, getting her hands under Maggie's arms to help her up.

Maggie collapsed into the armchair, eyes closed, trying to move as little as possible; just trying to breathe. Justine wrapped her in the blankets as the water began to boil. She added a few drops of the eucalyptus oil and dragging the wooden box next to Maggie's chair, placed the pot on it.

"Maggie, if you lean over the pot and inhale the steam, it will help you breathe."

Justine removed the pot's lid and the room filled with the astringent scent of eucalyptus. Maggie crinkled her nose.

"It's eucalyptus, Maggie. It's made from a tree that grows in Australia. It's really good for your lungs. I promise."

Maggie pried open one eye to look up at Justine who smiled at her encouragingly. Then she leaned over the pot and tried to inhale. Justine draped the towel over Maggie's head to create a vacuum and prayed for her to get relief.

Justine waited and Maggie tried and after an interminable period of time, Maggie finally tossed the towel off her head and lay back against the chair. Her face was flushed from the steam and her lips not quite as blue but she looked weaker than before.

"Is it helping?" Justine asked, leaning in to hear the reply.

"A little," Maggie whispered.

Justine placed the pot back on the brazier to reheat the water and create more steam. She watched Maggie struggle for air feeling the panic begin to rise again inside her. Finally she couldn't stand it any longer. Placing the hot infusion back on the wooden box, she leaned over and spoke to Maggie:

"I'm going to get something that will cure this, Maggie. Okay? Do you hear me? I'm going to get it right now."

Maggie nodded, not opening her eyes.

"While I'm gone, please keep breathing the steam. Okay?"

Maggie nodded again and Justine fled down the stairs and out the front door. She felt as if Death were pursuing her in his black hooded cloak with his sharpened scythe held in his outstretched, skeletal fingers. She was frantic and terrified and thus didn't care when the icy, sharp wind hit her face and chased her around the corner of the building.

Twenty-Eight

Her heart beat louder and her feet ran faster as she felt the unseen energetic field dragging her forward into a vortex of absolute, tomblike silence and overpowering intensity. Then, just when she thought Death had caught up with her, her whole body smashed into the invisible membrane, viscous, hard and porous all at the same time. And then just as abruptly, she broke through onto the hot cement alleyway having made a dizzying 180° turn. Almost smashing into the two hulking garbage bins, her bones felt like liquid and she had to steady herself from vertigo. But her mind remained focused.

Her nose was assaulted by unpleasant but familiar odours of car exhaust and 21st century pollution. It was evening and the air was thick with humidity, the streets slick with a recent summer downpour. It was still light and steam rose off the pavement. She walked quickly to the steps of her building and up to the front door. She hadn't thought what she would do if she encountered Margaret or Ducky. She hadn't thought at all.

The new keypad had been installed and she pressed the numbers Ducky and she had agreed on, praying they were the same. A taxi passed, slowing near the corner. She could feel the eyes of the passengers on her, dressed in an eider down dressing gown with wide silk embroidered trim, a lacy full length nightie peeking out beneath and bootie like slippers on her feet.

The door clicked and she summarily 'broke into' her own building. In contrast to the same house she'd left only moments before, the entry was spacious and open, smelling of fresh paint and wood stain. Her feet raced back up the same grand staircase to the third floor but now she ascended the newer stairway up to Ducky's attic apartment.

"Ducky?" she called out, tentatively pushing open his door.

She desperately longed to see him but hoped he wasn't there. If he were home, she wasn't' sure she'd have the resolve to go back.

Peering around the door, his apartment was exactly as she'd last seen it - as yet untouched by the renovations. No one was there so she crept inside, feeling like a thief in the night. Hurrying into his bathroom she was aware of passing the exact location where Maggie at this very moment was clinging to life by a thread.

But it isn't at this very moment, is it? She admonished herself, because her conscious mind refused to shut down.

The truth was that Maggie, who was relying on Justine to save her life, was very much dead, and had been for decades. Justine shook her head because there was no way to explain this very real paradox. The best she could do was follow her heart and her heart was determined to keep Maggie alive.

She bent down to open a narrow cupboard under the sink. This was where Paul kept the things he needed when he stayed with

Ducky. Paul was a bit of a hypochondriac and most of the contents were medicinal. She located the basket of inhalers. Paul didn't actually have asthma, he'd recently had bronchitis and kept an 'in case' supply. There were more inhalers than he would ever need even if he got sick again.

Grabbing one of Paul's ubiquitous silk pouches, Justine filled it with the inhalers. She would have liked to take more of the medicines – more need for them where she was going than Paul would ever have - but she had no idea what they were for and wondered if Paul did either. She did grab a big bottle of Vitamin C.

Then, as an afterthought, she removed the beautiful lace and silk bloomers Maggie insisted she wear at all times and stuffed them into the empty basket. Paul would appreciate the thought.

Grasping the pouch firmly in her hand Justine stopped for a moment inside Ducky's room. Eclectically furnished with antiques from various eras, she'd always felt snug and safe here. Sighing, she tucked her free hand into the deep pocket of her dressing gown and was surprised to feel something cold and hard inside. Pulling it out she discovered the Meissen statue from 'her father's' room. She'd forgotten stashing it there.

Over the gas fireplace, hung a watercolor by a well-known 20th Century English artist, that Justine had scraped the money together to buy for Ducky's 60th birthday. It depicted a bucolic confluence of sky, sunshine, snow, sheep, stream, an ancient stone wall and a locomotive steaming through on a sleek arched bridge. It suited Ducky's diverse taste.

But it wasn't the painting Justine was staring at; it was the elegant statue sitting on the mantelpiece. About 3 inches tall, the porcelain figure was an 18th century gentleman in a long red jacket with intricate white lace at his neck and wrists over a delicately painted white vest with dark blue flowers. His tiny alabaster face was so skilfully painted that his expression brought a lump to Justine's throat. His eyes looked to his right with longing and absolute love. His right hand was upturned and outstretched as if waiting. And now she knew what he was waiting for.

She carefully placed the Meissen statue from her pocket next to Ducky's figure. Moving them together, the tiny hands connected and fit together as if they'd been created that way. The two men's eyes met and she knew they'd been made for each other.

Much as she would have liked to wait for Ducky's return, sitting in his comfy 19th century gentleman's reclining armchair, upholstered in tan hide, with her feet on the footrest and a cappuccino on the drink stand, she forced herself back downstairs. As she approached the first floor foyer, she saw a shadow approaching through the opaque, cut glass windows in the front door. Turning sharply towards the back of the house, she passed swiftly through the wide-open space of living and dining rooms treading lightly on the hardwood floors. She pushed through the heavy plastic sheets hanging across the entry to the kitchen.

Everything in the kitchen sparkled, from the stainless steel appliances to the granite counter tops, which beautifully contrasted the distressed white cupboards and the continuation of hardwood floors. But Justine noticed it all only in passing as she slipped out the back door and tiptoed down the back stairs.

The garden had not yet been landscaped and remained forlorn and over-grown. Justine had only been in the back garden a few times and only after they had purchased the brownstone.

Now what? She wondered, glancing frantically around the enclosure.

She could hear voices, one of them Ducky's. She wasn't sure if he'd seen her but it wouldn't be long before he'd sense something and come looking. The voices got louder and closer.

Justine headed for the wall that ran along the alleyway, surveying the thick blankets of ivy, which cascaded over the brick from the rear of the garden halfway along the wall and all the way to the ground. Justine grabbed one heavy end of ivy and pulling it upward with all her might, managed to create a space between wall and plant into which she could disappear. Just as the gnarled mass settled against her, Ducky appeared at the kitchen door.

"I could swear I saw something. Or someone," he said to whoever he was with.

The sound of his much-loved voice almost caused Justine to push through the bramble and rush into his arms. But something stronger than Ducky's love compelled her to stay hidden. It wasn't just Maggie, it was the answers that lay on the other side of the dateline.

She pressed herself deeper into the darkness. It was oppressively hot and she shut her mind to whatever creepy crawlers might reside here. She became aware that while one side of her back was against the brick, the other side had slipped into a depression in the wall. Inching further along and testing gingerly with her hands, she felt an archway built into the wall and inside it, a wooden door.

Ducky had descended into the garden. The other voice was Paul's, more strident and higher pitched. No longer focused on potential intruders, they seemed to be discussing the upcoming design for the outside/inside terrace/deck. Their voices were distant and muffled.

She gave the garden door a shove, but it wouldn't budge. Feeling further down, she came upon a keyhole in the door, a large antique sized keyhole. The door was locked. How long the door had been locked, she didn't know.

Aware of the ridiculousness of the situation, Justine considered giving up and revealing herself. She stuck her hands indecisively into the pockets of her robe. One pocket was empty but in the other she was amazed to retrieve the set of keys Maggie had given her. The enormous coincidence was not lost on her. Grasping the keys, she made up her mind:

If I am meant to go back, Justine told herself, *one of these keys will open this lock.*

She waited, feeling lightheaded from the heat as night descended and Ducky and Paul eventually went back inside.

It took only three tries and one of the large keys slipped easily into the lock, turned with some effort and opened the hidden garden gate.

Twenty-Nine

Ducky couldn't shake the feeling of a presence in the house. Justine's note explaining her disappearance made him decide to tell everyone she'd gone to New Orleans on a buying trip for his shop. He thought about Justine's mother. The suspicions he'd always had about her arrival and disappearance had been so far fetched that if someone had suggested them to him, he would have looked for the men in white coats. But these fanciful notions went some way to explain Justine's absence and her possible presence tonight. His mind refused to go any further than that. He was worried to his core about her, but something prevented him from going to the police and reporting her missing.

He hadn't even communicated his concerns to Paul. Next to Justine, Paul was the most important human being in Ducky's life. Growing up in an age when his sexual orientation might have meant a lifetime alone, his relationship with Paul was a precious and treasured gift. But Paul was prone to hysteria over the slightest thing and this 'thing' was not slight.

Paul continued chatting as they made their way up to Ducky's apartment:

"This climb is really getting old," Paul complained. "Maybe you should consider moving down a level – or two. It's not too late to change the floor plans…"

Not waiting for an answer, Paul continued talking as they entered the apartment making his way to the bathroom. Ducky could hear him undertaking his nightly ritual of cleansing and toning and moisturizing. But Ducky was stopped in his tracks, feeling as if the earth had shifted on its axis, staring at the two figurines on his mantelpiece.

"O-M-G!" Paul exclaimed loudly. "Where in the hell did these divine things come from?" He stood in the bathroom doorway with Justine's bloomers draped suggestively over one finger, but seeing Ducky's face, he whispered, "Duck …? What's up?"

The best Ducky could do was move closer to the fireplace, signalling for Paul to join him. They stared at the pair of porcelain figures.

"Where…?" Paul asked.

But Ducky reached out his hand and Paul grasped it and they stood together, utterly transported.

Thirty

Justine was practically out of breath by the time she made it back to the attic. Judging by the summer darkness, she'd probably been 'on the other side' maybe two hours, but the clock on the second floor landing indicated less than an hour had passed and the winter dawn had not yet arrived. Crossing the dateline was the most horrifying thing she'd ever experienced in her life and she'd just done it twice in whatever amount of time was correct.

"I'm sorry it took so long, Maggie," Justine panted, falling to her knees physically and psychically winded.

Maggie was unable to respond, but her eyes opened hopefully at Justine's arrival. The scent of eucalyptus faintly filled the air but the pot had gone cold and clearly she'd been unable to reheat it.

"Maggie, I want you to put this in your mouth," Justine said, shaking the red, plastic inhaler and placing it in Maggie's hand.

Maggie looked at the thing, not understanding. Justine removed another inhaler to demonstrate.

"Place this side in your mouth. Press this button here and inhale as deeply as you can."

Maggie shook her head.

"I know you can't inhale," Justine said, gently, "This will force open your air ways and allow you to breath. I promise you."

Maggie looked at the foreign object in her hand and then up at Justine. She was exhausted and the bright blue eyes intently sought assurance. For a moment their eyes held, then Maggie brought the inhaler to her lips, pressed the button and inhaled, deeply.

Her eyes widened in surprise and she sat up abruptly as if she'd been shocked back to life, which in a way, she had. She took another deep breath, this time on her own and smiled from ear to ear.

"You can use it again if you need to," Justine said, smiling back.

Maggie shook her head, closing her eyes and relishing the ability to breath freely. She giggled with the sheer sudden pleasure of it and Justine giggled too. Maggie opened her eyes, looking at Justine. She laughed and Justine laughed too. The terror and anxiety of the past few hours melted out of them and the warmth and joy of relief filled the room with their hilarity.

Clutching the inhaler to her chest, Maggie asked, "What is this and where did you go to get it?"

"It's called an inhaler, Maggie. It's got medicine to reopen your lungs when you get an asthma attack. I brought back as many as I could so you've got them for the future."

"But I've never seen such a thing before."

"It doesn't exist. It won't exist until 1955."

Maggie shook her head, refusing to accept the implications.

"Have a look at it, Maggie. Have a close look."

Maggie opened her hand cautiously and studied the object.

"It's made of something called plastic. Have you ever seen plastic like that before?

Fingering the bright red inhaler, Maggie shook her head.

"I think plastic was discovered some time ago but it didn't start getting mass produced until the 1940's or 50's," Justine explained. "Look at the writing on the side," she suggested.

Maggie read the stamped date, "February Two Thousand and … Oh, dear God!"

She dropped the inhaler as if it were cursed, stood up, stepping away from the thing, digging in her apron for her handkerchief.

"I'm sorry to upset you," Justine said sincerely, picking up the inhaler. "Really I am. As I said last night, this is the most inconceivable thing in the whole universe. BUT. IT'S. TRUE. I wouldn't have saddled you with this if I didn't want to stop lying to you. And if I didn't need your help."

Justine's voice broke on the last sentence and Maggie came to her.

"Oh, Miss Justine. I'm sorry for being so stubborn. Me Mum always said it would keep the men from marrying me. I'm that grateful to you for saving me life!"

She handed Justine her hanky and Justine laughed, taking it gratefully and wiping the tears from her eyes. Maggie wrapped her arms around Justine and they held each other, each dealing with the overwhelming impact of the past few hours and days in their own way.

"What were you doing up here anyway?" Justine wanted to know.

"Cleaning, Miss. It's the last day of the year and I clean this whole house from top to bottom," Maggie replied with satisfaction.

"Not anymore. You've got asthma!"

"But, that's me job!"

"It was probably the dust that brought it on."

"Do you think?"

"Has it happened before on these cleaning sprees?"

"I don't know what a 'sprees' is but, come to think of it, it has done before. Not as bad as this time, mind you. I think that was due to the ... what you told me."

"Look. Take your time with what I've told you. You don't have to believe it. It's just important that you know it's true. For me. Okay? Because I do need your help."

"You have that, Miss Justine."

"So – true or not – everything has changed with my – with my – crossing. Everything here and everything over there. I don't even know what that means but .... the first thing we're changing is your job. You are too smart and too capable to be a house cleaner. And now that we know it's dangerous to your health, we'll find someone else. I am officially promoting you to house *keeper*. That means you now run this place."

"Well, then," Maggie said standing up proudly and dusting off her apron, "why don't we go downstairs for a nice, hot cup of tea."

"Or Coffee? And biscuits? I'd die for your biscuits right now!"

"Please don't talk about dying, if you don't mind."

"Oops. Sorry. Stupid me. Come on, it's freezing up here!'

Thirty-One

The sun arose on the last day of the year, determined to shine in spite of ominous, swelling dark clouds. Justine and Maggie sat companionably in the kitchen window overlooking the garden. The back half of the yard was a working garden with rows of frozen plantings, patiently waiting for spring to bring forth life again.

Justine sat dipping her fresh biscuit into hot, milky coffee, slurping the buttery, flakiness into her mouth, then closing her eyes and tilting her head into the faint sunlight, savoring the taste as it melted down her throat.

"I'm not a great cook," Justine murmured "but I'd love to learn how make these."

"I'll show you – if you'll teach me to write."

Justine's eyes popped open. "But I thought you could?" she said, sitting up and looking at Maggie, whose face was burning with her own impertinence.

"I can almost read. Reading and numbers. I'm good at numbers. But I had to leave school before the writing."

"Okay, then. It's a deal," Justine agreed, extending her hand. "I'll teach you to write and you will teach me to bake."

Maggie shook Justine's hand with gusto, blushing and grinning.

"You will have the more challenging task, I assure you!" Justine warned.

But Maggie was busy clearing the breakfast things, humming happily to herself. Justine smiled, leaning back into the sunshine when she noticed Alexander's daughter making her way across the garden. The girl paused to inspect a trailing vine and allow the sun to shine on her face then she opened the garden gate, and disappeared through it.

"I've never been in the garden," Justine said. "I think I'll have a look."

"I was going to make up some more biscuits," Maggie said, mixing spoon in hand. "I expect that brood downstairs'll be wanting breakfast."

Justine grinned at Maggie's expectant face. "I won't be long. And it'll take more than one demonstration to teach me the art of biscuit making. You'll be writing books long before I've made anything edible."

Justine slipped out the back door, taking the icy steps gingerly, surveying the garden enclosure. An elaborate stone fountain with two chubby nymphs cavorting atop was center stage in front of a white gazebo and bench, surrounded by rose bushes trimmed back to their scraggly, thorny nubs also waiting for the warmth of spring.

While the view beyond wasn't a solid wall of brownstones backing onto their own gardens as in the future, it was a very similar space to what she'd 'escaped' from only hours before. These comparisons gave her a sense of displacement as well as intimacy, drawing her in and pushing her away. She'd always felt deep down that she didn't belong somehow and this feeling was exacerbated now.

A winding brick path led to the garden gate, which she knew hadn't changed because Maggie's key fit it. She cautiously pushed open the gate directly into the stables. She didn't hear the screeching noises or feel the energetic pull so she figured it was safe to enter the stables from this direction.

There were two stalls housing the sickly horses Puttuck had sold her. In the far stall, Alexander's daughter was slowly brushing the Grey's mane, whose back was covered with sores. The Chestnut's head hung over the wall that separated them, as if lending support to his ailing friend.

The girl looked up alarmed, her narrow face overpowered by her two dark, round eyes. She wore her hair pulled back in a tight bun like her mother's – but while it flattered the older woman's high cheekbones and sensuous lips, it accentuated the girl's gauntness. The clothing Maggie had found for her bunched around her tiny waist and drooped down her slender arms. She didn't appear much healthier than the horse she was stroking.

"It's okay," Justine said gently. "I didn't mean to startle you."

Justine came around to have a better look at the horse's condition and the girl moved closer to the horse. Justine could have sworn the horse moved closer to the girl.

"He's pretty hurt, isn't he?" Justine observed. "We could do something for his wounds. Would you like to help me make something for him?"

The girl nodded, still eyeing Justine cautiously.

"I'm Justine. What's your name?"

The girl's large eyes wandered back to the horse.

"Come on, then," Justine said, offering her hand. The girl put down the brush and moved silently toward the gate. She turned to make sure Justine was following, but said nothing. She seemed to float across the garden, as if she weren't corporeal, moving quickly for one seemingly so weak.

Although Justine had already ingested two of Maggie's biscuits, the kitchen aromas as they entered, made her mouth water.

"Oh, good morning to you … Anzelika," Maggie said, pronouncing the name with some difficulty, but proud to have remembered and gotten it right. "You'll be wanting some breakfast, then," she said, bustling around the kitchen, setting the table with one eye on the bubbling pots.

But Anzelika didn't answer or seem interested in the food. She waited.

"We were going to make something for the horses wounds," Justine explained, glancing at the child. Anzelika looked down, not moving. "I need some sugar and some soap and a bit of old bread, if you have," she added, staring at Maggie to communicate that the child needed this attention.

Maggie glanced sideways at the girl who continued to wait without moving.

"Right," she said. "Soap's on the sink. Old bread would be in the bread box and sugar's in the lock up," she stated, fingering her keys, finding the correct one by touch.

Justine showed Anzelika how to shave the soap and add sugar and a bit of water to make a paste, then spread it thickly on the bread, to create a poultice. As soon as they were done, the little girl was out the door, back into the cold stables applying the salve to the horses' wounds.

Justine stood by, watching. Later she would believe Anzelika spoke to the horses, letting them know that she was helping them, and that they expressed their gratitude. In fact, the whole enterprise was undertaken in silence and, of course, the horses didn't speak.

Even when every wound on both horses had been seen to, Anzelika seemed to want to remain in the cold stables.

"Why don't we go and eat our breakfast," Justine suggested "and then you can come back and see how they're doing?"

Anzelika seemed not to hear. She was in another world, her head resting against the Grey, listening to the horse, rather than Justine. Justine reached out her hand to touch the child's arm. Anzelika jumped, shifting frightened eyes onto Justine that burned with accusation and fear.

Justine, stepped back, appalled. "I'm so, so sorry," she said.

Moments passed in which Justine was aware only of the horses moving, imperceptibly. Then she took a breath and Anzelika, once again, headed to the gate, glancing back to see if Justine would follow.

Everyone was nervously gathered in the kitchen when Justine and Anzelika retuned. Rosa looked as if she hadn't slept with dark circles pooling beneath her red-rimmed eyes, holding onto Sasha's hand and Alexander sipping coffee not taking his eyes off his wife.

Witnessing this sombre tableau, Justine became aware that everyone was waiting for her, as mistress of the house, to take the lead.

She made an announcement, "I'm going across to Dr Feingold. Would anyone like to join me?" Noticing Maggie eyeing her apparel, Justine added, "And yes, Maggie, I am wearing this outfit!"

Alexander followed her out of the kitchen.

Mrs Feingold answered the door immaculately dressed in an emerald green ruched silk dress with delicate white lace at the wrists and neck. She glanced imperceptibly at Justine's dressing gown, causing Justine to admonish herself for not heeding Maggie and putting on proper clothing.

Dr Feingold escorted Alexander into the examination room to see his daughter, leaving Justine in the foyer with his wife. Unable to find a graceful way to explain her attire, Justine apologized for disturbing the Feingolds on the last day of the year.

"But it's not *our* new year," Mrs Feingold, replied. "That won't be until September 30th. And it will be our year 5666."

Justine's eyebrows raised in disbelief. Mrs Feingold laughed, causing her inscrutable face to crinkle into appealing folds and lines.

"We began counting with the arrival of Adam," she explained. "You with the death of Jesus. Our calendar follows the course of the moon. So unlike your January 1st, our year begins on a different day every year."

Justine felt silly not to have known this. Paul was Jewish although always telling everyone he was a 'lapsed Hebrew'. She glanced around awkwardly for something to say and noticed a large room at the rear of the house that seemed to be set up with rows of desks and chairs.

"Are you a teacher?" Justine asked.

"Would you like to see?"

Like every thing else in this house the classroom was simply but efficiently fitted out providing a sense of elegance and purpose. Tall windows cast sufficient natural light to make the room pleasing even on this overcast, winter day. A black board hung on the opposite wall behind the teacher's desk. Chairs were pushed into individual desks with chalkboards lying neatly on each.

"What a lovely room. Do you teach school here?" Justine asked.

"Hebrew School," Mrs. Feingold explained. "Sometimes I teach but it is mostly my husband, the Rabbi.

At that moment the Rabbi, Dr Feingold, appeared, his eyebrows furrowed.

"The baby Liliya is improved but still in great danger," he began. "I have suggested to Mr Alexandrovich that she remain with us at least another night."

"That sounds like a good idea," Justine conferred.

"Mr Alexandrovich doesn't agree."

At that moment, Alexander appeared, his eyebrows also furrowed.

"Liliya should be with her mother," he said quietly, but in no uncertain terms.

"Yes, Alexander, she should," Justine replied.

Mrs Feingold looked askance at Justine but said nothing. Everyone waited. No one moved.

"The doctor wants to keep her here," Alexander said, defending his decision even though Justine was not arguing with it.

"The doctor is a good man. Would you agree?" Justine asked.

Alexander nodded assent.

"Would you agree this good doctor wants what is best for Liliya?"

Alexander didn't nod but also didn't disagree.

"You are a good man. You are her father and I know you want what's best for her."

Again everyone waited. Alexander struggled with himself.

"If Mrs Alexandrovich would like to come here and be with Liliya, she is most welcome," Mrs. Feingold suggested.

Everyone looked to Alexander. Hunching into his broad shoulders, he nodded once and left the room, followed by Dr Feingold.

"Thank you," Justine said, turning to Mrs. Feingold who was contemplating the two men heading down the corridor.

"It's difficult being a woman in our day and age," she mused, "but sometimes I think it is really rather difficult to be a man."

Justine was struck not only by the kindness Mrs. Feingold had just displayed but also by this insight.

"What do you mean?" she asked.

"Well, women are oppressed and we need to free ourselves. That's a very simple equation. Men, on the other hand, have to continually find the balance between their protective warrior spirit and the part of them that is – well – that is more like us."

She turned her intelligent, brown eyes towards Justine.

100 years from now, women are still oppressed, Justine thought. *But nothing like now. And yet, here's this educated woman, speaking with a wisdom my so-called-feminist friends would be wise to heed.*

"I'm Rachel, by the way," Mrs. Feingold continued, extending her hand.

Justine shook it gladly.

"We will – you know – free ourselves," Justine assured her.

"I'm glad of your certainty," Rachel replied.

Thirty-Two

When they returned, Maggie had readied the breakfast and welcomed a dressmaker into the house. Mrs Leonie Partridge from Ayrshire in Scotland was another one of Maggie's many accommodating acquaintances. She brought odds and ends of leftover clothing and was attempting to dress Sasha and Anzelika. Unlike her name she was a tall, thin women with nimble fingers who spoke in a stream of unintelligible Scots and didn't seem the least bothered that no one responded.

With the news that Liliya was better, Rosa at last allowed herself to sit and eat and then help Mrs Partridge find proper new clothes for her whole family.

Meanwhile, Justine had discreetly removed two Vitamin C pills and was crushing them in the mortar.

"These won't be discovered for another 25 years," she whispered to Maggie, "But they'll really help little Liliya. I managed to convince the doctor to add some to whatever she's drinking."

Maggie studied the pills with a mixture of curiosity and concern. "What is it?"

"It's called Vitamin C. We get it from the foods we eat but when we don't get enough, our bodies can't fight sickness so well."

As if on cue, Sasha coughed deep in his chest. His head was at that moment, stuck inside a very large woollen sweater he'd been trying on. He frantically grappled to extricate himself, coughing and spluttering and finally emerged, red faced and miffed.

One look at him and Maggie let out a loud guffaw and Justine tried to suppress her own giggles. Sasha stared back at them, attempting to appear offended but with his hair awry, succeeded only in looking more comical. Rosa covered her mouth, trying not to laugh but when he turned indignant eyes on her, his father clapped him warmly on the back, chuckling and mussing his hair even further.

This caused Maggie to laugh even louder. Justine and Rosa were unable to control themselves and also burst out laughing. Alexander wrapped his arm around his daughter Anzelika, who didn't laugh but seemed to relax somewhat and he too joined in. Sasha, unable to maintain his indignation in the face of so much hilarity, strode from the room.

For some reason this was the catalyst that broke the spell of worry and fear and everyone laughed and relaxed.

Justine popped a Vitamin C pill into her mouth and one for everyone in the room into the mortar, hoping she could convince them to take it.

As the morning waned into afternoon, Maggie began cooking the New Year's dinner of roast ham, potatoes and other delicious smelling things. She shooed everyone out of the kitchen. Rosa went to visit her baby, Anzelika disappeared back to the stables seeming to prefer the company of animals so Justine insisted Sasha bring her a brazier to keep the place warm. Justine asked Alexander to make up a fire in the parlour and they sat in armchairs sipping hot drinks laced with whisky.

As expected it began to snow again all but obscuring the sunshine. But Justine was filled with such a sense of peace and contentment she welcomed the light and warmth from the fire instead. Even the absence of her mother's portrait didn't bother her so much. She felt a greater sense of purpose and meaning on the eve of 1906 than she'd ever felt before. She would find James and recover the painting and force him to tell her how to contact her family. Of that she was certain.

Feeling this way made her want to dig deeper, become more immersed, and find out more. Glancing at Alexander she asked:

"Why did you immigrate to the United States?"

"It is a long story," Alexander replied.

"We have all year," Justine joked.

He chuckled and Justine was warmed by her ability to make him smile.

"My father was Mayor. It was not a large town but I was the second son. My brother would inherit. I was sent to the army. Alexander III was Tsar."

"Were you named after him?"

"He was a weak man and a fool," Alexander spat.

"I'm sorry. I didn't know…"

"I was named after his father, a good man as rulers go. Alexander III led a corrupt government. He diverted attention from this by blaming the Jews for everything - including the killing of Christ."

"Christ was a Jew."

"Yes. But reason doesn't often matter. His propaganda began the Pogroms. We were ordered to terrorise Jews all over the country – harassing, burning villages, terrible, terrible things – even killing."

"I'm sorry. That's awful."

"It was much worse than you can imagine."

He finished his drink and Justine poured directly from the whisky decanter into his cup. They sat staring into their drinks.

"How did you and Rosa meet?" Justine asked.

"In 1891 there was a famine in Russia. Then a cholera epidemic. It took my whole family." He paused, remembering. "I left. I ended up in Italy. I was young and with my size, I was able to find work. Rosa was a housemaid for a rich English lady. This lady wanted to rebuild an old villa and hired me. Rosa and I – well – she agreed to marry me."

He took a deep breath, staring into the fire.

"That was the happiest time of my life."

Telling his story was costing him but he went on:

"When Rosa became pregnant the old woman got angry and fired her. She kept me because I'd learned to speak English. Sasha was born and we were so happy. But when Anzelika was born, Rosa was very sick and I quit the job to be with her. It was very hard for a long time and so we decided to come here."

"What happened to Anzelika?"

Alexander looked at her sharply.

"I'm sorry. I shouldn't be so nosy. It's none of my business," Justine said, abashed.

"How did you know something had happened?"

"She doesn't speak. She doesn't like to be touched. She seems to prefer the company of horses to humans."

Alexander put his drink aside, grasping the arms of the chair until his knuckles turned white.

"On the ship coming here we were forced to sleep separately, men and women. Anzelika wandered into the place where they kept the animals. She was – she was – attacked by some men."

He stood up trying to contain the rage that was still with him.

"She was 10 years old!" he hissed between clenched teeth. "What is wrong with such people? She was an innocent little girl and I was not there to protect her."

He strode angrily out of the parlour and out the front door. Justine sat very still in the wake of these revelations; struggling to process all that she'd heard.

Thirty-Three

Passing through the kitchen, Maggie insisted that Justine dress for dinner and that she would meet her upstairs in half an hour to do so. Justine put her hands up in surrender and went quickly out to the stables to check on the horses but also to see Anzelika.

It was warmer inside with the brazier burning. Buckets of water were strewn about and Sasha was cleaning up and putting things away. He stopped when Justine entered, uncertain if they'd done something wrong. Anzelika was brushing the Grey and did not register Justine's entrance, her eyes closed with a look of peace on her gaunt face. The Grey's head was stretched over the divider and was nuzzling the other horse.

"I came to check on the horses wounds," Justine said, " but it looks like they're very well taken care of."

The wounds were clean and would heal. What the horses needed was rest and good food and Anzelika was seeing to that.

"Thank you for looking after the horses, Anzelika," Justine said. "They look better already!"

Anzelika stopped brushing, looking down at the ground. Although she didn't speak, Justine had the sense that she appreciated the gratitude.

"I confess I didn't understand why Alexander chose this horse but it looks like they're friends. Is that right? Would you say they're friends with each other and that's why your father wanted them to be together?" Justine asked, looking at Anzelika.

The child didn't look up but her hand moved to caress the horses' flank.

"Maggie has made a beautiful meal. Can you both come back inside and clean up?" Justine suggested.

Justine was happy that Maggie had moved the meal into the formal dining room without feeling the need to ask permission. She'd transformed the room into a beautiful environment to celebrate. A set of formal china dishes graced the white tablecloth, sparkling next to the silver cutlery and crystal goblets. A centrepiece of evergreen spilled from a cut glass vase and a crackling fire danced in the hearth.

Alexander and Rosa had returned while Justine was dressing and he nobly took his place at the head of the table, with Rosa on his right. Justine sat at the other end with Maggie on her right and the two children in the center.

Sasha helped Maggie serve the feast she had prepared. As platter after bowl of food arrived, Rosa began to cry silently, tears of gratitude and Alexander reached out to grasp her hand. When Maggie and Sasha were seated, he bowed his head and began a prayer in Russian. When he stopped speaking, Rosa spoke a prayer in Italian through her tears. When she finished Maggie said words in Gaelic. Justine didn't understand the words but felt the meaning and was very moved. So moved that she did something she'd never done before, she also prayed:

"Blessed be the Earth for providing us this food.
Blessed be the Sun for helping it to grow.
Blessed be the Wind and Birds for carrying its seed.
Blessed be the Rain for the water's loving flow.
Blessed be the hands that prepared this meal,
May those hands and our hands
Bodies, hearts and minds be well and quick to heal.
Blessed be our friends, our families,

And all of our loved ones, now and in the future.
Blessed be our mother earth, our father sky and sun. Amen."

After the meal, Maggie announced that she was going to midnight mass and everyone was most welcome to join her. When Rosa understood it was a Roman Catholic Church, she smiled for the first time. Maggie found her a warm coat and boots and linked arms as they walked down Hicks Street, joined in a mutual desire to worship on the eve of a new year.

The street was covered with a soft powdering of snow but the sky had cleared and the stars could be seen overheard sparkling in their deep blanket of midnight blue. The air was crisp and gusts of breath punctuated their progress along Clark Street. Justine had passed the Basilica of St. James a few times on her way to a summer yoga class held in McLaughlin Park. One of the many undertakings she'd started and not completed. And as they turned into Jay Street, the memory of repeated false starts, nagged at her. She'd let herself down so many times with uncertainty, procrastination and a restlessness she couldn't identify or feed.

In Justine's time, the single steeple of the red brick Church was considered old but tonite was only its third year. It's double doors opened directly onto Jay Street and there was a steady flow of parishioners packing the hall. Maggie greeted people and was greeted by others as she led the way down the center isle to an empty row. The church was filled with candles, flickering like an ethereal presence against the high majestic arched windows, warm yellow stone walls and marble tile inlaid floors.

Justine was not a churchgoer. She didn't even consider herself a believer although crossing back in time had certainly put into question everything she'd once held as true. Squeezed in between Maggie and Sasha on the hard wooden pew, she marvelled at the altar with its golden domed apse and the arrival of priests clothed in white and gold vestments. With their entry, the choir, seated at the rear on the second floor balcony, filled the space with sacred resonant chanting. Pomp and ceremony, rituals and song; no one did it better than the Catholics, Justine had to admit as she let herself be transported on this last day of the year, 1905.

Thirty-Four

Sunday, 1 January 1906

As eager as Justine was to find James, there was nothing she could do on New Year's Day. So she slept in, took a long, hot bath, allowed Maggie to feed her sausages and eggs and more delicious biscuits, which she attentively watched being made from start to finish.

Rosa and Alexander went to see baby Liliya so Justine brought out the small chalkboards she'd borrowed from the Feingold's and began Maggie's lessons. When Sasha seemed at loose ends, Justine suggested he might join in. They were seated at the kitchen table when Anzelika made her appearance from the stables. Curious enough to linger by the stove, at Justine's prompting, she too joined in.

All of them had some basic form of interrupted education and were old enough to quickly grasp what Justine showed them. The afternoon passed with A and B turning into X, Y and Z. But it was their pleasure at writing their first word that was most rewarding.

"Okay," she prompted them. "Now you can write A, B and C, we can spell a word with that. What does your father drive, Sasha?"

"A cab?"

"Yes. And cab is spelt C-A-B. Can you write that on your boards?"

They wrote. They showed her. She explained how to run the sounds of each letter together to pronounce and read the word. At that moment, Alexander and Rosa returned and Sasha proudly showed them his chalkboard:

"Look Papa. It says cab. We wrote the word for cab!"

Alexander ruffled his son's hair, smiling his approval.

"*Neuzheli*! You are a teacher as well as a doctor," Alexander said to Justine, jokingly. Then more seriously, "How will I ever repay you?"

"One day, Alexander Alexandrovich, I will tell you and then our debt will be settled. Alright?"

He nodded. "I look forward to that day."

"How is Liliya?"

"She will stay one more day with the Doctor. Then she will come home," Alexander, explained, his use of the word 'home' having yet another profound impact on him.

"How is it in your apartment?" Justine asked Rosa. "Is there anything you need?"

Rosa hesitated, then spoke eloquently with very few words. "I am mother and wife. I can cook. I can clean. I am very good for iron."

"Would you like to find a job, ironing?" Justine asked. "Or would you like to help with the cooking?"

Rosa nodded affirmation of both suggestions.

"Will you cook Italian food?"

Rosa nodded affirmation.

"Then I would like it very much if you would cook for us. Perhaps tomorrow you can buy what you need?"

Rosa nodded affirmation, smiling. Maggie on the other hand, looked at Justine sternly.

"Wait until you taste Italian food!" Justine enthused overlooking Maggie's objection. "The sun will shine in your mouth! And perhaps Mrs. Partridge can help Rosa find work?"

Maggie nodded assent, going to the stove to assert her authority in the kitchen for one more night.

"Tomorrow I will need to travel into Manhattan. Are the horses up to it, do you think Alexander?"

Before he could answer, Anzelika had scribbled on her chalkboard and pushed it across the table to Justine. On it was written the word,

'NO.' Justine smiled to herself. The written word gave Anzelika a means to communicate. She held the chalkboard up for Alexander to see.

"But Miss Justine needs to travel and for that we need the horses," Alexander explained to his daughter.

"Alexander, when I asked you to select a second horse, why did you pick the Grey?" Justine interrupted.

"You think I made a bad choice?"

"Well, he didn't look like he was going to make it out of Puttuck's stables, let alone be able to draw a carriage."

"The Grey and the other – they work well as a team," Alexander said in his own defence.

Anzelika headed to the back door.

"Where are you going, Anzel?"

She turned to look at her father with sorrowful eyes, then exited to the stables.

"She's like a horse-whisperer," Justine said.

"I don't know what this means. Sometimes I don't know anything when it comes to my daughter," Alexander said, sadly. "But don't worry, tomorrow there will be horses."

"She speaks to those horses and they speak back," Justine said.

"Yes," Rosa agreed sadly, remembering. "Always with the animals."

"Maybe we should listen to her?" Justine commented, shrugging. "But you are the boss, Alexander. Whatever you think best."

Thirty-Five

The next morning Justine was up bright and early. She had a plan and was determined it succeed. She and Maggie conferred on her choice of clothing and they selected a most elegant and expensive day dress; a waist length fine woollen black jacket with wide velvet lapels over a deep pink silk vest. Underneath she wore a white blouse with a high lacy neck and the same pink silk and lace appearing at her wrists and in the deep pleated panels of her long black skirt. The crowning glory was the angled black silk hat with the same seductive pleated silk peaking out from the inner lining and a large dyed pink ostrich feather on top.

It felt like a beautiful costume. It looked like something Paul would design and adore. Justine wished she had her iPhone to take a quick selfie and text it to him. Instead she focused on who she was meant to be in this outfit in this time and place. She'd learned this technique in one of the acting classes she'd started and not finished.

When she met Maggie at the front door, Justine was ready. They walked to the corner and down Orange Street to the Margaret Hotel. The weather was trying to decide what to do with dark clouds occasionally obscuring cold, blue skies. It was brisk and walking arm-in-arm with Maggie felt good after a whole day indoors.

They entered the hotel and Justine strode across the Hotel lobby trying not to be distracted by the thick Persian carpets covering white marble floors and the splendid crystal chandeliers hanging from the high, pillared ceilings. It was simple, grand and breathtaking elegance. She was aware of the impression she was making in the eyes of men and women in the hotel lobby; an attractive woman of substance, not to be trifled with. As she approached the front desk, she hoped the eagle-eyed concierge felt the same.

"Good morning, miss. How can I be of service?" he asked, peering at her through gold spectacles perched on a short, beaked nose.

"I'd like to use your phone – your telephone – if I may," Justine replied. The correct words continued to come out of nowhere, altering the way she normally spoke, but aligning her more conclusively with where she was. She heard herself speaking and knew it was she, and at the same time was acutely aware that it was also not she.

She blinked at the man, awaiting his response. Which seemed to take an inordinate amount of time although it was probably no more than a couple of seconds. His sharp eyes took her in without seeming to look.

"Are you a guest at our hotel?"

"No I am not. I have however recently moved into the neighbourhood." She glanced into his eye to underscore the import of her being a nearby resident. "I have not yet had a telephone installed in my home but I find I am in need of making an urgent local call."

"I see," said the concierge. "Well, in that case, please follow me."

He escorted her to a wood panelled office and offered her a seat at the desk and use of the telephone. Maggie followed, standing in the doorway. He didn't seem to want to leave them alone in the office so both women waited patiently. Becoming uncomfortable, he finally took his leave. Justine broke character and gave Maggie two thumbs up, smiling and relieved. Maggie didn't know what this meant exactly, but closed the door and nodded encouragement.

Justine got through to Mr. Brewster's secretary after waiting for the Operator to connect her.

"Good morning, Miss Singleton and Happy New Year. This is Justine, we met last week ... "

Justine was aware that no one used their first names, at least not without adding a surname, but this past week had put her identity into question and she was uncertain what to call herself.

Miss Singleton began making excuses, trying to dissuade Justine from bothering her boss.

"Yes I'm sure he's very busy today.... I don't need to speak with Mr Brewster," Justine assured her. "I was actually hoping that you might be able to help .... Well, there is a most beautiful portrait of my mother at the .... Oh, you've seen it? ... Yes, a remarkable resemblance ... well, I wish to contact the artist ... Yes, exactly. I'd like to commission a portrait... Yes, his address would be very helpful."

Justine nodded her gratitude to the concierge on their way out, handing the address to Alexander who was waiting with the carriage and two black horses he'd borrowed from one of his seemingly abundant contacts. Once inside she and Maggie burst into giggles.

"You do a grand lady, most believably," Maggie commented.

"Even though I'm the daughter of a..."

"You hush, Miss Justine. Your father was a great man and your mum a most beautiful woman."

"What about the church? What about sin?"

"Oh, dearie me. I – I don't know..." Maggie said wringing her hands. Then she saw Justine grinning slyly. "You're teasing me, aren't you? You don't care what the church thinks!"

"They loved each other, Maggie. That's for certain. And they made me from that love."

"It's not that simple, you know. It's never that simple."

Thirty-Six

Alexander steered the horses across the Brooklyn Bridge and up 2nd Avenue. Turning into 7th Street, he pulled up in front of McSorley's, an Ale House Justine was certain she'd been to before. Built in 1854 its paned front windows and low, black door with four storeys of brick front above, were charming in her time but had a nefarious feel about it now. In fact the whole neighborhood looked tattered and disreputable.

When she stepped from the carriage it was into snowdrifts hastily pushed off the streets and away from shop fronts, covered in layers of grime with horse droppings and bits of garbage frozen like still life into the mounds. Alexander did his best to make sure she and Maggie didn't slip and fall into the mess, while offering the physical protection of his size.

The address Miss Singleton had provided was two doors down from McSorley's in the same row of brick buildings. As they passed the frayed red curtains in the window next door they glimpsed a number of women sitting in the front room in various stages of undress. Maggie gasped, averting her eyes.

"Are you certain you want to do this," Alexander asked, peering in the window of the next shop.

Books and art were visible through a window that looked like it hadn't been cleaned since the shop was built, 60 years earlier. Investigating a bit closer revealed titles like, '101 Arabian Nights', 'Delta of Venus', a set of postcards with an ancient Japanese courtesan on the front and otherwise beautiful oil paintings of nudes displayed in suggestive ways. It was an early 20th century porn shop.

Justine knew she should be horrified but it really was rather tame by comparison to what was permissible in her century.

"I have to find him," she insisted to Alexander, pushing open the door.

The shop was no more than a large closet and dimly lit. Locked cupboards lined one wall, along with glassed cases displaying more suggestive reading material. The air was putrid with body odour and stale urine. The proprietor was asleep on a filthy cot in the corner, snoring loudly and smacking his lips with a half empty whisky bottle ready to fall out of his sleeping hand. Justine gave the bottle a nudge and it crashed to the floor startling the man awake. He blinked his sleep-encrusted eyes a number of times then dry scraped his hand down his face. When he finally focused his eyes landed on Justine in all her pricey splendour.

"You have something that belongs to me," she said loudly, leaning over his corpulent body.

"What? Who the fuck are you?" he asked, rolling himself indignantly into a sitting position while trying to keep his sore head away from the volume of her voice.

"You've got a lot of garbage in this place. A lot of sick, pathetic trash. But that," she said pointing to the painting on the wall, "That belongs to me!"

"Doesn't." the man said. "He gave it to me, cussed cockchafer. For the rent."

"Who?"

"Him, what lives upstairs. That drunken sot."

"You should talk," Justine spat back, glancing at the broken whisky bottle.

"Listen, I don't know who the fuck you are but you ain't getting nothing here."

"Alexander," Justine shouted and in moments the small room was filled with the height and bulk of Alexander Alexandrovich glaring down at the now frightened pornographer.

"Here's what's going to happen," Justine said slowly as if to a stupid child. "Mr Alexandrovich is going to take my painting and put it in my carriage. Then we are going upstairs to speak with your tenant. We will come to some arrangement, I am sure. Do you understand?"

The fat man eyed Alexander up and down.

"Mr Alexandrovich was a soldier in the Russian army. You do not want to antagonize him," she assured the shop owner and exited the shop.

The door to the apartments was right beside the shop entrance. Maggie was waiting anxiously in the street.

"I'm sorry Maggie, but I'm going upstairs to find James – Mr Grey."

"And I'm going with you," Maggie insisted, setting her jaw.

Unlike the tenements they'd rescued Rosa and her children from, this building had windows on the stairwell letting in a modicum of light. But the layers of dust, the stench of rotten garbage, mould and things best left to the imagination was almost overwhelming. Justine lifted her long skirts as she climbed, each floor increasing her anger at James. By the time they arrived at the top floor she was out of breath and out of patience.

She knocked. Waited. Knocked again. Then turned the knob and let herself in. It was the attic and the single room was cut short by a long, low ceiling slanting to the floor, only relieved by two windows set in the roof. Like all the other windows in this building, they were caked with grime, obscuring much of the natural light. The room was strewn with paintings, canvasses, rags and buckets to catch the water dripping from holes in the roof. It was frigid with cold and reeked of oil paint and turpentine.

"Hello?" Justine said into the gloom.

At first glance it seemed no one was at home until a pile of rags in the corner shifted and moaned and the figure of James Grey was revealed.

"Go away," he pleaded in a thin, pained voice.

Justine strode over and knelt down to peer at him. He looked terrible, whether from drink or illness she couldn't tell.

"What have you done? You're the color of your name," she said.

The sound of her voice caused him to crack open his eyes. As bad off as he was his green eyes held the vast ocean in them and momentarily took her breath away. Then he closed them and turned away.

"You stole my painting," Justine informed the back of his head.

"My painting," he mumbled. "I was never paid."

"Please explain," Justine said, pulling at his shoulder to make him face her, "You owe me that."

His eyes opened again, focusing on her, seeing her for the first time. He looked away in shame, his long fingers brushing his parched lips. He shook his head as if the burden of his indebtedness was wasting him almost as much as his overall ill health. Justine's anger began to melt.

Maggie approached with a cup of water from the pitcher on the sink. She helped him to sit up and brought the cup to his lips. He drank, hungrily.

"She disappeared," James explained hoarsely. "Broke his heart. He died. Wife ignored my requests." He paused. "My painting," he managed finally, collapsing against Maggie.

Justine looked to Maggie for confirmation. Maggie shrugged to suggest he could be telling the truth.

"So you stole – took – the painting to pay that filth downstairs?"

"There is a part of me that still clings to life," he whispered. "I don't know why," he added and without warning, burst into tears.

Instinctively, Maggie wrapped her arms around him, letting him weep into her shoulder, offering her precious handkerchief.

Justine on the other hand was appalled. She paced the room, waiting for him to finish. Either this man was the biggest con artist she'd ever met or he was still drunk or he was delirious. She wasn't buying the crying act.

She studied some of his sketches and paintings. He might be conning her, but he was definitely an artist. His portraits in particular, like the one of her mother, were imbued with great love for his subjects. She was captivated by one of an elderly man with a gruff expression and a haughty stance. James revealed the subject's humanity in the vulnerable drape of the hands and the slight bend of age in his shoulders.

"Listen to me carefully," she said to James, kneeling down to make sure he understood. "I want to know where to find his wife and his children."

He shook his head.

"What? You're not going to tell me?" she asked indignantly.

Again he shook his head. Then his green eyes peered back, challenging her.

HA, she confirmed, standing up again. *Con artist.*

She tried another tact. "I have taken my painting back and I will settle your debt with that scumbag of a landlord."

He struggled to sit up but, exhausted by the effort, fell back into Maggie's arms.

"He's not well, Miss," Maggie asserted, cradling his weight.

Staring down at the Madonna and Child pose they were creating, Justine assured her, "He's well enough"

"I will also provide you with a place to live and work," she offered – and waited.

This time he sat up, glanced up at her and smiled. His white teeth parted his full lips with mischief, making him look like a naughty boy. If she wasn't so outraged with his blatant scam, that smile could have seduced her right back into his bed.

Thirty-Seven

Now that Justine had an address, she was filled with anticipation and anxious with apprehension. Real people to whom she was related lived in this city. But her relationship to them was fraught and she had no way of knowing how she would be received. The overwhelming desire to be welcomed battled with the aching dread of being rejected. She needed to think about her next move but kept seeking distraction. And there were plenty of things to divert her.

First, was settling James Grey into the attic. Due to the spiral staircase, this was not as easy as moving Alexander's whole family into the basement. But Justine would not consider having him in the main house. The temptation of those green eyes was too great and she now knew what kind of man he was.

Initially Maggie had baulked at the idea of yet another person living under this one roof and a man at that. But James had turned the full force of his charm on her and now she was personally taking charge of the move. The portrait of Justine's mother was once again hanging over the fireplace in the parlour. The only items Maggie permitted from the hovel they'd found him in, were his artist's tools.

Justine put her foot down at Maggie's insistence that the attic needed cleaning and Alexander and Sasha volunteered to scrub and dust. Once up to Maggie's standards, they arranged furniture so that James now had a place to sleep and light pouring in from clean windows at which to work.

Once he'd bathed, been fed and given a hot drink with Vitamin C in it, James was feeling considerably better. This led Justine to surmise that his current 'illness' was due more to the drink and than to anything more injurious.

Maggie convinced Justine it was necessary to fit him with decent clothes in order to return him to his sense of self.

"That green jacket has seen better days and smells of that awful place he's been living in. A man doesn't like to appear without means," Maggie explained. "It makes him feel less of a man."

"A man is who he is, with or without means," Justine retorted. "Just look at Alexander."

But Maggie pursed her lips, refusing to budge and Justine agreed to new clothing and a proper bed for the attic.

"Beware of his charm," she cautioned Maggie.

"He's Irish," Maggie scoffed. "I know their every trick."

Mrs. Partridge was summoned and was measuring James for a proper suit of clothing at the same time discussing with Rosa how and when ironing would be required. Rosa was unable to comprehend anything that was being said to her in that steady flow of lowland Scots but nodded accommodatingly and Mrs. Partridge seemed very satisfied.

Liliya was returned to the fold. Still fragile, she lay in a basket in the warmth of the kitchen and Justine managed to slip more Vitamin C in the medicine Dr Feingold had prescribed. Her cough had subsided but she wasn't yet out of danger.

Justine visited the Doctor and his wife to settle her accounts and to return the chalkboards. This time she arrived properly dressed and was escorted into the parlour. It was yet another elegant room decorated with thick, Persian carpets and a small grand piano.

"Do you play, Doctor?" Justine asked.

"I am a lover of music," he demurred. "My wife is the pianist."

Of course she is, Justine thought. *Was there anything the perfect Mrs Feingold, didn't do?*

But before these jealous, unkind thoughts could go any further she noticed a painting on the wall between two glass and wood curio cases.

"Is that ...?" she asked, getting closer to the lovely painting. "Oh. It is. *The Sleepers and the One who Watcheth.* I love this painting."

Against a backdrop of stars a lovely couple sleeps while an angelic figure watches over them. Ducky had given Justine a very good reproduction when she was a child. The painting had been both comforting and calming to her when she feared sleeping and awakening alone.

"I'm surprised you are familiar with the work of Simeon Soloman," Rachel commented.

So enthralled was Justine to see the exquisite original, that she almost blurted out about having a reproduction. But Rachel was standing next to her gazing at the painting.

"He's not very well known. And certainly not in this country," Rachel commented.

"He's English, right?" Justine said to cover her bewilderment.

"Yes. And Jewish. When we were in England, we got to know his family."

Justine stared at Rachel trying to ingest this information. This was one of her most private and precious memories from childhood and here was the original and this woman had personally met the artist's family. But Rachel seemed to be waiting for an explanation, her implacable eyes gazing at Justine.

"The man who raised me is – was – is a great appreciator of art."

"Did he take you to England?"

"What?"

"I'm not sure how you could know the painting otherwise?"

"Rachel perhaps we could conclude our business," Dr Feingold said, "and allow our guest to get on with her day."

Justine could have kissed him. She took one last glance at the painting then stepped away from Rachel's inquisitive stare.

Thirty-Eight

The next day she still hadn't settled on a plan. But now anticipation was turning to anxiety. She asserted her authority over
Maggie and headed alone in the carriage back into Manhattan.

Alexander's silent presence was reassuring and the long drive to Murray
Hill gave her time to think. She knew she had to do this meeting alone.
Not only because of the terrifyingly personal nature of it, but also because
Maggie's expected disapproval might actually make her hesitate.

Snuggled into the furs her father had provided for the carriage, she stared
out at the New York of 1906. She'd remained in this time because of the
upcoming encounter. And it went far beyond destiny or kismet. It even
went beyond karma or what she understood that to mean. There probably wasn't even a word to describe what was about to transpire because
the meaning and the experience of time travel had never needed to be
described or expressed. At least not as far as she knew.

She thought about Maggie with her deep loyalty and strong will.
And Alexander with his innate nobility and capacity to endure. She
tried not to think about James but his body appeared unbidden in
her mind's eye and was difficult to push away. And Rosa and Sasha,
the troubled Anzelika and little Liliya and even Dr. Feingold and his

haughty wife. In such a short space of time they'd become deeply embedded in Justine's heart.

Travelling up the Bowery again, she was faced with the intractable and pervasive suffering of this age. Even on this cold winter's day, the streets were alive with people struggling to survive. She noticed a one-legged newspaper boy leaning on a crutch with his papers clutched in his other hand, the hardened look on his young face testament to his misery. Alexander and his family, James, even Maggie were in her life because she wanted to help, she felt compelled to do something about their suffering.

Heading up 5th Avenue she saw a row of heavy, horse drawn wagons removing loads of snow from the streets. The men driving the wagons cleared these streets for the wealthy and entitled. Their strong calloused hands capably steered the heavy-footed horses. They would go home to streets clogged with the detritus of poverty.

So is it any different in the time I come from? Justine wondered. *There's unnecessary and tragic misery then too. Maybe it's hidden and less life threatening than now, but it's there.*

She thought of Margaret and Joe and was reassured with the knowledge they had a roof over their heads. But she was also aware of how her intense self-involvement kept her preoccupied with things the media told her were important. Yoga and meditation made her feel good but it didn't really help anyone else. In this time, without that constant distraction, she was more able to think for herself and to see, to really see.

Approaching 40th Street she gasped at the site where the New York Public library was being built. This magnificent iconic structure wouldn't be completed until 1911, but the marble columns were all in place proudly becoming the pinnacle of Beaux-Arts design. Ducky loved this building and the proud lions that Justine knew would eventually grace the grand front steps. The reality of it now and in the future; the solid stone functioning reality of it took her breath away.

She was witnessing the sometimes tragic contradictions and extraordinary paradoxes of life in the democracy that was the United States of America.

5th Avenue was a busy street with traffic going in both directions and it required a steady nerve to turn the carriage into 41st Street. Arriving at Park Avenue, Alexander pulled to the curb behind another carriage in front of a renaissance-inspired palazzo of iron spot brick with terra cotta trim on a high brownstone base. Its massive size was enough to impress but the pillared entrance portico, which was mimicked in the stone balcony directly above loomed ominously over anyone daring to approach.

Justine sat inside the carriage contemplating this intimidating structure, hesitating in her resolve when the front door opened and a tall, elegant young man stepped out. Pausing to pull on his gloves he was dressed in an expensive mid-calf woollen coat with a luxurious close clipped fur shawl collar, high necked shirt with bow tie and a derby hat. She didn't get a good look at his face as he descended the front stairs but the shock of seeing him, of the distinct possibility that he was her half-brother sent electricity up her spine.

A smaller man, dressed somewhat less elegantly in a short brown coat and bowler hat, got down from a carriage to greet him. Justine got a sudden glimpse of the man's face. His flat pugnacious features, wild eyes and sly grin seemed improbably, hauntingly familiar.

The men entered the carriage and it was driving off as Alexander opened the door and saw her face. Unlike most people he didn't inquire if she was all right because clearly she wasn't, instead he asked:

"Can I help?"

Looking into his fierce blue eyes, if anyone could help it would be Alexander. His sincere willingness and strength gave her courage. But she had to do this on her own.

"If you are waiting for me here, that would be very, very helpful," she said taking his hand to step out of the carriage.

Thirty-Nine

Jaw clenched, Justine used the large brass knocker to make her presence known and just as she was about to lose her nerve, a young maid answered.

"Good Morning," Justine said "Is Miss McGowan in?"

"Is she expecting you, Miss?"

She could hear a piano being played suggesting that someone was indeed at home. The electric shock waves were still tickling Justine's spine so she propelled herself on a flurry of words and gaiety:

"Oh my, I do so love piano," Justine fluttered, peering past the maid. "Someone plays quite well. Don't you think?" she added. "I'm sorry, what's your name," she asked, smiling sweetly at the young girl.

"Matilde, Miss."

"Well, Matilde, I'll just poke my head in ..." she inserted herself past the maid, all her senses alert for the direction from which the music was emanating. "Such an accomplishment, playing an instrument. Don't you agree?" she babbled on, side stepping Matilde's alarm.

Large double doors led off on both sides of the grand marble foyer. But the music was coming from the second floor.

"Miss. P-Please," the maid stammered, pursuing Justine up the sweeping staircase.

The house smelled musty as if in need of a good dusting.

"Not to worry," Justine chattered on, reassuring her. "It's perfectly all right if I just drop in to say hello."

Large double doors also opened onto the expansive second floor landing and she moved towards the right where the music was coming from.

"I'm a relative," she whispered conspiratorially to Matilde then flung wide the doors.

The two-story balcony windows flooded the space with grey, winter light, which dimly lit a large room burdened with dark, overly patterned furniture positioned more to fill the area than for comfort. Heavy drapery decorated every window and numerous fussy gilt mirrors hung on striped and flowered wallpaper. The room was in need of a cleaning or an airing at least. Large, showy statuary stood in corners and at odd angles and an abundance of expensive but gaudy knick-knacks acted as decoration. The overall affect was ostentatious chaos.

A young woman in her late teens was seated next to a slightly older man who was playing the magnificent grand piano so skilfully. When

Justine opened the doors the young woman's head ducked reflexively and her shoulders hunched up in fear. The man stopped playing mid-chord, leapt off the bench, putting self-conscious distance between himself and the woman.

Justine's initial impulse was to apologize for interrupting but she was jittery with nerves and continuing the forced act of gaiety was the best she could do.

"Good morning. Good morning," she called out gaily, sweeping into the room. It took time and care to navigate around all the furniture, so she kept up the banter. "I see I've surprised you but I think you're going to be even more surprised when you find out who I am." She made it to the piano without knocking anything over.

By this time the young woman was looking up at Justine, her wide brown eyes rimmed with abundant blonde eyelashes were full of fright and curiosity. She wore her light blonde hair piled on her head with lots of little curls framing her face. And it truly was a classically sweet face, with a pink bow mouth, a perky, upturned nose and just enough baby fat in her cheeks to add to the overall girl/woman affect.

The man, by contrast, had black hair with dark, penetrating eyes, high cheekbones and a finely etched mouth. Justine judged him to be nearer her age, possibly 30. He watched her warily as if wavering between standing his ground and fleeing in terror.

"It's all right," she assured them both. "You must be Caroline," she said to the girl. "Am I right?'

Caroline nodded.

"But I don't think you're Hunter …?" she queried the man.

Justine noted both their postures go rigid at the mention of her half brother's name. The man shook his head managing at last to speak.

"I am Dušan Kucera," he said almost defensively.

"I am delighted to meet you and so sorry to interrupt. Your playing is just awesome."

Justine heard the much-overused word spill from her lips. She *never* said awesome. Although in this case it was abundantly true.

"… and do you play?' she chattered on, raising her eyebrows inquiringly at Caroline.

"Yes. No!" Caroline spluttered. Then looking adoringly up at Dušan, she enthused, "Dušan is my teacher. He plays better than anyone in the world!"

"I would have to agree," Justine replied, smiling warmly.

Caroline blushed but was clearly pleased.

"Excuse me, Miss," Matilde interrupted.

Everyone turned to look at the maid, but before she could continue, Justine rambled gaily on:

"I'm afraid I rather barged in here this morning and poor Matilde is worried that I shouldn't be here …"

Justine heard herself speaking strangely again, but couldn't stop. Her flow of words seemed to have the affect of directing everyone toward her desired end.

"Do you think we might have tea?" she asked imploringly, glancing wide-eyed from Caroline to Matilde and back again. "Then I can share with you my exciting news."

Like a deer in headlights, Caroline nodded unblinking first at Justine and then at Matilde.

"Splendid," Justine enthused. "Tea, please, Matilde and perhaps some lovely cakes if there are any. To celebrate. Shall we sit together over here in the sunlight?"

Justine motioned to a relatively comfortable grouping of Louis XVI style green painted armchairs near the balcony windows. Sitting first, she swivelled in her seat waving her arms encouragingly at Caroline and Dušan, ushering them towards the two empty chairs.

"Come. Come. Sit with me. I'm so delighted to be here and to meet you."

Obediently, Caroline sat on Justine's left, watching her with childlike expectancy. Hesitantly, Dušan sat next to Caroline perching on the edge of his seat. Seeing the anticipation on their faces, Justine realized she needed to keep up her prattle until Matilde had come and gone.

"So, Mr Kucera, you are a friend of Caroline's family?"

"Oh, NO," he replied startled. Then collecting himself explained, "I am only Miss Caroline's piano teacher."

"Dušan – Mr Kucera was - is – *was*, a concert pianist in Prague," Caroline stammered proudly.

"That was long ago and in another place," he murmured.

"I know exactly how that feels," Justine replied, patting him on the wrist.

He glanced at her comforting hand as if kindness were something foreign to him.

Matilde returned with a beautiful Beleek porcelain tea set with dragonfly handles, decorated with a portrait of a 19th century woman. She placed the soft turquoise and gold trimmed plates carefully on the table along with teacakes and fruit tortes. The set was only a few years old and was naturally in mint condition. But Justine viewed it from Ducky's perspective. Though a bit gaudy and not at all to her taste, she appreciated it's artistry and value.

"This is just beautiful, Matilde. Thank you so much," Justine effused.

Matilde smiled secretly to herself, bobbed a little curtsy and left the room. The time had come for Justine to drop her bomb.

"Well, isn't this charming…" Justine began, reaching for the teapot and pouring tea into three cups. "Do you take milk, Mr Kucera?"

she asked, needing to slow herself down enough to say what needed to be said.

"No, thank you."

"Caroline?"

"Yes and two sugars, please," she replied, crinkling her pug nose childishly at her love for sugary things.

Justine took a sip of tea, allowing the sweet, milky brew to make its way soothingly down her throat. She was beginning to understand why Maggie reached for this stuff like medicine. Placing the delicate porcelain carefully on the table, she took a deep breath.

"The best way to say something is just to say it," she announced. "So here goes ..." Turing to face her she said, "Caroline, I am your half sister."

Caroline looked up from her cup, startled and confused.

"My mother is – my mother was your father's ...."

"Oh. Oh, my. OH." Caroline said as the penny began dropping.

She looked at Justine, her brown eyes staring incredulously then casting about the room as if for an explanation, then arriving back at Justine again, wide-eyed with wonder.

"Oh, my," she said again.

Dušan gently touched her arm with concern, asking "Is this good?"

Turning her wide-eyes onto him, Caroline whispered in awe, "I have a sister, Dušan. I have a sister of my very own."

Caroline reached for Justine across an unknown valley of time and with an as yet unrevealed abyss of hurt and need and Justine reached back. They held hands and wept and laughed and wept some more.

For Justine in that moment time collapsed in on itself and with Caroline's words time blew up like a volcano. Imploding and exploding. The little abandoned girl she'd been, suddenly belonged. The yearning for meaning that had dogged the last decade of her life, suddenly crystal clear. The disappearance of her mother less painfully acute with the arrival of this person, this sister, who welcomed her with open arms and wide-open eyes.

Using Dušan's handkerchief to blow her nose, Caroline said,

"I never actually met your mother but I remember her portrait. It used to hang in my father's office. I'd never seen anyone so ... exotic," she explained. "I'm sorry. I don't mean to offend."

"No, no," Justine assured her, chuckling, "she was definitely out of the ordinary."

"She was the most beautiful woman I'd ever seen," Caroline told Dušan. "And the resemblance is – well – anyone can tell Justine's her daughter. My father loved her completely. He told me so."

"I'm sorry. That must have been difficult – for your family."

"My family was already difficult," Caroline said, her face darkening. "I was glad my father found happiness."

"Mr Brewster, the lawyer, told me he died."

"Yes. He waited for her, but she never came back. His heart broke. That's what I think. I was 10 years old. I miss him every day."

"That's how I feel about my mother," Justine said.

"Dušan also lost his father," Caroline added, sighing.

"It's why we had to leave Prague," Dušan explained, glancing at Caroline meaningfully. "It brought me here,".

"Then something good came of the loss," Justine agreed, noting how Caroline glowed at his glance. "I know what that feels like too."

They sat together in companionable loss. The sun had vanished behind darkening clouds and the room filled with the silent shadows of those not present. Matilde entered to refill the teapot, then added a log and began stoking the fire. It was a large fireplace with an ornate mantel and soon the room was warm again.

"Matilde, would you mind bringing my driver inside and give him some of your lovely tea. It's got so cold again. His name is Mr. Alexandrovich."

Matilde glanced at Caroline for approval.

"Matilde, this is my sister — my half sister, Justine," Caroline explained grinning with all her small white teeth.

Matilde looked at Justine, glanced at a series of photographs perched on the mantelpiece, frowned, nodded and left the room.

"More tea?" Justine asked.

"And cakes," Caroline insisted, selecting two teacakes, hesitating, then taking a fruit torte as well. "There's so much to celebrate," Caroline enthused, taking a healthy bite and licking her lips like a cat with a bright pink tongue.

"What about *your* mother?" Justine wanted to know.

"She died last year," Caroline answered around a second mouthful of torte.

"I'm sorry."

Justine was having difficulty rationalizing the time frame Caroline was describing. Justine had seen Mrs. McGowan throwing jewellery at James Grey... when was it? 6 weeks ago? The first time she crossed the dateline. And Caroline was 17 years old now, and Justine in her 28th year. It didn't make sense. *Time is a human invention*, she reminded herself, *and seems to be full of inconsistencies.*

"She was a grand lady from a grand family and I was a disappointment to her," Caroline demurred. "She wanted me to be someone else. More like my brother. The best thing she ever did was find Dušan to teach me the piano. I'm afraid I'm not very good at that either, but ..." she ended by looking with loving gratitude at her teacher.

Justine stood up taking the opportunity to study the photographs on the mantel. He was a bear of a man, her father, tall and broad shouldered and unmistakable in the pictures. In one he held baby Caroline on his knee, smiling proudly at the camera. His face was not handsome but kind and she imagined his small nose crinkling when he smiled just like his daughter's did now. Seeing him for the first time made Justine's heart ache. He looked like someone she wished she had known.

In another photograph, his size towered over the woman standing next to him and the grim look on both their faces over shadowed the picture.

A log slipped in the fireplace. Glancing from her father to the woman, Justine felt herself sliding off balance. The woman, Mrs. McGowan, held herself erect, not so much looking into the camera as staring it down as if defying time to define her. Justine knew exactly what she was thinking in that moment as if she were inside the woman's head. She clutched the mantel as her brain tilted inside her skull and then, after a moment, righted itself.

Dušan was at her side, holding her elbow to steady her. "Are you quite well?" he asked.

"Yes, thank you," she said. "It's just seeing my father ..."

She let him guide her back to her seat.

"I wish I'd known him," she confessed.

"He would have liked you. No. He would have loved you," Caroline confirmed.

"Some music would be nice," Justine suggested, needing to distract herself.

Dušan moved to the piano and Caroline followed, happily sitting beside him.

"*Zigeunermelodien*, Gypsy Melodies," Dušan announced in his soft, resonant voice. "Composed by Antonín Dvořák, my countryman." He closed his eyes and began to play.

Forty

Justine closed her eyes and let the haunting music wash over her. It reminded her of finding her mother one afternoon in the kitchen listening to a tape recorder. The music was similar and her mother was crying. This memory was not long before she and her mother travelled to New Orleans. Not long before her mother disappeared.

Justine's reverie was interrupted by distant yelling, growing closer. It was a man's angry voice, shouting:

"Is that filthy foreigner still in my house?"

And then the doors flew open and a tall man stood wavering in the entry, wild eyed with fury and with drink. It was the man Justine had seen departing earlier. It was her half brother, Hunter. Only now he had no hat or coat and was far less stable on his feet.

"You getting cosy with my sister again you damn, cussed low-life ..." he shouted, lumbering his way across the crowded room, knocking furniture over in his rage.

Dušan leapt up from the bench, keeping the piano between him and the mad drunk. Caroline was frozen in her seat. It was the same frightened pose Justine had found them in. This scene had apparently happened before.

Justine stood up, moving swiftly to block her brother's progress, shouting:

"Why are you making such an ugly and unnecessary racket?"

The sound of Justine's voice stopped him and he swung around to look at her, holding on to a chair for balance. His eyes were having trouble focusing and he peered at her.

"Who the fuck are you?" he spat.

"Hunter," Caroline pleaded, "She's our sister."

Hunter swung around questioningly to stare at Caroline then whipped his head back towards Justine. This action caused a wave of vertigo and he almost fell over.

"Why don't you sit down, before you fall down," Justine suggested.

"The Bitch had a Bastard?" Hunter screamed in outrage, moving towards Justine.

What happened next came from a deep, unknown place of pure survival and the training Justine had once started. As Hunter whisked his hand back to strike, Caroline screamed but Justine was moving into his on coming body, dipping her head and grabbing his outstretched arm, spinning him around on his own forward volition. He fell to his knees, crying out as she twisted his arm up and back and held it there.

She waited until her breathing calmed and he stopped struggling. Then she knelt over and whispered into his ear:

"Violence is never the answer. Understand?"

He nodded and she let go of his arm. He collapsed to the floor, spent.

Justine stood up, aware that eight sets of eyes were watching her. Matilde was standing in the doorway, Alexander behind her and Caroline and Dušan were motionless near the piano.

"Perhaps it's time to go," Justine said to no one in particular. "Will you be alright, Caroline?"

Caroline nodded. Justine looked into her brown eyes and understood that Hunter's rage was for others, not for his sister. Justine brushed a lock of hair from Caroline's face and caressed her lovely cheek.

"I will see you very soon," Justine assured her.

Caroline managed a smile and nodded again.

"Can we give you a ride somewhere, Mr Kucera?"

He grabbed his coat and hat, lowered his head as if in apology to Caroline and followed Justine and Alexander out of the room.

Standing in the shadows of the landing was the same stocky man Justine had seen Hunter with earlier. Studying her, his dark eyes glinted with interest. He was leaning on the banister and tipped his hat insouciantly as she passed causing the hairs to stand up on the back of her neck.

Half way down the stairs Justine stopped and turned back to the man.

"I know you. You're Kendall Shaw," she said, glaring up at him.

He covered his surprise with a nonchalant snort.

"I know what you've done," she presaged "and I know what you're going to do. It doesn't end well." In her research for Ducky, Justine often strayed into other nonrelated topics. This man's history happened to be one. "Stay away from my brother!" she warned, with the power of her knowledge.

He descended two steps as if to challenge her. Justine stood her ground. But when Alexander approached, Shaw backed down, snorting and shrugging as if none of it mattered.

The carriage swayed rhythmically as Alexander steered back down 5th Avenue. A bleak winter darkness crept across the sky. Dušan sat in defeated silence staring out the window. Justine waited for her heart to calm before she spoke.

"That's happened before, I take it?" she ventured.

"There is nothing I can do," Dušan apologized.

"No, of course not."

"I tried to speak to him once. He threatened to fire me."

"He doesn't hit Caroline, correct?"

"No. Never. And he's only managed to hit me once. When he's drunk he's not so graceful so I am able to avoid his swings. But I think he has beaten Matilde."

"What?"

"Sometimes she seems to be in pain. I suspect she doesn't want Caroline to know. So she hides it."

Justine thought about this for a long time as the temperature dropped and the silence between them deepened. Bullies were always hiding something. Some shame or repressed anger. What skeletons were in her brother Hunter's closet? She had to find out and she had to stop him.

"Can you not meet with Caroline somewhere else?" she suggested.

"She is not yet of age."

"And ...?"

Dušan looked at her quizzically. "Mr McGowan, her brother, is in control, of course. Of everything."

Of course. In her self-righteousness, Justine kept forgetting that the status of women was not what it would be a century from now.

"He barely tolerates the piano lessons," Dušan continued. "He has always been – well, … strange – but after the death of their mother, he seems to have lost his way."

"That's a very sympathetic assessment of a man who clearly loathes you."

"He is troubled. We are all troubled in one way or another. Don't you think?"

Justine shrugged. She wasn't feeling inclined towards compassion for a drunk who hit women.

"I do not know how you were able to stop him like that," Dušan said "but someone who can do that has learned it or been taught. Because they are troubled. No?"

Justine smiled. She liked this man. She liked him very much.

"Why don't you ask her to marry you?"

He sighed as if the will to live had just gone out of him. His strong features went slack and when he finally looked at her, his eyes were etched in pain.

"I would like to. When she comes of age. It is what I want more than anything in the world. But how could I look after her properly? I could not ask such a light to live in such darkness," he said, gesturing out the window.

They had arrived at the Bowery, and the carriage came to a stop. It was dark here, but not from the lack of illumination, there were numerous pubs and cathouses with lights to attract clientele. Remembering Alexander's appalling living conditions, Justine was sad this is where a man like Dušan was forced to live. The whole area was filled with the darkness of despair.

"Can you get a new set of clothes made for you by tomorrow afternoon?" she asked, suddenly.

"Well - I have a friend who is a tailor, but .... as I've just been explaining...."

"Please go to your friend," she instructed, pushing money into his hand. When he tried to refuse she insisted, "Please. This is for Caroline. I will send Alexander to collect you here at 1:00."

He was about to say something, decided against it, stuffed the money into his coat pocket and stepped into the street.

She liked having money, Justine admitted to herself, snuggling deeper into the carriage furs. She liked that she could help others without another thought. She knew there was more money needed to complete the plan that was formulating in her mind and that meant a visit to Mr Brewster.

Forty-One

The time it took to navigate the horse and carriage to the lawyer's door was interminable. This mode of transport was losing its romance. Justine was ready for something faster. As she and Alexander rode together in the caged elevator up to the Mr Brewster's office, she broached the subject:

"We need an automobile, Alexander. Can you drive?"

"No," he said. "But I can learn."

"Good. Tomorrow, I would like you to buy one of those electric automobiles."

He shook his head in wonder. "You move so quickly, Miss Justine."

"I'm sorry, Alexander. There is a lot I have to do."

"No. I like it very much."

She glanced sideways at him to see if he was making fun of her. Instead she felt as if the lift suddenly lost traction and was plummeting to earth because it was as if Ducky suddenly stepped into Alexander's body. He reached out to steady her and his face transformed from Alexander's to Ducky's and back again.

Then just as suddenly everything returned to normal.

"I'm sorry. I felt dizzy."

But, of course, nothing was normal. Justine had inexplicably travelled back in time and people in this time seemed to morph into people from her future life.

"Maybe I *am* moving too fast."

Miss Singleton wasn't happy to see Justine especially without an appointment and her suspicious glances at Alexander indicated what she thought of him.

But, if Mr Brewster was perturbed at her late arrival, he had the grace not to show it. When he heard what she had in mind, however, he was more forthcoming with his views.

"As your lawyer it is my job to do as you instruct. I believe it is also my duty to advise you. The house and money was left for your mother so that she would be cared for, for the rest of her life. Those were Mr McGowan's instructions. That, I believe, is what he would want for his daughter. That is – for you."

"I understand and I'm grateful that you have seen to his wishes all these years. The money *will* be used for his daughter – his *other* daughter. For her happiness and security. From what you said and what you've done, there is a large amount."

"Yes, that's true, but …"

"I am fine, Mr. Brewster. I am more than fine. Trust me."

He studied her for a moment.

"If you will excuse my impertinence I don't believe I've ever met a young woman quite like you."

"I'm afraid I keep being told that. And I'm sorry. Perhaps it's because we do things differently where I come from."

"Apparently. While it was not my place to put you in touch with your brother and sister, I am delighted you have met. It was also not my place to reveal some of the things I have said this evening. However, Henry McGowan was my dear friend and I have been very concerned about what has happened to his children."

Justine was about to ask about Hunter but the lawyer put up his hand to stop her.

"It is not my place to gossip or offer an opinion. After listening to what you have in mind I believe Henry would be pleased. And I believe you when you say you will be fine. I will do as you ask."

He stood up, guiding her to the door. Miss Singleton remained steadfastly at her desk in spite of the late hour, with one distrustful eye on Alexander.

Justine turned to Mr Brewster lowering her voice, "Exactly as I asked. It's very important that no one *ever* know." .

"I pride myself on honesty and exactitude, Miss Justine. I believe that has been the key to my humble success."

"That and the loyalty of Miss Singleton," Justine added loud enough for the secretary to hear.

By the time they returned to Hicks Street it was late but they were welcomed with the mouth-watering aromas of home made Italian food. They discovered Rosa at the stove stirring a pot of something tomato-ey and garlicky and Maggie standing by with Liliya in her arms, keeping a guarded eye on Rosa's every move. Sasha was practicing his letter writing and James was at the table sketching this domestic scene.

Anzelika was called from the stables, a stray puppy in her arms. She seemed less tense with the dog nearby and Maggie assured Justine it had been thoroughly washed. So the puppy was allowed to remain and lay curled in her lap all through dinner. And to Rosa's delight the food was a great success. Justine ate with relish. James and Maggie were hesitant, never having eaten anything so foreign, but once they got the handle of twirling spaghetti onto a fork and scooping up the delicious sauce, they were Italian food converts.

That night Justine lay in bed mulling over the events of the day. The fact of Caroline and Hunter's existence was truly miraculous and validated her decision to stay. However, the dislocating experience she'd had viewing the picture of their mother was confusing and troubling. Turning over to gaze out the window, which Justine kept open in spite of Maggie's repeated drawing of curtains and blinds, she thought about Hunter. Why was such a handsome, wealthy young man so angry? And what was he hiding from by drinking to such excess? And had she really subdued him with a move she'd learned in a self-defence class? That made her chuckle. One of her half-baked lessons had paid off. She thought briefly of Kendall Shaw and the coincidence of recognizing him from her research. He gave off a very bad vibe and she decided not to dwell on him.

The bedroom door opened suddenly, someone entered and swiftly shut the door again. Heart beating, Justine was already sitting up ready to defend herself, as the figure moved quickly to the bed. Then, in the moonlight she saw it was James.

He sat on the bed not speaking, just watching her. His eyes glinted emerald and his rich, dark hair fell softly across his forehead. Her head told her to pull back - that he had no right to be here like this. But her body was already leaning in to him as if she'd been waiting for his arrival. He touched her face, running his finger along her lips, causing her heart to beat not in fear but with anticipation and desire.

Then she slapped his face. His head whipped around from the impact but when his eyes returned to her face, they were narrowed and his lips were turned up in a grin. He forced her back against the pillows and climbing on top of her pressed his mouth against hers, then dragged his teeth and tongue along her neck. She arched her back, yearning towards him as he ripped open her nightgown and grabbed handfuls of her breasts all the while watching her with his green, wolf-like eyes.

She'd never made love open-eyed but she found herself drowning in those eyes, consumed by his look and his hands and the musky scent of him. But she couldn't wait for his lust to rise. She didn't want to be led. She had to have him. Reaching up she pulled open his robe, revealing his long shirt beneath.

He helped her rip his clothing from his body revealing the smooth, taut skin and hardened artists arms. She ran her hands hungrily over his skin, feeling the muscles tighten beneath the flesh. She bit his neck and shoulders, gently at first then with greater intensity, until he cried out. They were both breathing hard, staring hungrily into each other's eyes.

"I've never known a woman like you," he said.

Then he plunged himself into her and they rode a tsunami of rising pleasure and cascading passion, teetering on the edge of explosion, pulling back, seeking a deeper, more intense communion – Justine on top, James beneath – James forcing her on to her back and plunging into her again and again – culminating at last in a ferocious union as he spent himself and she received him.

Forty-Two

"I think this is a very good idea, Alexander," Justine confirmed.

The sun had come out and was fast melting the snow. They were standing in a soggy field north of Brooklyn Heights, a farmhouse off in the distance. There were cows grazing nearby. But it was the four brand new automobiles glinting in the sunlight that Justine was referring to. She'd never seen a car she would immediately describe as cute but the two smallest Baker Electric automobiles, the Runabout and the Stanhope, were cute and compact and fit for two.

Mr Boniface had been talking fast and lauding his wares for the better part of ½ an hour. His loud, red plaid jacket, mismatched brown hounds tooth vest and trousers together with his swaggering stance mimicked car salesmen to come.

"The Stanhope's capable of a swift 14 miles per hour," he was saying. "But, naturally, the larger Inside Drive Coupe seats four and goes farther and faster." He opened the door of the bigger car, eyes twinkling, to reveal a plush red leather interior. "This ain't no electrically driven carriage," he assured his listeners, "this here's a real automobile. But it's noiseless and gives off no offensive gas fumes - which I know the ladies like. And they are speedy and always ready for the gentlemen."

He climbed inside gesturing for Justine and Alexander to have a look. Stretching out his stocky legs in demonstration, Mr Boniface continued, "You can appreciate the increased roominess; full limousine back; longer wheel base, graceful, low-hung body lines with both interior and exterior conveniences and appointments. The Mister will appreciate the lever steering from the rear or the wheel steering from the front," he continued, not taking breath, "the lady will appreciate the revolving front seats. You can face front as you drive or...." he swivelled the seat around, smiling a set of yellow teeth, "... face back if you wish to gossip with your friends."

Being a savvy salesman he noted that this last comment had not impressed 'the lady' so, leaping out of the Coupe, he steered them towards the Extension Front Brougham model, which boasted a driving seat high up behind the passengers mimicking a hansom cab.

Justine murmured, "If you were to paint it yellow, you could call it a yellow cab."

Alexander glanced at her sideways. "I am not ever sure when you are joking with me."

"Well, I wasn't actually, but that's another matter. As I said, I like this idea. How much do they cost?"

Mr Boniface was swiftly at their side, his voice lowered now in keeping with the seriousness of moving from looking to costing. They listened attentively.

When she'd asked Alexander to find an automobile to buy he had instead made her a business proposal. He'd done so with solemn dignity, not asking for anything so much as offering to create something. While he didn't know it, he was proposing to begin a motorized taxi service. History would prove this to be an excellent entrepreneurial undertaking. And Justine knew it.

They already had horses and a carriage. Anzelika would have to accept that the animals would soon be ready to take up their reins. Alexander insisted Sasha could drive the carriage. With a motorized vehicle Alexander could see to Justine's transport as well as begin a small cab service of his own.

"I think Mr Alexandrovich would like to consider his purchase," Justine proposed. "Perhaps you could give us a minute or two," she suggested sternly to Mr Boniface, preventing him from speaking again.

The fields surroundings the 'car lot' were grey and barren, covered with deep patches of muddy snow. An eagle circled overhead. Justine marked its graceful dips and curves, riding the currents of imperceptible breezes.

Alexander found and presented her with a beautiful brown and white eagle feather.

"For you," he said.

"It's a portent!" Justine enthused, taking the feather. "It's a very good sign."

Living in New York her whole life, Justine had never learned to drive. After a quick lesson from the now impatient Mr Boniface, Alexander took the wheel, steered them out of the paddock and drove his new automobile home. Being electric, it was quiet and emission-free. *What a travesty petrol driven cars were*, Justine thought, enjoying the ride.

When they arrived, Justine suggested a drink to seal their new business deal. Once seated in the parlour, she turned to Alexander:

"Do you remember when you said I could ask a favor of you and you would do it?"

"*Konechno*. Of course," he replied.

"Here is my favor. I would like Sasha and Anzelika to go to school."

"School? But Sasha is ready to go to work."

"I know. And I realize this was part of your business plan. But Alexander, without an education Sasha will struggle like you and Rosa have. With an education his possibilities open up. He's a smart boy – like his father – why not give him a chance?"

Alexander thought about this as Justine poured two glasses of the vodka he'd bought for this occasion. She'd placed the eagle feather on the table to commemorate the day. Then he shook his head:

"But Anzelika? She is a girl. She does not speak. How can this happen?"

"I have an education, Alexander. So does Mrs Feingold. The world is changing and women have a contribution to make. I think Mrs Feingold could teach her. I think Mrs Feingold could help her."

232

In spite of Justine's negative reaction to Rachel Feingold, she believed this was true. The woman had an interest in human psychology even though it hadn't yet been officially invented and she was clearly an extraordinarily intelligent and wise person. And a teacher. Justine believed not only *would* she help Anzelika but that she actually *could*.

"Just because Anzelika doesn't speak doesn't mean she isn't smart. Would you agree she has some kind of amazing gift with animals?"

"This 'gift' is what got her into trouble!" he said, growing angry.

"No, Alexander. Bad men is what caused her trouble. And you know that."

He stood up, moving to the fireplace. This was a very touchy subject but Justine knew she was right.

"If you just leave her, what will her life be like?

He clenched his jaw repeatedly but didn't speak. This was something he'd chewed over many times.

"She has a gift, Alexander and I believe our gifts must be shared with the world. That's how we make it a better place."

"You are *silniy chelovek* Miss Justine. You have a power, a *gift*. You are not only generous but very convincing."

She'd been told many times by Ducky how powerful she was, "You could run a small country," he'd said. She'd never known what he was talking about. All her insecurities and self-doubts seemed to over-shadow everything else. Now, however, reflected in Alexander's admiring eyes, she was starting to believe it.

Outside, a rising number of voices drew them to the parlour windows. Everyone had gathered around the new automobile, including Anzelika, the doctor and his wife and other neighbors Justine hadn't met.

She raised her glass to the new car, "To the Yellow Cab Company," she said.

Alexander shook his head, baffled. "Strange name," he said. But he raised his glass, "To the Yellow Cab Company," and they both downed their drinks.

Justine happily displayed the interior of the car to an uncertain Maggie and an excited Sasha. Alexander spoke with Rachel Feingold, who listened intently, conferred with her husband then nodded her head at Alexander. He gestured to Anzelika who approached shyly, her puppy nestled in a sling she'd tied around her neck and her arms wrapped protectively around the book Justine had given her. Justine watched Rachel speak to Anzelika. The girl nodded and more surprisingly, smiled. When asked, she showed the precious book to Rachel and together they paged through it.

Forty-Three

Later that day, driving in the new vehicle, Maggie kept laughing with delight then sucking air with fright at how fast they were able to go. Justine was relieved she didn't have to worry about the cold impacting Alexander.

She thought of all the many inventions this century would bring that would delight and help human beings and the few creations that would utterly decimate and destroy forever what they understood as humanity. She wondered if those inventions would ever have evolved if their creators were sitting where she was now.

Ducky had travelled to Ground Zero in Hiroshima to visit the site where the first atomic bomb had been dropped and to Ground Zero in New York, where the most heinous act of terrorism had occurred. The experiences convinced him that every world leader should be required to go to these sites, to stand in the place of our greatest horror in order to step back from such a thing in the future.

In no time they were pulling into Mill Lane, an alley off Stone Street, which was itself too narrow to be called a road. The sign above the single wooden door read, *Mercy Home for Girls*. Justine knew before following Maggie inside, she wasn't going to like this place.

They didn't have long to wait inside the dim entry before an exceedingly plump, florid and sour faced woman appeared, introducing herself as Mrs Archer. She sized them up with one not too subtle glance, evidently deciding on graciousness and welcome over disdain and dismissal.

"And how can I be of service to you ladies?" Mrs. Archer inquired, smiling obsequiously at Justine.

"We've come to hire a young girl to do the cleaning and such," Maggie informed her.

"Well you've come to the right place," Mrs Archer confirmed continuing to look only at Justine. "We have plenty of girls." Continuing to ignore Maggie's presence, she gestured for Justine to precede her into the next room. "Would you like to come through to the office and we can discuss terms," Mrs. Archer suggested.

"No, actually, we'd like to meet the girls first," Justine, responded. "Miss O'Reagan is very particular about how her house is cleaned."

Maggie glanced dismissively at Mrs Archer and strode past her down the hall with Justine following behind.

"Wait, you can't go down there," Mrs Archer called after them.

The windowless hall ran down the center of the unheated building with doorways leading off, like in a hotel. *Or a prison*, Justine thought. The presence of barred windows in each door triggered that impression. She peered into one window and stepped back in shock, then twisted the door handle, finding it locked.

"You can't go in there," Mrs Archer shouted, waddling as quickly as she could to catch up with them.

"Why is this door locked?" Justine demanded.

"Why? Because ..."

"To keep the girls safe," a male voice explained.

Justine spun around to discover a rather short man, almost as wide as he was tall with mutton chop side burns and very bad teeth.

"I am Mr Archer, manager of this establishment. May I be of assistance?" he inquired with even more sickening guile than his wife.

"We are here to hire a live-in cleaner," Maggie repeated "And we'd like to meet the girls."

"But it seems you've got them locked up - like animals." Justine added.

"For their safety, as I explained," Mr Archer insisted. "May I suggest we conduct this interview in our offices?"

That's what I said," Mrs Archer whined.

He motioned for Maggie and Justine to move back down the hallway and deciding now was not the moment to pick a fight, Justine relented.

"I told them to go into the office," Mrs Archer complained to her husband, following him down the corridor, "But they burst in here instead."

"Go and get #5," he hissed at her.

Unlike the rest of the building, the office had a fire going in the hearth and worn, but comfortable furniture. Mr Archer indicated they should be seated but Justine was agitated by the dark, windowless cell she'd seen through the bars filled to capacity with cots and girls.

"It's day time, why are the girls locked in like criminals?"

"I take umbrage at your suggestion. As I explained …"

"I am not a fool, Mr Archer. It's day time and I can't imagine what danger these girls might be in …"

But the door opened and four girls of varying ages entered, followed by Mrs Archer.

"Here we are," she announced, proudly, pushing the last girl, no more than a child, into the room.

Justine's heart rose into her throat at the sight of them: forlorn, dirty, underfed and with a look of terror focused in Mr Archer's direction. One was clearly a red head but the other three could have been blonde or brunette, it was impossible to tell, their hair was so lank and unclean.

"Do you feed them?" Justine asked. "Do they have somewhere to wash?"

"Please understand," Mr Archer purred, "We are a charity and there's never enough."

"Looks like there's more than enough for the two of you," Justine commented, glancing at Mr and Mrs Archer's corpulence.

"Are they healthy?" Maggie asked, speaking over Justine's last comment.

"Well, of course they are," Mrs Archer replied, indignantly.

Justine noticed the dark skinned face of a young woman peeking around the door. When Mrs Archer noticed her as well she moved to close the door.

"Back to work, Sianna," Mrs Archer barked. "You're not wanted here."

"Wait, just a minute," Justine said, pushing past Mrs Archer to re-open the door. "Sianna, is it?" she asked. When the girl nodded, Justine suggested "Why don't you come inside, please, we'd like to meet you."

Sianna put down the heavy metal bucket she'd been carrying and entered the room. She was clearly mulatto, with dark caramel skin and the most extraordinary blue/green eyes. While skinny like the others there was a strength to her body and a power to her presence.

"You don't want no nigger," Mr Archer confirmed.

Moving to escort Sianna from the room, he placed a proprietary arm around her shoulders that was a bit too intimate for Justine's liking. She was tempted to sock him in his fat, hairy face when Maggie spoke up:

"How do you know what we want?" Maggie retorted. "If you think so little of her then I imagine you'll be happy to have her come with us!"

Archer's flabby face went slack with surprise but Mrs Archer seized the moment. Grabbing Sianna by the arm, she shoved her in Maggie's direction.

"An excellent choice. Take her," Mrs Archer said, narrowing her eyes at her husband in triumph.

"I ain't going nowhere without Camille," Sianna announced. Her voice was deep and rich and though the look in her eyes was cautious, her stance was insistent.

"Shut up, girl," Mr Archer hissed.

"Who's Camille?" Justine inquired.

"*Entrez,*" Sianna commanded. "*N'ayez pas peur, fifille.*"

If the sight of the first four girls had upset her, this child nearly broke Justine's heart. She looked 12 or 13 at the most, and could best be described as fragile from the delicate bones of her grubby face to the tiny hands clasped protectively in front of her. She moved cautiously past Mrs Archer, grabbing onto Sianna's outstretched hand. Suddenly Justine felt Maggie do the same thing, clutching her hand as if to share her own shock at the sight of the poor child.

"You are in no position to make demands, Sianna," Mr Archer warned.

When he spoke, Camille's face went sheet white causing the dark blue circles beneath her eyes to deepen.

"If these ladies take a second girl, that's up to them," Mrs Archer insisted, not looking at him and smiling ingratiatingly at both Justine and Maggie.

"Maybe you should take Camille back to her room," Mr Archer suggested sternly. There was a threat in his stance and Mrs Archer visibly cringed.

"Both girls can come with us," Maggie interjected. "If they want…"

"Well, I …" Archer, stuttered in surprise.

Justine squeezed Maggie's hand in thanks and acknowledgment. This was not an easy decision for someone like Maggie. Justine knew the prospect of bringing a dark-skinned young woman into her home was completely foreign, but overriding that was Maggie's enormous heart and ingrained sense of fairness. They both knew it would be easier for the other girls to find employment and they both knew Mr Archer's relationship with these two was somehow harmful and dangerous.

"Would you like to come with us?" Maggie asked Sianna.

"Yes, m'am, we would," Sianna confirmed, guiding Camille towards the door before anyone had a chance to change their minds.

Justine liked this young woman's courage and greatly admired her loyalty to her little friend.

"Go on Maggie, I'll settle things here," she said, turning a challenging eye on the detestable Mr. Archer.

On the ride home Little Camille huddled into her friend. Sianna sat erect staring wide eyed out the window as the world whisked by at greater speed that either of them had ever travelled. It was a revelation for Justine to witness them experiencing motorized travel for the first time. This century would bring so many new inventions. Looking ahead, she felt more acutely than ever before the painful wisdom of hindsight.

Forty-Four

At Justine's insistence, Maggie made up a hot bath, made sure both girls cleaned themselves and washed their hair. Seeing what came off of them, Maggie was beginning to appreciate Justine's preoccupation with human cleanliness.

Maggie sat with the girls in front of the fire as their hair dried, feeding them hot beef stew. Little Camille fell asleep before her hair was dry so they carried her up to the third floor where Maggie installed them in the small rear bedroom.

"You're safe now," she assured Sianna.

Sianna climbed into the double bed with her little friend and dropped into a deep sleep.

Maggie joined Justine in the parlour, stoking the fire and sighing deeply.

"You did a very good thing today, Maggie," Justine said, handing her a glass of whisky.

"I don't know nothing about anything," Maggie said "but there was something very wrong going on at that place. I wish we could have taken all them girls home with us."

"Birds of a feather, Maggie, my friend. That's you and me. But I think this house is full now, don't you?" Justine chuckled.

"There but for the grace of God," Maggie mused. "It makes me skin crawl to think what might of happened to me if you hadn't shown up when you did."

"Do you believe in karma, Maggie?"

"I don't know what that means."

"It means – it means, well, um, it's a concept that springs from Eastern Religions like Hindu or Buddhism. It was what Zhang Zhu said to me."

Maggie crossed herself and Justine laughed.

"There are some who believe that Jesus travelled to India and studied with the great spiritual masters there, you know," Justine explained.

"No I don't know. And I'd almost rather not."

"Fair enough. In Hinduism, it's believed that our soul or spirit - that inexplicable part of us that we call 'life' – that energy that animates us and makes us alive – never dies."

"Oh, Mother of God, there you go again, saying the most blasphemous things!"

Justine was beginning to understand that Maggie said such things to fend off the *evil eye*. It was reflex, but not necessarily belief. So she continued.

"… and that energy or soul or spirit, travels from one incarnation to the next – animating one lifetime after another. Reincarnation."

Justine waited while Maggie finished her drink. She was chewing her bottom lip; something Justine had seen her do when she was wrestling with a difficult thought or idea.

"Shall I go on?" Justine asked.

Maggie stopped worrying her lip but withdrew her handkerchief, holding it like a protective device rather than fretting it. She nodded.

"So during these different incarnations we manage to do good things and we also seem to succeed in doing some very bad things. The sum of these actions is called our karma and it travels with us into the next life and the next."

"Like fate?"

"Yes and no. Fate suggests we have no free will. But we do.

"So we chose to do bad things or, like today, we choose to do something good?"

"Yep. Today we created good karma, I think."

"Well, I'm relieved about that," Maggie said wryly as she got up to pull the curtains.

The fire crackled. Gazing out the window, Justine thought about the Archers and the Mercy Home for Girls. The snow had begun to fall again covering the city in a blanket of white. *All that white purity will never be able to clean away the evil humans do,* she thought.

"I found this in the little one's clothing," Maggie said, pulling a long length of white lace from inside her apron.

"Is it hand made?" Justine asked.

"How else would it be made?" Maggie wanted to know.

How else, indeed? Justine reminded herself, taking the lace from Maggie and spreading it out.

"It's exquisite. It must be almost four feet long. Do you think Camille made this?"

"Or stole it ..."

Justine looked at Maggie who was pursing her lips in order not to say more.

"I'll ask her tomorrow," Justine said. "If she made it, which I prefer to think, she's got a real skill."

Maggie recognized that Justine did not approve of her suspicions. So she changed the subject.

"You know Mrs Feingold's agreed to teach us to read?" Maggie said.

"Who's us?'

"Well – all of us illiterates," Maggie laughed, returning to the fire. "She taught me that word today. I like it. I want to learn to speak properly. I'm not going to be illiterate no more."

"Any more..." Justine corrected.

"Yes. I'll not be saying 'no more', any more," Maggie agreed.

Justine got up and hugged her. She liked the solid feel of this woman and the way she smelled of freshly baked bread. But most of all she liked her big, warm heart.

"What's that for?" Maggie asked, blushing but smiling with pleasure.

"I like you Maggie O'Reagan. I like you a lot."

"Well, the feeling's mutual."

"Shall I tell you something?"

"If you must," Maggie said sardonically.

"In the 1980's there will be a President of the United States by the name of Reagan. Ronald Reagan."

Maggie stepped back, grasping the mantel. She was chewing her lip again as her eyes darted around the room.

"I wish you wouldn't say things like that," she whispered.

"I'm sorry. I thought you might like to know."

Maggie reached for the whisky decanter, pouring and drinking quickly.

"Is it true?" she finally spluttered.

"Yep. And he was re-elected. They called him, 'The Great Communicator'."

"Ronald was me father's name," Maggie confessed in a very small voice, staring at Justine with wide, blue eyes. "William Ronald O'Reagan. Everyone called him Willy, but …." She stopped talking swishing the whisky around in her glass. Then she smiled and a tear rolled down her cheek. "No relation, I'm sure, but – if it's true – I'm glad to know."

Forty-Five

Driving alone with Alexander the next day, Justine was aware of how completely relaxed they were in each other's company – as if they had known one another for a very long time.

Closing her eyes, she thought of Ducky and that made her heart ache. The inability to describe the distance between them, intensified the longing. *Over a hundred years*, Justine thought. *I don't even know what that actually means anymore.* She inhaled deeply, trying not to let the lump in her throat develop into tears and then she smelled him. Ducky always used Ivory soap and the unique way it blended with his own aromas was a cherished memory from childhood, making her feel safe and loved. That exact scent wafted into her nostrils now and her eyes popped open.

"What kind of soap do you use, Alexander?"

They had driven quickly across the bridge and were now heading north up the Bowery in the midst of traffic. Horses pulling carriages seemed so vulnerable now from inside a machine but Alexander was utterly at home behind the wheel and seemed to be enjoying the speed and dexterity of the vehicle in contrast to guiding animals.

"Soap? I'm sorry I do not smell good?" he asked, sniffing the air and frowning.

"No. You smell nice - like someone I know and I wondered if you used the same soap."

"I use what Rosa gets," he said, shrugging, but glancing at her quizzically.

"I know, I say some very strange things!"

Alexander drove past Madison Square Park, pulling up at the corner of 26th in front of the Café Martin. As Justine approached the front doors, she smiled up at the familiar elegant façade, recalling that this had once been Delmonico's and that the French brothers, Jean and Louis Martin had taken over the lease, refurbishing the old building, giving it its current Art Nouveau design. Then she stopped as if she'd hit a hard wall. How did she know that? The doorman held the doors open and a well-dressed couple nearly collided with her as they made their way inside. Justine shook her head to clear it, aware that the doorman was staring at her uncertainly.

"Good afternoon, Pierre," Justine said, utterly unsure how she knew his name.

"*Bon après-midi, Mademoiselle,*" Pierre replied, ushering her inside.

Justine moved forward as if she were walking through a jar of glistening honey, as if everything had slowed down and was highlighted and emphasized by this fact. Ornate, breathtaking, and voluptuous were only some of the words to describe the interior of the Café Martin. And those same words might also describe its clientele. Here was gathered the *belle monde*, the fashionable elite, enjoying their wealth and privilege and grabbing the opportunity to put it on show inside this exquisite display case.

Approaching the *maître d'*, Justine heard herself say, "My regular table thank you, Philippe," then waited impatiently while the white haired man bowed his head and made a show of searching through his reservation list. "I'm meeting my .... " she almost said 'daughter' – then paused, confused, glancing around the expansive café. "I'm meeting Caroline McGowan," she managed to confirm.

At the mention of Caroline's name, Philippe looked relieved, "But of course, the McGowan's always sit upstairs, *n'est-ce pas?*"

He waited momentarily for Justine to agree, then guided her solicitously through the white table-clothed dining room, and up the Persian carpeted stairs with intricate iron worked railings, past the feathery potted plants and immense white marble columns to a table on the mezzanine overlooking the entire dining room.

Justine had selected the black and pink outfit with it's wide matching hat complete with plumage. She was vaguely aware of the stir her entrance created in the café as diners casually charted her progress, leaning in to one another, whispering and glancing up towards where she sat gazing down upon them.

She was less concerned with people's stares than with the persistent sensation of floating dislocation, coupled with the absolute knowledge that she had been here many times before, sitting at this very table filled with the awareness of her own entitlement and somehow angry with all of it.

She noted the wave of gawking heads turn subtly towards the door as Caroline appeared, following the officious Pierre through the same sea of onlookers. Poor Caroline, she was painfully aware of their looks and only just made it breathlessly to the table.

"Hello Caroline," Justine said, grasping her sister's arm firmly to instil courage. "I'm so happy you came."

Then motioning to Pierre she asked that tea be brought immediately. She noted his barely hidden look of disdain at being given a food order and how he nodded obsequiously nonetheless.

"Are you alright, Caroline?" she asked once they were alone.

"Yes," Caroline confirmed, her breathing beginning to slow. "I just – well – I haven't been here in such a very long time and – I used to come with Mummy and we'd always sit at this very table…"

Justine was trying very hard to stay in the present moment but Caroline's explanation was causing her heart to beat rapidly and there wasn't room for that inside the corset and petticoats and tight fitting bodice.

"I hope I haven't distressed you by sitting here. I hope those were good memories,"

"Well, she was a difficult person to please and I'm afraid I didn't do a very good job," Caroline confessed.

Justine felt an inexplicable pang of guilt grab at her chest as if she was somehow responsible for Caroline's sense of failure. "I can't understand that at all. You're very pretty and kind and clearly very loyal and loving. What better qualities could a person possess?"

"*You* are very kind. You are one of those people who's very certain of themselves …"

There it was again. Someone reflecting back to Justine something she'd never felt about herself. *Well, then,* she said to herself, *if that's what they think, that's who'll I'll be.* Suddenly everything came back into sharp relief and Justine returned to her sense of self.

"I'm very certain of one thing," she said, smiling. "I am SO happy to have finally met you and I think you're wonderful!"

To say that Caroline beamed was an understatement; she sat up straighter in her chair and glowed from head to toe.

"And I have a surprise for you," Justine added.

As if on cue there was an almost imperceptible shift of energy in the dining room as the sea of on lookers noted the entry of a dashingly slender, dark haired man and monitored his progress in Pierre's wake. Caroline watched from above as the elegantly dressed man made his way up the stairs, her eyes almost popping from her head as he approached the table, where he paused to bow in greeting, first to Justine and then to Caroline.

"Good afternoon, Mr Kucera," Justine said, nearly bursting with excitement, "I'm so glad you could join us."

Dušan Kucera took the seat next to Caroline. His gracious manner suggested he was comfortable and accustomed to such affluence, but his face belied his terror and joy at being so close to Caroline in public. Nothing was said as tea was served. Justine was only partially aware of the stir that continued amongst the other diners. She was busy congratulating herself for pulling this off.

Menus were offered and the three took time to study them as their hearts continued to race. Justine was entranced with the Café Martin luncheon menu. Under the heading 'Plats du Jour' was the translation in parentheses: (Ready Made Dishes). On offer were intriguingly named international dishes such as: Cold Poached Eggs *a l'Estragon*, *Omelet a l'Espagnole*, Irish Stew and the suspicious sounding *Tête de Veau vinaigrette*.

What little French she had, Justine could have sworn that *Tête* was the word for head and suspected the *Veau* to be one animal or the another all done in a vinaigrette sauce.

"I feel like sweets," she announced. "I feel like treating ourselves and celebrating! How about the *Pâtisserie assortie* and the *Macédoine de fruits au kirsch?*" She had no idea what the second one was but liked the sound of it.

"I – um – I love the *Crème au Caramel*, "Caroline proffered, shyly.

"Then you shall have the *Crème au Caramel*" Justine agreed, signalling the waiter. "Mr Kucera, do you have a particular request?"

"To be honest, I have all the sweets I could ever possibly hope for," he replied, glancing timidly at Caroline, who giggled and blushed and giggled again.

"You look so – so … I don't know …" Caroline responded.

"Dashing?" Justine offered. "Debonair?"

"Handsome," Caroline confirmed.

This time Dušan seemed embarrassed, nervously straightening his newly tailored deep auburn velvet vest. The rich color highlighted the chocolate brown of his eyes which longed to linger on Caroline's face but feared to do so.

The pastries were served, the tea topped up and the conversation flowed as Justine asked questions and Caroline and Dušan loosened up in each others company – delighted to be out in the real world together for the first time.

Dušan was a highly intelligent and educated man who'd grown up in what was then called Bohemia. As nationalism heated up, Jews became scapegoats, he explained and Dušan's mother was a Jew. His father was the conductor of a regional orchestra and Dušan had studied and loved music from a very early age.

Caroline knew his story and often filled in snippets he left out for the sake of brevity. She needed to share everything with Justine as a way of asking her to love Dušan as much as she did.

"In 1899 the Hilsner Affair started when a Bohemian Jew named Leopold Hilsner was accused of murdering a young girl," Dušan explained.

"Falsely accused," Caroline averred.

"The trial went on for months in the newspapers, which helped to feed the anti-Semitic fire."

"Dušan's parents were persecuted and his father lost his job."

"Hilsner was convicted and sentenced to death, but was later proven innocent and pardoned by King Karl. Despite the proof – the pogroms began. My parents fled to Germany but they insisted I come to this country."

"One day Dušan is going to bring his parents here."

"I would like them to meet you," he said to Caroline. "They would love you. I know it."

Without thinking he had taken her hand and they sat gazing at one another as if the rest of the world didn't exist.

A palpable shift in energy caused the gawkers to gaze towards the high arched windows that framed the Café's entrance. Caroline's attention strayed as well and she stood up suddenly almost knocking over her teacup. Justine followed her look and there in the entry stood the tall angry figure of her brother, Hunter, glaring upwards towards where they sat.

Caroline was already hurrying down the stairs before Justine or Dušan could decide what to do. It happened so quickly that onlookers were deprived of an extended show, but the gossip had already begun by the time Hunter grabbed Caroline's arm and escorted her out of the restaurant.

The look on Dušan's face was so full of angst, Justine was almost moved to tears. She touched his arm.

"Mr Kucera, I am assured by Caroline herself that her brother has never harmed her in any way."

Clenching his hands in unexpressed rage, still staring at the now deserted entry he said, "Not physically, no. The whole family has harmed her in so many other ways. "

Yes. Caroline definitely was suffering from emotional abuse and Justine was determined to put a stop to it.

"I will follow them," Justine assured Dušan. "I think it would be best if you went home."

He looked at her, appalled with himself. The cost of physically reigning in his outrage was a stiff bow, "Forgive my rudeness, Miss Justine. I am so very grateful for – for everything."

Forty-Six

As Alexander drove the car uptown, Justine reflected on how quickly things change. In one moment she was in 21st Century New York in the dead of summer and the next in 1906 New York in the dark of winter. In one moment two people were basking in the light of their love for one another and in the next a dark cloud blotted out the light. Time, life, love – they were concepts inside our head and hearts but had no substance you could hold on to.

Alexander dropped Justine off at the front of the mansion on 41st Street and drove the car around to the back to see if he could plug it in somewhere. This time, striding up to the impressive front entrance, Justine was not intimidated, she was determined. She knocked and waited thinking she could hear crying from the open second floor windows. She tried the door handle and finding it unlocked, let herself in.

She followed the sound of voices up to the second floor and into the chaos of the sitting room. Caroline was huddled in a chair near the French doors, which were open in spite of the cold. She sat shivering, wiping tears from her red-rimmed eyes. Hunter was across the room, holding on to a bleeding hand, staring out the window. Between them lay a path of angry destruction - furniture knocked over, a smashed vase, a shattered mirror.

Justine made her way swiftly across the room, side stepping shards of glass and righting a side table in order to get to Caroline. Wrapping her coat around her sister's shoulders, she closed the French doors and guided her to a seat by the fire, making sure she was not physically harmed. She poured a shot of whiskey from the cut glass decanter that had not been broken in the fracas and offered it to Caroline.

"Drink it, sweetheart," Justine encouraged her gently. "It'll warm you up and make you feel better."

Caroline obediently took a sip, squinched up her face at the strong taste, then finished off the alcohol. Justine glanced over at her brother, who had not moved from the window. As she looked at him that sense of dislocation returned and she found herself approaching him as if she wasn't in her body. She heard her voice say in a somewhat imperious tone:

"What have you done, Hunter?

He turned around, taking in the destruction of the room but she was already at his side, holding his wrist to get a better look at the injury to his hand.

"I told you violence wasn't the way, didn't I?"

His look was as confused as she felt but he allowed her to guide him to the chair opposite Caroline. Finding a teapot with hot water, she used this to wash his wound and a linen napkin to staunch the bleeding. He let her administer to him as if he were a child. She poured him a shot of whiskey, saying:

"I suspect you've had too much of this as it is …"

Then she sat down and waited. Hunter downed the whisky in one gulp then without looking up growled:

"Get out of here. I don't know who you are and I want you out of my house."

"No, Hunter. I'm not leaving. I'm beginning to understand what the problem is, but your way of solving it is destructive to yourself and others. Your reign of terror is over."

He stood up smashing the whisky into the hearth, causing the fire to flare. Caroline screamed.

"LEAVE ME ALONE," he shouted.

Justine stood up, looking him right in the eyes. "SIT DOWN, HUNTER MCGOWAN. NOW," she roared.

Justine had never in her entire life screamed at anyone like this. She'd wanted to. She'd felt the anger rising inside of her like searing hot liquid, but then she'd always squelched it. Now it exploded like hot lava, filling the room and demanding obedience. Hunter sat down. The power and unfamiliarity of what she'd just done ricocheted inside her body.

Caroline was shivering again, this time out of fear. Justine put a calming hand on Caroline's shoulder and bent down beside Hunter:

"You were very close to your mother, weren't you?"

She knew this as if she'd been there when Mrs McGowan was alive.

Hunter wrenched his arm away, growling, "Don't speak about my mother!"

Shame, the realization flashed in her mind. *He's feeling shame at the mention of his mother.*

"Hunter, the loss of your parents has left you feeling abandoned and out of control. But your attempts at regaining control are not working. They're hurting you and frightening Caroline."

"Don't tell me what to do," he said, but the strength was leaking out of him.

At that moment, Alexander appeared at the parlour door. The look on his face told Justine something was very, very wrong. She quickly followed Alexander down past the entrance foyer, discovering how large this house really was as they passed along a passage leading to the rear of the house and down more stairs to the servant's quarters and the kitchen.

Unlike the rest of the house, this area was designed for function and was utterly lacking in beauty or comfort. The cold seemed to have lingered here from winters past. It was a large kitchen to accommodate the huge dinners and balls the McGowans must have held in this massive mansion. That only two very unhappy people lived here now seemed to underscore the overall ominous feeling of the place.

Sitting at the butchery board was Matilde, holding her face. When they entered she looked up suddenly and Justine gasped. The whole left side of Matilde's face was bruised black and purple and her eye was swollen shut. She stared at Justine with her good eye, not knowing what to expect.

"She was locked in her room," Alexander explained. "Judging by the bruising, this must have happened this morning."

Justine approached the young, frightened girl cautiously, speaking gently, "Matilde – do you remember me? I'm Miss Caroline's sister?" The one good eye continued to stare. She was still in shock. "This is Alexander Alexandrovich. We are going to help you. Is it alright if I sit down next to you?" When she didn't object, Justine sat down on the bench. "Who did this to you?" The frightened eye looked away. "It's alright. Matilde. You don't need to be afraid. Was it Mr McGowan?" Matilde slumped over, unable to hold the terror inside any more. "It was, wasn't it? It was Hunter who hit you?" Justine reached for the girl as she nodded and began to shiver. "Ok. Listen to me Matilde. Did he do anything else? Did he – did he hurt you in any other way?" Matilde's lips were moving but Justine couldn't hear what she was saying. She leaned closer to the girl's face.

"He's tried," Matilde was whispering. "He's tried before. But he can't. You know. And then he gets angry. And then he hits me." And then she burst into tears, collapsing into Justine's arms.

"It's alright now. You're going to be ok," Justine consoled the young woman, seething with anger at Hunter's shameful behaviour.

"His friend was here too," Matilde whispered through her tears.

"What friend?" But a cold chill ran up Justine's spine because she knew the answer "You mean, Kendall Shaw?"

"He watched and he laughed and that's when Mr McGowan punched me. He's never hit me in the face before."

When Matilde spent herself crying, Alexander wrapped her in his coat.

"Are you okay to wait here Matilde?" Justine asked. "We're going to take care of this."

She stood with Alexander in the doorway to the parlour, waiting until Hunter became aware of her presence.

"You are going to leave this house, Hunter McGowan, at least for a couple of days. What you have done is inexcusable. You've crossed the line. For the safety of your sister and her maid, you need to re-move yourself from here."

Caroline looked from Justine to her brother, confused. "Hunter what's happened? What have you done?"

Hunter stood up and strode to the window.

"If you do not agree to leave here now, Hunter, I will tell your sister – everything."

263

He moved towards her, glaring and breathing hard. Alexander stepped to Justine's side, towering over both of them. Hunter glanced up at him then back at Justine.

"I would strongly advise you not to go to Kendall Shaw," Justine added.

She held his gaze until he looked away, realizing she meant business. Then he strode from the room. The scent of whisky and men's cologne lingered in his wake.

"Hunter?" Caroline stood up to follow him.

"Please, Caroline ..." Justine stood in her way.

"What's happened? What's Hunter done?"

"It's alright," Justine tried to sound soothing.

"NO. It's not all right. Tell me what's happened. I'm not a child."

"No. You're not Caroline. And it's time you stopped acting like one."

"How dare you speak to me like that? You're not my mother!"

Justine felt dizzy and terribly, terribly calm all at the same time. Caroline was glaring at her with a look very similar to Hunter's.

"Ever since you arrived, everything's turned upside down," Caroline sobbed, unable to hold onto her anger for very long.

"That's true. And I'm sorry if I've upset you in any way," Justine offered, looking at her sister with genuine regret.

"Oh dear," Caroline's cried, eyes widening in sudden realization. "He's hit Matilde hasn't he?"

Justine nodded.

"It's my fault. It's all my fault," Caroline wailed.

"Why do you say that?"

"Because, because I've been to scared to see it."

"Matilde has been hurt but not badly and it's not going to happen again," Justine assured her. "Come and sit down now, Caroline, we have things to talk about."

Forty-Seven

"Do you believe in reincarnation, Alexander," she asked.

They were driving down Park Avenue and Justine was unable to shake the sensation of dizziness, which was turning into nausea, coupled with a deep inner composure. Something had happened at the Café Martin and again in the McGowan drawing room, that Justine was struggling to make sense of.

"I don't know this word," Alexander replied.

"It means 'past lives'. It means we have lived before and come back again and again to inhabit different bodies in different lives."

"The Bible does not mention this," Alexander commented.

"Well, it does, actually. But only once. Other references were removed during the Council of Nicaea. But that doesn't make it untrue. The Bible was written a very long time ago, *about* the life of Christ but not *by* him."

"You don't believe in the Bible?" he asked, glancing back at her - not shocked but surprised.

"I believe the parts that make sense to me. The rest of it's just a story."

Alexander considered this as he steered into 21st Street narrowly missing a service wagon, stalled in the intersection.

"I have seen so many bad things that people do," he said, finally. "The night those men attacked little Anzelika, I knew God had abandoned me. I stopped reading the Bible."

"Those things that you saw, Alexander, and those evil men — Ducky would say that's the part of us that has forgotten we are God."

"Don't ever let Rosa hear you speak this way …" he warned, chuckling.

"Or Maggie," Justine added, grinning back. "Oh, turn right," she instructed as they came upon Gramercy Park West. "Yes. Stop here."

She gazed out the window. This was the house she most loved in all of Manhattan. She'd come upon it one night on her way to an event at The National Arts Club, which was housed around the corner in a Victorian Revival brownstone. That night she'd caught a glimpse inside this Greek Revival red brick townhouse. Glittering chandeliers lit up the high ceilinged grand drawing room spilling light out through the floor to ceiling French doors opening onto the most romantic cast iron lacework veranda, which faced directly onto Gramercy Park across the street. She'd stood there captivated by the elegance and simple grandeur of the house and ended up arriving late to her event.

That was in the future. Today Justine was contemplating buying this house and her heart was beating excitedly inside her chest. The fact that it was for sale could be called synchronicity or kismet but those words defined events happening in the same time frame. She'd fallen in love with this house over 100 years from now, and now, in the past, she was going to buy it.

Gramercy Park was blanketed in drifts of white, untouched snow. The sun had parted the grey clouds and light seemed to twinkle off of every single snowflake. It was dazzling. It was as if God was showing her the way. Justine giggled.

"God is here, Alexander, don't you think?"

He nodded, gazing out at the exquisite view. "Yes. I think he is," Alexander agreed.

The last couple of hours had been difficult but the delight of this moment was irresistible. They sat together just enjoying the view until it was time to meet Mr Brewster at his office and complete the deal.

Forty-Eight

Maggie and Sianna had been cleaning from early the previous morning. Maggie intended to make up for lost time and though Sianna was diligent she had her work cut out for her trying to keep Maggie away from the dust as per Justine's instructions. Maggie took great pride in a clean and tidy house and continuously found reasons to interfere with what Sianna was trying to do.

The next morning at breakfast the conflict continued. In spite of whatever hardships Sianna had suffered in her life, she was cut from a similar stubborn cloth as Maggie. Sianna was attempting to do everything and insisting on doing it her way. Justine recognized that Maggie was not going to relinquish her cleaning duties without a fight and Sianna seemed to be bringing on the battle.

Today was to be Sasha's first day at driving the Yellow Cab horse and buggy and he and Alexander were outside cleaning and polishing the harnesses and tack. James had left immediately after breakfast, Rosa was in her basement apartment, cleaning and ironing.

Camille had found a kindred spirit in Anzelika and they were already fed and on their way out to the horses when things came to a head between Maggie and Sianna.

It started when Justine showed Camille the length of lace and asked if she had made it. Sianna was cleaning nearby and interrupted,

"… a course she made it and what're you doing with it?"

Sianna's aggressive tone was followed by an attempt to grab the lace out of Justine's hand.

"It was in Camille's dirty clothes," Justine replied, stepping back and holding on to the lace.

"It's not yours," Sianna insisted, glaring at Justine.

"It's not yours either, Sianna."

"Wha'da you know about it?'

"You watch your tone, missy, "Maggie interrupted. "I don't like the way you're speaking to Miss Justine."

Sianna glared at Maggie and Maggie glared back. Then suddenly Sianna's shoulders slumped and the fight when out of her.

"That Archer," she said, her voice now a monotone, "he uses girls for makin hisself money. I didn't want him to find out what Camille can do."

"Okay, Sianna," Justine replied. "Your loyalty is admirable. You're not in that place anymore. You can trust us."

"I just hope we can trust you," Maggie added, still watching Sianna with suspicion.

Forty-Nine

Justine waited on the sidewalk for her sister and Matilde to arrive. She'd said only that it was a surprise. Both girls were in high spirits as the carriage delivered them to the house on West Gramercy Park. Matilde's eye had turned from purple to a sickly color of green, which meant it was healing but caused Justine to wince nonetheless.

"How are you Matilde?" she asked

"Better, thank you, Miss."

"I love this neighborhood," Caroline enthused, stepping down from the carriage. "Dorothy Pembroke's parents have a house on the other side of the park and Florence May, who married Augustus Davis, just moved here recently."

"I'm VERY glad to hear that, dearest Caroline." Justine replied.

"What's the surprise? What's the surprise?" Caroline demanded, breathlessly.

There were times when the girl Caroline was completely overtook the woman she was becoming. Her eyes twinkled in excitement and her hands clasped together in anticipation.

"Follow me," Justine instructed leading the way up the front stairs to the porch wrapped with iron lacework and in through the impressive double front doors.

Caroline 'oohhed' and 'aahed' as they entered the grand Drawing Room. The grandeur of the 13-foot ceilings and French doors opening onto Gramercy Park, was breathtaking. The room was empty, making the swirling arabesques of the ceiling and the Corinthian pilasters all that more outstanding. They followed Justine into the Library next door, with Caroline delighting at the carved shell wall recesses and the high wooden shelving.

"But why are we here?" she wanted to know.

"Wait until you've seen all of it," Justine insisted as they followed her through the main foyer, past the formal dining room with it's polished panelling and custom sideboards into the kitchen at the back of the house. This is where Matilde expressed appreciation:

"A kitchen next to the dining room," she enthused "… and such a kitchen! Everything so new and so *gemütlich*!"

"And the plumbing is already in place for an indoor lavatory and washroom!" Justine explained as they made their way up the curving central staircase to the master bedroom with its northern view of the intricate wooden spires of Calvary St. George's Church on 21st Street and a garden view to the south.

"It was too big to remove, so they left it," Justine explained pointing to the large bed tucked center stage in the room. The bedstead was made of iron dipped white with polished brass railing swirling in a design of butterflies.

"But it's absolutely beautiful and perfect in this room, don't you think?" Caroline cooed.

"Yes. I agree," Justine replied, more and more pleased with herself. "Let's go back downstairs, shall we, and I'll tell you the surprise."

Matilde managed to heat the kitchen by starting the gas range and they sat at the butcher-block table, Caroline bursting with anticipation.

"As you know," Justine began "Your father left you some money, which you will inherit on your next birthday… which if I'm not mistaken is in July."

"What? Yes. July. Really? I didn't know. About the – about - the money." Caroline admitted.

"Oh. I see. Well, Mr Brewster was your father's long time lawyer and his friend, right?"

"Yes. I met him once or twice, I think…"

"He is also my lawyer – now – and naturally, he is acting on behalf of your father's will and requests. He informed me that you have an inheritance."

"No one told me. Why would they not tell me?" Caroline asked, as the fact of her Mother's and possibly her brother's betrayal began to arise in her mind.

"Sometimes people do things for unfathomable reasons," Justine answered, sadly.

Caroline's long, blond eyelashes blinked trying to hide the hurt that was her constant companion in relation to her family.

"But listen Caroline, the good news is that you could buy this house. You could buy this house and start your own life. Start making your own decisions. Starting with having the friends you want to have and seeing the people you want to see."

Caroline looked up at Justine and the thought of Dušan Kucera flickered across her half smiling lips. Then she frowned.

"But how could I? What would Hunter say? Or do?" she added, glancing at Matilde's black eye.

"Perhaps if you were to live here," Matilde ventured gently, "and start your own life, as Miss Justine suggests, then Mr McGowan would have to do the same."

"You are a woman now, Caroline. In 6 months, the law will recognize you as such," Justine, instructed. "Hunter will no longer have legal control over you. Until that time, I can act as your guardian."

Caroline's eyes widened.

"I think after the events of the past few days, this may be the best solution." Justine added.

Caroline looked around the kitchen and out into the back garden. She looked into Justine's eyes and sighed.

"I don't know," she said finally. "I can't just leave Hunter – alone. He's always been high strung but since Mama died, he's become, well, you've seen what he's become…"

"How about if I promise to make sure that Hunter is not alone. That he's looked after and, maybe even that he's able to find some happiness…."

"You could do that?" Caroline asked doubtfully.

"I could try," Justine confirmed. "I have a fairly good idea of what it might take."

"Oh my," Caroline exclaimed. "If you can try, then so can I, I guess."

"That's my girl!" Justine congratulated her. "I've made arrangements for you and Matilde to move in today."

"Today?"

"No time like the present," Justine encouraged.

"But …"

"No buts, Caroline. Not any more. You can do this."

"Oh, my. Oh, my. Oh, my…" Caroline fussed. Then she became very still as an idea occurred to her. "What if?" she said, standing up suddenly. "Do you think..?" she wondered out loud, heading out of the kitchen with Justine and Matilde following.

She raced into the drawing room, striding across to one set of French doors, where the sunlight was pouring in. She turned towards Justine and Matilde with a look of wonder on her face.

Indicating the place where she stood she asked, "Do you think this would be a good location for a grand piano?" Not waiting for an answer she hurried on as if her idea was so daring she had to speak it before she became afraid. "If there was a piano here, then Dušan – Mr Kucera – Dušan, could give his lessons here. He could attract better students in a room like this, don't you think? Students worthy of his talent." Her face was aglow with the possibility, until another thought occurred to her. "Would it be proper, do you think? Would people talk?"

"What would be wrong about allowing a great musician to use your home to further the outreach of his art?" Justine answered. "And, Caroline, at the end of the day, we have to answer only to ourselves."

Caroline looked at Justine, tears filling her eyes and she sobbed, "I am so glad you're here and you're my sister." Then she ran across the room and into Justine's welcoming arms.

Fifty

Alexander was driving the car slowly east along 29th Street, past the Church of the Transfiguration. Designed in the early English Neo Gothic style the dark brick sanctuary was set back from the street behind a garden. Justine had gone to free concerts in the church and sat in the garden with her laptop.

It stuck her how much time she'd spent in the past – even before coming here. She and Ducky had their heads full of the past...

Tonight it appeared as if an additional chapel was being built. It would be called the Lady Chapel, she recalled.

They passed the ostentatiously crafted façade of the Second Empire styled Gilsey House Hotel on 29th at Broadway. She seemed to remember in her time it housed shops with cheap crap for sale. Looking up Broadway afforded Justine a view of what was known as the Great White way. Broadway was lined in both directions with illuminated signs glittering invitations, alluring clientele to all forms of legitimate vice and illegal entertainment; high-stakes gambling parlors, brothels, saloons and dance halls.

She couldn't remember who said: *The more things change, the more they stay the same.* She sighed. This was the gateway to the Tenderloin. In some research she'd done, Justine recalled that the phrase was coined when the new chief of police reputedly said: *'I've been having chuck steak ever since I've been on the force, and now I'm going to have a bit of tenderloin'*.

It made her shudder now as Alexander headed the car towards the outskirts of the Tenderloin district. Continuing along 29th the lights grew dimmer and the commercial buildings turned residential, but did not house families or homes. Stopping outside a dark, red brick row house Alexander turned to her with real concern.

"Is this it?" Justine asked, peering out at the darkened doorway and the bars on the shuttered windows.

"I should go in with you," Alexander insisted.

"No. I think you can appreciate why you can't go in there and why I have to do this without you."

She got out of the car and leaned in the window to speak with Alexander.

"Why don't you go someplace warm and get a drink. Come back in a couple of hours."

"No. I will wait for you here."

The implacable set of his jaw told Justine he was not going to budge. She felt bad about the temperature. It had begun to snow again. But she was infinitely grateful that he would remain.

There were no lights or enticing signs here. This place of business did not wish to advertise itself. The entrance was below street level, accessed down a dark flight of steps. When Justine pulled the doorbell, all she heard was the grinding of its metal gears. There was no perceptible ringing or indeed any sound at all. It was pitch black in the doorway, utterly silent and freezing cold. She was about to depart as much in dread as from the cold, when a small window in the door slid open at eye level. A woman's face peered out, clearly surprised to see Justine.

"Whadya you want?" the woman asked in a gruff voice.

Justine held up a large wad of money, "I want to buy what you have for sale."

The woman's eyes went wide at the sight of the money then squinted disbelievingly at Justine again.

"Open the door," Justine demanded "before I freeze to death out here and you have to call the police to collect my body!"

The door creaked open and not waiting for permission, Justine pushed in, brushing past the woman. Standing in a narrow entry with a dim electric light overhead, there was a musty smell of cheap cigars and mould, which could have been emanating off the woman or was the pervasive aroma of the house.

Justine had chosen to wear an obviously expensive evening dress of black silk embroidered with red and black sequins, elbow length sleeves and long red gloves. She was wrapped in a short matching jacket with fur trim around the neck and wrists.

The woman made a none-too-subtle but highly experienced survey of Justine with her wolf like, watery eyes.

Perceptibly impressed, she said, "I'm Mrs Tittle. Why don'cher come in ta the parlour."

Smiling ingratiatingly, and exposing a few missing teeth, Mrs Tittle was a thin woman at the far end of middle age. Her small bosom brushed up against Justine as she turned to lead the way. Justine shuddered to think the brush might have been an invitation.

Through a door off the hallway Mrs Tittle led Justine into a small parlor with an even smaller fire going in the hearth. The velvet-flecked wallpaper had seen better days and a dark water stain in one corner of the ceiling had caused it to peel.

"I'll see what we've got for you," Mrs Tittle purred in her gruff voice, indicating Justine should sit in the high backed tufted chair, poised like a viewing station.

Justine managed to grab the woman's bony arm before she disappeared, "I don't want children," she cautioned.

Mrs Tittle curled her lips into a knowing grin glancing with interest at Justine's grip on her arm. "I'm sure we can find somethin' to yer liking," she said, fading into the darkness of the hallway, chuckling lasciviously to herself.

Justine didn't have to wait long before the small room began to fill with an array of men from a big shouldered oaf with a square, slack jaw to a fragile creature, more female than male, with long wavy hair wearing a an intricately designed silk chemise draped off one naked shoulder. A seriously drugged looking fellow was pushed into the room by Mrs Tittle and then almost collapsed into Justine's lap. Mrs Tittle righted him with surprising force for someone so slight.

"Andre, here does the dirty better 'n anyone," she announced, patting his cheek a number of times with a slapping sound. His bloodshot eyes popped open staring at Justine without seeing. He reminded her unnervingly of those Zombie movies popular in her era.

Mrs Tittle draped herself on the arm of Justine's chair, leaning in conspiratorially. "He'll do anything yer wantin'," she said, her breath smelling liked almonds and decay. "And I mean *any*-thing." she added, looking evocatively into Justine's face. "And yer can do anything ter him. He don't care. He likes it all," she snorted, her sharp tongue licking her lips like a snake.

Justine looked away so Mrs Tittle got up, standing next to the large man, reaching her hand into his trousers.

"Olaf, might be what you're lookin' for," she suggested running her hand up and down along his member. "He'll fuck any one and any thing," she expounded, salaciously. "And he's got a really big one," she added, producing his large, hard penis for Justine to admire.

Justine wanted to run screaming from the room in revulsion and anguish. It took all her will power to remain seated when a young man quietly entered the room carrying a tray filled with glasses and a decanter of whisky. His hair was blond, shoulder length and curled around his strikingly beautiful face. Long lashes framed dark eyes.

High cheekbones defined full lips. He was tall, and though thin had wide shoulders and narrow hips.

Ignoring the young man, Mrs Tittle continued her pitch, "Delphine is our prize, of course," she said, wrapping a possessive arm around the delicate, girlish man. "Would you like to see more?" she asked, ready to strip the silk chemise from his body.

"No." Justine said firmly, indicating the boy with the tray. "I think he will do."

Mrs Tittle looked with surprise towards the young man then her lips pouted with concern. "Raphael? Oh, I don't think so," she argued. "He only fucks with boys. You'll not find him entertainin' at all." She moved quickly to extract the tray from Raphael and shoo him from the room.

"This is what I want." Justine demanded, rising from her seat.

Raphael paused at the door, glancing curiously at Justine. She noted his intelligent eyes. Mrs Tittle shot Justine an angry look, fighting an unknown battle inside herself.

"You drive a hard bargain, Mrs Tittle," Justine said, curling her lips into a grin. "I'll pay twice what he's worth," she announced, slowly drawing money out of her bag, waiting for Mrs Tittle to agree.

"Alright then," Mrs Tittle conceded at last.

"I want a room where we can be absolutely private," Justine stipulated, quickly. She offered half the cash, which Mrs Tittle didn't hesitate to pluck from her grasp. "That's half," Justine explained. "If I'm satisfied, I'll give you the remainder." Mrs Tittle pursed her thin lips, fingering the money, debating. "I drive a hard bargain too, Mrs Tittle," Justine noted.

"Humpf," Mrs Tittle replied.

"I'll want dinner as well. And wine," Justine ordered.

Mrs Tittle nodded and swept from the room, stuffing the money down her minimal cleavage. Justine looked at Raphael. He shrugged and led her across the hall into an identical room, this one with a table, two chairs, a cracked full-length mirror and a bed.

"Please make a fire," Justine said, watching as he moved silently to the hearth. It was then she noticed he was barefoot. "Where are your shoes?" she asked. "Your feet must be freezing!"

"Yes," he agreed, watching while the kindling caught fire. He turned to face her, his face impassive, awaiting her next instruction.

There was a knock on the door and a young boy entered with a tray of food and wine. Placing it on the table, he glanced curiously at Justine. He was probably no more than 12 but looked much younger. This was the child she'd asked not to see. He left the room, shutting the door behind him.

Justine waited a moment, then wrenched the door open. As expected, Mrs Tittle was standing in the hallway ready to eavesdrop.

"I said ABSOLUTE privacy!" Justine bellowed, glaring into Mrs Tittle's wolfish eyes.

"I was wantin' to make sure the food was to yer likin'," Mrs Tittle said, defensively.

"No. You were wanting to spy," Justine retorted and slammed the door. It felt good to behave badly in this house of sadness and sin.

She draped her coat on the door handle, covering the keyhole from other prying eyes. Raphael watched with interest. She approached him, placing both hands on his shoulders, drawing him to her as if she were going to kiss him. Instead she moved her lips to his ear.

"Is there another spy hole?" she whispered.

Raphael bent down, reaching into the fireplace, repositioning a large log over a hidden viewing hole that would have displayed all activities in and around the bed. He stood to face her, silently watching and waiting.

She motioned for him to sit with her at the table. "You look hungry," Justine said softly, pushing the tray of food across to him. "Please. I'd like you to eat."

The delectable aroma of stew filled the space between them. She knew he was hungry but he continued to watch her. In the firelight, his unflinching eyes were flecked with gold.

"Please. I mean it. I'd like you to eat. I'm going to tell you a story. Then I'm going to make you an offer. I need you strong and aware in order to make a decision. For that, I think you need to eat."

Used to taking instructions, he picked up the spoon and shovelled in a mouthful. He closed his eyes as he chewed, savoring the flavours and swallowing with pleasure. He looked up at Justine and she smiled encouragingly. He took another bite and then another. It was clear he hadn't eaten a proper meal in some time.

As he slowly and completely devoured everything on the plate Justine relayed the necessary history. When she poured him a glass of wine, she had his absolute attention. He asked one or two questions, which she answered as best she could.

"Now I need to know a bit about you, Raphael. Beginning perhaps with why you have no shoes."

"I am owned by the owner of this house," he explained. Though what he said was appalling, his English was flavored with an appealing taste of French and his expression was matter-of-fact. "I tried to escape. They took my shoes."

"In order to make my offer," Justine continued, "I need to know - why are you here? Why does the owner, own you?"

"As she said, I only fuck boys. This was a disgrace to my important family in France. They sent me away. By the time I arrived in New York, I had no money..." he finished by shrugging his shoulders and sipping more wine.

Her instincts about him were proving right. His intelligence was real; partly education, partly breeding. His only issue so far was his sexual orientation, which he clearly had no problem with and which Justine believed was exactly what was needed for the offer she was going to make him. She poured him more wine. And explained what she had in mind. He stopped drinking and listened attentively to everything she said.

"If you think you can do exactly as I suggest," she said, finally. "If you think you can handle this job and try to create a positive outcome – then we can plan how to make it happen."

"You came to a very strange place to find what you are looking for," he commented.

"No, I came to the only place there is to find what I'm looking for."

He thought about that for a moment, then sighed. He'd seen more than anyone needed to see in one lifetime. He'd experienced more pain, both physical and emotional, than most could handle. Yet there was a peacefulness about him that confirmed to Justine she'd found what she was looking for.

"If it makes any difference … things get better … in the future … for men like you." She said it without thinking and he looked at her strangely.

"How do you know?"

"I just know," she said.

They agreed that he would escape later that night. Alexander would be waiting for him nearby so he didn't have too far to run in bare feet. Alexander would take him to a men's public bath then, in the morning, to a tailor for a suit of clothing and then to his final destination. Justine promised there would be a bank account opened for him, with money that would allow him a certain amount of freedom. And in return he would promise to undertake the job she had proposed.

She poured herself some wine and sealed their agreement with a clink of glass and a whispered promise. When she stood up he arose as well. He wrapped his arms around her and held her for a long time. She could feel his heart beating through his thin clothing. She held him too. She was making something right in this moment. She could feel it. He was embarking on a fresh, new path. There was gratitude on both sides. But there was something more.

He pulled back and held her shoulders, looking deep into her eyes. Justine looked up at him but then something mystifying happened – his eyes turned from brilliant blue to deep, almond brown and Justine felt as if she was very small in his hands, as if she were a little girl again – as if she were 6 years old looking into the eyes of her mother.

The room tilted with vertigo so she held on to him. She was standing in a shabby room in 1906 with a young French man but she was also in the presence of her mother. That was how it seemed. The more she looked into those eyes, the more she knew she was somehow seeing and feeling her mother, her mother's soul in his eyes. Later when she thought about it, bizarre as it seemed, she was aware that in that moment, she was rescuing a part of her mother. Her mother's Soul. Her mother's Soul's manifestation.

Then he stepped back and crossed the room, gathering her coat from the door handle and helping her into it.

"I was born to do this," he whispered. "I have all the skills it will take. Thank you. Thank you for finding me."

The moment was ripped apart by a blood-curdling scream emanating from another part of the house. A man's voice roared, followed by the sound of running. Justine pulled the door ajar just in time to see the boy they called Delphine, run past half-naked and covered in blood. He was pursued by a man brandishing a whip. When Justine recognized the man's face she quickly shut the door. She was certain he hadn't seen her, which was a great relief. But seeing him shocked her to her core. It was Kendall Shaw. He was evil. Of that she was now certain.

Glancing suddenly at Raphael, she asked. "Do you know that man?

"Kendall Shaw. His father is very rich. He does as he pleases." Raphael said as an explanation for the man's horrific behavior and added, touching his head, "*es putain de malade dans ta tête.*"

"He *is* sick in the head. Does he know you?"

"No. The owner has protected me from him and his kind. For that I am grateful."

Fifty-One

The furniture had not been put back and lay like dead bodies where it'd been knocked over, revealing patches of collected dust. The broken vase and mirror remained in shattered shards on the floor. The room was cold and felt empty - not just of people but of life.

Alexander built a fire in the hearth. On this occasion he'd refused to allow Justine to go alone. They sat quietly, sipping whisky, waiting. It was the evening of the third day after Justine had banished Hunter from his home and she expected, she hoped, he would return.

"Why do you do all this?" Alexander asked.

"All what?" Justine replied, though she knew precisely what he was talking about.

"Everyone you meet. You help. I am not complaining. I am very grateful. I am curious."

"When we first met, Alexander Alexandrovich, I might have said something like: it's the right thing to do. But now I believe there's something else going on. Something to do with – something to do with the past, with past lives – with reincarnation."

289

He looked at her sharply but she was staring into the fire, wrapped in the thoughts that were now surfacing into consciousness.

"If I hit you, Alexander, I cause you pain. That pain remains like a scar, like an energetic scar the binds us and will not let us go – unless – unless and until I do something to heal it. If I hit you once, in another life, then the next time, when we meet again I have the possibility to redress, to heal that pain …. To resolve the karma between us. To calm and settle the energetic field that we are all a part of….."

When she finished speaking she looked up wide-eyed from her reverie, as surprised by what she'd just said as he was. But before either could say another word, there was the sound of someone entering the house below and ascending the staircase.

Hunter appeared in the doorway to the parlour. He looked as one might expect after days away from home, bedraggled in his elegant clothing, forlorn, his eyes puffy and red – but he didn't seem surprised to see them sitting there.

Justine was about to speak when Kendall Shaw appeared, striding into the room as if he owned it, his pugnacious features sniffing the air like a mastiff, weighing the threat.

Justine felt the temperature drop and a chill run up her spine. She was about to stand and confront him, when Alexander placed a warning hand on her arm and stood himself; his size and imposing manner, a warning to everyone in the room.

Shaw, paused, then chuckled in a practiced fashion, feigning indifference.

"What it is you want, Mr Shaw?" Justine asked, trying to regulate the trembling in her voice.

Shaw removed a cigar from his jacket, taking time to light it, while everyone watched and waited. He blew malodorous smoke, casually into the air.

"Yer boy here has run up a bit of a tab," Shaw said finally, jerking his head at Hunter.

His voice was incongruously high and breathy and Justine had to fight back hysterical laughter upon hearing it. She glanced at her brother, standing hang-dog in the doorway, realizing Shaw's claim to be true.

"Then I'm sure he'll pay his debt and you can leave us alone."

Shaw tilted his head, peering at Justine, sizing her up and undressing her with his eyes. The look was meant to disarm her, but Justine came from another time, when a man looking at her like that might actually prompt derisive laughter. But she recalled poor Delphine's terrified face and bloody back, running down the hallway. She held his gaze, the bile rising in her throat.

"He wants my Grandfather's gold watch," Hunter mumbled.

"Makes it sound like I'm stealing it from you, Hunter, old friend," Shaw piped in, blowing smoke in the air. "But it's not like that, is it?" he continued, moving towards Hunter. Alexander shifted his weight, which was enough to halt Shaw. "Don't want this here big fella to get the wrong idea, do we now, Hunter, me boyo? It was a fair game. You made a bet and, well, as sometimes happens, you lost. I'm just here to collect." The last was said mostly to Alexander.

Hunter moved suddenly from the doorway. His hurried footsteps could be heard on the hardwood floors. A door opened. Then silence.

"I told you to stay away from my family," Justine spat at Shaw.

"I've been to a so-called *fortune teller* before," Shaw taunted her. "Named Bella in the Bowery. Didn't know what the hell she was talking about. Neither do you."

He sucked on his cigar waiting for Justine to take the bait. She watched him.

"I can't help it if he can't stay away from me, now can I?" Shaw implored, grinning and blowing smoke in Hunter's direction.

A door slammed followed by footsteps returning, not so swiftly this time. Hunter reappeared in the doorway a polished gold pocket watch in his hand. Alexander allowed Shaw to approach Hunter and take the watch. He opened it, nodding with satisfaction.

Turning to Justine, Shaw smiled a set of very bad teeth, lifting his hat he was about to speak when she stood up to face him.

"I told you I know who you are," Justine warned, "The evil you do will catch up with you. And very, very soon."

He turned visibly white, "What do you know?" he demanded.

"Your family owns property in Haverstraw, New York, I believe," Justine said, recalling an insignificant article she'd read in a local newspaper while researching for Professor Linklater.

"What of it!"

"There's going to be a landslide there, killing 21 people."

This was a man whose religion was greed, but he was also a creature of his time. Her prediction clearly unsettled him. He narrowed his eyes at her.

"What else do you know?"

"That you are a piece of unholy filth. You got what you came for now get out of this house."

Shaw's jaw tightened and his hands clenched but this time when he moved, Alexander reacted quickly, seizing the smaller man by his jacket lapels and frog marching him from the room.

Hunter slumped into the seat in front of the hearth. Justine studied him as he gazed unseeing into the fire, shivering slightly as the cold left his body.

"I'm sorry," Hunter said at last, his hand indicating the room and the man who had just left.

"Me too," Justine replied.

"My father didn't like me very much."

"I'm sure that's not true."

"That watch was the one thing he wanted me to have."

"It's been a very hard time for you since your parents died…"

"Where's Caroline?"

"She and Matilde have moved out, Hunter."

He glanced at her and then his eyes drifted around the room as if seeing it for the first time. The shards of glass lay like reproof of his anger. He slumped in his chair.

"Where?" he wanted to know.

"I won't tell you that until I am sure you won't hurt them."

"I would never hurt my sister," he said, the old outrage flaring for a moment.

Justine reached across a comforting hand. "I know," she said.

He stared at her hand on his arm and a tear rolled down his cheek. A discreet knock on the door was followed by Raphael entering with a tray laden with a late 19th century Moscow tea set with green and gilt geometric motifs on a pale green background. It was exquisite porcelain, Justine observed much like Raphael himself, now cleaned and clothed.

He expertly began to set the table. "Your driver suggested you might need this. I made hot cocoa," he murmured, "I hope you like it." This last comment was said with a subtle glance into Hunter's face. There was a brief moment when their eyes connected and Justine believed she felt an electric current. She hoped she felt an electric current, anyway.

"Hunter, this is Raphael. I took the liberty of hiring him so that you wouldn't be alone – with no one to attend you."

Raphael stood back, humbly awaiting Hunter's approval. The blond sweep of his hair and the deep clefts of his cheekbones were highlighted in the fire's glow. His beauty was breathtaking. It left Hunter unable to look away and momentarily speechless.

"I've made a fruit torte if you are hungry," Raphael offered into the silence.

"That would be lovely," Justine answered. "Would you like some torte, Hunter?"

Hunter was nodding before he could speak but eventually managed a simple, "Yes. Torte."

Raphael bowed his way out of the room. Justine didn't know what to make of Hunter's silence. She prayed it meant approval of Raphael and acceptance of his employment.

"In light of what's happened - I thought a man would be a good idea," she said cautiously. When he didn't comment, she went on. "Raphael is intelligent, skilled and very likeable. Don't you think?"

"You remind me of my mother," he replied. "She thought she knew what was best for everyone." His tone was matter-of-fact but Justine knew better than to take the bait. She waited. Hunter sipped some cocoa. "If his torte is as good as this cocoa, I'll keep him."

Fifty-Two

The morning exodus from Justine's house to the Feinstein's across the street was now a regular routine. All Rachel's students gathered in the front foyer, Maggie threw open the door and in one mad rush they raced across the street alleviating the need to put on and take off coats and hats. Maggie, Sianna, Camille, Anzelika and Sasha were all being taught to read, write and do arithmetic.

Anzelika was intent on preparing to go to a proper school and Justine hoped Sasha would join her. Sianna had accepted the invitation with her customary bluster and Camille, who already knew how to read was grateful for help with her English. Rachel, it seems, spoke fluent French. And as for Maggie, she was so ecstatic to be mastering the written word that she was only too pleased when Rachel asked her to help teach the others to count.

Rosa was in her apartment ironing and Alexander was either driving his taxi or overseeing his team of Italians, working on Caroline's new bathrooms.

Justine stood in the doorway warmed not just by the welcome winter sun, but by the joy of watching this exodus. Rachel also stood in her open doorway, allowing James to depart and her students to arrive. Justine waved, suppressing the impulse to call out and Rachel responded with a courteous nod of acknowledgement.

James made his way up the front steps carrying a medium sized, wrapped canvass and his knapsack of brushes and paints.

"Did your session go well?" Justine asked, closing the door behind him.

Emboldened by the freedom from paying rent, James was now approaching potential clients again, offering his services. Dr. Feinstein, it seems had jumped at the opportunity to have a portrait painted of his beautiful wife. And Justine was more than a bit curious.

"Very well," James replied, grinning slyly as he mounted the stairs.

"What does that mean?"

"That she's a lovely subject whose husband can pay well!"

At the spiral stairs leading to his attic studio, he turned to face her, his eyebrows raised in question and his head cocked to one side.

Justine was aware his was toying with her, but she couldn't stop herself.

"Can I see it?"

"No. It's not done."

He hefted his things and expertly climbed the tenuous stairs. Justine knew she shouldn't but she hiked up her cumbersome skirts and followed him.

She emerged from the trap door as James was covering the painting. He looked up at her in mock surprise. The glimpse she caught of the portrait was stunning. He'd chosen to focus on Rachel's face, which filled the canvass with its proud but perfect proportions.

"Is there something you need?" he asked, grinning suggestively.

The brazier had not been lit, but it felt warm in the room, which was filled with the scent of paint and maleness.

"You've settled in nicely," Justine commented, changing the subject and glancing round the attic.

"Thanks to you," James replied, removing his jacket and bending over to light the brazier.

From other rooms in the house Maggie had appropriated a comfortable armchair and side table, a proper bed and a washstand. The bed remained unmade with its dark red comforter draping voluptuously to the floor. The rest of the space was filled with canvasses and a sizeable easel, positioned near the large windows overlooking the street. Sun pored in adding to the overall cosiness.

She watched him, knowing she should leave.

"I'd like very much to paint you," he said.

"What? No," she insisted, feeling his eyes on her making it impossible to move.

He was close enough now to brush his fingers along her cheek, sending flashes of heat through her body.

"You are the most extraordinary woman I've ever met."

"Rachel Feinstein is an extraordinary woman," Justine argued, tearing herself away.

"Yes. But she is not unique. If you let me paint you, you will understand what I mean."

He waited, his hazel eyes full of fire.

Sometime later, the house still empty, Justine was sitting on James' bed, the brazier glowing nearby. Her lower body was draped in the plush, red comforter. She was intensely aware of her nakedness though James had seen her in far more intimate deshabille.

She'd agreed to pose for a portrait, anticipating something like the one he'd painted of her Mother. But, after much persuasion, she'd finally agreed to sit for him nude, turned away just enough that her face and breast were in profile and her hair loose and cascading down her back.

She couldn't help being seduced by the secretive and taboo nature of their relationship. She felt more exposed as he studied her than she ever had with a lover. His eyes made love to her while his hand told the story with his brush on the canvass. At the same time this liaison troubled her, tying her to this time and place in a way that felt precarious.

She shivered, aware that her nipples stood up even more erect.

"Are you cold, me darlin'?" James asked.

Every time he spoke with his rhythmic Irish brogue, she felt it deep in her groin. This physical melting in his presence robbed her of control and left her longing for more. He got up from his stool, making certain to cover the painting from her curious eyes and came to sit on the bed beside her.

"Let me warm you," he murmured in her ear.

His warm hand cupped her breast, pinching the hard nipple as he nuzzled her neck. She wanted to protest. She felt she should refuse him. But the all-consuming desire, the insatiable need that burned through her had already taken hold. She arched back as he grasped both her breasts, pushing his fully clothed body hard against her. She exhaled in a loud and pleasurable sigh as the heat rose between them.

And when they were finished and the breath was still coming fast in her throat, he rushed to his easel saying, "Turn and look at me. Just as you are. I want you - just like that..."

The way he'd taken her, the urgency in his thrust and the surrender in her whole body rid her of inhibition. She looked at him, utterly raw and exposed, her lips still swollen from his mouth and her body still aching with pleasure and satiation. And he painted, his face diffused with the pleasure he'd just experienced and the flow of his creativity.

Time passed in this heightened state until the chill in the room brought her back to her senses and the need to get warm and get dressed. She reached for her chemise.

"You are a naughty, evil man James Grey," she scolded him.

"So I've been told."

"Do you seduce all your subjects?"

"Not the men, to be sure," he chuckled.

"My mother?" It was a question she'd wanted to ask and not wanted to know the answer to.

"Your Mother was a tempting lady ... but I did not have the plea-sure ... that I've had with her daughter."

As she buttoned her blouse, she trailed her fingers over the places where he'd bit her in their passion.

"What was she like?" It was another question she hadn't found the courage to ask until now.

"I think she was hot-blooded and passionate in a world that con-demns such things – particularly in women," he said. "You are like her in that way. But unlike her too ..."

No, I just come from a time when it's acceptable, Justine thought.

"There was a sadness about her," James continued. He paused from cleaning his brushes, trying to remember. "I know she loved your father. It was he who commissioned the painting and came for that first session. That look in her eyes, that glistening I tried to capture in the portrait … that's how she looked at him." He chuckled. "No one needed to make love to her to reveal what she thought and felt."

"Can I see my portrait?" Justine asked, changing the subject, which had become a bit too revealing.

"No."

His back was to her now as he concentrated on cleaning his brushes. He was an intensely focused man when it came to the things he loved, painting and lovemaking.

"What were you doing out there – that first time – that first time I saw you?" he queried, casually over his shoulder. It was obviously something he'd wanted to ask for some time as well.

She knew he was asking *why* she'd appeared outside in the cold half naked, not *where* she'd appeared from. Nonetheless the question took Justine off guard and she didn't know what to say. Her silence caused him to turn and look at her.

"If I told you, you wouldn't believe me," she said. It was the truth.

"You're the most unusual woman I've ever met. I probably would believe anything you said."

"What's so unusual about me?" she asked, changing the subject.

"I've never met a nice young lady so willing a partner in bed," he replied, looking at her the way he did when he was painting as if he could see into her soul. "I'd have to say you've been with a man before but you don't seem concerned about your reputation or the consequences." This was true of course and nothing to be ashamed of in the 21st Century. However, she looked away confused. "It's refreshing and very alluring," he went on. "It's why I wanted to paint you. And to bed you."

The conversation was veering into dangerous territory, either leading back into bed or into truth telling. Justine wanted to avoid both. So she changed the subject again.

"Please can I have just a quick look at the portrait? I promise not to say anything."

"It's bad luck."

"How so?"

"If you look on an unfinished image, it imprints on your mind and you never come whole to another session."

"That's Irish blarney," she told him.

"And what would you know about the blarney?" he asked, half serious.

"That it's just something someone made up."

"Life's just something we make up as we go along," he said, turning away from her so that she wasn't sure how he really felt about what he'd said.

Fifty-Three

After finally extricating herself from James' studio, Justine found herself standing in the window overlooking the alley. It was the first time since arriving she'd looked out at this view of the innocuous set of stable doors, shut tight to protect the horses from the cold. But she knew it was an entirely different doorway as well. Unseen. Unthinkable. A doorway that traversed time.

On the other side was Ducky. Thinking about him made her heart ache. Being here made her heart expand and flutter. She knew this relationship, or whatever it was, with James Grey was not a good idea.

We'll have no more of that, Missy, she told herself, hearing Ducky's turn of phrase.

She longed to speak with him, to ask him what he thought - about everything that had happened – about the strange 'awareness's' she'd been having. Why had Raphael looked like her Mother? And what about the eerie *knowing* she felt inside herself of Mrs. McGowan – as if she *was* Mrs McGowan. And of Ducky, himself, who Alexander continued to feel like. Ducky's last name meant *son of the King* and Alexander seemed to be that noble manifestation.

Over the years she'd been trying so hard to come out from under Ducky's sometimes overbearing protectiveness that she feared she'd pushed him away. Now she wished more than anything just to be close, to hear his thoughts, to listen to his gentle voice.

Even with all the people she'd gathered into her life in a very short space of time, she knew she really was very much alone. *Life is just something we make up as we go along*, James said reminding her that she was here on borrowed time. Being here was no longer a dream from which she might awaken. The people who lived under this roof were as real as the people who lived here in her time. Everyday there was something new to experience, some sight she'd never seen that filled her with wonder or broke her heart, making her understand that life was precarious in every age. But she also knew that she couldn't, *wouldn't* stay here forever.

These thoughts filled her with a sense of urgency and as she stood at the window a plan began to form. The more she thought about what James had said, the more she knew this was what she had to do. Meeting her brother and sister had been exhilarating, frustrating and even dangerous but the possibility that her mother was here some-where in this time was also very real and so compelling that she made a decision on the spot.

Fifty-Four

Justine was not surprised when Maggie insisted on accompanying her on this journey. Navigating the unfamiliar territory of 1906 was sometimes exhausting and often exacerbating so she felt relaxed as she waited while Maggie negotiated their train tickets.

She overheard the ticket salesman proudly explain that, "The scheduled time for the New York-to-New Orleans run is, as advertised, a 40-hour, unprecedented trip. The *New York & New Orleans Limited* is equipped with club cars and an observation car," he added confidently, certain this would seal the deal.

But Maggie was a canny Irish girl and not impressed with the high cost of such a luxurious journey. So the ticket salesman offered an alternate route:

"Well, there's the Baltimore and Ohio Railroad to Washington D.C. From there you could catch the…"

But something assaulted Justine's memory and before she could control herself she shouted loudly, "NO! Not that train!"

People standing nearby turned to stare at her. A stocky man in a brown coat buying tickets at a nearby window reacted, motioning for his ticket salesman to wait a moment. His head was turned away from Maggie and Justine, his bowler pulled down over his brow, but his whole body strained to hear what she would say next.

Staring fiercely into Maggie's surprised face, Justine exclaimed ominously, "We cannot take that train!" Then addressing the ticket salesman, she instructed more calmly, "We'll take two tickets on that lovely train to New Orleans, thank you!"

The trip was a gruelling 40 hours, with plenty of stops. The rumble of the train was very conducive to sleep and Justine slept like she had never slept before, tucked in their private, 2-person sleeper. Her exhaustion seemed to come from deep inside and having nowhere else to be, she gave in to it. Sleeping and dreaming. She dreamt of Caroline as a small baby with dimpled, chubby cheeks and fair, curly hair — but she viewed her with a kind of repulsion, refusing to acknowledge the baby's cries for attention. Justine awoke, confused and heartsick. Other dreams were about Ducky, speaking Russian or Maggie sitting on her front stoop drinking coffee and holding forth in a loud, confident New Yorkese. These dreams were amusing but somehow filled with portent.

On the occasions when she and Maggie made use of the dining car, Justine had the distinct impression they were being watched. But looking around the car she saw only other innocent travellers like herself and Maggie.

The car was elaborately decorated with gilded ceilings. Passengers sat in leather arm chairs at tables covered in white linen and were served by discreet, black waiters. The last attribute made Justine uncomfortable and she found herself overcompensating by thanking the waiter repeatedly.

The second night, a man at a nearby table looked up from his newspaper and both Justine and Maggie overheard him comment to his wife that there had been a terrible train wreck on the Baltimore and Ohio Railroad the day before on it's run to Washington.

Maggie stared wide-eyed at Justine. "How did you know?"

Justine shrugged, "I read it somewhere, I think."

Maggie closed her eyes, making the sign of the cross.

The gruff chugging of the engine and wailing of the whistle, mirrored Justine's own sluggishness as three and a half days later the train pulled slowly into the red brick Louisville and Nashville Passenger Station in New Orleans. Maggie had already packed and collected their belongings and was waiting impatiently for assistance in disembarking as the train came to a final exhausted stop.

Fifty-Five

The Station had been built 4 years earlier and was located at the foot of Canal Street just behind the Iberville Wharf. The muddy Mississippi waters were visible even in the early evening light, busy with boats and paddle wheelers docking for the night.

It will be flowing past this very same point, when I come here as a 6-year-old with my mother, Justine thought. *Some things never change…* And that thought gave her comfort and energy. She tucked her arm companionably through Maggie's as they approached a stand of horse and carriages.

In 1906 New Orleans was experiencing a relatively milder winter than New York and the gaslights along Canal Street seemed to twinkle in welcome as they made their way to the French Quarter. Streetcars rumbled past and Justine could feel a more sedate pulse in this southern metropolis.

Turning into Royal Street was like leaving one country and entering it's more robust, eccentric neighbor. It was dark by this time but lights and music poured out of numerous doorways. This was the *Vieux Carré*, a 78 square block within the city of New Orleans that has always been a world unto itself.

Crossing Conti Street, Justine knew where they were before they arrived at their destination. What would be a front door in the future, was now an entry for horses into the inner courtyard. But everything else about the building was much the same. Bordering the entry were two bay windows, displaying antiques for sale. That too had not changed. The three-story building was fronted with the same delicate 18th century ironwork balconies overhanging the sidewalk.

As she dismounted the carriage, déjà vu didn't begin to describe what Justine felt. Looking up were the same set of five tall French doors on each floor. She stared at the one on the far right. Inside that room was where her entire life had changed. This was where the dark hole inside her heart was born. But that momentous event hadn't happened yet. Except that it had. In the future. To her.

But she was here now and whatever lay ahead, coming here was something she knew she had to do. Steeling herself, Justine and Maggie made their way into the inner courtyard. Bricks covered the expanse in a herringbone pattern with a row of circular planting areas containing palm trees and probably vegetables in the warmer weather. An older woman appeared in the doorway, summoning them inside.

Negotiating for the same second floor room was not problematic once Justine produced the required financial incentive. They followed the old woman up a dark set of internal stairs and once she opened the door to the room, Justine's heart stopped and she experienced difficulty swallowing.

Everything was in exactly the same place: the two beds against one wall, a nightstand between them, the tall French doors opening onto the balcony overlooking the street with an over stuffed chair and table beside it.

"The facility is down the hall," the old woman was saying. That too had not changed. Her mother had instructed her to use the sink in the corner of the room if she had to pee, cautioning her not to leave the room. She'd used it only once in the endless hours she'd waited until Ducky arrived. Now, there was only a stand with a pitcher of water and basin to wash in as well as the ubiquitous chamber pot.

Justine unconsciously reached for the heart shaped locket hanging around her neck, fingering it in memory.

"We'd like to bathe," Justine heard Maggie explaining to the old woman.

She wandered to the windows, feeling dislocated. Everything seemed smaller than she remembered with that odd inversion of the physical world that happens when you return to a place you knew as a child.

She stepped out onto the balcony. In the future, many of the streets of the French Quarter were cut off from traffic and the sounds filtering up from the street were revellers raucously calling out to one another at night and visitors speaking in loud American voices during the day. Now there was the clatter of horses' hooves followed by the whoosh and rub of metal as the street car rumbled past. That too seemed a strange inversion of things.

"Would you like to have a bath?" Maggie asked gently.

"Yes, please. Most definitely!"

They followed the old woman back down and through the courtyard. It was dark but the sky was full of stars and the evening was rich with the sound of music and laughter floating on the night air. The old woman passed through a door that was actually more of a gate into a smaller courtyard, roofed by a massive oak tree. They made their way across the hard packed dirt, when the old woman seemed suddenly to vanish. In fact, she'd made a sharp right turn behind a low wall and disappeared up a covered set of stairs.

Feeling their way in the shadows, Justine finally shouted out, "Please wait. We can't see where you're going!"

The woman paused long enough for Maggie and Justine to stumble up the stairs, then she turned without comment leading them along an exterior terrace. They almost collided with a young, black woman, who suddenly opened one of the doors off the terrace. She was carrying a heavy load of what looked like multicoloured fabric, gauze and sparkly bangles. In the darkness her face seemed misshapen somehow. Apologizing profusely, with a distinct note of fear in her voice, the black woman stood in the doorway waiting for them to pass. Justine glanced into an unlit corridor running through the gloomy interior of the building.

The old woman, who was moving through the darkness with surprising speed, turned right, heading down another set of stairs. Maggie was just able to see her disappear into an archway at the bottom.

Grabbing Justine's hand to guide her, this time Maggie shouted out, "If you don't slow down, dearie, we're going to have an accident!"

They made it to the bottom of the stairs and found the woman waiting as if nothing untoward had occurred. She stood inside a doorway out of which steam was pouring as it hit the cooler night air. Shouts of protest emanated from inside and the old woman gestured for them to hurry inside.

They stepped into what Justine could only describe as a Turkish bath, having been to something similar in the East Village. The sight of naked women soaking in tubs, being scrubbed by black attendants or lounging on chaises unconcerned by their nudity caused Maggie to inhale with horror. The old woman shut the door and the steam embraced them.

It took some coaxing, but Justine was finally able to convince Maggie that as cleanliness was next to Godliness, this bathhouse must be a virtuous place. Justine said this with fingers crossed because the dissipated attitude of the other women, suggested they might in fact be women of the night. So, while Maggie would not let anyone administer to her, she did sink into the hot tub of water and seemed genuinely to enjoy it. And Justine was equally grateful for the heat and to cleanse the days of travel from her skin and mind.

Fifty-Six

In the morning, Justine's hasty plan was to head east out of the hotel and question every shop, restaurant or hotel owner. The first shop proved how ill conceived her plan was.

The Martin Lawrence Gallery was still owned by the same family over 100 years hence. Ducky often did business with Sean Lawrence as his antiques came with excellent provenance and were sold at a fair price. But this fact was neither relevant nor helpful today as Justine and Maggie entered the shop.

"A delightful good mornin' to you, ladies," the well dressed, grey haired shopkeeper drawled, oozing Southern charm. "I am Martin Lawrence, proprietor. How can I be of service?"

Meeting the original owner might have been thrilling under other circumstances but they were here on an uncertain and delicate mission. The recognizable aroma of old leather and dust filled the shop and was reassuring, giving Justine the courage to proceed.

"What lovely things you have for sale," Justine said.

"Each and every item imported from the Continent and complete with provenance," he replied with easy pride.

Justine cast her trained eye around the shop, moving to a nearby glass display case. Inside was jewellery of all kinds, but what caught her attention was a particular pocket watch. He wouldn't admit it, but Ducky collected timepieces of all kinds. He insisted they were acquisitions for sale in his shop. But as he never encouraged anyone to buy them they became a kind of collection.

"That's very beautiful," Justine said, pointing to a small cut enamelled watch.

"Early 17th century German," Mr. Lawrence, explained, removing the item from the case and placing it temptingly on a black square of velvet for Justine's closer inspection. "Very, very rare, indeed," he continued, genuinely appreciating the item as much as he was trying to sell it. "The cameo is the Holy Roman Emperor, but inside is the real gem," he explained opening the delicate shutters to reveal colourful cut enamel pictures with figures and birds and flowers. "This is the allegory for Wisdom," he said, "... and this, Justice."

"Something we all need," Justine conferred. "It's exquisite," she whispered, touching the delicate piece.

"The engraved décor on the watch is by the Parisian master Barbaret."

"I'll take it," Justine, replied. "I trust you will give me a good and fair price."

Lawrence nodded in recognition of her trust towards him and set about wrapping the watch.

"I've not seen you in my shop before," he commented. "And yet I know you to be a skilled buyer..."

His voice was soothing and she was about to confer that her step-father, Ducky, shopped here all the time, until she remembered where she was, and when.

"Actually," she said, "I wonder if you can help us ... we're looking for someone ..."

"Yes?" he asked, focusing on what he was doing.

"It's my mother. I believe she may be living here ... in New Orleans."

"New Orleans has a population of over 200,000 souls," he instructed. "What makes you think I would know your Mama?"

"This was the last place she was seen," Justine replied somewhat obliquely.

The man raised an eyebrow, pursing his lips.

"That is, not here - in your shop," Justine blundered on, "But nearby ..." She stepped closer to him in case his eyes were not so good. "I'm told she looks very much like me," she pleaded.

Her earnest tone caused Mr. Lawrence to pause. He blinked once, then squinted at her, finally shaking his head, "I'm sorry," he demurred, "I'm afraid I've never seen a woman who looks like you."

"Never?" Justine persisted. "Please think hard, Mr. Lawrence. It's very important. Did a woman, who looks like me, ever live or work or shop around here?"

"I'm really very sorry," he replied becoming somewhat agitated.

A middle-aged couple entered the store. Mr. Lawrence glanced toward them, smiling acknowledgment.

He told her the price of the watch and waited expectantly while she withdrew the money. When he handed her the small package, Justine looked beseechingly into his face.

"It could have been some time ago. Please," she persevered.

"I'm very sorry, Miss. I'm afraid I can't help you," he said, lowering his voice, which had grown impatient.

Justine realized he had in fact never seen her mother. Waves of disappointment, loss and sorrow flooded through her. She hung her head, accepting defeat and Mr. Lawrence moved expertly toward his new shoppers.

Much of St. Louis Street was taken up with warehouses and stables, with a few tailors and a small café. As they entered and exited one place after another, this unsuccessful scenario was repeated many times that morning and into the afternoon.

Turning into Bourbon Street was like entering a different world. While the streetcars on Royal Street took passengers into the city for work, those on Bourbon travelled in the opposite direction. Advertising themselves with posters, colourful signs and even touts, the street was lined with any number of taverns, nightclubs and houses of ill repute. Returning home after a long day, one could easily hop off the streetcar and avail oneself of one form of entertainment or the other.

Near the corner of Bourbon and Conti Streets, Justine entered what was clearly a brothel with women in various stages of undress lounging in rooms like shop displays. Maggie was so shocked, she didn't wait for Justine to ask the now familiar questions. With a loud prayer to Mother Mary, she retreated to the relative purity of the street.

Justine heard a throaty laugh and turned to see a corpulent woman with enormous bosoms bulging out of the deeply cut dress she wore. Those large mounds of flesh baubled with her laughter. Overtly aware of the impression she made, the woman waddled past Justine, laughing and wobbling.

"Don't think we got what y'all's lookin' fer," she chortled.

"I'm looking – I'm looking for a – a certain person," Justine stammered.

The woman stopped, turning to examine Justine more closely.

"Boy or Girl?" she asked.

The woman's dark eyes were mere slits peering out above the fat of her cheeks. Justine wasn't sure she could actually see very well, so she stepped closer to show her face.

"I'm looking for my mother," she said. "I'm told she looks a lot like me."

The woman scrutinized Justine as if she were sizing up a heifer for sale. Then she smiled, revealing a missing front tooth.

"Try the Chateau d'Arlington, dearie. Over in Storyville. Josie's stable is only foreign exotica. She'd likely hire yer mama."

When Justine finally appeared, Maggie demanded breathlessly, "You don't actually think your dear mother worked in a place like that, do ye now?

"No," Justine replied defiantly. "But I have to ask. I have to ask as many people as I can. I don't know what else to do." But the fat Woman's words burned in her ears.

Fifty-Seven

It was late afternoon by the time they turned back into Royal Street. Passing a solid, two story building with three elegant, arched windows, Justine was about to remark that this was clearly a private residence and they shouldn't bother, when she suddenly felt sharp, high pitched reverberations piercing her ears and her body being compelled towards the small non-descript building next door.

But it wasn't the low, narrow, building with an equally narrow doorway that was pulling her. It was the three foot wide, shadowy alleyway separating this non-descript building from it's impressive neighbour out of which the sounds were emanating and into which she was being drawn.

Of course no one else in the busy street heard these unearthly sounds but Justine knew what they meant. The energetic pull was getting stronger and the sounds were getting louder. With her last bit of conscious choice, Justine hurled her body in the opposite direction – into the street – just as a streetcar hurtled past, leaving her unable to halt her collision course with its deadly metal surface. The screech of the streetcar's warning whistle coincided with two arms forcibly grabbing her, just in the knick of time, out of harm's way.

Surprised not to be fatally crushed upon the tracks, Justine turned to see who had saved her and was shocked to stare into the pockmarked face of Kendall Shaw. In the seconds it took her mind to register his presence, she was looking deep into his dark, sly eyes. At that moment an electric shock registered deep inside her womb, and she cried out.

Next she heard Maggie shouting and together they managed to dislodge Shaw's grasping hands. Maggie pulled Justine across the street, directly in front of an on-coming truck and caravan.

They narrowly missed being hit as Maggie dragged Justine inside a doorway and pushed her up some stairs. It wasn't until Justine was seated at a table by the window, that she became aware they were upstairs in a pub of some kind. She was staring out the window as the truck and caravan pulled out of view and saw Kendall Shaw glancing around, clearly wondering where they had disappeared to.

"This is for women only," Maggie reassured her. "He can't come up here even if he figures it out!"

But Justine's eyes had moved from the hated figure of Kendall Shaw to the ominous divide of an alleyway, across the street. She vaguely heard Maggie ordering tea and whiskey because she could not tear her eyes away.

Wedged between the squat building on the right and the grand three-story on the left, the alleyway, though unusually narrow, looked innocuous enough. But she knew, staring into the sliver of darkness – this had to be her mother's doorway, her mother's portal to the future. This very passageway is where, in the future, Ducky had found a woman, strangely dressed and very, very frightened huddled against that wall, that equally innocuous wall. And that woman, her mother, was pregnant with Justine at the time.

Her gut lurched and she thought she would throw up. But Maggie was placing a shot glass firmly in her hand and without thinking Justine downed the contents.

"Another, I think," Maggie instructed the barmaid. Then, reaching for Justine's hand, she asked, "How're ye doing, Miss Justine?"

The whisky was still burning down Justine's throat but had brought an instant calm to her insides. She turned wide-eyes on Maggie, "You saved my life!"

Maggie waved the notion aside, focusing on pouring hot tea and milk with plenty of sugar. Gently prying the shot glass from Justine's tight fist, she placed the cup firmly in her hand.

"Drink this down it'll bring ye back to yerself."

Justine obeyed, allowing the sweet, soothing liquid to further compose her spirits.

"I saw that man at Union Station," Maggie confided "and then again on the train. I had the feeling he was following us, but I didn't want to alarm you."

The shots of whisky arrived and they gulped them down at once.

"He is. Following us," Justine confirmed.

"Why? What does he want? Are we in danger, do you think?"

"He's someone Hunter knows. I wouldn't call him a friend, because a person like that doesn't have friends. He wants me to tell his fortune. He wants me to predict his future. I don't think he wants to hurt us," Justine said, trying to sound certain for Maggie's sake.

"And …. Can ye do that, then? Can you see into the future?"

"No. Of course not. Any more than you can. I just – well – there are things I know because they happened in the past – *my* past. General things. World events."

"But you – you did foretell something … about him…?"

"Yes, well, that's because I read it in an old newspaper; a newspaper that hasn't been printed yet. "

Maggie shuddered.

"I'm sorry, Maggie. I'm so sorry to have dragged you into this."

"Well, I'm not sorry at all," Maggie insisted. "I've always been a bit of rabbit, darting for cover at the least danger. With you I'm becoming more like a fox – fearless and wily."

"To Maggie the fox," Justine repeated, raising her teacup to toast her friend.

Maggie blushed, her freckles turning red as her hair and merrily clinked Justine's teacup with her own.

Fifty-Eight

The next day, at Justine's suggestion, they spilt up. Maggie headed to the City Hall on Lafayette Square to see if she could find any record of Justine's mother. Justine headed into Storyville. While she preferred safety in numbers, Justine didn't want to subject Maggie to what she suspected she might find in this notorious neighborhood.

It didn't take long for her suspicions to bear fruit. When she gave the desired address to the cabbie, he turned full around in his seat to stare at her.

"Is there something wrong?" Justine inquired

"I 'ain't never taken a nice lady like you to Basin Street. 'Specially not at this time of day!'

Unsettled by his obvious apprehension, Justine summoned a retort, "Well, there's always a first time for everything."

The driver shrugged guiding the horse up Conti Street.

She didn't want to believe that her mother may have lived and worked in this sad, sorry, corrupt and utterly debased corner of the world. So rather than heading directly to Josie Arlington's establishment, she'd made her way in and out of other places. The treatment she received ranged from open offers of sex and debauchery to outright aggression.

By the time Justine found her way to The Arlington, it was late afternoon and her feet hurt. By now she understood that she could just walk directly into any place in Storyville. Appearing to be grand mansions from the outside these we not residences, they were places of business.

She'd seen things she wished she'd never seen before and witnessed the depths to which humanity could sink in the pursuit of pleasure and decadence. The Arlington boasted plush rooms filled with plump velvet furniture draped with plump prostitutes of varying ages and ethnicities.

A fire had ripped through Josie's establishment the previous year and Josie herself suffered a mental collapse. An imposing black man at the front door informed Justine of these facts. He was clothed in an interpretation of butler garb, complete with tails and a bright orange waistcoat, and spoke in hushed tones as if he were referring to the queen. He directed her to the office/boudoir of Madame La Croix, a buxom florid woman with a deep, masculine voice.

Justine didn't need to stand close to show her face, Madame La Croix sized her up from top to bottom the moment she entered the stuffy, over stuffed room.

"We've got anything and everything and we've got the best of it…" Madame La Croix began her spiel. Having been offered everything and anything under the sun, Justine interrupted her:

"I'm not buying. I'm looking for someone. It was suggested she might have worked here."

Madame La Croix snorted, "Humph. Didn't think your finery was real. I can always tell.

"My finery, as you call it, and my money are both very real." Justine retorted, pulling bills from her sleeve where she'd stashed them for safekeeping.

Madame La Croix coughed, deep in her throat, hawking up a wad of mucous, which she expertly spit into a brass spittoon. Justine hated this place and everyone in it. It was like a human sewer into which the unfortunate and the detritus of humanity spilled.

There was a knock on the door and a thin black girl with strange golden eyes, peered around the door. Madame La Croix nodded at her.

"If you'll excuse me. I'll be back directly…." she said and hoisting her ample size out of the chair, left the room.

Moments later, just as Justine was about to depart in frustration and disgust, Madame La Croix returned excited and beaming,

"I think we can help you," she said, gesturing for Justine to follow "if you'll just come with me…"

Justine followed, not remembering that she'd never actually said who she was looking for. Madame La Croix' excitement was intriguing and this sudden change of events startling, after so much disappointment.

They were half-way up the grand staircase when Justine asked, "Where are we going?"

Madame La Croix was quite out of breath climbing the stairs so she simply gestured impatiently for Justine to follow. They were nearing the landing and Justine slowed, warily. But she didn't have time to speak or to protest, when two large men grabbed her by the arms, dragging her down a passageway.

"The Silent Room," she heard Madame La Croix instruct the men and Justine was tossed unceremoniously into a room at the end of the hall. The door slammed and she heard the key turn the lock.

She tried the handle. Unable to open the door she shouted," Let me out! You have no right to lock me in here!"

"It's called the Silent Room," a small voice spoke.

Justine spun around to find the thin, black girl clinging to one of the bed's four posters, golden eyes wide with terror. Justine scanned the walls, which were padded and then covered in pin-tucked purple velvet wallpaper. The door was fitted with flaps covering the seams. When she strode to the windows, not only were they securely locked, they were also fitted with thickly padded drapes.

She looked back at the child, still frozen in fear. Panic was beginning to travel up Justine's spine.

"What's your name?" she asked the child as calmly as she could.

"Nadine," the girl managed to answer.

"Why are we locked in here, Nadine?"

Nadine's eyes shot around the room, landing on metal handcuffs attached to the bedposts and an assortment of whips hanging from the walls and an ominous, ornate armoire against the opposite wall. Justine was beginning to get the picture. The Silent Room was designed to muffle whatever sadistic acts were undertaken here.

The girl spoke again in a horrified whisper, "That man paid big for you – and me."

Suddenly Justine remembered Delphine, the feminine male prostitute, running down the hall covered in blood and she was absolutely certain who the terrified girl meant when she whispered, 'that man'.

"Hide," she instructed Nadine. "Quickly!" Dragging the bed skirt aside she practically pushed the frightened child underneath. "Don't make a sound," she cautioned. Whatever he was intending, it wasn't going to involve this child.

Justine's mind was racing but the act of protecting the child had cleared it of fear. A plan was emerging when she heard the lock turn and the door open. Kendall Shaw entered, locking the door behind him.

He hadn't turned back into the room when Justine was on him. Knowing she wasn't strong enough to fight him, she took another tack. Wrapping her arms around him from behind she took his ear lobe in her mouth. The act almost made her gag, but forcing down the bile she stuck her tongue into his ear then whispered,

"I've been waiting for you. I can't wait anymore…"

She bit his ear lobe enough to cause pain then quickly pulled away. He spun around to see her removing her short jacket and unbuttoning her blouse. She forced herself to look at him with passion and desire. She'd seen enough movies to have an idea how this was done. She'd slept with enough men to know what it was supposed to feel like.

"I want you. I want you to fuck me - so much," she growled.

The surprised look on his face turned to something resembling a teenage boy eagerly spying on a naked woman for the first time. He licked his lips, grinning. She ploughed her advantage, moving swiftly and seductively towards him, her blouse now open and her breasts spilling from her chemise. She grabbed his arm, dragging him to the bed.

"You're so strong and manly," she convinced him. "I want you to take me. Take me now."

When she pushed him onto his back on the bed, however, something changed in his face. He didn't like the direction this was heading. But before he could protest, she'd climbed on top of him pressing down with the full weight of her body, rubbing her breasts in his face. This caused him to relax for a moment. She could feel his excitement hardening between her legs and she almost vomited.

Turning her head aside to gulp some air, she saw Nadine's big eyes peeping over the bed and her delicate hands grasping the shiny metal handcuffs.

Justine grabbed Shaw's face so that he would not see the child and pressed her lips to his. She felt his hands grabbing chunks of her hair, pulling her head painfully back. She was about to lose her advantage.

"*NO!*" she commanded with all the volatility her disgust could produce. "If you want me, you let ME!!" She slapped his face.

He was again momentarily thrown by her ferocity. She pushed back so that she was sitting up, tore his hands from her hair forcing his right hand into the cuff held open in Nadine's trembling grasp. The impact of the movement caused the metal to clamp shut.

His eyes went wide and his face turned dark. He was about to protest when Justine began laughing, deeply and loudly. The sound was coming right out of her fear. But it silenced him.

"I'm going to do things to you, you never dreamed of," she snarled at him.

There was one more hand to secure and Justine couldn't allow Shaw time to think or struggle. She pulled her chemise off, exposing her breasts. It wasn't the first time a man had seen her breasts and it certainly wouldn't be the last. And if those big mounds of flesh could distract him long enough she was grateful for once for their abundant proportions.

It had the desired effect. Shaw grabbed a breast with his free left hand and at the same moment Justine pushed down with all her might, snatching his offending hand off her flesh and forcing it towards the second handcuff. He struggled, playing along at first, but when he saw her angry determination he started fighting back in earnest. He was strong but the handcuffs were securely fastened to the bed posts.

"You filthy sonofabitch," Justine screamed.

Nadine jumped up, biting the thumb of his right hand so hard Shaw cried out. This allowed Justine to force his left hand into the other cuff, which Nadine expertly locked.

Justine felt like high-fiving this quick thinking, courageous little girl but Shaw was roaring foul language and thrusting his trapped body upwards in an effort to eject Justine. She just managed to stay on top of him, spinning her body around as she shouted:

"Nadine, get me those curtain sashes, quickly!"

The little girl scampered to the window, ripping the heavy golden cords from the wall and delivering them to Justine. With her last bit of strength, Justine managed to secure one of Shaw's legs to the bedpost. This effectively disabled him so she climbed off and he began screaming for help.

"This is the Silent Room," Justine reminded him as she forcibly tied his last leg to the bedpost. "No one can hear you scream," she added.

The line from the movie *Alien*, felt very satisfying to threaten this despicable excuse for a human being with. Then she stuffed his mouth with her chemise.

Justine strode to the corner of the room and vomited. It was such a relief she didn't miss a beat and began pulling on her blouse and jacket asking Nadine:

"Is there a way out of this place besides the front door?"

The girl pointed a shaky finger towards the next room, but shook her head as if it was fruitless to try.

Justine knelt down, looking Nadine in the eye. Placing firm hands on her shoulders she said, "You are the bravest little girl I've ever met. We're going to get out of here."

Shaw stopped struggling and was staring at Justine with raw hatred as she approached the bed.

She leaned down, hissing into his ear, "This is what it feels like to be utterly helpless. Not very nice is it?"

As she reached into his pants to withdraw the keys, she noticed a pocket watch in his vest. Snatching it, she recognized Hunter's Grandfather's Le Roy & Fils gold anchor chronometer. Stuffing it into her corset, she said:

"You wanted to know your future, Mr. Shaw? Here it is: Later this year you will commit a final heinous act. Then you will fall from a high place to your death. And may you rot in hell. Which, in my opinion, is where you belong!"

She opened the door and Shaw began to struggle again, making noise. Justine drew Nadine into the hallway, quickly securing the door behind them. It really was a silent room. Shaw's cries for help were completely muffled.

Fifty-Nine

There were voices approaching from the stairs. Before Justine had time to panic, Nadine's small hand was pulling her through a heavy velvet curtain and into a passageway separating the Silent Room from the room next door. They stood in the darkness, holding their breath.

The voices sounded like a woman, with a high-pitched laugh, and a man. They did not come as far as the secret passageway or the Silent Room. Instead they entered another room and shut the door.

Justine thought about heading out the way she'd come in but she knew the butler wouldn't be as accommodating this time. Madame La Croix had clearly sold Justine and little Nadine to Shaw to do with as he wished. In a place like this, his business was more important that their lives.

Justine peeked out of the curtain. The hall was empty. Signalling to Nadine they scurried into the next room, which was thankfully empty. But for how long, Justine had no idea. She rushed to the one window, grateful that it gave easily, sliding open on its sash. The cold evening air felt good but looking out her heart sank. They were three stories up and there wasn't an easy way down.

She turned to question Nadine but the child was shivering in the cold, her eyes wide with fear. Justine looked out again this time noticing a thin ledge running along the façade of the building. Following the ledge Justine leaned further out the window. She thought maybe there was another, lower building butting up against the Arlington at right angles, but she couldn't be sure.

If I can make it to that roof... she told herself.

This window had no ropes and while she would have liked something to secure herself with, the thought of returning to the Silent Room was out of the question. There wasn't time to think as voices could be heard somewhere in the house, maybe coming to this very room.

Her long skirt was definitely too cumbersome so as she was removing it, she whispered to Nadine, "Can you climb on my back and hold on really, really tight?"

Nadine looked at her, not understanding.

"I'm getting out of here and I'm taking you with me."

Justine knelt down, offering Nadine her back. The little girl climbed on and Justine was grateful she weighed so little. Wrapping her long skirt around the child and securing it by the front buttons around her neck, Justine moved back to the window.

"Hold on tight," she whispered to Nadine. "Don't let go. And whatever happens, don't look down."

That last caution came from her memory of the rock climbing class she'd done. Yet another false start. Justine didn't like heights. However, she liked this house of horrors even less. Gingerly, she placed one set of toes and then the other onto the narrow ledge. Nadine's thin body shivered but she held tight and her immediacy gave Justine courage.

With only her fingertips clinging to whatever purchase she could find, Justine inched her way along the side of the building. She was reaching with her left hand for the sill of the Silent Room's window when another window to her right was flung open and the same high-pitched laughter, shrieked across the cold, evening air.

Justine stoped abruptly, one had grasping the windowsill and the fingernails of her other hand digging desperately into the wooden siding, her toes clinging painfully to the ledge. Her sudden halt caused Nadine to lose her grip. The little girl was only able to catch herself by grabbing Justine's neck. They hung, frozen, waiting. Nadine's hands made it impossible for Justine to turn her head to see if they had been spotted and her fingers were making it increasingly difficult to breath.

After a moment there was the sound of a chamber pot being emptied into the street and more raucous laughter, followed by the window slamming shut. Justine prayed they'd not been spotted as she moved cautiously to grasp the windowsill with both hands. She was going to pass out if she didn't get Nadine to let go of her neck so she reached around, supporting the little girl's bottom.

"Can you lower your hands, sweetie?" Justine croaked.

As Justine mercifully made it to the next windowsill, her toes felt like they might break so she forced herself to think about Shaw and wonder if he was still tied up inside the room. She had no idea how much time had passed or how much time he'd paid for use of the Silent Room. She didn't know if at this very moment their escape had been reported.

The window was near to the corner of the building, so she forced herself to look down, praying there was in fact a low building onto which they could climb. There was, but it was further down than she'd expected. Her strength and will were about to give out when she noticed an iron drainpipe running from the roof down the corner of the building. From the sale of human flesh, Josie Arlington had the money to have things like drain pipes installed on her mansion.

Justine reached for the pipe, using it to pull her to the end of the narrow ledge. Now her brief rock climbing experience came in handy as she pushed away from the building, squatting and planting her feet firmly on either side of the pipe and with a combination of sliding and pressure walking, she made it to the roof of the low building.

From there she was able to jump down into the dark alley and catch Nadine in her arms. Justine was so relieved to be free and on solid ground, she hugged Nadine tightly to her chest and let tears fall down her face. Then she took a deep breath, grabbed Nadine's hand and they ran and ran and even though Justine was wearing only her underclothes, she didn't stop running until she felt they were far enough away from the reach of the Arlington and it's denizens. She hailed a cab and ordered it back to Royal Street. Fortunately, she still had money stashed in her corset. Money, in Storyville, was enough to explain all types of behavior including a woman out of doors in her underwear.

Sixty

It was time to leave, of that she was very certain. That Justine was in New Orleans in 1906 was troublesome enough, but the notion that her mother was also here and that Justine could somehow find her had been a hare-brained scheme from the outset.

Back in their hotel room, she was packing her small suitcase, having difficulty fitting things as well as Maggie did. *Where was Maggie, anyway?*

She was relieved to have rescued Nadine from the Arlington, but she wasn't sure what to do about her now. Nadine sat quietly in the chair hungrily eating the rice and beans Justine ordered for her. It was a chair in exactly the same spot Justine had sat when she was Nadine's age – after her mother had left and Ducky was on his way to rescue her.

Ducky'd know what to do… Justine thought as she tucked the pocket watch she'd bought for him next to the one she'd taken from Shaw safely inside her leather satchel.

Her reverie was broken by shouting in the courtyard of the hotel, followed by Maggie bursting into the room.

"He's here and he's angry as sin!" she blurted out.

"What? Who?"

But Justine knew who and she also knew, what. From the sound of the ruckus downstairs, he'd be up here any minute and there'd be hell to pay. Nadine had already jumped out of her chair at the sound of Kendall Shaw's shouted threats.

"We have to get out of here. Now!" Justine declared.

Maggie hesitated, eying their belongings spread around the room.

Justine tossed the leather satchel over her shoulder and flung open the French doors to the terrace. "This is serious, Maggie. We have to go. Now!"

Nadine was already out the doors and onto the terrace. Justine impatiently held the doors waiting for Maggie. Another man's voice joined Shaw's and that was enough for Maggie to rush onto the terrace followed by Justine.

Justine closed the doors behind them, pointing towards St. Louis Street and the three raced to the end of the terrace. The terrace of the adjacent building was higher up and there was a gap between. After her perilous climb out of the Arlington, Justine was ready for anything.

Maggie watched aghast as Justine bent down and Nadine obediently clambered onto her back. Justine climbed onto the rail, stretching her arms across the gap, grasping the railing of the opposite terrace.

There wasn't time to remove her skirt, which interfered with seeing where to put her feet. She reached out cautiously testing for a foothold. Feeling her sole connect with something, she bent, pushing with her other foot and hoisting her body safely across. Justine turned to Maggie, whose face was white with fear.

"You can do this, Maggie," Justine encouraged her. "You have to do this!" she insisted, glancing back along the terrace to the doors of their hotel room.

At any moment a very, very angry Kendall Shaw was going to appear and Justine had run out of clever ways to deal with him.

Justine reached out her hand, Maggie grabbed it and was across the two-storey gap before she had time to think. And there wasn't time for anything other than running, which they did, following the terrace around the corner, temporarily out of sight of their pursuer.

But Justine knew Shaw would follow this same route so she pushed open a door, finding herself in the hallway of the building, which shared the courtyard with their hotel. She'd peered down this hallway on their way to the bath the night of their arrival. It was dark inside, but Justine had seen doors, so feeling her way as quickly as she could she wrenched open the first door, went inside, followed by Maggie.

There was a dim light coming from an adjacent room. They were in some kind of storeroom.

"Who's there?" a woman's voice asked as she cautiously appeared in the doorway, staring suspiciously at Justine and Maggie.

"I'm so sorry," Justine said. "We're in trouble …"

"I don't want no trouble here," the woman cautioned, venturing further into the room and switching on a lamp.

She was a black woman; the same black woman they'd almost collided with the other night on their way to the baths. Now in the light they could see the terrible damage, which had been done to one side of her face.

Nadine, who'd been clinging to Justine's back, hiding herself, suddenly let go, plonking to the floor.

Stepping out from behind Justine, she asked in a small voice, "Mama?"

Seeing the little girl, the woman's eyes went wide. Her hand rose to her mouth and with a shocked intake of breath, she asked "Baby? Is that you my Nadine?"

Nadine's mother swiftly hid them in a small closet obscured by shelves of fabric and accessories. They didn't have long to wait before they heard Shaw and his men bursting into the storeroom.

Repeating exactly what she'd done only seconds before, Nadine's mother entered the front room, asking, "Who's there?"

They could hear Shaw's demanding voice and Nadine's mother's reply. Shaw responded to her with a threat. They could see under the door that she'd switched on the light. Then there was silence.

After a moment, the door to their hiding place opened and Nadine's mother said, "Come here my baby, it's safe now."

She sat holding Nadine as if she would never let her go. Her name was Rachel, she explained. She used to work at a Bawdy House in Storyville. When she accidently got pregnant by a customer, the Madame took care of Rachel and Nadine was born.

Rachel laid her wounded face on the child's head. It was clear Nadine was the best thing that had ever happened to her. When Nadine turned seven, Rachel went on to explain, the Madame's boyfriend demanded Nadine go to work. When Rachel refused to allow her daughter to be prostituted, he'd punished her with acid to the face.

"What did the police do?" Justine wanted to know.

"No one cares about a useless niggar woman," Rachel said. "'Sides, the Chief 'o Police was there every night…"

Nadine was sold to another house while Rachel was recovering, and she'd been desperately looking for her daughter ever since.

The night had turned cold so they'd moved into Rachel's living quarters and were huddled around a small brazier.

"Why d'ya think those men hightailed it out of here?" Rachel continued. "Some people think my face is a curse. When I turned the light on … it scared the shit out of 'em!"

She said it matter-of-factly. She had clearly been a beautiful woman. The undamaged side of her face proved that. An uncomfortable silence followed.

"I was looking for *my* mother as it happens," Justine offered, gazing into the fire. "Instead, the Madame at the Arlington sold me to that man, along with Nadine."

Rachel hugged the little girl protectively, shaking her head in despair.

"I don't' think she's been … taken," Justine added. "I think she's seen and heard more than any person of any age should see or hear – but I don't think …" Justine paused. She wasn't really certain of anything. "Anyway, she's one of the bravest little girl's I've ever met. She made it possible for us to escape."

"Thank you. Thank you for bringing her back to me," Rachel cried, holding Nadine close, tears in both their eyes.

There was a sound coming from the hallway, a barely perceptible creaking of floorboards. Everyone froze. Rachel placed Nadine on her feet and went quickly to the door, peering out.

"Just this old buildin' protestin'," she declared. But the scarred skin stretched across her face highlighted the danger they were in. Studying Justine and Maggie, Rachel said, "Maybe there's somethin' I kin do ta help y'all…"

Sixty-One

Two hours later, Justine and Maggie stepped into St. Louis Street dressed as men.

Rachel, who lived and worked in the small warehouse owned by a Mardi Gras costume designer, was an expert seamstress and quickly cobbled together two very convincing disguises. Using long strips of cotton, she wrapped and compressed both Maggie and Justine's large breasts then tucked them into shirts, vests, ties, jackets and overcoats. Pants and shoes were easy to find and fit.

Justine was about to hastily cut her hair when she saw Maggie's horrified face.

"I've been growing this since I was a girl," Maggie confided, touching her golden red head. "Me brother used to call it 'the Devil's Mane'."

Justine couldn't see an alternative and Maggie was on the verge of tears when Rachel appeared with more cotton wrapping and a large derby hat. Sitting her down, she expertly wrapped Maggie's locks tightly against her head, then forced the hat on top. Doing the same for Justine was easier as her hair was shorter.

"We look the part, don't you think?" Justine commented, as they stood looking at themselves in the full-length mirror.

"We look like a couple of fat young rascals," Maggie replied.

They both stared uncertainly at their images. Their wrapped breasts caused them to look a bit portly and Maggie's slightly enlarged head added to the impression of size, though she stood at slightly less than 5 foot.

This is going to have to work, Justine thought, as she couldn't come up with a better alternative.

She was grateful for the relative cover of darkness as they headed down St. Louis Street towards the river. Justine was naturally accustomed to wearing trousers but for Maggie it was a new and, at first, challenging reality.

"I feel so exposed," she whispered to Justine.

"Well, you're completely covered from head to toe and I think you'll find men's clothing to be liberating because they're much less cumbersome. But there's something more pressing I need to tell you."

They'd reached Decatur Street and turning right were headed in the direction of the train terminal.

"We don't have any more money," Justine confided.

Maggie stopped walking trying to comprehend this situation.

"I think we should keep walking, Maggie dear. We don't want to bring attention to ourselves," Justine warned.

Maggie fell in beside Justine who was taking bigger strides as if she could outpace their dire situation.

"The money was in the room safe and I only had time to grab this satchel," Justine explained indicating the leather bag, slung over her shoulder.

"What are we going to do?" Maggie wondered.

They continued in silence all the way back to the New Orleans Union Train Station where they'd arrived. Standing outside the substantial brick building, Justine felt a sense of real panic for the first time since arriving in this time. If she couldn't get back to Brooklyn, she wouldn't be able to get home to her own time. The portal on Royal Street that she was certain had brought her mother to the 20th century was too risky a proposition. Kendall Shaw was back there and on the warpath. And then there was Maggie – Maggie who was stranded here in this inhospitable town because of Justine.

Just as the anxiety was threatening to overtake her, a young boy spoke *sotto voce,* trying to get her attention:

"You boys lookin' for a game...?"

She glanced at him with irritation. He was a scrawny, dark little boy dressed in a soiled suit and hat, looking like an undersized imitation of a grown man. Justine almost burst out laughing until he sidled up and spoke to her again:

"I kin get you into the best river game ..."

His cherubic face was smiling encouragingly as he motioned for them to follow. Moving away from the station, revealed the docks of the mighty Mississippi lined with boats of all kinds. The boy was indicating a particularly grand steamer complete with paddle-wheel.

"Where's it going?" Justine wanted to know.

"Goes all the way to St. Louis and back," he replied, proudly. "You can play all night, eat like a king, win big and sleep like a baby..."

He was about to continue reeling them in, when Maggie interrupted:

"What're they playing?"

Whereas Justine had a naturally low register, Maggie's voice tended to the upper range, especially when she was nervous or angry. The boy looked at her oddly, but replied:

"Every kinda poke you wanna poker..."

"You can get us in?" Maggie asked.

Justine watched her friend in amazement.

"Yes, sir..." the boy assured her.

"Because we don't have any money," Maggie declared.

The boy's shoulders sagged. His fish just got loose of the line.

In the distance, Justine heard shouting. It could have been anybody about anything but it conjured the salacious face of Kendall Shaw locking the door to the Silent Room.

"We have items of value," Justine offered. They needed to get on that boat and out of New Orleans.

This time Maggie looked at her in amazement. The shouting was getting louder and closer. Justine moved encouragingly towards the steamer. The boy considered for a moment.

"Worse that can happen is they won't let us play…" Justine suggested, hopefully.

The boy considered this.

"What's your name?" Justine asked, tyring to engage him.

"Josiah," he replied

"I'm Justin and this is my brother, Mag." Justine told him. "We'd sure like to get on that boat…"

"…and into that game," Maggie added, lowering her voice to sound more masculine.

Josiah looked from one to the other.

"I'll ask my Dad. He's in charge."

He led them up the gangplank, which rose from the dock to the third level of the steamers boiler deck. The two lower levels were packed to bursting with whatever was being transported north and the gangplank was steep. Two strong, young men wouldn't have trouble running up it but Maggie and Justine were not boys. They made their way cautiously. Josiah waited impatiently and was joined by a tall, black man.

"Two more players?" The man asked.

"One..." Maggie replied edging almost protectively ahead of Justine.

"They got no money but they got... um..."

"Items of value..." Justine supplied, catching her breath.

The man eyed Justine and Maggie. He was clearly Josiah's father, with skin as black as the night and big broad shoulders. But his manner wasn't suspicious or threatening, more curious.

"I think that'll do..." he said finally. "Show them to the gaming room, son."

"Thanks," Justine said, surprising the man as he headed down the gangplank.

Justine caught sight of him expertly unhitching the ropes tying the boat to the shore. The boat immediately started to move. They'd escaped. So far. So good.

She focused on hurrying behind Josiah along the boiler deck with its wide white wooden planks running the entire length of the ship. Every ten feet or so a low metal urn was secured to the boards. They passed two men leaning against the tooled wooden rails, smoking. One of them hawked into his throat and expertly released the mucus – displaying the function of these urns as spittoons. The boat was heading out into the wide river.

Justine whispered to Maggie, "Can you actually play poker?"

"Me brothers taught me."

"Maggie, these players are professionals, probably professional criminals."

"You never met me brothers," Maggie retorted.

Sixty-Two

Josiah swung open a door escorting them into an elegant saloon with seating at white clothed tables beneath low hung wrought iron chandeliers, glittering with crystals. Delicious smells emanated from a kitchen, making Justine's mouth water and reminding her that she hadn't eaten since breakfast. They crossed thick Persian carpets past a long line of windows, draped in white silk. Against the bright white, five black waiters stood in silent contrast.

But Josiah continued through the dining room to a set of stairs at the rear. These led up to a door. As they ascended the stairwell, Justine felt as if they were walking to their doom. Josiah knocked, waited for permission to enter then swung open the door. Cigar smoke poured from the room.

It was a small room with bare floorboards and a stacked iron stove at one end, somewhat overheating the room. Smaller windows without curtains ran along the length of the room interrupted by stacked chairs and a small bar with decanters and glasses. A black steward stood ready to provide drinks. At the center was a large, round table with a thick carpet-like cover. Sitting around the table in high backed wooden chairs was an assortment of men. To Justine's eye each one looked more disreputable than the next.

No one turned to acknowledge their arrival. The players were focused on their cards and on the game. Maggie and Justine stood awkwardly in the doorway as Josiah approached an older man sporting a white goatee with a horseshoe moustache, so called because it looked like a horseshoe hanging upside down on his face. He glanced at Justine and Maggie, his clever eyes sizing them up, then dismissively focused again on his cards.

They were left standing just long enough for Justine to lose patience:

"Excuse me," she said, "I'm Justin and this is my brother, Mag. As I'm sure Josiah just told you, my brother wants to join the game!"

A thin man with his back to them, turned full around in his chair to see who had spoken, his sharp blue eyes taking them in with a piercing glance. His head was bald but his face was covered with a full moustache and beard and he chewed a fat cigar with his yellowed teeth. He reminded Justine of a snake, probably poisonous.

"Bring me a whiskey," he shouted, turning back around to the table.

The waiter moved quickly to fulfil his request. Justine wasn't sure it was so wise to try and get Maggie into this dodgy game with this unpleasant and probably dangerous group, but they had no other way to get home.

She'd never liked arrogant men. And although she'd never had the courage to do anything about it, after Kendall Shaw, she'd had enough. She waited another beat, then announced:

"Well obviously our participation in this game is not wanted, so we'll be on our way."

She turned back towards the stairwell ready to leave.

"Josiah tells me you boys have no money," someone challenged her.

She turned to see Horseshoe squinting at her with a wry grin. The man sitting next to him was also now looking at her. His fat neck spilled over his tight collar and sweat had formed on his shaved upper lip.

"Then you've also been told we have items of value…" Justine retorted, holding Horseshoe's gaze.

"What items?" Fat Neck wanted to know.

By this time the others at the table were paying attention. These included a middle aged man with a thin moustache and equally thin, hunched shoulders who sat in his shirt, thin tie and suspenders with his hat pushed back on his head nervously not looking at anyone and next to him a boy, probably Maggie's age, with a smug grin on his stupid, pimply face.

Justine approached the table reaching into her leather satchel. Opening her palm so that everyone could see, she explained:

"It's 17th century. Belonged to the Holy Roman Emperor. That's him there in the cameo."

"Never heard of him." Pimply Face said.

"Then shut your stupid mouth!" Fat Neck snapped.

She was quite confident none of these poker players had any idea of the true value of Ducky's watch. When she flipped it open to reveal the jewelled inside, everyone leaned in with interest. Fat Neck reached for the watch, but Justine quickly withdrew her hand.

"Is my brother in the game?" she asked.

"Of course, dear boy," Horseshoe advised, smoothly. "No need to be coy."

"This is a poker game, my dear man," Justine replied. "It's all about being coy."

Horseshoe's eyes tightened but Justine refused to look away or be intimidated. He raised his voice over his shoulder, "Bring these boys a drink," he ordered.

The Waiter moved to pour and Justine, still looking into Horseshoe's eyes said, "We drink white spirits. Only white spirits."

"Yes, sir." The Waiter replied.

"Only white spirits ..." Pimply Face quoted, teasingly under his breath.

Justine shot him a threatening glance.

"That a problem?" she asked.

"Not at all, dear boy," Horseshoe advised. "Player's got his lucky charm. Ain't that right?"

Justine eyed him, but didn't reply, moving back and whispering to Maggie:

"Can you do this? You don't have to."

"White spirits?" Maggie whispered back, incredulously.

"One or two and then water. I don't want you getting drunk."

Maggie nodded, comprehending.

"Who's in charge on this boat?" Justine asked. "I want him here to hold this watch."

"He don't trust us," Pimply Face sniggered.

"Should I?" Justine asked.

"No, sir," he snorted, "Cuz I'm gunna take everything you got!"

Josiah scurried out of the room in search of the Purser.

Maggie walked to the table and sat down in the only empty chair, which was between Fat Neck and Pimply. She placed her hands on the table and stared at them.

"Bring me another drink," Snake Man shouted, impatiently.

The Waiter practically ran to place Maggie and Snake Man's drinks on the table.

"How come you got bandages on yer head?" Pimply Face asked, staring at the white fabric holding Maggie's long hair in place. Maggie didn't look up and she didn't move but Justine feared what confidence Maggie was displaying was quickly disappearing.

"Had a head injury," Justine spat at him. "As if it's any of your business!"

Pimply leapt out of his seat ready to attack Justine, but Fat Neck pulled him back down.

"This is a *friendly* game," he instructed the boy, but his eyes took in Maggie's 'bandages' and he smiled to himself.

Everyone waited. Horseshoe lit a cigar. Thin Man tapped nervously on the table. Fat Neck sipped his whiskey, while Snake Man downed his drink in one gulp, still chewing on a cigar. Pimply glared at Justine who was watching Maggie quietly sizing up her opponents from under the brim of her hat.

A uniformed man entered the room, followed by Josiah's father.

"How can I help you gentlemen?" the man asked Horseshoe.

"Good evening, Mr. Gordon," Horseshoe replied. "These young men have an item of value they're putting up to get them into this here game. They wish it to be secured."

"You gentlemen in agreement with this arrangement?" The Purser asked the others players as he eyed Justine and Maggie.

There were general noises of assent.

The Purser considered for a moment. "I trust the running of this ship to Henry here," he said, pointing to Josiah's father. "If I trust him with that I can trust him with this valuable item." He glanced around the room, waiting for anyone to object.

Henry shifted uncomfortably. Justine was acutely aware of a black man's precarious position in this day and age and what might happen to him if he failed in his duty. She didn't like putting him in this position.

"Doesn't that sort of put Henry in danger as well as my 'item'?" Justine interjected. "Don't you have a proper safe on board?"

"The safe, proper or not, is for paying passengers only," the Purser retorted, becoming annoyed with what he perceived to be a young man's impertinence. "So young man, if you'll hand the item over to Henry, here – it will stay with him for the duration of this game."

"What's it worth?" It was Snake Man, speaking in the same aggressive voice he used for the Waiter.

The Purser looked at Justine. She mentioned a sum above what she'd paid for the watch, hoping it was enough to get Maggie a stake in the game. No one questioned her assessment.

As she handed the bag with Ducky's watch to Henry, she whispered, "I'm so sorry to do this to you…"

Josiah's father gravely received the bag and nodded acknowledgement.

"You Gentlemen need anything else…" the Purser added as he was leaving, "… you know where to find me."

"Can we get back to the game now?" Pimply whined. "Cuz I'm gunna whip your ass…" he spat directly at Maggie. When Maggie didn't look at him or reply, he demanded, "What's wrong with you? How come you don't talk none?"

"He's got that head wound, don cha know," Fat Neck chuckled, reaching for the deck of cards, shuffling and dealing.

Justine was apprehensive about Maggie who appeared to be half-asleep in her chair, a strand of fiery red hair threatening to escape its wrapping, her body slumped onto her arms resting on the table, holding her cards with her eyes half-shut.

Justine turned to the Waiter, "Would it be possible to get something to eat now that we're in the game?"

The Waiter hesitated uncertain what to say.

"You go on, Carleton," Henry said to the Waiter. "I'll look out for these gentlemen."

Sixty-Three

To say Justine was anxious and overwrought was an understatement. She'd never been a gambler, literally or figuratively. Paul bought a lotto ticket every week but Justine thought it was a waste of money. Gamblers liked the thrill and possibilities of the unknown. Justine longed to feel in control of things, of life. In light of where she now found herself, that longing seemed a bit absurd.

From what little she knew about the game of poker, Maggie seemed to be losing. The pile of wooden chips, which had been placed in front of her, originally equalled the value of Ducky's watch. That pile was now greatly reduced.

Justine turned away from the game feeling helpless and out of control. Henry was still standing by passively watching, his dark eyes hooded, as if he'd disappeared into himself.

"Your son is very clever," Justine said, needing to focus on something other than the consequences of Maggie losing.

Henry slowly turned surprised eyes towards her. It wasn't so much her non sequitur as that she was speaking directly to him in a conversational manner. He was used to receiving orders from white people, not making conversation.

"I suspect he must be very smart," she went on.

"Yes, ma'am," Henry said, "I mean, sir," he corrected himself, then looked quickly away.

"Oh, dear. It seems Josiah's father is clever too."

Henry didn't look up.

"How did you know? Does anyone else suspect?" Justine was whispering now, leaning urgently in towards Henry. "Oh, dear God ..." she added, glancing back towards the men at the table.

"They don' suspect nuthin'," Henry assured her. "They thinks about winning and losing. That's all they thinks about."

"We we're being followed by a really terrible man. This was the best way to escape..." Justine spluttered.

"It's ok, miss. You're secret's safe with me."

Carleton returned with plates of sandwiches, enough to feed an army.

"There's food here, gentlemen," Henry announced, "If you'd like to help yerself..."

Food it seemed was the only thing important enough to draw the men away from their game. Everyone but Thin Man stood up. Justine grabbed a couple of sandwiches and motioned for Maggie to join her outside on the deck.

It was chilly outside but Justine hoped the air would be good for Maggie. But even before the door had closed behind them, Maggie was transformed.

"That skinny fellow's the one to watch," she confided to Justine. "Can't exactly read that one. The others, mind you," Maggie chuckled, "they're not bad – but they never played an O'Reagan before." She finished by taking a healthy bite of the thick sliced bread.

"But Maggie," Justine hissed, "You're losing – badly!"

"Appearances," Maggie replied. "Just appearances…" Her breath came in bursts of mist against the cold.

The dark Mississippi rolled beneath them stretching out in all directions; black and silver waves trailing in the wake of the powerful steamboat and the wavering light it cast.

They were near the front of the boat, and the only sound they could hear was a distant rhythmic slapping of the paddle wheel against the current. The shore was indistinct, without signs of life. Everything else was darkness leaving Justine feeling more out of time than ever before.

"I hope you know what you're doing Maggie because, speaking of appearances, Henry knows we're not men…"

Losing didn't seem to worry Maggie. This did. "Oh, Mother of God..." she muttered, her mouth full of ham and cheese.

"He promised not to say anything."

"I don't trust the lot of them ..." Maggie worried.

At that moment Henry appeared.

"We'll be dockin in a couple of hours," he said. "Unloadin' goods ..." His words were simple enough but their meaning seemed to hold some import.

"Thank you, Henry," Justine replied, not knowing what else to say.

"They're wantin' to get on with the game," he added to Maggie, holding open the door.

Maggie went back inside and Henry let the door close behind her. The whites of his eyes were like orbs in his very black face. He stepped closer to Justine and began to speak in a very low voice, quickly and earnestly. When he was done, Justine understood the peril he was putting himself in telling her what he had – as well as the very real danger she and Maggie were facing.

Henry slipped back into the gaming room. Justine stood in the darkness for as long as she could tolerate the cold. She thought about a man like Henry, a good man, a hard worker, providing for his family as best he could, a man who suffered daily indignities springing from institutionalized racism and discrimination. And his son Josiah was growing up facing these same injustices. And though things would change, they would change slowly. All men would not be created equal even 100 years from now. She followed Henry back inside.

Things were beginning to shift at the poker table. Maggie was sitting up a bit straighter in her chair and there was now a small pile of money in front of her. Carleton was serving drinks. Henry had promised to make sure Maggie's was only water.

The other men seemed changed as well. Pimply Face was quiet, his face sulky and morose. Snake Man was leaning into the table now as if to exert some negative force on everyone. Fat Neck was sweating more profusely. Horseshoe was sitting out a round, smoking and sipping whiskey. He seemed to be deciding his next move, his squinty eyes moving from poker player to poker player and then to Justine. When he looked at her, she quickly looked away and then immediately regretted doing so. Her resolve was fast unravelling. Only Thin Man seemed unchanged. He was neither drinking nor smoking and his intensity had not abated.

Josiah appeared in the room covered in dirt and grease. He'd clearly taken on his father's responsibilities while Henry held onto Ducky's watch. Henry began speaking quietly into Josiah's ear. Josiah nodded once, glanced at Justine and left the room.

So, the dye was set. Justine had agreed to Henry's plan.

Sixty-Four

The night wore on with Maggie slowly but irrevocably increasing her wins and the others becoming gradually more aware that she had hoodwinked them all. The room was electric with expectation. Helplessly watching from the sidelines, Justine knew they were hurtling towards a showdown. These men were not accustomed to being sharked at their own table and it was only a matter of time before they turned on the culprit.

Maggie seemed blissfully unaware of the tension mounting in the room. She continued to say next to nothing but played her cards with precision and seeming prescience. She had made their money back on the watch and then some, when the boat began to slow.

Pimply Face threw his cards on the table, "Shit, Fuck you Fucker," he shouted at Maggie, standing up and grabbing her by the coat.

Thin Man spoke for the first time, his voice soft and menacing, "Fair and Square," he warned. "Fair and Square."

Fat Neck responded immediately as if under orders, pulling Pimply Face off Maggie and tossing him back in his chair. "We're dockin'," he spat.

Everyone put their cards down except Maggie, who was confused. Justine was about to step in, to do what, she didn't know, when the Purser appeared.

"Cards down, Gentlemen," he announced. "We're docking. No gambling until we're afloat again." He cast his officious eye around the table and Maggie obediently laid down her cards. At the same time she drew her winnings close.

"Give me a drink," Snake Man shouted.

"Where'd you learn to play?" Horseshoe asked Maggie. He and Snake Man had lost a considerable amount of money.

Maggie shrugged.

"The man asked you a question," Pimply Face growled at her.

"Deeds – not words," Thin Man exhorted, gathering his winnings and rising from his chair.

Justine was shocked to see him remove a priest's collar from his pocket and secure it around his neck. From under his shirt, he exposed a golden cross on a chain, hanging around his neck. He kissed it perfunctorily, donned his long black cassock and a hat and made his way to the door.

"It's been a pleasure, gentlemen, as always…" he said, and departed down the stairs.

Maggie stared after him, rattled and scandalized.

"I hate him," Pimply Face spat in the direction of the Thin Man/ Preacher.

"That's a Holy Man you're speakin' ill of," Horseshoe commented.

"He's not holy. He's a hypocrite," Maggie spluttered.

"Yeah? And what're you?" Pimply Face accused her.

"What're you talking about?"

"You stole all my money! You must've been cheating!"

"You're just an obviously bad player," Maggie told him. Her face was getting redder and redder and she'd forgotten to lower her register.

Justine was looking anxiously from Maggie to the door and back again. Where was Henry?

"What's wrong with you?" Fat Neck wanted to know, pushing Pimply Face aside and stepping up closer to inspect Maggie. "What's wrong with your voice? You sound like a girl..."

"That's because he is a girl," Horseshoe explained, snorting and adding sneeringly "So's the other one."

"What?" Fat Neck spat, peering at Justine and then back at Maggie. "Girls?"

Snake Man shot suddenly from the bar to Maggie, ripping her hat from her head. Part of the wrapping came undone and her long, red hair uncoiled down her back. Maggie instinctively stepped back but Pimply Face was there preventing her escape.

Justine knew it was now or never. She pulled a gun out of her leather satchel and pointed it at the men.

"Stop!" she shouted. "Don't anyone move or do anything stupid."

All eyes turned towards Justine. Pimply Face dropped his hands from Maggie's arms and raised them in the air.

"That's right," Justine said to him. "Everyone take a step back." Her nerves caused her voice to come out louder and deeper than normal but this had the desired affect. "Back off. Now," she stressed. The men stepped back.

"Take your winnings, Mag." Justine instructed, tossing the satchel onto the table. With shaking hands, Maggie swept the money into the bag and grabbed her hat. "Now come over here," Justine instructed.

Justine didn't know what was going to happen next, but she knew they had to get out of this room and away from these irate men. She began moving backwards towards the door keeping the gun pointed at everyone in the room, moving Maggie with her onto the landing.

"I'll find you," Fat Neck threatened.

"And then I'll kill you," Pimply Face added.

"They mean it," Horseshoe warned. "I'd recommend leavin' that money here and then leavin'..."

"I'd recommend not trying to follow us," Justine warned. "I'm as good with this gun as Mag is with poker."

In one swift movement, she was out the door slamming it behind her and was relieved to find a key in the lock, as Henry had promised. She managed to lock the door just as one of the men angrily rattled the handle.

Maggie raced after Justine down the stairs, not into the dining room but down two more flights.

"Can you really shoot?" Maggie asked, stuffing her hair back into her hat.

"Of course not," Justine replied.

"Where'd you get the gun?"

"Costume. Fake. Just like the rest of our get-up!"

"Jesus, Mary and Joseph. What if one of them'd called your bluff?"

"What if one of them'd called yours?"

"They did," Maggie chortled with a rising edge of hysteria.

They'd reached the bottom of the stairs and Justine slammed open the door onto the steerage deck where the cargo was stored. Maggie's laugh caught in her throat. A faint light filtered onto huge shadowy bundles wrapped in canvas, crushed one on top of the other and stacked to the ceiling.

A narrow passageway had been left between these walls of cargo, which Justine and Maggie now navigated as quickly as they could. There was a smell of livestock, tobacco and mould and the threat of something or someone hiding in the darkness behind the next bundle.

"Where are we going?" Maggie wanted to know.

"Off this boat," Justine replied.

And just as she spoke a figure suddenly appeared out of the shadows. She was about to scream when she recognized Josiah. He was signalling them to follow him into a small space behind a high stack of soot-covered bundles. And just as suddenly, Josiah vanished.

Justine recognized the black soot as coal dust and rummaged around for something to cover their mouths. But Maggie was ahead of her, producing her ubiquitous handkerchief and offering it to Justine. But Justine shook her head pushing the white cloth over Maggie's mouth. This fine toxic dust could bring on an asthma attack easier than a dusty house.

"Do you have your inhaler?" Justine whispered.

But before Maggie could respond, they heard loud voices. One seemed to be coming from the deck above and from its whining edge, it sounded like Pimply Face:

"Did you see them boys?"

The reply came from Henry who sounded as if he was right on the other side of their hiding place.

"No, sir. I been here unloadin'... Then I'll come back to the game."

"Not necessary, Henry. Game's over ... 'til we find them boys." It was Horseshoe. "Then we'll have some sport!" he added and both men laughed.

"Josiah's lookin' too just like you ordered." Henry confirmed.

Then it was silent. Maggie tried to strangle a cough. Justine could hear her heart beating. The longer they waited here, the greater chance one of those vengeful poker players finding them. She didn't want to imagine what would happen then. Maggie coughed and Justine feared this time someone must have heard it. She held her breath.

The silence was ripped apart by the powerful screech of a train's whistle, followed by the ship's engines firing up, rattling the floor beneath them.

Justine grabbed Maggie's hand and pushed out from behind the bundles of toxic coal, running headlong into Henry who had come to fetch them.

"Quickly now," he said, gesturing for them to follow.

The whistle let off another almighty shriek as they stepped onto the open deck. And there it was, a great black bulk of coal driven train backed onto a track that stretched over the water and connected with a wide platform, that had been lowered from the ship. Bundles and goods had already been transferred and stored inside the train's dark, voluminous rear car.

"Go on now," Henry said, nodding towards the open train.

Justine reached for the small packet she'd prepared for this moment. "I can't thank you enough, Henry," she said, stuffing the packet into his hand. "Helping strangers is a very rare thing."

He could feel the money inside and he too reached for a small package inside his jacket, "Thank you, miss. That goes both ways."

Justine accepted the silk pouch containing Ducky's watch. Then impulsively she hugged him. "Things do get better," she told Henry. "In time."

He looked at her quizzically, but when the train screeched again, Justine and Maggie ran across the platform and into the cargo car of the train. Henry pulled up the ramp and the moment it disconnected, the train began to move with a loud chugging of engines and rasping of metal wheels against metal tracks.

Justine caught a glimpse of Snake Man standing on an upper deck, casually smoking. She wasn't sure he'd seen her, because he didn't seem to be looking.

Henry had explained that as the train moved slowly away from the river, workmen would come to secure the rear cargo doors. They had a very short window to make it into the passenger car.

Sixty-Five

Even though the water was beginning to cool, Justine lingered in the bathtub. The new electric heater was warming the room and she felt content beyond measure. Maggie had bathed then come and washed Justine's hair, a luxury Justine knew she would miss. There was something else she knew now for certain, but about which she didn't wish to think. It was dressing as men that had made it finally apparent to her.

She thought instead about their arrival back on Hicks Street, filthy but flushed with freedom. The train pulled into Grand Central at 2:00pm and Maggie insisted on making numerous stops just to savour one last time what it felt like to walk around in trousers.

Bursting with excitement and relief they noisily entered the Brownstone. No one seemed to be home until James appeared from his studio, surprised at first, then amazed and then something else.

"Where the devil have you two been?" he asked, sizing up Maggie's legs in her trousers.

"You might ask," Maggie replied haughtily, brushing him aside.

"What would yer Mother say if she saw you right now?" he taunted, following her into the kitchen.

"Me mother would ask could I please find her a pair of trousers cuz she's the one's been wearing them anyway…!"

Maggie's manner was brusque to the point of impertinence. She embellished her replies to all of James' questions and had a clever retort to all of his jokes. His eyes continued to travel over her vaguely disguised voluptuousness as if he were seeing her for the first time. He was clearly drawn to this bold, perky version of Maggie O'Reagan, dressed as a man and acting like one too.

Justine left them in the kitchen, happily making her way to her private bathroom. She considered the irony of her current situation in light of what might be a budding relationship between Maggie and James Grey.

Justine smiled, splashing water onto her face. Then she sighed. She knew she was pregnant. She knew it for sure. And James was the father.

Later that afternoon, a beautifully embossed invitation arrived by delivery boy. Alexander and his family were gathered in the kitchen finishing lunch and Justine requested Maggie read the invitation out loud.

Clutching her handkerchief in one hand as she tried to keep the note from shaking with the other, Maggie read:

"The residents of #11 Hicks Street are all requested to attend a special event at the home of Caroline McGowan." Maggie looked at Justine mystified. "What's it mean," she asked.

"It means my sister Caroline wants all of us to come to her house."

"All of us?" Alexander asked.

"It says *'all the residents',*" Justine confirmed, smiling.

Alexander thought about this for a moment, then nodded his head in agreement.

Caroline's considerate invitation and Alexander acceptance pleased Justine very much. A family had formed and this confirmed it.

The following Saturday everyone scrambled to present themselves in their very finest. Maggie insisted Justine wear the light pink and lace confection with the long train. Looking at herself in the mirror, she had to admit, once again, Maggie had excellent taste. The Gibson Girl fashion suited Justine to a tee with her hair piled high on her head and a wide belt cinching her waist. She wouldn't let Maggie cinch too far, however. Not now. Not for another 8 months or so.

Maggie had gratefully accepted one of the dresses in Justine's Mother's closet. The dark green embroidery on ivory silk highlighted her eyes and her rich red hair.

"I'm so glad you didn't cut it," Justine commented as Maggie stood beside her in the mirror inserting a large filigree silver ornament into her waves.

"I would have died," Maggie confessed. "If that horrible man didn't kill us, I would have died anyway…"

James was waiting at the bottom of the stairs his keen eyes watching the two of them as they descended. Justine allowed Maggie to precede her. She didn't want his eyes discerning anything other than their beauty. He too was dressed for the occasion in a dinner jacket worn with a matching fancy waistcoat, high-necked shirt and bow tie. Without a word he took each of their arms, escorting them to the front door.

As they descended the front steps to the street, Alexander stood tall in his finery, opening the door to the automobile. His family had a head start in the carriage with Sasha driving.

"Good evening Alexander Alexandrovich," Justine said. "You look very dashing this evening."

"I don't know this '*dashing*'," he replied but bowed his head in acknowledgement nonetheless.

Sixty-Six

There was a chill in the air and snow lay in piles here and there but the late afternoon sky was clear, turning from deep blue to royal purple. It felt like one of the most perfect evenings Justine could remember.

They pulled up at Caroline's new home in Gramercy Park almost at the same time as the carriage with Rosa, Anzelika and baby Liliya. Other guests were arriving and the street was becoming increasingly congested. Alexander took over the job of head valet, directing traffic in a low commanding voice, restoring order as James escorted Justine and Maggie to the door.

The house was transformed, with tasteful, warm furnishings that were clearly Dušan's elegant touch with a bit of Caroline's feminine whimsy. A butler took their coats and guided them through the archway above which was hung a stone Rubenesque cherub smiling cheekily down at them. This led into the large living room where Caroline and Dušan were greeting guests.

Caroline's baby face, not unlike the cherub's, broke into a delighted smile when she saw Justine, her turned up nose wrinkling into her sparkly blue eyes.

"Oh, there you are. I am so glad you're here!" she gushed, wrapping both arms around Justine and hugging her tight.

"Everything looks so beautiful, Caroline," Justine gushed back. "Particularly you!" What Caroline actually looked was grown up, in a light blue silk dress with black velvet trim.

"It's all Dušan. He helped me choose the furnishings," Caroline demurred.

Probably the dress as well, Justine thought.

"And all his talented friends helped with sourcing and manufacturing," Caroline went on, indicating a lively group of people gathered in the center of the room. "But it was my idea about the piano," she added, proudly.

"I remember," Justine said. "It looks wonderful there by the French doors.

"And the acoustics are wonderful too," Dušan added, bending to kiss Justine's hand in welcome.

Chairs had been placed in a semicircle of rows facing the piano.

Pointing to the front row, Caroline whispered, "I've saved a seat for you next to me."

Soon everyone was seated and as Dušan approached the piano, conversation fell away. It was an eclectic gathering to say the least. Four musicians stood around Dušan holding a variety of stringed instruments. They could have been mistaken for labourers or gypsies in the unusual and colourful way they were dressed. They certainly didn't have the sombre stance of orchestra musicians.

But this diversity was also reflected in the audience. Three women, who were probably the musician's wives, wore colourful, intricately embroidered blouses over wide skirts with hair pulled back into simple, but unfashionable buns. Some held small children in their laps. Alexander and his family added to the mix. And there was a small group of wealthy girlfriends of Caroline's dressed and fluttering like butterflies around a distinguished grey haired man, who seated himself in the last row, nearest the door.

Candles in a tall candelabrum burned brightly on the piano and when the butler turned down some of the other lights it drew the audience into a cosy embrace. Without introduction Dušan sat at the piano and with a nod of his head launched into Dvořák's Piano Quintet in A. The otherwise rough looking musicians were transformed into angels, passionately transporting the audience with their craft.

When the piece was over everyone took a breath, as if returning from the heavens, before applauding sincerely. Dušan stood with great dignity, presented his fellow musicians and then spoke:

"Many of us are here today because we were forced to flee our homelands."

Alexander shifted uncomfortably in his seat.

"We came seeking freedom," Dušan continued. "And we are grateful. Today's small concert is how we are expressing our gratitude.

Thank you to Caroline McGowan for providing such a wonderful space. And thank you for being here."

He sat. Nodded again and the musicians broke into a hauntingly beautiful and wild rendition of Gypsy music. When they finished the audience again applauded, this time with great enthusiasm.

Then the musicians moved to the side of the room.

Standing behind the piano, Dušan spoke reverently, "I wrote this piece for Caroline, the woman I love."

Caroline gasped, blushing sweetly. Dušan sat and began to play what Justine would always remember as the most achingly beautiful piece of music she'd ever heard. Caroline's hand found Justine's and held on tight.

When he was finished, no one spoke or moved as Dušan rose from the piano, kneeling in front of Caroline.

"You are my heart and my soul," he said. "Would you do my the honor of becoming my wife?"

Caroline gasped again, squeezing Justine's hand so hard she nearly cried out as she stared wide eyed at her sister. Justine's heart was beating fast with this wonderful turn of events but she managed to smile back, encouragingly. Everyone held their breath.

"Yes," Caroline cried, turning back to Dušan. "Oh, my Yes!"

Dušan produced a small, but exquisite diamond solitaire, placing it on Caroline's finger. Taking both her hands he brought her up to meet him, kissing her full on the lips. Then everyone applauded while the musicians broke into more festive gypsy music.

Caroline's girlfriends clustered around to view the ring and giggle their delight.

Dušan moved to sit with Justine.

"It is a miracle, beyond anything I could have hoped for," he confided to her. "A distant relative, someone I was not even aware of, left me an inheritance. It is not a lot, but it gave me the courage to propose. I hope you approve."

Mr Brewster had done his job well. Dušan was not aware where the money had actually come from and never would be. It had produced the desired effect.

"I am so pleased for you, Dušan," Justine enthused. "I couldn't be more pleased for both of you!"

"I worry about Hunter," Dušan confessed.

"Caroline will soon be of age to make her own decision," Justine consoled. "But I will speak to Hunter, if you wish."

Before he could reply, the Butler approached with a business card on a small silver tray. Dušan studied the card, looking dismayed.

"The Philharmonic-Symphony Society director had to leave," the Butler explained "but he wishes to meet with you and asked that you give him a call."

This time Caroline grabbed Dušan with great excitement, "Oh Dušan the Philharmonic!" she exclaimed. "I just knew Victor would love you as much as I do!"

"Who is Victor?" he asked.

"*Mr.* Victor. The director," she laughed. "Of the Philharmonic-Symphony Society! He wants to meet with you!"

"But I had no idea he was here."

"I know. It was a secret, which is why I didn't formally introduce you. My father was a big contributor to the society and, well, I thought I would invite him to your first concert," Caroline babbled happily. "I had no idea you were going to propose – but I'm so proud he got to hear your original music. Now he knows what a genius you are!"

Dušan was stunned, flushed and confused but he didn't have time to reply because one of his fellow musicians was raising a toast in Czech, followed by hearty cheers and more lively music.

It may have been the music or the highly charged emotional atmosphere but Justine suddenly felt unwell. She made her way through the shiny marble foyer feeling as if her feet were dragging beneath the weight of her body. She headed into the kitchen were Matilde stood at the counter washing dishes. She stopped, staring at Justine:

"Miss Justine? Are you unwell?"

"Just a bit overwhelmed, I think, " Justine assured her but allowed Matilde to pull out a chair into which she gratefully slumped.

The world was spinning, slowly, slowly and Justine couldn't get her eyes to focus. She was vaguely aware of Matilde using the end of a box to fan her face. The cool air felt good and she closed her eyes, giving up on focusing for the moment.

When the breeze stopped, Justine peeled open one eye. Matilde was bending over her a look of great concern sharpening her features.

"Please to drink this, Miss…" she suggested, offering Justine a glass of cool water.

Justine drank and felt her insides calming. She sat up slowly and opened her eyes. The world seemed back to normal.

"Are you better now?"

"Yes, Matilde. Thank you."

But she wasn't. She knew she wasn't. She knew time was running out.

"And how are you, Matilde?" Justine inquired, needing to shift the focus.

"Ah. Thank you … " Matilde replied. "For this…" she explained, indicating her kitchen and the lovely home it housed. "We are all good now, I think. And little Miss Caroline – getting married! Ach. This is *zher, zher gut!*"

Yes. It was good. It meant there were a few more things Justine needed to do and then – and then it was time – time to go.

Sixty-Seven

This time, she'd formally requested a meeting with Hunter. She needed him to feel respected so rather than barging in as she'd done in the past, she arrived at the appointed time. Raphael met her at the door and managed to whisper his delight at seeing her before escorting her with appropriate dignity into a small sitting room on the first floor at the rear of the house.

Overlooking the formal gardens it was much cosier than the grand reception room upstairs. It clearly had been decorated for a man, with golden tiffany lamps casting warm light on two rich leather armchairs positioned in front of a raging fire. Her father must have spent time here. This thought made Justine want to linger and to touch things but Hunter's defiant presence hunkered in a chair, refusing to stand and greet her, made Justine focus on the matter at hand.

She circled the opposite chair gazing at her half-brother, who refused to look at her. In spite of his obstinacy, he looked better than the last time she'd seen him. The dark circles were gone from beneath his eyes and there was a flush of health in his skin.

"May I sit?" she asked.

He waved a hand in the direction of the empty leather chair. The chair was designed for lounging or for long limbs to sit upon. It was not for bodies restricted by corsets and Justine was forced to perch on the edge of her seat, putting him at an advantage. Nonetheless, she was determined to have a civilized conversation with her brother.

"How are you Hunter?"

"Fine. Couldn't be better."

In spite of his ironic tone, he was actually speaking the truth.

"You look well. You look very well," she confirmed.

"Where is my sister?" he asked, turning to look at Justine for the first time.

"It's actually about Caroline that I've come to see you," Justine replied, regretting the subject had been broached so soon.

But she could understand. After the death of his parents, Hunter was the head of the household and Caroline was supposed to answer to him. Justine's arrival and Caroline's subsequent disappearance effectively curtailed his power and he wasn't taking it well.

She could feel him trying to keep himself in check and sensed the effort it was requiring. Hunter had a temper. Hunter's temper had always gotten him what he wanted, but he was learning that there were negative consequences to his outbursts as well.

"I have some wonderful news, Hunter," Justine said cautiously, trying to keep her voice even and her smile sincere. "Caroline's getting married."

"What?" he exploded, sitting up in his chair. "To whom?"

"To Dušan, of course."

"That gypsy gold digger!" he raged, slamming his hands on the arm of the chair.

"My mother came from gypsies, Hunter," Justine warned. "And Dušan's people are Jews."

"Even worse," he declared, standing and striding to the window.

"How can you say such a thing? Or even believe it? You of all people!"

"What do you mean by that!"

Justine bit her lip in order not to say more. They glared at each other across the room until he turned to glare out the window.

She took a deep breath. It was a different time, she reminded herself. He was just saying what he'd been taught by a society that embraced the beliefs Hunter was espousing – beliefs that included harsh judgement of his sexual orientation as well as condemnation of Gypsies and Jews; beliefs that would eventually lead to concentration camps.

Justine slumped in her chair, the weight of this realization, filling her with disgust and despair.

"She's just a child," Hunter insisted. "She's been seduced," he declared, turning to face Justine with the force of this new argument. "I will not allow my sister to marry this flea-ridden musician."

What fleas had to do with anything, Justine wasn't sure but by the look on Hunter's face he was building to a tantrum and Justine was no longer strong enough to deal with him.

"Calm down, Hunter," she implored.

"I will not calm down!" he shouted. "Stop telling me what to do in my own home!" Then he was moving swiftly towards her, leaning down and screaming in her face, "TELL ME WHERE SHE IS."

"If you don't calm down, Hunter, I'm going to leave. Right now.

"I demand that you tell me where I can find her or..." His eyes were wide with rage, his body hunched and ready to strike.

"MONSIEUR! S'IL VOUS PLAIT ..." Raphael's voice came sharp and pleading from the doorway.

Hunter looked momentarily confused, glanced once in Raphael's direction then strode back to the window.

Raphael was immediately at her side, leaning in solicitously, "Ça va, Mademoiselle? Are you alright?" he whispered.

"Yes, Raphael. Thank you. I'm fine. Hunter was just surprised by my news. His sister Caroline is getting married." She said it firmly as a statement of fact, not to be argued with.

"But this is wonderful news," Raphael confirmed as he moved a straight-backed chair in front of the fire. "Would you prefer to sit here?" he asked, reaching out his hand to help her from her precarious position.

As he did so, he kept glancing towards Hunter as if gauging his mood.

"Two people who love each other joining their lives is always a cause for joy and celebration, ne c'est pas, Monsieur?" Raphael asked, gazing at Hunter with his dark blue eyes.

Hunter turned, looking at Raphael with what Justine could only define as longing, though it could have been interpreted as pain. His eyebrows were drawn together and his eyes were moist. The fire seemed to go out of him. His shoulders slumped and he hung his head.

"I have brought coffee and cakes," Raphael went on in a soothing voice as he collected his tray from the hall table.

After setting out the china and sweets he approached Hunter gently, standing more closely to him than might have been considered proper for a servant. He spoke so softly Justine couldn't hear what was said.

"Monsieur also has news," Raphael explained to Justine, stepping aside to allow Hunter to speak.

Hunter reached for a cigarette from a silver box on the mantel. Raphael produced a lighter. The first inhalation seemed to restore Hunter's decorum.

"We're – that is, *I* – am going to Europe. Raphael will accompany me," Hunter explained.

Raphael was pouring coffee and Justine could just make out the hint of a relieved smile at the corners of his full lips.

"That's a wonderful idea, Hunter," Justine enthused.

Hunter seemed surprised by her enthusiasm. He sat in his chair, a look of wide-eyed questioning on his face revealing the boy he still was under the bluster and anger.

"Raphael speaks four languages, so he's going to take me around and show me places." He added, eager to move on from his previous outburst.

"I'm envious, Hunter. I really am. Europe with a knowledgeable guide….! It sounds so romantic."

The word had slipped out before she realized how precariously near to the truth it was.

"Do you take anything in your coffee, Mademoiselle?" Raphael interrupted, covering the moment.

"Milk and sugar, thank you," Justine replied quickly "…and are these more of your delicious French pastries?"

Raphael nodded offering the tray for her to select one. They busied themselves with a discussion of the cakes, praying that Justine's faux pas had gone unnoticed.

"I'm going to sell the house," Hunter announced.

It was clearly said to shock, so Justine rallied to react appropriately.

"What? For Heaven sake - why?"

"I don't know how long we'll be away. I just want to do it."

"I think it's a good idea, Hunter."

"You do?"

"I do. You're young. It's an unnecessary burden."

"Yes. A burden."

"I say that because I sense you were not especially happy here ..."

"No ..." He hung his head as if that truth shamed him.

"Would it be alright if Raphael sat down and joined us for coffee?" Justine asked, trying to refocus Hunter's attention.

Hunter glanced up at Raphael, then shrugged. Once Raphael poured himself coffee and sat, Hunter seemed to relax. They drank and nibbled cake and spoke of good coffee and how it should be made and cafes in Paris or Rome where you could find it.

Justine thought her heart would explode with joy. This was what Hunter's life should be. Sitting together with the man he was clearly besotted with and who seemed to truly care for him as well, drinking coffee and enjoying a conversation about travel and the future.

"So when are you leaving?" Justine asked.

"In a few weeks."

"Caroline's wedding is on March 3rd" Justine said, casually producing an invitation, which she offered to Hunter. He sipped his coffee, ignoring the invitation. "She really wants you to be there Hunter. She wants you to give her away."

"I would have been happy to give her away to an appropriate spouse," Hunter spat, getting up and grabbing another cigarette.

"What exactly do you mean, 'appropriate', Hunter?"

He spun around, red in the face, hissing, "What are you suggesting?"

She looked away, letting the unspoken truth fill the silence.

"*Vivre sans aimer n'est pas proprement vivre,*" Raphael quoted. "To live without loving is to not really live. Moliere."

He stood up and began clearing the cups and plates. Hunter watched his movements hungrily until he noticed Justine looking at him. He turned, tossing his cigarette angrily into the fire.

"We love who we love, Hunter. And that makes it good and right." Justine said, simply. "Caroline loves Dušan and he loves her."

Hunter shrugged and shook his head as if the thought was distasteful.

"Would it help if I told you Dušan's recently come into some money and he seems to have so impressed the manager of the New York Philharmonic that he's been offered the job of concert master?"

"Why do you just accept the unacceptable?" he asked, almost pleading.

She looked directly at him.

"Because to me it isn't unacceptable. Because diversity and difference is what makes the world a beautiful and interesting place. Because I judge people based on their character, not their religion or ethnic background – or anything else!"

"What's that supposed to mean?"

"Just what I said." She approached him as she spoke. "I'm going to give you an example. Your friend Kendall Shaw. On the surface he fits into what you would probably define as acceptable. But he is one of the most evil men I've ever met."

"How do you know?"

"I know, Hunter. And I think you do too."

"Well, I don't believe you. About the Piano teacher." Hunter insisted, petulantly, turning away.

"Why would I lie about Dušan?"

"Because you love Caroline and you hate me!"

The outer edges of her vision began to lose definition. The irritatingly acrid aroma of cigar smoke filled her nostrils and Hunter's face morphed into a little boy.

"Don't be silly. I love you both," she heard herself say.

Her lips moved to form the words but her voice wasn't her own. It was deeper, harsh and full of disgust. She felt a violent anger ricocheting inside her head, directed at the source of the cigar smoke, her husband Henry McGowan. She resented him so much, this man she had married.

Justine felt the solidity of the ground beneath her giving way. Then Raphael was at her side, his warm hand on her arm, guiding her back to her chair, bringing her back to herself.

When her vision cleared, Hunter was staring at her shaken and uncertain.

"You sounded like ... like my mother..."

"I'm sorry, Hunter. I'm so, so sorry." She knew she was speaking for someone else, for the woman she'd once been, for Alicia McGowan, Hunter's mother. This knowledge was absolute. It fit as cleanly into the puzzle of her life as her being here in 1906.

"Our father was forced to marry an 'appropriate' person," Justine continued. "She ended up hating him. Your mother hated your father."

That's what she'd just felt. Hatred and disgust. And she knew it was true. She waited for the flicker of acknowledgement in Hunter's eyes.

When he blinked, she asked, "Is that what you want for Caroline?" She stood up, placing the invitation on the coffee table. "You're a good man, Hunter. You're just a bit confused. Those people, your parents, they set a very bad example of what love is and what's right and wrong. You need to make a decision here and I hope you do so with your heart and not with your head."

Sixty-Eight

"Will he be there?"

Justine had just arrived to find Maggie sitting at the table in Caroline's kitchen as the two discussed plans for the wedding. Lacking a mother who might have assumed the role, Maggie had stepped in to help organize, making everything run much more smoothly.

"I don't know," Justine replied to her sister's urgent question. "I honestly don't know, sweetheart."

Caroline looked crestfallen.

"He's confused." Justine explained.

"He's angry and he hates me."

"No. If he hates anyone, it's probably himself."

"What's that mean?"

"I tell you what," Justine offered, "if your brother can't give you away, how about your sister?

"You mean …?"

"Why not? I'm family. I'd be proud to walk you down the aisle."

"What would the Minister think?"

"The Minister's already made a great dispensation, don't ya know …" Maggie interjected. "This would be a small thing by comparison."

"And that from a Roman Catholic," Justine conferred.

"Don't you be speaking ill …" Maggie warned.

"Far be it from me …" Justine countered, smiling at her friend.

"It *is* a great thing he's done, agreeing ta marry a non-believer in his church!" Maggie instructed.

"Yes, it is. And I'm glad Caroline gave up the idea of being married in her own church and found the Calvary Church instead."

"I can see it from my bedroom." Caroline enthused. "Dušan said it was a sign!"

"And I'm delighted Dušan believes in a Great Spirit over a specific God and is happy to be married by an Episcopal Minister," Justine added. "And I'm happy to give you away, Caroline. If you agree."

They'd given Matilde the day off and, in her customary manner, Maggie had taken over the kitchen.

Moving to the stove to reheat water for tea, she said, "We've got another problem."

"My dress," Caroline moaned. "No one's available."

"More like no one wants the challenge of creating something for such an important personage at such short notice."

"I'm not important," Caroline insisted with complete innocence

Justine and Maggie exchanged a look. It was this genuine lack of guile that made Caroline so appealing and sometimes, so frustrating.

"Hmm …" Justine said. "I've got an idea…"

With a worried look, Maggie watched Justine pick up the telephone, whispering under her breath, "Jesus protect us."

The next morning, Alexander arrived with Camille and a youngish man dressed in a relatively new suit, with a pink cravat at his neck and his long hair brushed back and greased to his head. He cut an unusual but jaunty style.

"Caroline," Justine said, "This is *Madame Camille*. She is a personal friend and an accomplished dress designer and lace maker." Justine prayed the first statement was as true as the second.

"So nice to meet you," Caroline enthused, willing as she was to accept everyone. "Thank you so much for being available to create my wedding dress."

"It is *mon plaiser, Madamoiselle*," Camille replied, trying to overcome her nerves and appear to be what Justine said she was.

"And this is Madame's assistant, *Monsieur Delphine*," Justine went on, introducing Delphine in his new incarnation.

Justine had arrived the afternoon before at the door of the house where Raphael had previously been held captive. She was surprised when Delphine himself answered the door. As it was Sunday everyone, it seemed was out or asleep. Mrs. Tittle was, in fact, attending church. Justine didn't think any amount of holy water could absolve that woman but she said a grateful prayer for her absence.

Justine ascertained her suspicion that Delphine did have sewing skills and had designed and created the outfits he wore in his current job as a male prostitute. Then she presented her proposal to him, underscoring that he was to do exactly as he was told and not breathe a word about his former occupation.

Delphine assured her with a wry smile that he was more than accustomed to doing as he was told. He went back inside the house and returned with a sewing machine. While it wasn't his, he assured Justine that he had more than earned it.

Justine insisted that Camille come alone, without Sianna, who was presenting more and more of a challenge for everyone. On the ride to Caroline's house, Delphine had thoroughly endeared himself to Camille not only because of his funnily accented but mostly fluent French, but because he really was qualified to act as her assistant. After a visit to the bathhouse and tailor, he presented himself as Monsieur

Delphine with an absolute determination to succeed and an ingrained ability to please.

Camille spread out drawings of wedding dresses on the table and Caroline was pouring over them with animated 'oohs and aahs'.

"They're all so beautiful, I don't know which to choose," she enthused.

"If I may, *Mademoiselle* …?" Delphine asked.

"Yes. Please," Caroline agreed.

Delphine held up two of Camille's drawings. "I can say with absolute conviction that either of these beautiful confections will look stunning on *Mademoiselle*. This one will flatter her lovely, long neck and this will accentuate her attractive curves."

These comments might have sounded inappropriate coming from any other man. Somehow Delphine said them in a way that was truthful, acceptable, helpful and flattering all at the same time.

"Where did you find him?" Maggie asked, surprised at her approval of Delphine.

Justine smiled smugly.

Sixty-Nine

Justine had made a final visit to Mr Brewster to arrange for the transfer of ownership of the brownstone on Hicks Street into Maggie's possession. She'd apportioned some of her money to Maggie and some of it to Alexander. Her instructions were that Mr Brewster was to continue to oversee their financial affairs and invest the remaining money on their behalf. Her instructions were that on a certain date, Mr Brewster would relay this information to them. By that time Justine would be gone.

Alexander brought them home and was seeing to the delivery of a new automobile to add to his fleet. With Justine's support, he and Maggie had gone into business. Maggie wasn't as excited about the car itself as she was about the prospect of making money. She had absolute confidence in Alexander and as Justine was well aware, Maggie was a skilled gambler.

The house seemed unusually quite.

"Sianna?" Maggie called out, moving towards the kitchen. "Where is … ?"

Her words were cut short by what she saw.

"What's wrong?" Justine asked drawn into the kitchen by the shocked look on Maggie's face.

The kitchen had been thoroughly ransacked, with towels spilling from drawers and pots and pans pulled down and upturned. Maggie stood in the middle of the chaos, holding the brown ceramic jar into which she put the household funds. It was empty.

"Sianna?" she asked. "Or Sasha?"

"Before we jump to conclusions," Justine advised, "We should see if they're in school."

They hurried across the street and were let in by Dr Feingold, himself, who led them to the back of the house and into the classroom. It was late in the day and the room, though well heated was filled with the cold, grey light of a long winter's afternoon. Rachel stood at the blackboard looking unusually strained. Neither Sasha nor Sianna were present.

"I'm very sorry to interrupt…" Justine began but before she could finish, Rachel winced in pain, shut her eyes and held her jaw. "Are you alright?" Justine asked, clearly seeing that she wasn't."

"I think we will end our class today," Rachel said through clenched teeth to the few students present, ignoring Justine altogether.

There were a couple of new faces Justine didn't recognize, including two teenage boys and a girl about Maggie's age. Justine was delighted that Rachel was expanding her teaching to a wider community than just her neighbors across the street.

She stopped Anzelika at the door.

"Do you know where your brother is, Anzel?" Justine asked, gently.

The answer came in the form of clearly written letters on her small blackboard.

"With Papa," it said.

"Thank you. Your writing is very nice," Justine added.

She was rewarded with a rare smile, which softened Anzelika's features.

"Do you know where Sianna is?"

Anzelika shrugged, her face shutting down again. Sianna was not someone people warmed to.

"Gone," Rosa whispered as she joined her daughter in the doorway.

"What do you mean, gone?" Maggie asked

"She gone. Camille go with you. She get mad. She go."

"When?"

"This morning. I see her get into cab, with big bag…"

"Yes. I noticed her too," Dr Feingold said.

"Oh, dear God, she's got money to take a cab!" Maggie fretted. "What else did she take I wonder?"

"You not know, she go?" Rosa worried.

"It's alright, Rosa," Justine said.

"She's stolen from you?" Dr Feingold asked.

"Let's call it payment," Justine replied. "I don't want any trouble and it's probably just as well."

"That girl bad story," Rosa confirmed, shaking her head.

"Yes," Justine confirmed. "She was bad news."

"Yes. Bad news." Rosa agreed. "Thank you, Miss Feingold," Rosa raised her voice sincerely to Rachel, taking Anzelika's arm as they left.

The moment the students were gone, Rachel collapsed into a chair, her hand once again grasping the side of her face as she moaned in pain.

Dr Feingold moved to his wife, placing a comforting hand on her shoulder.

"She has a bad tooth," he explained, "Which she will not let me pull because she refuses to use Cocaine as an anaesthetic."

"Cocaine? Is that what you use?" Justine asked, surprised.

He spread his hands as if to say, 'what else'.

"For a clever woman," he said to his wife, "You're not very smart. This tooth is not getting any better."

"It's addictive!" Rachel managed to argue. "And very bad if ..." but the pain cut her short.

"It's very bad if you want to have children," Maggie piped in.

Rachel nodded gratefully in agreement. Dr. Feingold shot Maggie a frustrated look.

"Sorry," Maggie said "But me neighbor back home got herself in a very bad way..."

"There is an alternative," Justine offered.

Everyone looked at her expectantly.

"It's ... well, you may find it ... at the least unconventional ... at the worst a little strange. But it works. I can almost guarantee you that!"

As Maggie and Justine were exiting the Feingold's house, Alexander was pulling up in the carriage. Maggie wanted to return home to investigate Sianna's disappearance so Alexander drove Justine quickly to Grace Court.

He couldn't pull into the narrow alleyway where Zhang had his store so she got out and walked. She passed the quaint shop with the curved front windows, facing the corner. It was empty and dark. This oddly shaped building didn't exist in her time. Someone had torn it down and put up something ugly in its place.

Down the darkened alley, she knocked once and was startled when Zhang Ming answered immediately, as if he'd been expecting her. His dark, slanted eyes studied her then he nodded, approving her admittance.

The shop was closed so there was no warming brazier glowing in the corner. She stood in the dark with the exotic tang of Chinese medicinal herbs scenting the air.

There wasn't time for pleasantries, so Justine just launched into the reason for her presence:

"Do you or your grandfather practice Zhēn cì?"

Seventy

The herbal aromas clung to Zhang Zhu and filled the air as Justine, Ming and his grandfather rode back to Hicks Street. The little bearded man seemed dwarfed by the plush seats and velvet curtains of the carriage but Justine knew his size to be deceptive. His piercing stare didn't waver as the carriage bumped along the cobbled streets.

"Thank you, Zhang Zhu, for coming. I'm sure Dr Feingold will be delighted to meet you," Justine said, uncomfortably.

Ming translated but the old man continued to watch her.

"I'm not so sure about his wife, however…" She confided to Ming.

Zhang Zhu spoke and she sensed in her bones it wasn't about the Feingolds.

"He says, you should take your child and go home," Ming translated.

Justine's hand flew involuntarily to her womb, then, realizing she'd confirmed his suspicions, laced her fingers together firmly in her lap. The carriage stopped.

Justine grabbed Ming's arm before he could get out, "Please. No one else knows. I'd like to keep it that way!"

Ming nodded, stepping out to assist his grandfather.

They gathered in Dr. Feingold's office. The warmth and order of the room was a welcome change from the chill and uneasiness created by Zhang Zhu on the ride over. However, his presence and foreignness was clearly disconcerting Rachel, who'd not moved in her customary way to welcome the Zhangs.

"Dr. Zhang is a master of Zhēn cì." Justine explained. "In English, I believe it's called Acupuncture. It's an ancient Chinese practice of inserting really fine needles through the skin at specific points to relieve pain and promote healing."

When she'd said, 'inserting needles' Rachel had vocally gasped and Dr. Feingold looked very concerned.

Ming interrupted Justine with his soothing voice, "There is no pain," he said to Rachel. "I assure you. As Miss Justine said, my grandfather is a master of Zhēn cì. In China we do surgery using the needles and the patient feels nothing."

"I appreciate what you're offering and I am certainly professionally very curious ..." Dr Feingold began.

"Dr Zhang, why don't you demonstrate on me?" Justine offered.

410

"NO!" Rachel insisted, but this was as much as she could say before the pain in her tooth seared through her skull and she collapsed back in her chair.

Justine went to her. She hadn't warmed to this haughty, intelligent woman but a person in pain is always vulnerable and that overrode any prior feelings.

"It's okay, Rachel. I've had acupuncture before. It's completely painless and it can actually numb sensation so the Doctor can remove your tooth."

Still grasping her painful jaw, Rachel shook her head fiercely, her dark eyes boring into Justine in stubborn refusal.

"For a smart woman, you're being pretty stupid," Justine retorted, frustrated more with Rachel's discomfort than with her stubbornness. Before anyone could intervene, Justine plopped down on the fainting couch near the hearth, saying "Zhang Zhu, please show this stubborn woman what your needles can do!"

Everyone took a breath waiting for someone to speak or move. When no one did, Zhang Zhu took Justine's wrist, feeling for her inner pulse. Surprising everyone, Dr. Feingold took Justine's other hand and felt for her heart pulse.

Zhang Ming produced a silk box from inside his jacket and opened it on the table. His Grandfather selected a hair-fine needle from the box and inserted it into Justine's wrist, followed by one to the center of her palm and one at the base of the thumb.

In spite of himself, Dr. Feingold watched intently, observing Zhang Zhu and noting the change in Justine's pulse.

Zhang Zhu spoke and Ming translated.

"My Grandfather says there are points he cannot get to because of the clothing…"

"Shall I take something off?" Justine asked, beginning to feel very relaxed and forgetting where she was.

"Not necessary," Ming replied.

Zhang Zhu inserted three more needles to the inner wall of Justine's ear.

"You cannot feel these needles?" Dr. Feingold asked.

"No. It feels lovely …" Justine said, closing her eyes.

"Your pulse has slowed surprisingly," he murmured, in wonder.

"Yes …. slowed…" Justine murmured, feeling herself drifting.

She wasn't sure how much time had passed when she resurfaced from a deep slumber. Ming was standing over her twisting a needle in her hand. She glanced over to see Rachel on the examining table with needles inserted at various places on her body - just below her cheeks, along her jaw, towards the back of her upper arm, which had been removed from the blouse she was wearing. Her feet were exposed and lined with needles.

Justine looked away. Seeing Rachel's naked feet seemed strangely too intrusive. Ming removed the last needle from Justine's hand.

"Is the pain gone, my dear?"

It was Dr Feingold speaking gently to Rachel.

"Yes? Are you ready for me to pull that tooth?"

Justine sat up. Dr Feingold was holding a long metal instrument that looked like something used for torture.

Zhang Zhu spoke.

"If you don't mind, Dr. Feingold," Ming interrupted. "My grand-father would like to wait a moment longer."

Justine stood up. She still felt like she was floating, but knew she had to get out of the room. Whether the acupuncture had worked or not, Dr. Feingold was going to use that terrible instrument to pull that tooth and Rachel was going to let him.

Justine made it to the foyer when she heard Ming say:

"Yes, she is ready now."

She hurried out the front door and into the clear, cold night. She didn't hear screams but prayed for Rachel anyway and said another prayer of thanks for 21st Century dentistry and novocaine.

Seventy-One

"Someone needs to tell them what it's really like!"

Justine had just entered the small room adjacent to Caroline's bedroom. The fire was crackling in the small hearth and though it was still afternoon, the curtains were shut against the persistent winter's chill. Caroline had designed this room and thus it was filled with flowered upholstery covering soft, comfy sofas and chairs with lace doyleys on every possible surface. Much of that had been removed to fashion a temporary sewing room in which Camille and Delphine could create her wedding gown.

Delphine didn't look up from what he was cutting, leaning over the table in intense concentration. But there was no one else in room so it must have been he who spoke.

Justine halted by the side of the table and he glanced up, looking at her significantly.

"Someone needs to tell them the truth," he said. "About sex." He focused again on his cutting. "I was 6 when my uncle took me for the first time. It was painful and shameful…"

"And wrong," Justine interjected, outraged.

"Yes. Thank you," he conceded. "But the thing is later on no one told me how it could be. That it could be something nice and, well, loving…" He looked at her again. "Someone needs to tell young Caroline. They've been sharing stupid lies with each other all morning. "

He would have said more but Caroline herself entered, followed by Camille. Maggie was staying in the house to over see the wedding festivities and she sat in one of the chairs making notations in the small leather book, which, now she could write, was with her at all times. Camille sat in the opposite chair her tatting ring in her hand like a natural extension of her body. Caroline stood near the fire.

Justine didn't move, troubled by Delphine's words. Then she heard in her head a now familiar angry and resentful voice say, "No one told me anything. Let her figure it out for herself!" It was Mrs. McGowan, Caroline's mother. Of that Justine was now certain. As she was equally certain that she heard this voice because it was a part of her speaking. And her certainty was causing her to draw unexpected conclusions.

Matilde arrived pushing a tray of drinks, tea and sandwiches. Around her neck was a length of fabric fashioned as a sling out of which the head of a small, grey kitten emerged. It had mysteriously appeared a week ago, alone, shivering and hungry. Caroline and Matilde instantly adopted the bedraggled thing, naming it Susan B. Anthony after the infamous suffragette.

This small, furry female had indeed found emancipation in this house - it was eating like a queen and being carried about like a Kangaroo's joey. Witnessing how this place was fast becoming a home filled Justine with a deep sense of contentment. She was also heartened by the choice of name for the kitten. Her little sister's life was moving in an interesting direction.

"Would anyone like a refreshment?" Matilde asked. "In honor of our Irish friend, I have whisky and tea."

"I'd like a whisky, thank you, Matilde," Justine said, a bit too eagerly.

"I'll do the same," Maggie agreed heartily, not looking up from her notes.

Matilde poured a third whisky for Delphine placing it carefully on the table next to him.

"Someone should tell them," Delphine repeated.

Justine moved to the window away from the others, hoping there was someone else to take on this delicate task.

"What? Tell them what?" Caroline wanted to know with her puppy like enthusiasm.

Justine gulped down her drink, casting a resentful eye at Delphine.

"Caroline, sweetheart, come here with me," she said, sitting on the sofa and patting the cushion beside her.

Caroline plopped herself down. Her love for Justine was absolute and added to the burden Justine felt. How to speak about such things? She'd been given a cursory education about sex in school, but that was really more biology than the finer details of a relationship between a man and a woman.

'... *about love*' Delphine had said. Had she ever been with a man and called it love? She was carrying James' baby but that had been more passion than anything else. Certainly it had been the most passion she'd ever experienced - but not love. It was true that she probably knew more about the act of sex than anyone in the room, except Delphine of course. She glanced at him again, but his back was turned as he busied himself with his task.

She looked at Caroline's lovely, expectant face. Caroline was a virgin. It was to be assumed that the other women in the room were too. In fact, they would all assume the same about her. Delphine knew otherwise and had cleverly pushed her into this awkward position. However, when she considered the alternative – that Caroline would go to her wedding bed uncertain and afraid – Justine realized she had no choice. She wasn't Mrs. McGowan with a resentful axe to grind, she was Caroline's half-sister from another time when women knew about such things.

"I want to speak with you about tomorrow night," Justine began.

"You mean the party?" Caroline asked. "Maggie's got that all under control. Don't you Maggie, dear?"

Maggie was looking quizzically at Justine. "I don't think she means the party, Caro. I think she means tomorrow night. In there." Maggie's head nodded in the direction of Caroline's bedroom.

"Oh!" Caroline blushed, staring down at her hands now clutched in her lap.

Justine shot Maggie a hard stare then reached out to grasp Caroline's fist comfortingly in her own.

"It's okay, sweetie. I just want to try and explain so that it can be the 'nice and loving' experience it should be." She heard herself repeating Delphine's words.

Justine was aware that the energy in the room had subtly shifted. Matilde placed a cup of tea on the table for Caroline and was moving very slowly back to her tray, stroking the kitten. Camille hadn't looked up from her lace, but was sitting very still, as if listening with her whole body. Maggie leaned forward, openly interested but with eyebrows raised as if to say, 'well I should have expected this from you as well'.

Justine squeezed Caroline's hands again. When she began to speak, it was as if she were being guided because the words came easily, gently and appropriately and Caroline was able to eagerly listen and gratefully learn.

When she stopped speaking, Caroline asked a few questions and Justine answered as best she could.

She was aware that Maggie was sitting back in her chair, listening, absorbing but also regarding Justine in yet another new light. Would this subject be the one that broke the back of her willingness to accept Justine and continue to love her?

Camille mumbled something, not looking up from her lace.

"Sorry, Camille. I didn't hear what you said?" Justine replied, avoiding Maggie's eyes.

"She wants to know," Delphine piped in, "... if it's like you de-scribe only if there's love?"

No one seemed the least bit concerned that Delphine, a man, was privy to this entire conversation. He had that knack for blending in, in spite of how very, very different he was. They all turned to Justine, awaiting her reply.

Again she glanced at Delphine who shot her a mischievous grin. She was about to ask his thoughts on the subject, but instead found herself saying,

"The whole purpose is the expression of love and the desire for connection. It's not really worth it otherwise."

She was surprised at the conviction in her voice. When she looked back, Delphine had a tear rolling down his face. Quickly wiping it away he said:

"Thank you for your illuminating words. I wonder if you would you care to try this on?"

With a flourish he produced the item he'd been working on - a bolero style jacket in the same lavender silk as her maid-of-honor dress, with delicate black velvet appliqué detail shot with silver threads and tiny beads that glittered in the firelight.

Justine was relieved to move on from the topic of conversation and joined Delphine in front of the full-length mirror. He helped her into the jacket and she studied her reflection. It had never been easy for her to find clothes that fit and flattered at the same time. This piece did both. It was quite simply, exquisite.

Her hands explored the intricate work, caressing the sheer beauty of the piece. Her eyes met his in the mirror. Her peripheral vision diminished suddenly as if someone had dimmed the lights and his face seemed to morph into another well-known and much-loved one. Without thinking, tears chocking her words, she whispered:

"Thank you, Paul. It is the most beautiful thing anyone has ever made for me!"

"Well, I don't know who Paul is," Delphine, demurred "but I can tell you it was my great pleasure to create this!"

He was fussing with the drape of the jacket on her shoulders. She grabbed his hands, so very like Paul's with long, capable fingers that fluttered and flitted and created lovely things. The room returned to normal and Paul's older face softened back into that of Delphine and the nausea that accompanied these 'visions', was settling.

"Thank you Delphine. I will treasure this always!"

"*Mademoiselle*," Camille, said suddenly, standing up. "*Alors. C'est fini!*"

Camille beckoned Caroline. The lace she'd been working on was now attached to a hair comb, which she inserted into Caroline's head of long, curly hair. Then opening a slender box, she produced the length of lace Justine had discovered hidden in her clothing. Unfolding it reverently she attached it to the back of the comb, allowing it to cascade down Caroline's back, almost to the floor.

Camille guided Caroline to the mirror, showing how the small front lace would drape over Caroline's face until Dušan pulled it back once they were married. But it was the long length of veil that took everyone's breath away. Caroline kept twisting and turning to behold its beauty.

"Oh, my," she declared. "Just look how beautiful it is!"

Justine was trying to catch Camille's eye. This length of lace was a kind of family heirloom for her. But Camille, like everyone else, was watching the young bride and relishing her joy. So Justine focused on her sister, saying:

"Yes. Yes it is. Aren't we lucky to have such wonderful artists, designing your wedding dress!"

"And yours," Caroline gushed, but she couldn't quite take her eyes off the long, lacy veil.

Camille was speaking now in French and Delphine began to translate.

"She says that after the wedding, this veil should hang in your bedroom. It will bring blessings into your life."

Caroline gasped, looking wide-eyed at Camille, then spontaneously hugged her, engulfing the smaller woman in her arms.

"Thank you. Thank you. Thank you," Caroline spluttered. "This is going to be the best wedding I'll ever have!" Then, realizing what she'd said, she clamped an embarrassed hand over her mouth, blushing and giggling.

As Camille gently removed the veil, Caroline sighed, "It would be perfectly perfect if only …."

Justine wrapped an arm around her sister, "There's still time, sweetheart. Maybe he'll come…"

Seventy-Two

Justine felt the luxurious brush of heavy silk against her legs. This dress and Delphine's jacket were possibly the most beautiful things she'd ever worn. The bodice of the dress was simple lavender silk trimmed in black velvet with lace, draping and cascading from her cleavage. Her waist was enhanced with a wide belt of black velvet and the skirt draped to the floor, decorated like the jacket with black velvet appliqué, shot with silver threads and tiny beads.

She carried her cup of tea to the French doors overlooking Gramercy Square. A brilliant winter sun was sparkling on frost clinging to bare branches and lining park benches. A nanny pushed a stroller on the sidewalk below, her dark felt hat tied firmly beneath her chin. Justine touched her belly. Her heart was full with the simple pleasure of being inside this beautiful home, a building she'd so often admired, on the morning of her sister's wedding.

She wore a diamond bracelet and earrings, borrowed from the many beautiful pieces bought by her father and left for her mother. The diamond glinted now in the sunshine, casting a small colourful rainbow on the glass.

Justine had lain awake many nights since arriving in this time trying to understand the inexplicable things she'd experienced and observed.

Of course, being here was utterly unfathomable – nonetheless every-thing her senses told her was that it was real - she was here. What troubled her was an explanation for the absolute knowing she had of certain things and the uncanny way people's faces morphed in and out of faces she knew from her own time.

Justine sipped her tea, causing the diamond bracelet to move and the rainbow to dance across the glass pane. The rainbow comes from a single source, she mused, watching the sunlight glowing through the diamond. She felt she was on the brink of understanding something very important as she studied the light splitting into an exquisite array of uniquely different colors - all coming from the same source, but each color individual and distinct.

She jangled the bracelet and watched the rainbow skip across the glass – its colors remaining intact – separate from each other but from the same source. What's the source? She wondered. What's our Source?

Maggie bustled in, wearing a dark green raw silk dress designed by Delphine specifically for her. It fetchingly accentuated her hourglass figure and highlighted her alabaster skin. With her abundant red hair piled tastefully on top of her head and finished with a green velvet rib-bon, she looked very much the well-to-do woman that she now was. She handed Justine a pair of black leather gloves.

"You're going to need these," Maggie insisted. "I've never known a church to be warm. It's how the priests keep the parishioners awake." She bustled out again because, like her namesake 100 years from now, Maggie was always on the move.

Maggie went to church and believed in a God and a Soul. Her religion couldn't explain Justine's existence in this time, but maybe it could explain the other things Justine was pondering. Maybe the existence of a Soul was the explanation. Maybe the Soul was the Source – as the sunlight was for the rainbow.

What Justine sensed so powerfully was that Raphael was somehow from the same source as her mother and Margaret, who was now living in the basement apartment in the future, was from the same soul as Maggie. She knew, without knowing how she knew, that Ducky and Alexander were from the same origin as were Paul and Delphine.

And strangest of all was the knowing that she, herself was bizarrely but inescapably from the same whatever as Mrs McGowan, her father's wife and the mother of Hunter and Caroline. She knew things only Mrs McGowan could have known and she'd heard voices in her head that felt connected to what Mrs. McGowan thought and felt.

So, she ruminated, perhaps each one of us has a Soul that splits into a variety of lifetimes, and manifests like the unique colors of the rainbow.

She caressed the soft leather gloves and smiled. If this were true then she would never lose them. All these beloved people who were with her now, would be with her then. And if Mrs McGowan had made mistakes, then Justine was righting some of them. Redressing Karma. This wedding was proof of that.

The doorbell interrupted her thoughts but it was Matilde's sharp scream that sent Justine hurrying to the foyer. First she saw Matilde running in fear towards the kitchen, then she saw the tall figure of her brother, Hunter, followed by Raphael.

"Hunter!" Justine exclaimed.

He was scowling resentfully at the retreating Matilde then shifted his dark gaze onto Justine.

"Yes. It's me," he replied haughtily. "I was asked to escort my sister down the aisle."

He brushed past her into the living room, moving directly to the piano.

Sweeping his hands across its ebony surface he declared," Well, I see he's already moved in!"

"Hunter," Justine hissed moving quickly to his side. "If you're going to be unpleasant, you are not welcome here!"

"Good morning, Miss Caroline. You look beautiful." It was Raphael speaking pointedly from the foyer.

Hunter strode past Justine, coming to an abrupt standstill in the arched entry, staring up the staircase. Justine followed him and was equally taken aback by the vision of Caroline at the top of the stairs.

Camille and Delphine were arranging her wedding dress and veil to prevent a hazardous descent. She looked at once like an ethereal fantasy in ivory silk and cascading lace, her blond hair curling angelically around her cherubic face and at the same time more than ever like a grown woman, quietly confident and self-possessed.

"Hunter," she said, not with the gushing or giggling one had come to expect from Caroline, but with a calm delight and gratitude.

And it was clear from his silence and the tears welling in his eyes, that Caroline's brother was captivated by his sister's transformation.

They all watched as she made her way slowly and gracefully down the staircase, linking her hand around Hunter's arm.

"I'm SO glad you're here," she said.

With eyes only for each other, he guided her out the door to the carriage Alexander had waiting.

Justine sighed. "May I join you in a carriage?" she asked Raphael, as she collected her handbag and shawl.

The church was only a few blocks away, but Alexander had arranged transport for the wedding party so that the bride arrived with proper pomp and circumstance. No one did pomp and circumstance quite like Alexander Alexandrovich.

Once inside the carriage, Raphael couldn't help but ask, "Delphine...?"

"Yes. I got him out of that hell hole as well."

"I'm glad. He would have died there. But, why? Why have you done so much to help us?

"He's very talented," Justine replied, avoiding his real question. "He made my jacket, you know, and assisted with the wedding dress. I think he's got a career ahead of him – if ..."

The carriage lurched forward and they were thrown momentarily together.

"There isn't much time," Justine stated, as she reached inside her handbag withdrawing Hunter's pocket watch and an envelope. Handing the watch to Raphael, she said, "I would like you to hang on to this and give it to Hunter when you feel the time is right."

"How did you get this back?" he asked, amazed.

"It's probably better if you didn't ask," she replied, thinking momentarily of Kendall Shaw tied up in the Silent Room, then wiping the awful memory from her mind. "Hunter needs to know he's loved," was the most she would say.

Raphael pocketed the watch, nodding in agreement.

Justine studied the envelope, running her hand across its smooth surface. This is the beginning, she thought to herself - the beginning of the end of her time in this time.

"You'll see that I went to the post office and had yesterday's date stamped on this," she explained, handing him the envelope. "I want there to be no doubt about what's written inside."

"This sounds serious," Raphael commented.

"Yes. It is. This is for Hunter but I'm asking you to be responsible for it. On April 18th, I want you to open this envelope and I want you and Hunter to take very seriously what's in there! This is just for the two of you so I suggest you not share it with anyone else. You'll understand why once you've read it."

He looked at the envelope.

"Will you promise to do this?" Justine asked.

"Miss Justine, I'll do anything you ask."

She glanced at his exquisite face, etched now with lines of concern, his marble blue eyes full of past hurt and present hope. She believed him and was comforted that she'd made the right decision about him. However difficult Hunter might be, Raphael's gratitude secured his commitment.

"How's it going?" she asked, indicating the carriage in front of them, carrying Caroline and Hunter.

"We've had a drink or two together and he opens up a bit then. I will take care of him as you've asked, but - I can't stop myself from loving him as well."

She grasped his arm. "I couldn't have hoped for anything better and I pray he'll allow himself to feel the same one day!"

"I've never had such a conversation with anyone before," Raphael declared. "Why do you not judge me and find me evil?"

"It's a long story," she answered. "Suffice to say, I was raised by two men. Two men who love each other still!"

He looked at her strangely and she realized she'd said too much. Luckily they'd arrived at the church, curtailing the need for further explanation.

Seventy-Three

The Calvary was the church of the Roosevelts, The Astors, the Vanderbilts and now Caroline McGowan, soon to become Mrs Caroline Kucera. Its two magnificent wooden spires had been removed in the last century when they became unstable. But the proud octagonal bases remained, framing the heavy wooden doors, which were flung open to welcome the wedding guests.

Justine was glad she wasn't leading her sister down the aisle. While it went without saying that she would be here for this wedding, she wouldn't be here for much longer and she preferred the attention remain on Caroline and Dušan.

She allowed Raphael to escort her past the soaring stone arches, to the head of the nave where she sat in the front row. Morning sunshine shone through stained glass windows lighting up the towering arched wooden ceilings and warm ivory painted walls. The church was already full and Justine was grateful for the warmth of so many bodies.

The Priest, an older man with a round, cheery face was speaking with Dušan. Dušan looked every bit the fairytale groom with his dark hair combed back off his pleasingly angular face and dressed in morning suit, the tails of which perfectly draped his tall, lean figure. He noticed Justine and, unaware of Caroline and Hunter's arrival, was about to question her when the organ struck the first chord of the wedding march and all eyes turned towards the wedding procession.

Hunter gave his sister graciously away to her new husband without any indication of his true feelings for Dušan. When he came to sit next to Justine, she squeezed his arm gratefully. As the ceremony continued, she laced her fingers companionably through his, feeling the dry, coolness of his hands, holding on to his realness because she knew he was leaving immediately after the ceremony. This would be the last time she would touch him or see him, ever again. Hunter, my brother, she said to herself and her heart surged as tears rolled down her cheeks. And through the tears she saw Dušan pull back the small lace veil and lean down to kiss his bride full on the lips.

Justine remained seated as the music again began to play and the happy couple strode arm in arm back down the aisle. Raphael appeared beneath an archway and Hunter rose with a smile, his fingers going to his lips as if he were about to blow a kiss. Aware that Justine was watching him, he stopped himself.

She wrapped her arms around him, whispering in his ear, "Goodbye, Hunter. Bon Voyage."

He hugged her back then quickly made his way past Raphael and out of the Church. Raphael paused, placing his hand on his heart as if to say, 'thank-you' and to indicate the envelope was safely in his possession.

Justine raised her fingers to her lips and turning her palm towards him, sent him a kiss. Then he too was gone. Their boat sailed that evening to France. She sent them a prayer for happiness and safety. Maybe today, in the church, God was listening.

Maggie appeared at her side and Justine accepted the white handker-chief she offered to blot the tears and pull herself together.

"I feel like a walk," she announced. "I know Alexander has pre-pared transport ...."

"Actually, I felt like walking too," Maggie confirmed. "It's a per-fect winter's day and love is in the air!'

"That sounds a lot like sentimentality," Justine teased, as they linked arms and emerged from the church into a glorious crystal clear morning.

"We Irish may be practical, but we've got the soul of the poet!" Maggie declared.

New York winters could be harsh and prolonged and the winter of 1906 was no exception. But on a day like today with the sun shining benefi-cently down and the crispness in the air refreshing rather than bitter, it was good to be alive. To have such a day out of time, with people she'd come to love and cherish, was a gift beyond measure. Justine's heart lifted. This was what all the New Age teaching had been about – stay-ing in the moment. This moment, with the warmth of her friend by her side, strolling in trusting silence was one she would treasure for all eternity.

Using the lovely upstairs bathroom she'd convinced Caroline to in-stall, she thanked God and Alexander for indoor plumbing. When she turned off the water in the little sink she thought she heard crying in the room next door.

She made her way into the cosy sitting room next to Caroline's bedroom. It had been scrupulously cleared of all pre-wedding preparations except for Delphine's sewing machine. And it was he who Justine found huddled over his machine, weeping. She went to his side and wrapped a comforting arm around his too thin shoulders.

Delphine immediately straightened his back, hastily wiping tears from his cheeks, embarrassed by his vulnerability.

"I'm sorry," he blustered.

"What's wrong, Delphine? Today was a great success."

"Yes. Yes, it was. A success." He busied himself securing the sewing machine into its case.

"I'm glad to find you here," Justine said, gently. "I wanted to speak with you. Unfortunately, Camille's friend Sianna has left. Well, that's putting it lightly. She stole money from Maggie and has disappeared."

He stopped what he was doing to look at her, as if to say, 'what does this have to do with me?'

"Camille is – rather delicate. I'm not sure how she's going to take this news. I think she trusts you and you seem to have a good working relationship."

"Yes. We had a good working relationship." He sighed.

"What do mean – had?"

"Well, we've done what you asked and ... that's, that."

"You're not going to continue? But, I'd hoped this would be a future – for you both...!"

"You, what? Continue? How?"

"Well, I'd hoped you'd come back with us tonight to take care of Camille and then in the morning – there's a small shop for rent – it's in Brooklyn but that probably makes it more affordable..."

"A shop? For Camille and me? But – how?"

"Well, you probably should go downstairs and find out – Camille's being inundated by pushy mothers and wealthy daughters who want dresses as unique and beautiful as what you created for Caroline."

He shook his head in disbelief but rushed to the landing from where one could see down into the expansive foyer. There, indeed, was tiny Camille surrounded by loud and insistent women, clamouring for her attention.

"Ladies!" he shouted, clapping his hands to get their attention, in his best Monsieur Delphine voice. "Ladies, Madame Camille will be opening her new shop soon," he advised, descending swiftly down the stairs to place himself between poor, overwhelmed Camille and this gaggle of demanding women. "And when that exciting event occurs you will be welcome as our special première clientele!" Removing a notebook from his jacket, he continued. "Allow me in the meantime, to take down your names so that I can personally invite you to our grand opening."

Justine watched from the landing, smiling and shaking her head. Delphine's past survival depended on showmanship and his talent and that same ability to charm would secure his future. And he would protect fragile Camille with his life.

The party was underway in the living room, with Dušan's musicians providing lively ambience. Matilde had brought together a couple of Caroline's local friends' maids and they were serving tea and champagne.

Dušan led his new bride gracefully around the small dance floor. Justine was sitting near the piano, watching James dancing with Maggie. He was leaning close, whispering something in her ear that made Maggie blush and playfully reprimand him with a slap to his arm. But she didn't let go as he twirled her expertly around the floor.

"Would you care to dance with an old man?"

Justine looked up to find Mr. Brewster smiling down at her, offering his hand.

"I'd be honored, although I'm afraid I'm not a very good dancer," Justine confessed.

"Well, I'm told I lead sufficiently well…" he replied, humbly.

The truth was Justine had tried ballroom dancing lessons. The voucher for three more classes was at the bottom of a drawer somewhere in her apartment in the future. She sighed. So many unfinished plans. So many false starts. She stood up. Today, in her lovely lavender silk dress on the arm of a well-mannered man, she would dance.

They danced to a waltz; played skilfully by the musicians, with a tempo even a novice might follow. She actually liked to dance but never felt good enough about her ability or her body. Mr. Brewster guided her confidently around the floor affording Justine a bit of belief in her own grace and skill.

When the music ended, Justine thanked him sincerely and accepted a glass of champagne. He was about to propose a toast, when she leaned in and whispered:

"I need to speak with you privately. Would this be a good time?"

"By the seriousness in your tone, I suspect this is business...?"

"Of a sort ..."

"Then why don't we find a quiet room and I will get my son to join us, if you don't mind. He'll be taking over the practice soon ..."

"Of course..."

Justine led the Brewsters through the foyer to a room at the back of the house, which Caroline had saved for Dušan's office. He'd decorated it simply with Bentwood and leather chairs in front of the fireplace, a sleek desk with lovely lines in a rich textured wood against the wall and a baby grand piano near the window. The floor was covered with a plush oriental carpet. It was a welcoming, elegant room, which Dušan was extremely proud of. He'd come a long way from a difficult and tragic past through years of struggle and longing, to today and his marriage to the woman he'd loved in silence for years.

"Miss Justine, I'd like you to meet my eldest son, Richard Brewster," the elder Brewster said, proudly, "… my partner and soon to be sole proprietor of Brewster Attorney-at-Law."

The younger Brewster was a comforting carbon copy of his father. Taller and somewhat less portly, he exuded a similar air of confidence and genuine concern. His grip was warm and strong when he shook Justine's hand.

"I wish to assure you that my father is not relinquishing control quite so soon or so completely," Richard Brewster said with a wry grin and a knowing twinkle in his eye.

"It's important there be a smooth transition when I do finally retire," Brewster the elder asserted. "So I thought it important Richard be here today. Mr McGowan's family continue to be important clients."

"I'm very glad to meet you," Justine said to Richard. "What I'm about to say is difficult and will most likely sound very strange." She turned away to collect her thoughts. "Because I love and care about my brother and sister, I wanted to share this with you, so that you can continue to support and advise them into the future."

She was standing at the window looking out on the back garden. Winter could not hide the beauty that lay in wait for spring, with high bordering hedges, a central gravel pathway leading to an ornate fountain surrounded by rose bushes and a vine covered trellis. It would be glorious when the warm weather arrived. She sighed again. She'd done the best she could for her sister.

"I'm going away," she said. This was the first time she'd said it out loud. "I'm not coming back."

The finality of her words caused tears to spring unexpectedly to her eyes. She took a deep breath and turned to face the two men. Father and son waited respectfully for her to explain such an extreme pronouncement.

"I'm not well …" She let the statement hang in the air. They would fill in their own explanations. "I haven't told Caroline and I'm not going to," Justine continued. "I want her to enjoy her honeymoon to the full. I'm not going to tell Dušan either although I am going to give him a letter just like the one I'm giving you now," she said, producing an envelope from her bag, exactly like the one she'd given Raphael. "This is the last request I will make of my lawyers, who have served my father's family so loyally and well."

She handed the envelope to Mr Brewster.

"I request that you open this letter on the 18th of April this year. When you read what's there, I trust it will explain itself. I fully appreciate that this letter will challenge every rational notion you've ever had. I implore you to take it very, very seriously. It's all unequivocally true!"

Mr Brewster studied Justine for a moment.

"I've had some very unusual clients and rather strange requests over the years, Miss Justine, but I confess the short time I've known you has been the most curious of all."

"I'm sorry to have burdened you, Mr Brewster."

"On the contrary, you've been a breath of fresh air. And your arrival in the lives of Henry's children – that is, your arrival as one his children – has produced nothing but good."

Justine smiled, her heart filling with gratitude for this man.

"My son and I will honor your request and reserve judgment in the belief that your intentions remain good."

"Thank you Mr Brewster. Thank you so much!"

He reached out a hand to shake hers.

"You will be missed. Of that I can assure you," he said.

Instead of taking his hand, she felt compelled to wrap her arms gratefully around his ample form and hug him close. He stiffened in surprise, then chuckled and allowed his arms to reach around and pat her back, comfortingly.

"Would you ask Dušan to meet me in here?" Justine requested, before father and son departed.

Justine took a deep breath. Her plans were moving inexorably forward. Like time. And while she'd travelled back in time, there was no going back on her decision.

She'd convinced Caroline that she and her household should depart early. There was to be a celebration dinner and the dining room, though large, would not accommodate all the guests. Justine was concerned about the ramifications of leaving too obvious a trail of her existence in this time. She'd been able to persuade Caroline that her presence as the 'illegitimate sister' might upset some of her friends and that she should remain in the background as much as possible. She smiled, remembering how Caroline's new found confidence had made this a hard won battle.

Then yesterday, after much coaxing by Maggie, she'd relented to a photo session. It was Maggie's steadfast belief in James' newly acquired photographic skill that caused her to concede. It was clear Maggie was falling for Mr Grey's abundant charms.

An image of James' beautifully naked body and seductive green eyes arose uninvited in Justine's mind and her hand drifted involuntarily to her belly. She moved closer to the fire, away from such thoughts. Maggie and James could be good for each other, Justine told herself. Maggie's strength of character and love might just be able to reform him and Justine genuinely welcomed the thought of James romancing her friend. Maggie deserved the loving a man like that could give.

She sat in one of the Bentwood chairs, running her hands over the exquisite craftsmanship. Not for the first time, a beautiful piece of furniture made her think of Ducky. While memories of James might still be alive inside her, her whole being was longing for her original life, and her family in the future.

She smiled again, reflecting on the photo session, which James had set up in the foyer. It'd been rather strange as one had to sit very, very still for a very, very long time allowing for the necessary light exposure. Justine now understood why people from this era looked so serious in photos. In spite of the beautiful dresses she and Maggie and Caroline were wearing and the lush arrangement of plants and settee James had provided, the sitting and waiting were tedious. Ah, for the days to come of the smart phone and the selfie!

While James' mastery of the visual arts had the same seductive quality as his mastery in the bedroom, it wasn't enough to keep Justine from becoming somewhat giddy. Halfway through the posing she caught both Maggie and Caroline off-guard with bursts of hilarity resulting in at least two shots in which the sitters were uncharacteristically laughing.

Dušan's arrival interrupted her reflections.

"Are you alright?" he asked with genuine concern, moving swiftly to her side.

"Yes. I'm sorry. I didn't mean to worry you."

He sat in the opposite chair not fully convinced, his features sharpened with apprehension.

"I'm truly sorry to interrupt your special day. There's something I need to share with you. But first I want to say how very happy I am, Dušan. True love and marriage don't happen all the time."

His face softened. "It is I who am happy and grateful. To you."

"You and Caroline are going to Italy and then to Prague to see your family," she stated, conversationally.

"Yes," he chuckled. "My parents won't believe how lucky their wayward son has been – finding such a beautiful wife!"

Justine removed another envelope from her bag. Placing it in her lap she said, "You may decide what's inside this envelope concerns your family as well. I want you to believe me – everything written here is absolutely true."

"This sounds ominous."

She held his hands, feeling the strength of his pianist fingers, "As you know better than most, Dušan, life is full of surprises. Some are happy and others can be tragic. Caroline is my sister and I love her more than I can say. You are now my family too and that's why I'm giving you this." She picked up the envelope but, before handing it to him, she demanded, "I want you to promise that you will not open this until April 18th. The reason will be clear once you do. Will you make me that promise?"

He glanced at the white linen envelope then back at Justine. His dark eyes held a comforting depth of intelligence set off with sadness etched at the corners. Dušan was in his 30's and there was grey streaking his hair, adding to his already dignified demeanor. He took the envelope from her and much like Raphael had done, held it to his heart:

"I promise, Miss Justine."

Seventy-Four

That night, alone in her bed, Justine lay awake. Partly it was the muffled sounds from the floor above of Camille crying and Delphine comforting her. When Justine revealed to Camille that Sianna had gone, she seemed shocked but not upset. But when Maggie added that Sianna had stolen money, Camille became very distressed. Justine assured her that it was all right and Maggie softened enough to add that she never intended to call the Police.

Camille's upset was such that Maggie made no comment when Delphine escorted her to the room she'd once shared with Sianna and shut the door behind them.

Maggie was softening to many things and that made Justine's heart ache. She'd been considering the things she would take with her when she left – her mother's portrait and the one James had done of her – she wished there was some way to bundle Maggie up and take her too. Then she remembered what it meant to cross the dateline – the sheer horror of it. She shuddered to think of Maggie in the 21st Century. Justine's mother had adjusted, somehow, to her time in the 20th Century. But things were moving ever more rapidly every year now – technology, social trends, violence. The 21st century would not be easy to adjust to.

The next morning, Justine was greeted in the kitchen by an impatiently waiting group. Delphine and Camille already had their coats on in preparation for departure. Justine noted Camille's red-rimmed eyes. However, in contrast she had a rare look of excitement on her face. Clearly Delphine had found the right words to soothe and refocus her attention. Maggie was hastily washing up the breakfast dishes and was also dressed to go out. But it was Alexander's presence that particularly surprised Justine.

A lone plate with a buttered biscuit sat on the table next to a still steaming cup of tea.

"Biscuits!" she exclaimed, her mouth already watering.

"Not sure it's hot anymore. Some of us've been up for a while…" Maggie commented, wiping her hands and folding away the dishtowel.

Justine knew it was late and she'd promised to accompany Delphine but it had been a particularly bad morning. She'd awoken to the terrifying sensation that her heart was about to stop. Her body felt like lead and she literally couldn't get up. She waited in fear, forcing herself to move first one foot, then the other, travelling slowly up her body, moving a leg then the other until her heart began to beat again and she was able to rise. She mentioned this to no one. Instead, she grabbed the buttery biscuit, shovelling its flaky deliciousness into her mouth.

Gulping a sip of Maggie's richly satisfying tea, she declared, "I'm ready to go. Are you joining us Alexander?"

Justine hurried out the door, avoiding Maggie's disapproving stare.

They arrived at Hicks and Remsen Street just as the owner was un-locking the front doors, which uniquely faced the corner. He was a surprisingly young man in a striped suit and bowler hat with a dis-tinguished handlebar moustache. It was the same building Justine had noticed was empty on her way to Zhang's Chinese Apothecary. Not knowing who was in charge of this unexpectedly large group, the young man gravitated to Alexander.

"How do you do," he said, extending his hand. "Clarkson. David Clarkson Jr."

Alexander shook his hand and allowed Clarkson to lead the group inside.

The place had been empty long enough that dust had settled on the display cases. But Justine was happy to note that the front shop was already set up for a retail enterprise. Alexander immediately disap-peared into the rear of the building to inspect the plumbing. The oth-ers were more hesitant, never having been potential renters or owners of a business or anything approximating that.

But Delphine's ability to dream soon got the better of him and he began chattering away in French, selling Camille on the attributes of the place.

Maggie stuck close to Clarkson who was discomfited by Alexander's disappearance and uncertain as to whom he was renting. Maggie commented here and there when something didn't meet her high standards and her beady eye, unsettled Clarkson even further.

Justine allowed them to inspect the upstairs, leaning on the window ledge, enjoying the sunshine, but also feeling terribly tired and heavy.

Soon enough everyone returned to the main shop area. But before discussions could proceed, Alexander spoke:

"The upstairs is in need of a proper wash room and kitchen if they are to live and work here and a water closet will be required on the main floor. I will install these things and you will lower the rent."

He presented this fait accompli in his usual matter-of-fact voice, which if you didn't know him, could sound a bit like a threat. Alexander waited, looking down his long nose at the discomfited David Clarkson.

But before Clarkson could respond, Maggie piped in: "The whole place will need a proper clean and some of this furniture is desperately in need of repair. We will take care of the cleaning and repairs," she glanced at Alexander for confirmation, "and you will also include that in the lowered rent."

Maggie folded her arms over her ample breasts, daring Clarkson to contradict her. Clarkson opened his mouth, then closed it, staring from one to the other.

"We'd very much like to rent these premises," Delphine spoke up. "Madame Camille and I are opening a dress design shop with a clientele from some of New York's best families – the McGowans, the Walkers, the Posts, to name a few."

Delphine smiled his most winning smile and Clarkson, relieved to speak with someone not making demands on him, smiled in return.

On the walk back, Justine asked, "What was that all about? You ganged up on the poor man!"

Maggie paused to look in the bakery shop window and answered nonchalantly over her shoulder, "No, that was showing a united front. That was all about business!"

"What're you talking about?"

"Alexander and I are combining forces," Maggie explained, hooking her arm through Justine's as they continued down the road. "Mr. Clarkson will discover what we can deliver and he will very soon realize he is in need of our cleaning and plumbing services for all of his other properties!"

Justine laughed out-loud.

"Combining forces, indeed! That poor man didn't have a hope in hell of turning you down!" She squeezed her friend's arm. "You got Camille and Delphine a really good deal that'll give them a fighting chance of succeeding. You make an impressive team – but..."

Maggie interrupted before Justine could object, "I won't be doing the work," she assured her friend. "I'm going back to that terrible place where we found Camille and I'm going to hire a couple of good, reliable Irish girls to come and do the cleaning – at home and in this new business. They're not going to live with us, mind you, I will find them suitable housing."

"Sounds like you've thought this through. Good for you! I'd suggest reliable and confident girls…"

Maggie's eyebrows knit together, perplexed.

"You can be quite formidable, my friend," Justine explained, smiling and pulling Maggie close.

"I had a good teacher!"

Seventy-Five

With Maggie's encouragement, James was travelling to round up business for himself. Armed with his camera, she'd convinced him his photo portraits would be the perfect calling card for his painted portraits.

And good to her word, Maggie headed to the Mercy Home for Girls to find employees for her new enterprise.

The house was empty and quiet except for the brownstone's occasional creeks and sighs; sounds Justine had become accustomed to and welcomed. This house held and protected the people most important to her in her life, now and in the future, and she'd begun to think of it as a special friend.

She snuck up into the attic. There were two tasks she'd planned, each requiring privacy. One was to take the portrait James had done of her. Leaving it here could only create upset if it were ever discovered. And it would be the one thing created by her baby's father that she would take with her.

Tiptoeing into what was now James' bedroom and studio, she felt strangely disembodied. This space held Ducky in the future and had witnessed much of her early and recent life. This space was also privy to her interlude with James and perhaps the place her baby had been conceived. One was ahead, the other behind her.

She crept to the windows. In the future, a small balcony would be constructed, on which Ducky often sat when the weather was fine, enjoying a coffee and reading the paper. Perhaps a balcony had always been intended because the windows were large, more like French doors and framed with polished wood capped with beautifully turned knobs. This odd detail remained in the future in Ducky's apartment.

Justine pulled one of James' stools to the windows, standing on it in order to grasp the knob to the right of the window. She twisted with all her might but it would not budge. She'd seen these odd decorative pieces a hundred times in Ducky's room. She remembered a seam where the knob was attached to the frame so she'd assumed it twisted off. She climbed off the stool, moving to the knob on the left of the windows.

This time she used one of James' metal scraping tools to lightly tap at the knob. After much effort, the knob finally gave and she was able to twist it off. As a child she'd played with similar pieces stored in a forgotten box in Ducky's shop. They were partially hollow inside. She'd taken a 14-carat rose gold infinity engagement ring with a princess cut 1-carat diamond from her mother's collection. She plopped it now into the space inside the knob. It fit snugly into the cavity. She replaced the knob onto the frame and twisted it back into place.

Gathering her portrait, she left the attic.

In the next few days, she asked Delphine to fashion a large back-pack. Never having seen such a thing before, she described what was needed and he obliged. He and Camille were working harder than either of them ever had before to get Madame Camille's ready for it's gala opening.

"I'm sorry to make this request at such a busy time," Justine apologized.

Delphine gave her one of his mock exasperated looks.

"There will always be time for you, *Mon Cherie*" he said.

There wouldn't be time, in fact, Justine thought, watching him as he dragged fabric from a box and set to work on the one clear table in the shop. She was again reminded of Paul, as Delphine's wild energy focused completely on his task.

The new plumbing for the shop was almost complete and Maggie's team would soon scrub the place from top to bottom. Supplies were to be delivered and a date for the opening had been set. Justine would not be attending.

Her final conversation with Alexander was more difficult than she anticipated. She invited him for a whisky. Maggie stoked the fire, replenished the water in the pitcher then left them alone.

"Alexander," Justine began "I've come to trust you like a brother and care for you as a friend. So this is very, very difficult for me to say."

"Then you must have courage and speak," he insisted.

She took a deep breath. "I am going away."

He waited, sensing there was more.

"I'm going away forever."

"Why? Do you not like it here? Has someone done something to make you leave?" His voice was rising with suspicion and his body tensing to take action against her enemies.

"No. It's nothing like that. Being here has been the most wonderful experience of my life. It's been a blessing."

"As it has for all of us!"

"I'm glad," she told him, because she was glad and deeply gratified. "I'm going because – because I'm not well."

He turned darkly concerned eyes on her.

"Can Dr. Feingold not do something for you?"

"No. I'm afraid what is wrong with me cannot be healed here." She leaned towards him, speaking in a low voice. "I've not told anyone I'm going. I'll tell Maggie. Tomorrow. But I've not told anyone else."

She reached for the white linen envelope sitting on the table next to her.

"I've given this only to a few others – those whom I care about most deeply. That's why I'm giving it to you." She handed Alexander the envelope. "I ask that you open it on the afternoon of April 18th.

When you read what's inside you'll understand why I'm making this request. What's written there is absolutely true. I ask that you believe me and act accordingly."

He sat for a time with the envelope in his lap staring into the fire, his brow furrowed. He sighed.

"I want to understand the way of the world," he said, his voice heavy with sadness and longing, "but I think I never will."

He reached for his whisky, taking a sip then secured the envelope in his jacket pocket.

"Promise me you will take care of everyone…"

"It is how I will honor you from this day forward."

"I will miss you terribly, Alexander Alexandrovich," she confessed, tears filling her eyes. "But I know you are with me, now and always."

"I thought God had abandoned me and then you came along. Maybe God just wants his angel back."

He finished his drink. Pushing tears back with his fingers, he stood up, turning to her. Without thinking she was in his arms, hugging him and he hugging her back.

The next day, Justine paid a visit to the Feingold's. Rachel answered her knock and graciously admitted her, with her usual glacial welcome.

This was to be Justine's last visit and she wanted to make it warm and friendly. She followed Rachel into the sitting room.

"How's your tooth?"

"Fine, thank you."

"Fine, thanks to you," It was Dr Feingold, standing in the doorway smiling, warmly.

"I'm so glad I could help after all you and your wife have done for all of us!"

"I'm going to pay a visit to Zhang Zhu." Dr. Feingold, confided.

Rachel shifted uncomfortably in her seat.

"Rachel thinks it could harm my practice, but after what I witnessed his needles can do, I believe it's my duty to find out more."

"He also uses herbs for healing."

"So he said…."

Rachel turned to face Justine, curtailing this line of conversation.

"Yes. I'm sorry to barge in like this," Justine said. "Time has run out and I was hoping to speak with both of you. I know you're busy Doctor Feingold. It won't take long."

He came to sit with them, his face open and expectant, hers closed and suspicious. But Rachel Feingold's haughty façade didn't bother Justine anymore. What she understood was that everyone has insecurities and each of us covers it in different ways. Rachel Feingold was no exception.

In another era, Rachel would probably choose to pursue a full time career and find success and fulfilment in that way. In this time, it was expected of her to generate an offspring and it seemed she was struggling with this.

Justine produced her next to last white linen envelope, placing it on the table in front of them.

Seventy-Six

The most difficult good-bye came that evening. Justine and Maggie were sitting in the same seats as they had on her first night, staring companionably into the fire, sipping whisky. Maggie was telling her about the two girls she'd hired and how she was housing them at Camille and Delphine's shop until she could arrange something preferable. Maggie's cleaning service was launched.

"I'm SO proud of you, Maggie."

"I'm so proud of me," she concurred, smiling smugly and pouring more whisky.

"Maggie. There's something I need to tell you and I don't know how…"

"Oh, Mother of God, I knew this was coming …" Maggie moaned, fishing for her handkerchief and twisting it in her hands. Her eyes were tightly shut as if that could stop what ever was about to happen. "I've had the sense something terrible was about to happen. Something to do with you…"

"I'm going back, Maggie."

"I knew it. I just knew it!" Maggie opened her eyes to look pleadingly at her friend. "Why? Why do you have to go?"

Justine was about to speak but Maggie fiercely shook her head, "No. I know why. You're not from here and … and you belong there. But … but … I'll miss you so much," and she burst into tears, crying, "I don't know. I just don't know…"

Tears spilled from Justine's eyes and it felt as if her heart couldn't hold this sorrow.

"I'll miss you more," she said. "I've never had a close friend."

Maggie clamped her hand over her mouth to stop herself crying, offering Justine a clean hanky from her apron pocket. They sniffled and blew their noses and laughed a little. Justine poured them both another whisky.

"I've never been very good at friendship," Justine confessed. "I think because my mother disappeared, I was afraid to get close to anyone. So I was never very good at it." She squeezed Maggie's arm. "You made it easy, Maggie. You taught me how."

"And I was afraid of my own shadow before you arrived."

"You could've fooled me at that Poker Game!"

"And that's the puzzle. Because I learned from me brothers how to be brave. So I had that part of me. But it was hidden. Hidden under what everyone was telling me a nice girl should be! And here you come, one of the nicest girls I've ever met, and you're nothing like what everyone was telling me!"

"I think that's a compliment...?"

"'Tis."

"Well if you're ready to break away from the old, there's a movement underway in this century, Maggie dear, that will liberate and empower women. It's happening right now and you could be a part of it."

"Them Suffragettes?"

"Yes. Them Suffragettes. It'll take time, but in 1920 the US Constitution is amended giving women the right to vote!"

"I get the absolute willies when you do that."

"What?"

"That crystal ball gazing. Like some circus fortune teller..."

"Sorry."

"I mean, a part of me likes hearing that an O'Reagan will be President and women will get the vote. But that's the mad yoke part of me."

She gulped some whisky.

Justine removed her last white linen envelope.

Seventy-Seven

Justine and Maggie had spent much of the night talking and holding each other and weeping and laughing - making promises and holding each other again and weeping some more. She was drained. So was her friend.

They stood in the foyer. There was nothing more to say and yet it felt as if so much remained unsaid. When her mother disappeared, she'd had no say in the matter. Now it was she who was choosing to go and she felt acutely the burden of her decision. She also felt the dragging illness or whatever it was. It would take every last bit of determination to face the crossing.

They'd filled the backpack Delphine had made with her mother's portrait. It was heavier than she'd imagined. She wore another, smaller one slung across her chest filled with the other things she was taking with her.

It was time to go. She forced herself to turn away from Maggie and push open the front door. The darkest hour is just before the dawn, she thought scanning the black, moonless sky. Thankfully it hadn't snowed in a few days and the streets were clear. The bitter cold hit her face and grabbed her heart.

She stepped out the door. She could hear Maggie racing up the stairs to stand in the window, just where she'd been on Justine's first crossing. Justine moved as quickly as she could down the front steps and around the building.

Compelling herself to keep going, she dragged one foot in front of the other, approaching the stables. The wrenching pull took hold. She glanced up to the second floor window. Maggie's face was pressed against the pane and beside her was the figure of a tall man. Alexander, Justine thought before she was yanked forward into the web of time and …

… flung into the alleyway, barely avoiding a collision with the hulking, metal garbage bins. The heat and heavily polluted air precipitated a wave of nausea. Her whole being felt weighted and bruised but she forced herself forward, towards the street. A Yellow Cab drove past. The last light of day cast long shadows and she hoped its passengers hadn't seen her.

She made her way up the front stairs, pressed the security lock and practically fell from exertion into the foyer.

Disengaging herself from her baggage, Justine called out, "Ducky? Are you home?"

The house was silent. There was no sign of scaffolding or construction. The renovations must be complete. But she felt too unwell to investigate further. She dragged herself up the stairs and into her bedroom, pulling off her skirts and corsets and making for the shower.

As the water poured down, she managed to scrub herself, wash her hair and shave her under arms before the heaviness returned. Fearing she was going to faint, Justine was able to dry herself, put on track-suit pants and a t-shirt before the room started spinning and she passed out completely.

When she came to, she was lying on her side on the hardwood floor, uncertain where she was. Her body was too heavy to move and this caused her to panic. Her heart felt as if it was going to stop and at the same time, as if it was going to burst out of her chest. Remembering she was pregnant gave her the impetus to drag herself upright.

Her wet hair dripped into her face, but when she wiped it away her fingers were covered in blood. She knew there was always a lot of blood with head wounds, but the sight of it further disoriented her. She thought of Dr Feingold and the image of him with the tooth-pulling instrument flashed across her mind, increasing her panic. At the same time she knew there was something wrong with her thinking.

The room she was in was only somewhat familiar. On the wall was the familiar Simeon Soloman painting, The Sleepers and the One Who Watchest, but it seemed in the wrong place somehow. She recognized the quilted bedspread, a birthday present from Ducky. She was sitting on the floor near the bed and she reached out to touch the familiar colors of blue and grey, hand sewn by a women's collective. Her mind was wandering and her head felt dizzy again when the phone rang, startling her into standing up. It rang only once, signalling an answering machine had intercepted the call. But it was enough to prompt Justine into action.

She dragged herself to the phone, picked up the receiver and dialled 911.

Later they'd tell her she'd left the front door ajar and the Paramedics found her passed out on the floor next to the bed. They also mentioned that she'd come to long enough to tell them she was pregnant.

Seventy-Eight

But Justine remembered nothing. Until she awoke to brilliant green eyes looking down on her with concern.

"James?" she said to the kind face with the green eyes.

"Jaime, actually," the kind face said back.

"I'm so glad you're here, James…" she replied and fell back asleep.

Sometime later she awoke, feeling calm and safe, as if she were floating. The man with the green eyes was sitting next to her bed. She was aware he was holding her hand and it felt warm and comforting. She was glad he didn't let go, even when he noticed she was awake. Instead, he stood up to look down at her.

He wasn't James but she continued to hold his hand anyway. There was something about the way his longish, light brown hair fell over his forehead and of course the green eyes that reminded her of James. When he smiled it was with perfectly straight, white teeth and the lips were similarly etched and full.

"Who are you?" she asked.

"My name's Jaime Grey. I work here – well, I work here doing a variety of things."

"Where am I?"

"Mount Sinai Doctors Hospital."

She pulled her hand away and tried to sit up, "Hospital? Why? What happened?"

"It's okay," his voice was tender and reassuring. "You passed out and hit your head and you're pregnant so …."

Her eyes darted around the room, taking in the hospital décor, the monitoring machine and finally his words. She fell back against the pillow as it all came back to her like a book whose pages were fanned by a thumb; speed reading the story of her crossing and her return. She lay breathless until he took her hand again.

"You need to breathe, Justine," he said calmly.

The intimacy of his speaking her name was almost too much for her but the wisdom of his words got through and she took a deep breath.

"I don't know what you've been though but it seems to have put pressure on your system," he explained. "Breathing helps to relieve some of that pressure."

She liked his sensible, calm tone. She took another deep breath and squeezed his hand. Then a Doctor entered.

"Don't go," Justine pleaded.

"I'll just be outside," Jaime assured her.

She'd been in the hospital over night. They'd taken blood, done tests, checked all her vital signs and ascertained the health of her baby. They could find nothing wrong. She needed to rest. That was the doctor's advice.

She felt well enough to go home so she didn't argue. She didn't feel entirely real and everything had a dreamlike quality about it but she got dressed and made her way downstairs.

She got into a taxi waiting at the rank and gave her address. There was a knock on the window and she looked out to see Jaime, signalling for her to wind down the glass.

"I don't want this to sound impertinent or creepy," he said "but would you like me to take you home? Maybe you could use some help?"

She studied his face, familiar in so many ways. His eyes were clear and honest. And, yes, she could use some help although she wasn't sure he would understand how. She opened the door and moved over to let him in.

When they pulled into Hicks Street, he sat forward.

When they stopped outside her Brownstone, he muttered, "I don't believe it!"

Justine paid the driver, got out, slowly mounted the front steps and opened the front door.

Jaime joined her on the stoop.

"I grew up in this house," he said.

She looked at him. This was certainly co-incidental, even very, very odd. But Justine had experience stranger and odder things.

"Really? You grew up here?' She said. "I've lived here for almost 8 years."

"My father lost everything and we had to sell up and move. About 10 years ago."

"I own the house now," she explained. "We've renovated it so it probably won't look very familiar."

He followed her inside. The truth was it didn't look very familiar to Justine because she'd been gone for much of the renovations. The baggage she'd brought back with her laid strewn where she'd dropped it in the entryway. Justine wandered into the kitchen, which was now an open concept space separated from the living/dining room by a large, granite covered island. There she found a note from Ducky:

Should you return, I am with Paul in New Orleans, buying. Margaret and Joe are in Philly working with homeless org.

It was signed with a picture of a duck.

He knows, Justine thought.

She was about to pick up the phone to call his hotel in the French Quarter, when Jaime exclaimed:

"I don't believe this. Oh, my God. How is this possible?"

Justine found him still in the foyer, staring at the portrait of her mother. He spoke to her with awe in his voice:

"My Great Grandfather painted this."

The dreamlike quality of things sharpened. She stared at him sensing there was portent in their meeting just not able to grasp what or how. Then he was at her side, supporting her to the sofa, rushing to the kitchen for water, waiting while she drank it.

"I'm fine," she assured him. "Would you sit with me for a minute?"

He sat beside her, taking her hand as he had in the hospital. His fingers felt warm and real and she held them, not speaking.

Finally he suggested, "I could make you something to eat...?"

"That would be nice."

He got up, glad of something useful to do. While he was busy in the kitchen, she called Ducky, leaving a short message with the hotel concierge: The Parcel is back.

There wasn't much in the fridge so Jaime made omelettes, which they ate on the terrace overlooking the still unfinished garden.

"This is good," Justine commented.

"My mother wasn't much of a cook, so I had to teach myself."

She was aware of how comfortable and right it felt to have him here and yet how completely strange.

"I like what you've done with the place," he said.

"Not me. Ducky."

"Did you say, Ducky? Who's that?"

"My adopted father. He lives in the attic."

"My brother and I used to sneak up there all the time. My Dad said it was my Great Grandfather's studio."

"Yes. It was."

The words were out of her mouth before she realized the implications of what she'd said.

"You know about my Great Grandfather?" he asked, surprised. Then glancing towards the painting in the entryway, he added, "Well, of course you do. You have one of his paintings."

Justine kept eating, not looking at him, not commenting.

"I've been researching and collecting his paintings for years. I'd read about that one, but couldn't track it down. May I ask where you got it?"

"It's a long story …"

"I'm sorry. The Doctor recommended rest and here I am babbling away."

"Yes, I'd like to lie down now. But … would you stay here? I mean, can you stay? When Ducky gets my message, I'm sure he'll call. Maybe you could tell him I'm ok…?"

She was already moving slowly towards the stairs.

He let her go up alone, assuring her retreating figure, "I'll be here if you need me."

Seventy-Nine

She was dreaming. In the dream, she knew she was dreaming. And at the same time everything seemed very close and real. Then Jaime was there and he was speaking to her and she liked the sound of his voice. He'd made something to eat and she sat in her bed and ate and it tasted good. Then she slept some more. And dreamt some more.

Then she awoke and Ducky was sitting beside her bed.

"Hello, Parcel," he said, "You've been gone a long time."

She happily drank in his familiar face, feeling him do the same to her. She reached out to touch him, making sure he wasn't a dream. He took her hands in his and they sat that way for a time.

"You know, don't you?" she said.

"I'm not sure what I know. I never have been."

"If I tell you, will you believe me?"

"I will. Yes, I think I will."

So she told him. Everything. In bursts and starts. And when she tired, he let her sleep. And when she awoke, she carried on with her tale. He listened, nodding occasionally, his eyes tearing up when she spoke of the search for her mother. He held her hand when she expressed how difficult it had been to leave.

"There's more. There's a bit more ... but I am so happy to see you, dearest Ducky," Justine whispered, wrapping heavy, tired arms around him and letting him hold her close.

The next day she and Ducky were sitting on the terrace. Jaime was in the garden digging.

"Does he have a home?" Ducky asked.

"I don't know – I don't know much about him... except that he feels comfortable and right."

"Yes. Strangely, he does," Ducky agreed.

The both sat, watching Jaime shovel dirt, creating a deep trough from the central point of the garden towards the wall along the alley.

"He and Paul were out here early this morning," Ducky commented "discussing Paul's design for the garden. It seems Mr Grey is multi-skilled."

Justine was aware of how content and safe she felt. It was having Ducky by her side but it was also something to do with Jaime. He had his shirt off and she admired the curve and cut of the muscles along his back and arms as he worked.

But it was more than his physical beauty. There was something stable and familiar about him. He was easy to talk to and she felt she could be herself with him. Yes, that was it. She could be herself and he seemed to like who she was.

At that moment, as if he could hear her thoughts, Jaime looked up and smiled.

"Would you like some lemonade?" Justine asked.

He put down the shovel, wiping his face and mounted the stairs to the terrace. Justine noted that he put his shirt back on as he sat at the table. It seemed an old fashioned sort of deference to table manners and a sign of respect to Justine, Ducky and their home. She liked it.

"Paul and I discussed a raised bed at the back for planting crops," Jaime enthused.

"Crops?" Ducky asked.

"You know, veggies and stuff..."

"I'm certain that wasn't Paul's idea," Ducky chuckled. "Paul thinks milk is grown in cartons."

"Well, no, it was my idea...."

"I love it!" Justine enthused.

Jaime smiled, encouraged. "And for the rest, Paul's planning a beautiful traditional garden complete with roses and a water fountain," he explained.

"Just like it was," Justine murmured.

"I imagine so," Jaime said. "My Great Grandfather dabbled in early photography - but like his paintings it was mostly people, not places. I have one or two photos of this house… none of the garden."

"I'd like to see the photos," Justine said.

Ducky was studying Justine with what she called his imperial face. His head was back and he was looking down his long nose at her. Actually it was his thinking face, but Jaime became aware of a change in mood.

"Yes, well, I guess I may have over stayed my welcome … maybe I can bring those photos over some time soon."

"You have not over stayed anything," Ducky insisted. "I'm very grateful to you for looking after my girl – and this work in the garden – which Paul seems to have roped you into."

"No. We were talking and I got excited about what he's planning. I could see it, you see – and, well, the tools were here and, well, there's no time like the present…"

"No. No time like the present," Justine agreed, smiling back at his open, excited face.

Jaime stood up to go.

"You'll come back?" Justine asked.

"I could bring Chinese food," Jaime suggested. "Best Chinese near where I live…"

"Where do you live?" Ducky asked.

"Not far. Over near the University.

"I love Chinese," Justine conferred.

He smiled, nodded and left. They watched him go.

"You're interested," Ducky commented, wryly.

"I would be but – I can't be … " Justine got up to stand at the railing, looking down at the piles of dirt in the garden.

Ducky joined her. "What does that mean?"

"It was the other thing I didn't tell you." She took a deep breath. "I'm pregnant."

"What? Wait a minute. By whom?"

Justine couldn't look at him.

"Justine - was it someone – back then?"

"Yes."

"Who?"

She didn't answer.

"Justine, who's the father?"

"His Great Grandfather."

"Who?"

"Jaime's Great Grandfather. James Grey is the father of my child!"

"WHAT?" It was Jaime, standing in the living room, just inside the open sliding-glass doors.

Justine and Ducky turned to look at him.

"I - I was moving the things in the foyer and I found this …" Jaime held up the half-naked portrait of Justine, painted by James Grey. His eyes were wide in disbelief. "This – this isn't possible. This is you," he said, staring at Justine. "But it's painted by him!"

"Yes." Justine agreed.

"And did I just overhear you say he's the father of your child…?"

"Yes," Justine conceded.

Eighty

Jaime was not the sort of man to dismiss things offhand. He believed in giving an idea and people the benefit of the doubt. The contention that his great grandfather, James Grey, was the father of Justine's child was probably the biggest benefit and the most bizarre doubt he'd ever encountered.

They were sitting now in the living room on Ducky's Roche Bobois splurge. Not only was the sofa not an antique, it cost more than many of the items in his shop. The sleek lines, high-end materials and exquisite construction plus the multi-functioning backs, arms and configuration, appealed to his aesthetic. Ducky had never splurged on anything in his life.

He sat now ensconced in the sofa's corner unit, pouring tea from an antique porcelain tea set.

"When things become difficult," he was explaining as he carefully emptied dark amber liquid into three cups.

"... Tea settles the nerves." Justine completed his sentence.

She was feeling surprisingly calm as if sharing the strangeness of her life, lightened the load.

Jaime sat silently, apart from his new companions. They sipped tea. Hot and milky and a little sweet. Jaime had placed the portrait of Justine against the wall and it sat glancing at them seductively.

"You said you used to sneak into the attic and play there when you were a boy," Justine said softly.

"Yeah, me and my brother."

"Did you ever find anything up there?"

Jaime peered at Justine but didn't reply.

She got up from the sofa, grabbing a note pad Ducky always kept near phones. This one had Daffy Duck on the cover - a joke gift from Paul. She selected a mechanical pencil from the penholder and standing at the large granite island, began to draw. When she finished, she handed the sketch to Jaime.

His eyes widened. He stared at the drawing, then at Justine. Then he reached slowly into his pants pocket and removed a long gold chain.

"Absolutely no one knows I found this," he said, holding up the chain at the end of which hung a ring. "I was 8 and it was the first and only secret I ever had that was mine and mine alone. I never told anyone about it."

He stared at Justine then handed her illustration and the ring to Ducky. She'd depicted the 14K rose gold infinity ring with its princess cut 1K diamond.

"I placed that ring inside the left knob of the window frame over-looking the street," Justine explained.

"That's exactly where I found it!" Jaime shook his head as if this was all too much to comprehend. "My father talked about his Grandfather just enough to make him fascinating to a small boy. I kept going up there. It felt like his ghost was calling me."

"It was James Grey's Studio. It was where that portrait was painted."

They all looked at the painting. Justine's half turned face was suffused with pleasure and a hint of smugness as only James could paint it. Her wild hair and partially exposed breast completed the picture of post-coital satisfaction.

"But how is it possible?" Jaime asked.

"I don't know," Justine confessed.

"Her mother, it seems had the same ability," Ducky said, quietly.

He then described in much more detail than he ever had before, his discovery of Justine's mother, huddling in a dark alley just off Royal Street in the French Quarter. At the time her dress had seemed very odd, but her distress was so great that was what Ducky had focused on.

He'd purchased more appropriate clothing for her and eventually suggested that she come back to New York with him.

"She was so vulnerable and so strong," he remembered. "But there was a sadness haunting her, even through her joy. And she was so happy when you were born," he added, glancing at Justine. Ducky sighed. "It was hard for a man like me, back then," he confessed. "We became friends. I miss her every day."

Justine had never heard him speak like this before. It was the first time she realized; her mother's absence had been hard for both of them.

It was only later, Ducky continued – when he started putting together all the strange things about her behaviour, her surprise at hot water from the faucet and airplanes and telephones and so many, many things – that he allowed himself to question her origin.

"When Paul saw her original clothing," Ducky remembered "He said, '*These are so real, she probably came through a portal from the past.*'"

Ducky shook his head and shrugged.

"He didn't mean it, of course but Paul often has a way of stating the bloody obvious. But she wouldn't say where she'd come from and I didn't want to pry."

Of course, Paul hadn't given it any more thought except to take the clothes into his possession. But Ducky had thought about Paul's comment over and over as the years passed.

"When you showed up with that antique brooch," he said to Justine "I began to suspect something. But when you disappeared in your mother's clothing, I couldn't avoid the 'bloody obvious' any longer. It was as if I'd been anticipating something like this from the day you were born."

"But it's not possible," Jaime insisted.

"And yet it's true," Justine replied.

To confirm her statement, Ducky handed the ring back to Jaime.

Eighty-One

Jaime's continued presence felt as normal as the aroma of fresh coffee they were sipping. He liked his iced on a hot summer day. Justine was a purist. She'd learned from Paul to insist on only whole milk in her lattes, heated not more than 140° and to add a second shot for the richness and flavor.

They hadn't spoken of the paintings or her unborn child or the ring he still wore around his neck. In spite of the bizarreness of what had been said, Jaime came back the next day to work in the garden and everyone accepted this as normal.

Ducky was back at work and in the afternoon, Jaime suggested a stroll on the Promenade.

"If you feel up to it," he added, running the towel through his hair one more time.

He was doing an amazing job on the garden and Justine suggested he might like a shower. This too felt normal. To both of them.

The trees were lush as they walked in companionable silence, gazing across the East River to lower Manhattan. A soft breeze wafted up from Buttermilk Channel, easing the weight of humidity.

Maggie would have said. Not that I was listening…"

This time they both chuckled.

"What's Live Blood Analysis?"

"It uses Dark-field microscopy, which is a valid scientific tool, to examine and observe live blood cells. We might be able to see what's going on with you - why you feel so slowed - maybe uncover anomalies or inconsistencies... "

"Okay..."

"Are you up for it?"

"Does it hurt?"

"Just a really light pin prick to get a sample."

She studied him for a moment. This man whose features were so like his ancestor's, but who carried none of the wild, self-destructive energy of James Grey. His hazel eyes sparkled with enthusiasm for his idea. Her heart skipped.

Without thinking Justine reached out and touched his cheek.

"Thank you," she said.

His hand covered hers and they looked deeply into each other's eyes.

He didn't let go of her hand as they made their way along Montague Street, down Hicks to a narrow building at the corner of Grace Ct Alley. The sign read: Integrative Medicine and Natural Healing

"This is where Zhang Zhu had his shop." Justine said. "Not this building, of course but … he would be happy to know it's still a place of healing."

Jaime's friend, Jenny, was a middle-aged woman with a long, sliver braid falling almost to her waist and round John Lennon glasses perched on the edge of her nose. Her tiny office was located off the small, plant-filled waiting room.

She smiled when Jaime introduced Justine, "I knew he was waiting for his mate soul to find him," Jenny said, hugging Justine warmly.

"His mate soul?" Justine asked, somewhat embarrassed by the implication.

"Oh yes. It's definitely you," Jenny confirmed, cornflower blue eyes peering at her over wire rims. "You're the female dipole. He's the male dipole. You are most definitely mate-souls."

Justine glanced at Jaime, who shrugged, indicating this was normal Jenny-banter.

"I'm not talking about New Age soul-mates, you understand," Jenny went on. "That's just a romantic notion that distorts the truth - like much New Age clap-trap."

She sat at her keyboard, tapping information into her computer as she spoke.

"You see, mate souls don't always get along," Jenny explained. "But they continue to travel through time together. Sometimes intimately in each other's lives, sometimes tangentially. From your mate soul you learn much of what your Soul needs to learn. So it was important in this lifetime that Jaime find you and that you be together."

She turned to a microscope sitting next to the large computer screen.

"If you'll just sit there, sweetie, we can get this show on the road."

Under other circumstances, Justine might have felt uncomfortable but Jenny exuded such an aura of calm confidence it made her unexpected words sound possible and her assertions, pleasantly reassuring.

After quickly pricking Justine's finger and squeezing a few drops of blood onto a glass pane, Jenny placed the glass under the microscope.

Suddenly a full-color moving image appeared on the screen.

"Is that my blood?" Justine asked.

"Tis, indeed," Jenny confirmed. "We're looking at cell mobility and activity levels, number of chylomicrons, adhesion of platelets, microbes and other great stuff."

Justine was transfixed by the sheer poetry of what she saw. Rounded ovals clustered together against a back drop of infinite, smaller dots flowing at different speeds interspersed with strange masses of larger formations, sinuously moving through fluid, like an infinite, graceful dance.

"It's so beautiful," Justine whispered.

"It is, isn't it," Jaime agreed. He was sitting close and staring with her at the screen.

"It's who we are," Jenny piped in. "Everything working together in recognition of the one are many and the many are one." She adjusted the microscope lens. "If we could mirror the way the body works into the world, it would be a much better place to live in."

They left Jenny to her analysis of Justine's blood. It was late in the day and though it was still warm, the humidity had abated.

"How're you feeling?" Jaime asked. "If you're up to it, we could go to Fortino's for pizza."

"I'm up for it!"

The restaurant was located on a large pier overlooked the East River. The sun was setting in fiery shades of ginger and gold, casting shimmering pathways across the river, leaving lower Manhattan appearing like rectangular dinosaurs looming over the water.

"Do you agree with what she said?" Justine asked as they waited for their food to arrive. "About mate-souls?"

"The moment I saw you in the hospital, I knew you. I felt I knew you," Jaime replied without hesitation. "That feeling hasn't let up. In fact, it's intensified."

"I feel the same way."

"Can I add – feeling I know you doesn't take away from the fact that I'm also very attracted to you?"

Justine blushed, glancing away. He looked down, exposed by what he'd just admitted.

"I feel the same way," she murmured.

He reached out a grateful hand and she reached back. They sat gazing at each other, relishing the moment. The fading light highlighted the golden streaks in his hair and she thought she would never love another's face as much as she loved his right now in this moment.

"You're so beautiful," he said, echoing her thoughts.

The food arrived on two tiered trays of gluten- free pizza with organic cheeses and vegetables. The solar candles lit up as night descended.

"And *softly, slowly*, as my Grandma advised," Jaime said, biting into the pizza with supreme delight.

Eighty-Two

The following day, she was on her way back from her maternity yoga class feeling calm and alive, when she noticed Margaret climbing the front steps and called out to her.

"What's up, sweetie-pie?" Margaret asked, eyeing her up and down. "You look different? You're not...?"

"Hi Margaret. How was Philly? How's Joe?"

Margaret had the kind of x-ray vision that could see inside your mind. Justine wasn't ready to talk about the pregnancy. She didn't know what she'd say.

"That Joe, he loves that big 'ol La-Z-Boy chair so much, he's turned into a Lazy Boy! I can't get him out of it," Margaret sighed. "He's in there right now with the a/c on, watching TV. How far the great have risen!" She added, shaking her head and laughing her laugh that was more like a cough.

"He deserves it," Justine insisted. "You both do. Why don't you come up tonight? Paul's cooking dinner."

"Something fancy, schmancy I assume."

"It's Paul. What else? We'd love to hear about your travels."

"We'll be there!" Margaret headed back down the stairs. "Oh, I almost forgot. There's an idea I've been cookin' up. I want to run it by you and Ducky, when you have a sec."

"Do you want to make an appointment and have a meeting?" Justine asked, amused by Margaret's serious tone.

"Dear God, has it come to that?"

"Of course not."

"But on second thought, maybe I should." She was headed down the steps to her apartment, muttering to herself. Justine smiled. This was Margaret as she should be, energised and plotting the future.

Justine poured herself a glass of filtered water from the sink and one for Jaime who was hard at work in the garden. His shirt was off and sweat was running down the curves and ridges of his muscular arms and back.

She felt a rush of desire. *Softly, slowly*, she reminded herself. She'd spent a lot of time in the past and she didn't know what the future would bring, so she was content just to stay in the moment and let herself appreciate the beauty of him.

He looked up, feeling her eyes on him and grinned knowingly, as if he could read her thoughts. She held out the glass of water and he nodded, coming inside where it was cool.

"Jenny delivered her analysis," he said, gulping water and going into the kitchen for more.

He was as relaxed here as Ducky or Paul and the ease of it, pleased Justine.

"And ...?"

"There were anomalies, but nothing exactly health related."

"What does that mean?"

"Because we couldn't tell her your real history, it's based on what we did tell her, about your deep exhaustion ...

"It's not exhaustion, exactly," she interrupted him "It's more like - like my life force slows..."

"Yes. I think you said that to her when we were there."

"I couldn't say it in the hospital, because I was afraid they'd think I was crazy. But I felt like Jenny would understand."

"... And she did, as far as that goes. She's recommended some supplements, that won't hurt the baby and ..."

"... And?"

"She asked if any member of your family had the same complaint. I told her your mother had ..."

"Disappeared?"

"Look, I've known Jenny for a while. She knows about my father leaving and … I hope it was okay to tell her about your mother… not being around."

"Your father left?"

"My father was a hopeless drunk and a gambler. He lost everything in Atlantic City and instead of coming home and being a responsible adult, he took off. One day, out of the blue, my mother was told he'd lost the house and we had to get out."

"I'm sorry," Justine said, touching his arm.

"It was a long time ago."

She thought about James Grey who was also Jaime's ancestor. She prayed that if he and Maggie did get together, that she'd be able to keep him on an even keel. Justine realized she was thinking about these things as if they hadn't happened yet – and yet they had, decades in the past.

"So, you were saying about my mother …?" Justine asked, interrupting her own troubled thinking.

"Jenny said she'd never come across anomalies like this and it would be really helpful to have a sample of your biological parent's blood. The comparison could lead to a much better understanding of what's going on and possibly to a real cure."

Justine sighed. He took her in his arms and held her gently.

"It's okay," he said. "She was very confident these supplements and herbs will help."

"There's something I want to show you," Justine said, suddenly.

For some reason this felt like the moment so she went to her purse, which was lying where she'd left it on the kitchen counter. She withdrew a white linen envelope.

"I gave one of these to everyone – back then," she explained, handing the envelope to Jaime. "I couldn't bear them not knowing. I couldn't go without warning them."

Jaime fingered the fine quality linen then opened the envelope and read what Justine had written:

1906, April 18. San Francisco Earthquake occurs at 5:13am. A magnitude of 7.8
1907, June 15. Typhoid outbreaks in New York City linked to Mary Mallon (called Typhoid Mary)
1911, March 25. A fire at the Triangle Shirtwaist Company in New York City results in the death of nearly 150 young women and girls.
1912, April 15. The RMS Titanic sinks in the North Atlantic Ocean, four days into the ship's maiden voyage from Southampton to New York City.

1914 World War begins in Europe on June 28. Archduke Franz Ferdinand, heir to the Austro-Hungarian Empire, is shot to death. Jews will be targeted.

1929, Thursday, October 24. The Wall Street Stock Market Crashes at the end of the market day. Safe Funds: Vanguard Wellington and CGM Mutual Fund. Have cash stored at home. Have your invested money in foreign stocks, bank accounts, real estate and hard investments like gold and silver.

"I came back in March, 1906," Justine explained. "The earthquake was coming in April and I used that as a way to prove that the rest of what was written there would also happen."

Jaime folded the letter, placing it back in its still new, white envelope.

"I didn't want them to get hurt. I didn't want them to lose everything in the Crash. I wanted to protect them." Justine's voice was rising as she rushed to defend herself.

"It never occurred to me that this was something you could do," Jaime said, shaking his head. "I mean, none of it every occurred to me..."

"Do you think I did something wrong?" Justine interrupted, her voice now a whisper.

"Wrong?"

"I mean, changing time. Changing history. I don't know. Altering destiny in some terrible way...?

"I have no way of answering that," he confessed. "I believe it was done out of love so your intentions were right and good."

"Oh, God," Justine sighed. "What if I made things worse?"

She was looking at him now with real fear in her eyes. He held her shoulders and looked deeply into those eyes.

"Sadly, these things happened, in spite of your letter. Right?" he asked.

She nodded.

"And James Grey married Maggie O'Reagan," he continued. "I know this for a fact. They had children together. One of them was my grandfather. That history made it possible for our destinies to collide. Yours and mine. I can't find anything wrong with that."

He wrapped his arms around her and she let herself be soothed by his size and his assurance. One day she would investigate more deeply what might have happened to all those people, but for now she let her self be in this time and this place with this miraculous man.

Later that evening, everyone was gathered for the first time in the newly renovated space.

Paul was in the kitchen whipping and stirring and making a mess creating something he called, 'fabulousness'. It smelled delicious. Being Paul, when Justine returned he'd given her a big hug and kiss, behaving as if nothing was different. Paul's professional life was so full of drama and stress, that he preferred his personal life to at least appear tranquil and calm.

Ducky was expanding the dining room table to seat everyone, setting it with his eclectic collection of antique plates and glasses. He was humming to himself, something Justine had not heard him do in years.

Margaret was also in the kitchen, whipping up what she called her 'private recipe' for Margaritas.

"I guess you'll be wanting one with no alcohol, sweetie-pie?" she asked, staring pointedly at Justine.

There was a slight, almost imperceptible pause in the conversation.

"Yes, thank you, Margaret," Justine answered, staring back, challenging her to take it further.

"I thought as much," Margaret nodded, confirming her suspicions about Justine's pregnancy and switching the blender onto high.

Joe it seems knew a great deal about art and was engrossed in Jaime's explanation of his ancestor's paintings.

"She's a mighty fine looking woman," Joe commented, studying the portrait of Justine's mother. "Looks a lot like our Justine, here, doncha think?"

"Yes, she does a bit," Jaime, agreed. "In the research I've done," he added, hurriedly changing the subject, "I discovered her name was Bella. Bella Corso. It means beautiful traveller."

Jaime glanced at Justine as he revealed this piece of information. His intention was to communicate his love for her and his awareness that the translation of her mother's name had great significance.

She thought her mother's name was Belle. But hearing the name, Bella Corso, rattled something in Justine's memory. She couldn't quite hold on to what it was hiding just below consciousness.

"You found her name?" Ducky asked.

"In my research I discovered that once he got into photography, James Grey took photographs of all his paintings …" Jaime explained.

Justine, Ducky and Jaime realized this conversation was being conducted at two levels and was wandering dangerously into the area of too much information.

"Hors-*d'oeuvre?*" Paul asked, presenting a colourful tray of bruschetta and inadvertently rescuing the situation.

Eighty-Three

She forced herself to stop and take a deep breath. The horror sounds of coming through still screeched in her ears and the shock of arriving back in 1906 was no less this time than any other.

She reached a hand to her belly, closing her eyes, saying a prayer to the tiny being growing within. She had to believe he was ok, just as she had been when her mother crossed over with Justine still in her womb.

It was very late in the season, but a light snow was falling and Justine's breath came now in bursts of mist. The street was deserted but street lamps cast their unique yellow glow and an occasional window shed warm light from around closed curtains.

Her brownstone loomed solid and inviting but she wouldn't allow herself to focus on that. The pull of the people within was stronger than she'd imagined. What did get her attention was the land next door on the other side of the alleyway. A house was being built, its foundations and walls appearing like dark undefined beasts in the night. She knew that house. In her time it had been taken over by a wealthy developer and its tenents evicted.

She didn't want to be discovered by anyone she knew; explanations would be impossible as well as painful. She was aware of growing colder and wondered if she should walk to the Hotel Margaret to find a cab, when a lone horse and carriage turned into Hicks Street. She reached out her arm to hail him, but he seemed to be heading towards her.

The cab stopped and a young man leapt down from the driver's seat. A woollen hat was pulled low on his head but his ears were exposed and red with the cold.

"Can I help you, miss?"

"Yes. Can you take me to the Bowery?"

He paused, considering. It was a long way and an unsavoury neighbourhood.

"I can pay you extra for your trouble."

"Oh. It's not that, miss. Of course I'll take you. I couldn't leave you here in the street. It's just they're closing the Bridge for repairs and I hope we're not too late…"

He opened the carriage and helped her inside. Before he closed the door, Justine removed her gloves and scarf and handed them to him.

"Please take these. It's cold out there and I wouldn't be comfortable sitting inside when you're doing me such a service."

The young man looked at the items quizzically but before he could question her offer, Justine closed the carriage door. She saw him smiling as he wrapped the scarf tightly around his cold ears.

They made a quick ride to the Brooklyn Bridge, where lights were set up everywhere shining on scaffolding, making it seem like daytime. Justine heard the young man talking with a Guard. She held her breath and didn't let it out until they were well onto the Bridge on their way to Manhattan and her destination.

When she peeked out she could see that one side of the Bridge was completely empty of traffic with repair work underway. Even in 1906, New York's arteries couldn't be completely closed. The city would virtually die.

Sliding open the small window in the carriage top, designed specifically for this purpose, the Young Man asked. "What's the address, miss?"

"I'm not exactly sure," Justine confessed. "I'll know it when I see it."

Some time later, he slid open the window again, "We're turning into the Bowery now, Miss …"

"Thanks. I'll let you know when I see it."

He steered the cab into the lights and chaos of the Bowery's sleazy entertainment and questionable commerce. This was her destination because of something Maggie had said about Justine sounding like a circus performer, Kendall Shaw's comment about a fortune teller named Belle and the information Jaime had provided about her Mother's name.

Justine had a vague memory of a sign she'd seen out the window of Alexander's cab. It was the afternoon they'd rescued his sick daughter and he was driving fast in an area Justine had never been in before. Nonetheless, she stared out the window determined to see that sign again.

The young man slowed the horse to a walk causing other drivers to shout protests. He shouted back. This certainly hadn't changed in over a hundred years. But the fracas made Justine nervous and increased her sense of urgency.

At the next corner a well-lit overhang boosted a spruiker dressed in top hat and tails touting whatever entertainment was to be had inside. Justine knocked on the ceiling.

"What cross street is this?" she asked when the young man slid open the window.

"Grand."

"We've gone too far, I think," Justine said. "It must have been on the other side ..."

"You want me to turn around?"

"Yes, please. I'm sorry."

"Not a problem," the young man replied, though with the angry, night-time traffic it clearly was going to be a big problem.

Heading south Justine was a bit disoriented. That afternoon they'd been heading north from Pell to whatever dark and dismal street Alexander and his family were living in. She remembered sitting on the right side of the carriage, but maybe her memory was playing tricks.

She peered hopefully out the window as they passed Canal Street and then suddenly, there it was – just as in her memory – The Bowery Theatre with it's grand, neoclassical pillars and just beyond a narrow building with a sign reading:

GRAND CAKE WALK   SEE INTO THE FUTURE

MINSTREL   &   BELLA CORSO

BURLESQUE   FORTUNE TELLER

There was the name, just as Jaime reported. Bella Corso. She pounded on the roof and the cab came to an abrupt halt throwing her forward and then flinging her back.

"Sorry, miss you okay? Is this it?"

"Yes. This is it!"

He was down from his perch in an instant, opening the door and helping her onto the pavement.

"You sure about this, miss?" The young man asked, eyeing the dark, narrow building suspiciously. "Maybe I should wait for you…?"

"I would be very grateful if you waited," Justine replied, meaning it. "What's your name?"

"Sean, miss."

"Well, Sean – if you can wait here and be ready for anything, that would be much appreciated."

"Be careful, miss…"

Eighty-Four

She realized the signs were misleading. The advertised Minstrel show was taking place inside the theatre, while the fortune-teller seemed to be inside the narrow building.

Opening the door, revealed that this building was nothing more than housing for a set of stairs, which led to the floors above the theatre. Light emanated from a landing so Justine ascended. The stairway was dark, the wooden treads creaked and there was a musty smell - not very encouraging to anyone seeking to know their future.

At the top of the stairs, Justine pushed open the door into what appeared to be a small anteroom leading to another room. Worn wallpaper flocked the walls and a fat woman sat in an overstuffed chair with her feet on an overstuffed ottoman next to a small fire burning in the grate. She'd clearly just popped into her over painted mouth one of many chocolates, which sat in an open box on the table next to her. She looked up from the book she'd been reading with mild interest. Sizing Justine up, she became more interested and arose with some difficulty from her cozy chair.

"Come to have yer fortune told, have ya?" she inquired, sidling up to Justine and drawing her further into the room with one pudgy hand. "Ye've come to the right place," she insisted, smiling a set of bad teeth. Feeling Justine's hesitation, she rambled on, "First time is it? Nothing to be afraid of."

The woman paused, gripping Justine's arm a little harder.

"Payment up front," she insisted, handing Justine a grubby hand written price list and indicating the brass bowl on her table next to the chocolates.

Justine deposited the required coins and the woman opened the inner door. The first thing Justine felt was the cold in sharp contrast to the anteroom. Then she noticed the fabric hung haphazardly from the walls in an effort to create some semblance of a gypsy tent. Finally, she noticed the thin woman slumped over the table and her heart stopped.

"Bella?" the fat woman demanded in an aggressive voice. "You have a customer!"

"Leave us!" Justine demanded in an equally aggressive voice, glaring at the woman threateningly.

"I just want to wake her up ..." the fat woman insisted, moving to shake the sleeping woman.

"DON'T touch her," Justine cried.

The woman withdrew her hand in shock, staring at Justine.

"I've paid my money. Now get out," Justine insisted.

They glared at each other for a moment. Justine's heart was beating fast but she held the other's gaze. Finally the woman shrugged and moved to the door.

"I don't want to be disturbed," Justine warned.

The woman closed the door behind her.

Justine stood still, trying to get her heart to calm. The figure at the table had not moved but Justine could see her thin shoulder blades rising and falling almost imperceptibly with her breath.

Justine felt as surreal and unsubstantial as the fake hangings sagging on the walls. She opened the long cape Paul had made, with fake fur lining that was so real it almost smelled like fox, and removed it from her shoulders. She came around the table and draped it over the sleeping figure. Justine sat in the opposite chair and, with shaking hands, removed the golden locket from around her neck, sliding it across the table to the woman.

The woman stirred, her hands moving first to investigate the fur cape draped around her shoulders, then pushing herself up, she noticed the locket sitting on the table. Justine watched all this as if from far away, as if the little girl she'd once been was sitting in the room waiting to see what the woman would do, holding her tender heart in her throat – unable to breath.

The woman grabbed the locket, drawing it nearer to study it more closely, turning it over in her hand and finally popping it open with a knowledge of the secret clasp. Then her back straightened and her cat like brown eyes shot open to look directly into Justine's. Those eyes devoured Justine with an aching longing and a fearful disbelief.

"Mama?" Justine asked.

The woman's eyes filled with tears, spilling great droplets onto her cheeks. Her head shook from side to side as her mind tried to comprehend what was happening.

"Justine?" she finally managed to ask.

And then nothing could stop Justine from knocking over her chair as she raced around the table, pulling her mother up and into her arms. She was light as a feather and Justine felt as if she were not just holding her, but holding her up as their bodies convulsed with tears. Her mother's arms scrabbled to draw Justine closer – touching and holding on as if to prove her substantiality. And all they could say was, 'Mama' and 'My Baby' over and over.

Finally Justine pulled back, looking deeply into her mother's eyes.

"How?" Her mother's mouth formed the words.

"You know how…" Justine replied.

This statement brought back the reality of time and place.

"We should get out of here," Justine suggested. "Then we can talk."

"I have four more hours to work," Bella said, fear crossing her face.

"You're not working here anymore. Not ever again," Justine informed her.

The fur cape had fallen to the floor and Justine bent to retrieve it, wrapping her mother's impossibly small frame into its warmth.

"Paul made this especially for you ..." Justine explained as she fastened the clasp at her mother's neck.

"Paul?" Bella said the name as if it were in a foreign language.

"Yes. You remember Paul. Ducky's Paul...?"

Justine was moving her mother towards the door.

"Ducky ..." the name caused Bella to sway uneasily on her feet.

"Please hold on. We're going to get you something to eat," Justine said, opening the door. "Let me do the talking."

Supporting her mother by the arm she strode into the anteroom and right up to the fat woman sprawled in her fat chair, making it impossible for the woman to rise.

"I imagine you're just doing a job for someone else, but shame on you anyway. Forcing someone to work in these terrible conditions is criminal!"

The fat woman's mouth flapped open like a fish, as if to speak.

"NO," Justine stopped her.

Being younger and in better shape was having the desired affect, causing the woman to think twice about arguing or resisting.

"We are leaving and not coming back. I'm going to assume that this woman has not been paid properly for her services so I am going to take some of what is owed to her!"

Justine dumped the contents of the brass bowl into her small purse. She didn't have much money from 1906 and she'd need this for the duration.

"I have a man waiting outside," she warned the woman. "You don't want to follow us or encounter him, I can assure you!"

She escorted Bella out the door, shutting it convincingly behind them.

Eighty-Five

Once on the street, Justine was relieved to find Sean waiting as promised.

"Somewhere to eat something…?" Justine asked.

He pointed across the street, where she could make out the front of a tavern. It was snowing now in earnest.

"Please go inside and get yourself some dinner," Justine instructed, handing him some coins. "If we need to leave suddenly, can you be ready?"

Sean nodded, helping them part way across the street then returning to see to the horse and carriage.

Access to McGinty's Pub was down some well-worn stairs. The main area was lined with a long, polished wooden bar with a thick brass railing. The place was full, mostly with men. Their entrance caused a stir, bearded faces of differing ages turning to look and to stare. The warmth was a relief but the noise and the stench of beer and smoke was stifling.

A bar maid appeared from behind the bar, her greying hair suggesting she was no longer a 'maid'.

"Can I help you ladies?" she asked, suspiciously.

"We want supper and a drink and somewhere quiet where we can be alone," Justine informed her, eyeing the room full of curious faces.

The woman pursed her lips, studying Justine and the silent woman on her arm.

"What's wrong with her?" the barmaid asked, indicating Bella.

"She's hungry," Justine spat back, straightening her shoulders. "Look, I can pay. Do you have a private room, or not?"

The woman eyed Justine from head to toe and deciding she could in fact pay turned abruptly, leading them down a short hallway and into a very small room with tables and chairs stacked against one wall and two incongruous booths against the other.

"Poker night's tomorrow," the barmaid said in explanation of the empty room.

Justine seated her mother in one of the booths, then turned back to the barmaid, "Please bring us two dinners and two beers."

She turned dismissively away from the barmaid, waiting until she heard her leave. Bella was leaning on the table, holding her head in her hands. She was clearly not well and Justine's heart broke all over again.

There was so much to say, but as Justine sat beside her mother both women just held each other's hand, waiting.

After delivering the food and drink, Justine warned the barmaid, "I don't want to be disturbed. Do you understand?"

The woman nodded indifferently and left them alone.

"Eat, mama," Justine encouraged. "It's hot and it actually smells good!"

As Bella ate, Justine began to speak, trying to fill in the years, trying to connect with her mother through the story of her life. She spoke only about her own century and her words sounded hollow, insubstantial but her mother grew more animated as the food worked it's magic. She asked questions. She nodded in memory of people and places that were also familiar to her.

Justine wasn't hungry but she began to eat as a way of making it necessary for her mother to tell her story. Bella explained that she'd come back through the portal in New Orleans. Yes, it was on Royal Street. Yes, next to the antique shop. Neither spoke of the chasm of pain her departure had created in both their lives.

"I came to believe if I stayed in the future, I would die. The doctors couldn't diagnose what was wrong but it felt as if my heart was going to explode in my chest," Bella explained.

Justine had come to the same conclusion. Her symptoms were different; she'd felt as if her heart might just stop, prompting her to return to her own time.

"It never seemed fair that I could travel through time, but not stay there," Bella went on. "Even after I returned, there were times when I missed you so much I thought my heart would break. Knowing that in some ways you'd not yet been born as the future hadn't happened yet, made me feel so alone…"

"Why didn't you look for my father? Now that I was – gone – why didn't you seek him out?"

"Things got very bad in New Orleans. I came here, back to New York. But he was already gone – dead… and…"

Bella slumped over, sighing deeply.

Justine put her fork down, placing a hand on her mother's shoulder, "He loved you very much."

And that prompted Justine to explain that she'd been here, in this time, before. She didn't talk about the Brownstone – that would come later. But she did describe meeting her half-brother and sister and discovering how much their father, her father, had loved – her mother – had loved Bella.

Bella was in tears by this time and she and Justine held each other, the people gone or not yet born wafting like ghosts in the empty room.

When the emotion subsided, Justine knew that it was time to reveal why she was really here.

"I'm pregnant, mama," she confessed.

Eighty-Six

Sean placed himself at the end of the bar nearest the entrance. He was glad to be out of the cold and the pleasure of having money to order food and drink made him feel like a king. Sean Moran's secret dream was success. He didn't know how or as yet what, but his heart nearly burst when he thought about affording a proper roof over his mother's head and proving to his hateful, alcoholic father that he was nothing like him.

He was glad he'd decided to stay out for another hour tonight because it meant being there when this strange lady needed a cab. He thought of her as strange for many reasons but none of them were disparaging. Strange, because she'd given him these expensive leather gloves, which were unlike anything he'd ever owned, which made driving in the fierce cold much less painful. Strange, because she had a calm authority that he'd not experienced in a woman before. Strange, because there was something going on in that back room tonight with the other, older woman that had given the barmaid a bad case of nosiness.

Sean shovelled the last tasty morsel of beef stew into his mouth, keeping his eyes on the barmaid. She kept glancing down the hallway, moving towards it and then deciding against it.

"Can you be ready for a quick getaway?" the strange woman had asked him.

Sean wasn't as interested in what was going on in the back room as he was in making sure he was ready. Finally, the barmaid couldn't stand it anymore and grabbing an empty tray headed to the back room.

The door opened suddenly and Justine looked up from what she was doing to find the barmaid standing there with her mouth open.

"What part of 'we don't want to be disturbed' did you not understand?" Justine shouted, tossing a linen napkin over her mother's exposed arm and the hypodermic needle that was still drawing blood. "Get out of here. Now!"

The barmaid hesitated but was distracted by the sound of shattering glass coming from the bar area, followed by a man's loud voice. She glanced at Justine uncertain what to do, but headed back to the bar, leaving the door ajar.

"We better get out of here," Bella advised.

Justine focused her attention on delicately removing the needle, pressing a cotton ball to her mother's arm, capping the blood draw in its glass vial, placing it gingerly in the small, padded metal case and stashing them in the leather satchel she was carrying.

The noise from the bar was growing as more voices joined in. Justine helped her mother to her feet.

"Are you okay? Do you feel dizzy at all?" she asked.

"I can manage," Bella assured her.

Peering down the hallway into the bar, Justine saw the barmaid trying either to push Sean away or to hold him up. Sean was singing loudly and wobbling on his feet. Other customers were adding their comments to the general melee.

"Oh, God. He's drunk," Justine despaired, even as they continued moving towards the entrance.

At that moment, Sean caught Justine's eye over the barmaid's shoulder and winked. Like a choreographed dance, he swung his weight towards Bella, grabbing her elbow and causing the barmaid to lose her balance. He manoeuvred Bella out the door by the time the barmaid righted herself.

"Hey. You!" the barmaid shouted.

Justine turned. "The money's on the table," she assured the woman.

The barmaid was about to object when, glancing down at Justine's right hand, the glint of sharp metal caught her eye. Justine stood in the doorway holding the hypodermic like a weapon, daring the woman to challenge her departure.

The barmaid looked up, surprised. When she didn't move, Justine stepped into the street.

Sean was waiting with the reins in hand and Bella already inside the cab. Justine jumped in beside her mother and they took off at a gallop.

After turning a few corners and putting some distance between them and the Bowery, the window in the cab's ceiling slid open and Sean asked:

"Where to?"

"Brooklyn, Sean," Justine instructed. "And thank you. You do a very convincing drunk!"

Eighty-Seven

There wasn't much time left. Only as long as it took to cross the bridge. Justine reached for her mother's hand.

"How're you feeling?" she asked.

"Much better. Almost human again!"

Glancing at her mother huddled into Paul's fur cape, Bella looked fragile and unwell. Justine wanted to wrap her arms around her and protect her forever. As if understanding, Bella gave Justine's hand a comforting squeeze.

"What's in Brooklyn?" she asked.

Justine told her about the house her father had built for Bella, hoping, willing her to come back to him. Never knowing why she'd left. Never knowing about his daughter, Justine.

"He was a good man," Bella said. "He was forced by his family to marry the 'right' woman. She was - not a nice person - his wife."

Justine knew this. She had been that wife.

"But I suppose I would have been angry if my husband had a concubine," Bella conceded.

"God, what an awful word," Justine said.

"In this time, that's what I was..."

Justine glanced out the window. They were heading up to the Brooklyn Bridge. The work lights were ablaze and one side of the thoroughfare was still closed. The snow had stopped but they were proceeding slowly and Justine was glad.

"I'm taking you there, Mama. You have a place to live and there are people to take care of you and you don't have to work ever again."

Bella closed her eyes tight, reaching blindly for her daughter's hand. The pain, sorrow and struggle of her life etched in her clenched face and in the tears that spilled from her eyes.

"Ducky and I live in that house, now – I mean – in my time," Justine offered, trying to lighten her mother's burden. "We were renting apartments but coming back in time made it possible for us to buy it."

"I'm glad," Bella smiled. "That feels like continuity. I'll feel you in the house - like a kind of connection I thought I'd lost forever."

"And, we'll feel you."

Justine knew they were grabbing at very thin straws – trying to make this moment of actually being together – endure.

She continued by describing Alexander and his family and how they had come to live in the house on Hicks Street, how they were like family to her, to Justine.

She mentioned James Gray, focusing on her mother's encounter with him for her portrait, avoiding the fact of him as father of her unborn child.

"I remember a cheeky young man – with a great deal of talent," Bella commented.

"Yep. That's him."

Next, Justine explained about Maggie, including the fact that the house now belonged to her.

"I'm glad she owns the house," Bella assured her daughter. "I wouldn't want the responsibility,"

"But it's yours to live in ..."

"I understand," Bella interrupted, smiling and caressing Justine's hand. "Maggie sounds very special," she remarked, encouragingly.

"She's like the sister I never had or the best friend I've never been able to keep." Justine's words caught in her throat. This was going to be harder than she thought.

Bella sighed. "Life's more difficult than we ever imagined, isn't it?" she mused. "Then add to that dearly beloved people and places, who exist in another time..." She took her daughter's face in her hands. "I know you can't stay, my darling. I know. Let me save you the need to say it. I would give my life to make it different." She wrapped her arms around Justine. "But I confess, I'm comforted that you understand why I had to leave," she whispered. "And that you know how very much I've missed you – and will miss you." She held Justine more tightly.

"I've missed you my whole life…" Justine whispered back, letting the too painful tears pour down her face.

Bella took a deep breath. "I'm grateful to have had this one night with you, my daughter. I will cherish it forever." She pulled back, wiping Justine's tears gently with her fingers. "You've become such a confident and beautiful young woman. And about to be a mother, yourself…" Bella paused trying to get control of her own tears. "I'm so proud of you."

They were approaching the Brooklyn side of the Bridge. Justine slid open the little window and spoke to Sean:

"Would you please stop up the street from where you found me?"

"Yes, m'am."

Justine and Bella sat in silence, holding hands and listening to the clop, clop of the horses hooves. There was so much to say – and yet everything that could be said, had been.

When the cab stopped, Justine didn't know if she would survive the next few minutes. She pointed out the window:

"That's it. That's the brownstone."

Bella looked and nodded.

Sean had parked in the shadows, just before the street lamp. Justine turned to her mother, whose pale, ethereal face seemed to glow in the dimness. Bella's almond eyes looked at her daughter, drinking in her memory, making these last moments count.

"Please tell Ducky, thank-you," Bella said. "For everything."

Justine nodded.

"And Paul," Bella added, hugging the warmth of her new cape around her. "I love you," she added, touching Justine's face once again.

"I love you too, mama."

Sean opened the door and helped Bella to climb down. She grasped the locket in her hand, looking once more at Justine, then taking a deep breath, walked away.

Eighty-Eight

"Please get into the cab, Sean, if you don't mind," Justine instructed.

They watched Bella make her way across the street and up the steps of the Brownstone. When she knocked on the door, Sean got into the cab and Justine shut the door.

Justine watched as the door opened and Maggie appeared on the doorstep. It only took her a moment before she recognized Bella and pulled her eagerly into the house in much the same way she'd done with Justine that first night of her arrival here.

However, Maggie stepped back out, looking inquisitively up the street. From behind the cab's curtain, Justine knew she couldn't be seen but she felt acutely the moment their eyes met. Maggie paused, drew her handkerchief from her pocket and wiped away a tear. She raised her hand as if to wave, then re-entered the house.

"You did a really good job tonight, Sean." Justine said. It was easier to focus on him than to keep looking at the house. "And I'm very grateful."

"What an adventure!" he replied. "Can I take you home now?"

524

"No. I'm afraid not." She shifted to face him. "Do you know the Yellow Cab Company?"

"Yes, of course."

"Would you like a job with them?"

"Who wouldn't?"

"Come back to this same house tomorrow and ask for Alexander Alexandrovich. Give him this," she added, handing Sean the eagle feather Alexander had found the day they bought the first car in his fleet.

Sean took the feather quizzically and was about to speak when Justine continued, "Here is payment for tonight," she said, handing him whatever was left in her small purse. "Can I ask one more favor?"

"Yes, ma'm. It's my pleasure, but ..."

"I'm going to get out of the cab. I need you to drive away and not look back. Can you do that?"

"Just leave you here. Alone? I'm sure My Alexandrovich wouldn't like that!"

"No. He wouldn't." Justine chuckled. Thinking of Alexander and his fierce loyalty, however, was threatening her resolve. "Will you do as I ask?" she said, her voice taking on some urgency.

"Yes, if that's what you want."

She nodded. He stepped down from the cab, holding the door and helping her out.

"This has been the most amazing night of my life. Thank you," he said.

She waited as he climbed up and grabbed the reins. He got the horses going and, as promised, didn't look back. Alexander would like this boy.

When the carriage turned the corner, she walked quickly towards the stables. Out of the corner of her eye she caught a glimpse of a figure standing in the second floor window, watching, but the piercing sounds had already taken hold and, hugging her belly and the child within, she let herself be drawn through the horror, back to her own time.

Eighty-Nine

"There's a bird," Jaime'd explained when Margaret wanted to know what the hell he thought he was doing sitting in that godforsaken alleyway.

"What bird?" was her next question.

He knew it was foolish to try and pull a fast one on Margaret.

"And don't try and pull a fast one on me," she added peering over her horned rims at him.

"Ok. Not a bird. Would you believe a migratory butterfly…?"

"Yer sittin' in this barren alley hopin' to spot some butterfly on it's way to Miami…?"

"Something like that…."

"Oh, jeez. Never mind. You wanna sit in the hot sun…? Sit. Wadda I care." And she waddled back towards the street. "JOE?" she shouted. "We're going!"

Jaime watched as Joe appeared at the end of the alley, happily taking Margaret's arm, waving and smiling at Jaime and escorting her down the street. Jaime admired Margaret's efforts on behalf of the homeless and he was also a little intimidated by her.

He'd been sitting in the alley for the better part of the day. He'd missed Justine's departure so he didn't know what to expect for her return. And return, she must. Every time he let himself think about never seeing her again, he had a sense of what his father meant by being visited by the black dog. It was like a cloud darkening his heart.

'Would she just appear,' he wondered 'like out of thin air?'

It was an inconceivable question with an equally unimaginable answer. So he sat. And waited. And prayed. Just a little bit.

He bent to retrieve his water bottle and suddenly she was there – pale and shaken - but there.

Justine had never been so happy to see anyone in her life.

He gently wrapped his arm around her as if she were something very fragile and rare. She let her head rest against his chest as he guided her to the gate in the wall.

"They removed that ivy and look what they found," he said, indicating the gate.

Of course Justine knew the gate was there but she liked the comforting sound of his voice so she just let him talk. It was all she could do to put one foot in front of the other.

It was late in the day but the sun would be up for hours. The heat and humidity carried the scent of jasmine from the garden next door. Jaime carefully latched the new lock on the inside garden wall. Justine felt her head spinning and slumped against his strong frame.

He held her close, guiding her through the house, into her bedroom and into her ensuite bathroom, where he gently but swiftly began removing the layers of 1906 winter clothing. He steered her into the shower, where he turned on a steady stream of warm water.

Justine closed her eyes, letting the water flow down her body. After some moments she felt Jaime join her. His tall, naked presence melted the part of her that'd been holding on since watching her mother disappear into the house on Hicks Street. She let her forehead rest against his chest, felt her heart crack open and the tears flow down her face. She sobbed as his strong arms came around her and she could feel his chest rise and fall as he reacted to her pain with an expression of his own.

They stood together like this letting the water wash over them, washing away the sorrow, the loss and finally the tears.

Dressed now in summer pyjamas and a light cashmere robe - a gift from Ducky and Paul, proud grandparents-to-be - the hum of the hair dryer was comfortingly familiar, a sound from her own time. Justine closed her eyes as Jaime combed the brush through her hair, brushing and drying. She thought of her Mother and of Maggie, who at one time or another had also combed Justine's hair. It was a distant reflection, without emotion. She was drained of feeling, content to let this beautiful, sensitive man care for her and love her.

With Jaime's help, she crawled between the bamboo sheets of her bed, their brushed softness, caressing her skin and reminding her of how much more comfortable it was to live in this time. She was aware of Jaime collecting the leather satchel she'd carried with her, containing the glass vial with her mother's blood. Her heart leapt at the thought of her mother then surrendered into a deep and peaceful slumber.

She was awoken by the familiar sound of Ducky's gentle voice and the mouth watering smell of bacon and eggs.

She smiled before she opened her eyes and mumbled, "I love you, so much!"

"Well, that's a good thing because I love you as well, Parcel" he said, placing the tray of food on the side table and sitting beside her on the bed.

She opened her eyes and reached for his hand, warm and dry with those long elegant fingers. She noticed Paul inspecting the costume she'd worn, which Jaime had hung tidily on hangers, nodding appreciatively at his handiwork.

The sun was shining though the French doors, but for Justine the room was filled with an unseen light – the light of love and family. There was a place in her heart that had always been empty, first with the disappearance of her mother and now filled almost to bursting with the beloved people she'd left behind in the past. But she could manage that emptiness now with the presence of these two men, Jaime and the child growing in her womb.

Ninety

Justine and Jaime were walking down Hicks Street on their way back to see Jenny, who'd been testing Bella's blood. They had to dash across Montague Street and for the first time Justine felt her body and her gait adjusting to the growing weight in her belly.

The acrid stink of exhaust fumes mingled with other 21st Century pollutants, filling her nostrils. This would once have disturbed her but was now a welcome confirmation of where she was and when.

She thought about the past everyday and had to resist going to her computer to uncover what she might about the people she'd left behind. Had they heeded her warnings, specified in the letters she'd left with each one of them? If anyone could find a trail left by those people, it was Justine. But she needed more time here and now to feel grounded and not so torn.

"If we told Jenny about my mother – about me – do you think she'd believe us?" Justine asked.

The conversation with Jaime began the day she opened her eyes in the hospital and found his green ones gazing down at her. And it hadn't stopped since. She wasn't talking to herself so much any more because what ever she was thinking, she just naturally shared with him now.

"If anyone would believe, it would be Jenny," Jaime replied.

"Those herbs and things she gave me are really working. I feel like I'm back in my body and coming back into sync with my own time," Justine continued. "I don't know if that makes sense."

"We departed from sense and reason when you crossed the dateline," Jaime said, snuggling his arm around her. "But I'm really glad to hear it and so will Jenny."

"There are anomalies in your Mother's blood," Jenny was explaining, peering at her notes through her wire-rimmed glasses. She wore an oil of citrus that filled the room with its pleasant zesty aroma. She looked at Justine. "The same anomalies in your blood, but different."

Justine didn't look away. She also didn't respond.

"They're anomalies," Jenny explained. "I don't know what to make of them."

Justine nodded, waiting.

"When I look at blood, it's like I'm reading your life – it's like I'm reading your life on many levels – not just the physical."

Jenny paused to assure herself Justine understood what she was saying. Justine sat up and nodded again.

"When I looked at your blood," Jenny went on "it was just a gut instinct to suggest herbs and supplements that would increase your life energy. That's what your blood seemed to be lacking."

"That's exactly what they've done," Justine confirmed.

But Jenny wasn't listening. She was exploring out loud, unformed thoughts she'd been having.

"It was as if you've been in a time that was slower and that slowed you down. But not just physically..."

Justine glanced at Jaime who was hanging on Jenny's every word.

"And your Mother's blood seemed to suggest the opposite."

Jenny's fingers were absently touching her notes as if she were reading Braille.

"Your Mother's system is depleted by having gone too fast and there's been no support to slow her down... she's exhausted – but not just physically."

Jenny paused again, lost in thought.

"Everything you say is true," Justine confirmed.

"Anomalies," Jenny confirmed. "But I think I can make up a concoction that will solve things for you, anyway..."

Ninety-One

Not long after Justine's return, Margaret met with her and Ducky. It was a Sunday and Paul and Jaime were in the garden with a couple of plumbers, who were laying the irrigation system.

"I don't know where this sudden wealth came from and I'm not asking cause I'm very grateful for it," Margaret said, watching the activity in the garden with mild interest. "But if there's any more of where that came from, then I got a proposal to make."

She eyeballed Ducky first, waiting for a reply. He was looking down his nose at her but Margaret wasn't fazed by his imperious pose. She knew it was just Ducky, listening. She shifted her gaze onto Justine, who'd leaned forward with interest. Realising Margaret was waiting for a response, Justine blurted out:

"Yes, there could be more where that came from."

Ducky glanced at her sharply, then sighed and nodded – indicating to Margaret his agreement.

"I want to open a clinic and a support location for the homeless and struggling," Margaret explained. "Brooklyn needs a place where poor people can go and get the kind of help and support they need

534

without the red tape and the third degree. We help the community, the community improves and everyone's life gets better."

"It's a great idea," Justine enthused.

"We don't have that kind of money, ..." Ducky warned.

"There are ways it could pay for itself," Margaret countered. "And I know how we might get funding in the future. We just need to launch it. Prove it can work..."

Jaime and Paul came for refreshments and joined the conversation. Margaret had done a lot of thinking and researching over the years and she laid out her plans. They were good, solid plans. Paul presented concerns. Ducky asked questions. Jaime offered ideas, which Margaret instantly warmed to. But it was Justine who had the final say.

"I want you all to know that I have everything I could ever hope for or dream of right here and right now." She looked meaningfully around the table. "If you think this could work, then I am in 100%"

Simon Pankhurst had sold the diamond ring for a tidy profit, putting to rest Ducky's resentment towards him. The money was in investments and provided a nice nest egg for the future.

The ceramic egg was in a safe deposit box at the bank along with a few other small items Justine had brought back. The egg alone was probably worth enough to fund such a project. From an egg a life is born, Justine thought touching her belly, which had grown considerably with time.

And so the project was launched and from that moment on, Justine's life took another profound turn. She worked tirelessly in the creation and implementation of Margaret's dream. Jaime also got involved.

They were sitting in the small office at the back of the three-story warehouse that was being converted to house their new clinic and support center.

"All my adult life I've been looking for meaning and purpose," Justine confided. "With lots of false starts. Lots of uncertainty, resulting in lots of restlessness. When I was in the past, I never hesitated. I knew what I had to do and I did it." Looking around the warehouse, she added, "Now, meaning and purpose seem to have found me."

"Like I told you," Jaime replied, handing Justine the sandwich he'd picked up at his favorite deli, "When I was 18, my mother died. I created a smart phone app that sold pretty well and I've been living off the money since. It paid for college and left me free to explore a variety of jobs, paid or not. Working at the hospital was one of them. I've been looking too," he admitted.

Now he was turning his vast abilities into providing technical support for the new enterprise. He was fiddling with electrical cords at the back of a computer monitor.

"... and I found not only purpose and meaning, but family as well."

He poked his smiling face up from behind the screen and Justine smiled back, her mouth happily full of sandwich.

Jaime had more or less moved into the house on Hicks Street. He slept in her bed and they cuddled and caressed. Both seemed to want to delay actual sex until after the birth of the baby. She was reminded of what she'd said to Caroline: *The whole purpose is the expression of love and the desire for connection. It's not really worth it otherwise.* Every morning Justine awoke to the warm scent of his body nearby and the joy of another day shared with this perfectly, beautiful man. Everything about being with him was worth it.

"How would you call your relationship to him?" Justine asked after the sonogram revealed it was a boy.

"He's my Great Grandfather's child. Does that make him my grandfather?"

They laughed at the notion of an unborn baby already a grandfather.

"He's also the child of my lover," Jaime added, curling up beside her in bed. "Does that make him my child as well?"

"I'd like him to be your child," Justine confessed. "And the fact that you're related – well that makes it easier, doesn't it?"

"You are what makes it easy," Jaime whispered. "I want to be with you forever."

"According to Jenny, we have been together forever as mate souls, travelling through time."

"Do you think I was my Great Grandfather, James Grey?"

Justine turned over to look at him.

"I don't know. You look a lot like him. Those devilish green eyes. But you don't feel much like him."

"He was a sexy bastard, wasn't he?"

"He used his sexuality to get what he wanted. You're just sexy…"

To prove it she leaned over and pressed her lips to his, letting her tongue linger inside his mouth, relishing how he tasted of honey and maleness.

She was delighted with the daily challenges presented by Margaret's Community Center and Clinic. She found inner resources she didn't know she had to meet those challenges and create positive outcomes.

The day the clinic opened was near Justine's due date but she couldn't stay away.

"It's like giving birth, twice," she whispered to Jaime.

Ninety-Two

November 1ˢᵗ 6 years later

As she always did on this day, Justine thought about the morning of Alex's arrival. He was impatient to be born and it had been a short and easy birth. Afterwards, the midwife handed Justine this fragile bundle. She gazed down at her new baby and felt her heart stretching wider than she thought possible with love for him. His tiny fingers grasped her thumb and his determined mouth worked in concentration. In that moment, so replete with love and joy, she'd suddenly become aware that he was a re-incarnation of the soul of Kendall Shaw. She didn't know how she knew, but she knew and the realization rattled her to her core.

"Zhang Zhu made a prediction on the day I first met him," Justine confided to Jaime.

Jaime had supported her throughout the whole birth, encouraging her with his calm voice and strong hand to hold. He was sitting now on the bed, one of those strong hands resting on her knee.

"He said I would find myself, and my lover and my enemy and then I would find them again. They are you and yours," he said. "Now and in the future."

"What's it mean?"

She looked down at her new born, acutely aware that moments before he'd been inside of her; a part of her. His little body was fiercely alive and her feelings toward him didn't change. Rather, her heart opened wider into a wisdom that told her, he is here so that you can love him enough that he loves himself and can grow up to be a good and valuable man.

"Well, 'finding my lover' is you, of course," she said, squeezing Jaime's fingers. "And finding myself is what's been happening from the moment I crossed the dateline."

"… and your enemy?"

"Well, that was Kendall Shaw. And so is he," she explained, glancing down at her baby. "It's somehow my karma to be his mother. Just as it was my karma to be there for Caroline and Hunter."

She put her lips to the baby's tiny ear and whispered, "I will be the best Mommy I can possibly be for you. I love you no matter what."

That promise remained true to this day.

They'd named him James Alex Grey. Jaime's mother had been Alexis Grey. The name embraced a satisfying number of people from both their lives, past and present. They were his parents now and determined to be the best possible protectors and guides for this newly arrived soul.

Tonight was the evening of Alex's 6th birthday. That afternoon, Justine and Jaime had taken him to the Natural History Museum with a small group of his friends. Alex loved the dinosaurs.

When Jaime asked why, Alex replied, "Because they're bigger and badder than everyone else."

Justine knew they had to stay vigilant with Alex to keep these tendencies in check and offer more balanced alternatives to empowering him. She'd encountered the very worst of what his soul could manifest in Kendall Shaw. Luckily Alex was an endearing, clever little boy and loving him was easy.

Three years later saw the arrival of Bonnie Belle Grey, the result of Justine and Jaime's passion and love. Jenny confirmed that while Alex did not carry the anomalies in his blood, Belle did.

"Passed on through the female line, apparently," Jenny concurred.

Justine didn't like to think too much about what this might mean. For now, they kept Baby Belle out of the alley and away from the portal that existed there.

Everyone was gathered around the table to celebrate Alex's birthday. The sliding doors were shut but the lights in the garden Paul designed and Jaime built twinkled off the late autumn leaves.

Baby Belle, who at 3 was already a dark haired beauty like her grandmother, had her father Jaime's hazel eyes and was quickly learning how to use her beauty to get her way. She'd utterly seduced both her grandfathers, Ducky and Paul.

"I wanna cake," Belle squealed, as Ducky snuck another slice onto her plate.

Justine caught Ducky's guilty look and chuckled.

Ducky had sold Heights Antiques so that he and Paul could open an interior design business that was now flourishing. They'd just returned from an all expenses paid trip to the Loire Valley to furnish a newly purchased summer mansion for a wealthy client and friend. They were more relaxed and content than either of them had been in years.

Sadly, Joe had died earlier in the year. Living most of his later years alone on the street, he died a grateful and well-loved man with his new Hicks Street family by his side. Margaret decided to move out of the basement apartment and relocate to the new Clinic. She was in her element there, giving out advice at all hours of the day or night.

Time had brought about changes and as Justine looked around the table at the people she loved most in the world, the room filled with the warm presence of those she'd loved and left behind.

"Mama coming," Belle said, licking birthday cake from her stubby fingers.

"Who's coming, sweetheart?" Justine asked.

Recently Belle had started making these seemingly nonsensical pronouncements, which most of the adults around her ignored. However, Jaime pointed out a pattern of Belle stating something and then an event occurring that could fit in to what her limited baby language was trying to say. It was like she was prescient.

"Mama," Belle said.

"Yes, Baby girl. I'm your Mama." Justine agreed, reaching over to wipe her daughter's face and kiss the remaining sweetness on her chubby cheeks.

There was a knock on the door.

"Are we expecting anyone?" Ducky asked.

"I'll see who it is," Jaime said, getting up from the table.

Seconds later, Bella Corso, Justine's mother, entered the room, followed by a stunned and speechless Jaime.

She was dressed in a white gossamer lace tunic cinched at the waist with soft lavender over a narrow, draped silken underskirt of the same color. She wore no hat but her abundant chocolate hair, streaked with grey, was piled on top of her head. Her pale olive skin and thin, fragile carriage made her appear almost ghostlike. Her unexpected appearance accentuated this impression.

No one spoke. Justine's heart leapt into her throat as she stared at this apparition of her mother. Her mother stood speechless as well.

"Mama," Baby Belle gurgled with great delight.

END

About the Author

Born in Los Angeles, Carrie is the daughter of former schoolteachers. Every summer as a child, the family piled into the station wagon and explored the United States. On these long car rides, Carrie would gaze out the window at the ever-changing scenery and tell herself stories. When she was 9 and her sister was 11, Carrie's father and mother took sabbatical leave, purchased a Volkswagen van and the family toured around Europe for an entire year. Carrie's landscape and opportunity for storytelling expanded. When Carrie was 14, her father became an American diplomat and the family moved to Europe. Her new home was an apartment on the banks of the Rhine River and she attended school in the Netherlands in a castle built in 1715. Her canvas for narrative and dreaming broadened. She returned to the US to attend the University of California Los Angeles, getting a Bachelors degree in Theatre Arts and visited her parents in a variety of countries where her father was posted. Carrie moved to New York City in the edgy 1970's where she worked as an actress. She later moved to Tokyo where she taught English and acting and then to Sydney, Australia where she taught acting at the prestigious National Institute of Dramatic Art in Sydney. There she met her beloved husband, Charles, a New Zealander, filmmaker and kindred storyteller.

"Acting gave me the tools for understanding character and how to hear their voices. Teaching acting deepened my understanding of storytelling"

Carrie's life came full circle when she returned to Los Angeles in 2006 where she now lives with her husband and two cats and has a Life Coaching business. Carrie has been telling stories all her life. *The State of Grace, an adventurous memory,* is her first novel.

"Crossing the Dateline, my second novel, came to me in a dream," Hannah has said. *"Then I just had to write it all down."*